who ever reads this
I hope it inspires you

D1066639

For those who suffer… You Are Not Alone!

Where there is Darkness… There is Light.

Where there is Fear… There is Hope.

Where there is Hate… There is Love.

Where there is Madness… There ARE Miracles!

For L.

his website writeful journeys

The Domino Effect

How dare they I felt! I mean really now, who does this?
How can they just take a man's life away and not even consider
the fact that someone's world will be destroyed over this and those
around them? Perhaps it was Divine intervention since my crime
included stealing, deception and gluttony by over consuming
mind-altering drugs. My body ached for it so bad and I lost
control. I have a powerful mind and wondered how could the
flesh over power the mind? I'm a companion to my own demons,
trapped in fear. No matter how hard I tried to fight, I could never
win this on my own power. Those demons will dance and I
danced right along, enjoying the short-lived euphoria and it caught
up to me. Like being caught in a loop of insanity as those demons
danced in my head calling for more.

It was late February 2013, a day with all the bare trees
standing eerily against the cloudy frigid day. I was forced into

cuffs and in that moment was where I felt everything fall away and tumble down like a domino effect. One by one I saw everything I had being taken away from me…. The job I had, the one I was supposed to be doing right then, instead of those ridiculous crimes was gone! My freedom had been torn away as life continued to function all around in the dead of winter. To the police it was just another arrest. Another day at work where they get to go home but to me it meant my life was ruined.

The officer had me leaning forward on the hood of his patrol car, as I felt scared and sick. As he searched me, I felt the cold air blow my independence away. I saw people walking, working, and able to go home at any time to live out their lives, oblivious to the fact of what I've done and how my life was over.

I won't be able to relax in my bathtub and freely listen to music. I had freedom, a warm home, loving pets and so much more. All the things I took for granted was stripped from me. I would miss being able to stop and buy a soda, turn up the radio, admire nature, watch a good movie or sleep in a comfortable bed. All the little things we all forget to appreciate for the most part. I would no longer be able to admire the snow that swept across the area in a wondrous way.

Even with all that there was nothing that could compare to not being with my true love who I called Xanadoo or sometimes Goo or Doo or The Doo and… well… I gave her so many names over the years. The one woman I waited for all my life, I would not be able to touch, kiss or make love to. That's when a sick feeling of missing her settled in. Crying out in my mind that I want to go home to her!

As I was placed into the cop car all I could think about was her. The way we met and how everything fell into place was an unexpected phenomenon surrounded by a true love story. Xanadoo was all I had wished for in my days of darkness and now I may lose her! She had no idea how low I had sunk to obtain pills. I had risked everything in my life for an element that helped me escape reality for a short time. If I had everything why was I escaping reality anyway? I had to hold on to myself because I knew what lied ahead of me was going to hurt like hell!

I was brought to the police station of that small northwestern Pennsylvania town, which probably wasn't used to someone like myself playing doctor. Little did they know that my string of deception and lying to be my own doctor of medicine had gone way back a couple of months. At that moment they only knew of the two prescription sheets I stole from a doctor over state line in New York where I lived. Well at least where I used to live... I was pretty sure I wasn't going home any time soon. I was going to be a new resident of a Pennsylvania county jail for a while until the courts decide my fate. I heard my work phone ring and the arresting officer answered it and had to inform my boss that their driver, me, was in custody.

I heard my boss yell through the phone. "What! What! For what for?"

The officer said. "I am unable to tell you that."

"Holy shit! I don't need this!" He shouted. "Where is our company truck?"

"Downtown. We haven't towed it yet so someone will have to come down and pick it up. I will give you the address if you have a pen and paper."

As the officer gave my pissed off boss the info I thought how embarrassing! Dreadful and shameful feelings were all I felt in that moment. There goes my job as a driver!

Thoughts of how this all fell into place came to me…

About a week or so ago I had a day of pure bliss, even though, I had been withdrawing from the pills I had been abusing. The day was beautiful, clear and crisp. I drove the truck from a Buffalo delivery down Interstate 90 on the way to Erie, Pennsylvania. Music spoke to me as to say I had reached the end of my madness. There were no cars in either direction as the sun shone blurry all around. The passing scenery felt like I was in a foggy dream. It was a moment where I felt like I didn't exist in the real world. It was as though I was riding through a blank reality where I felt completely alone. Like I was in a momentary purgatory. I was never of this world and always saw weird, beautiful heavenly moments, especially with music.

As I drove through that incomprehensible void of existence there was a prison to my left and a sign that said…

"State Correctional Facility. Do not pick up hitchhikers."

I've been through that before like God granted me one last peaceful spiritual day before He brought the hammer down. That eerie day had to be a sign of my pending doom. Whenever I stop the toxins in my body, my mind and spirit always comes back alive. So do my senses and awareness around me.

The very next day I had made a delivery to that same prison and I don't deliver to many prisons! I mostly delivered to businesses and houses so this made it even stranger. I had to drive around the side to where the service department was, not to the main prison itself. I drove around the barbwire fence that circled the campus. After I dropped off the packages to one of the groundskeepers, I drove slowly looking past the barbwire fence and the site of the prison itself made me unwell. It was a huge two level gray concrete building with narrow vertical windows that gave off a creepy vibe. It was strangely quiet and no one was around. That was the moment when I knew what I was doing was wrong and that if I would not stop I would surely be doomed to a place like that. The Divine had given me the message to discontinue what I was doing but all I could do was try to strike up a deal.

I said before I drove out of the prison parking lot. "Lord, please allow me to pull the last of my refills on the pleasing painkillers and sedating muscle relaxers I am illegally obtaining. After I do, I promise I will never do this again!"

Little did I know that it really doesn't work like that. What a fool I was to defy a sign and feeling like that! On the way back from that delivery with my head heavy with worry about what I had been doing, I heard on the radio, Super Tramp, singing *"The Logical Song"*.

*"Then they sent me **Away** to **Teach** me how to be **sensible, logical, responsible, practical,** "* were the words that spoke to me.

It was like a voice speaking to me through music from a power bigger than me in sync with my thoughts. Like a strange spiritual synchronicity that was connected to my mind. It was something I could never explain as it happened all the time all my life. All I knew was I was able to hear it, notice the strange and constant coincidences that occur all around us. Would the angelic powers that surrounded me send me away to prison to save me from myself was what came to mind.

Another strange occurrence happened when I did a hospital run one night Goo and I got into a fight a few weeks ago. She got me so angry with her childish yelling drilling in my head. I just left and drove needing an escape! I had gone to my local hospitals a bit too frequently so I drove all the way out to Erie Pennsylvania about an hour away from where I lived in Western New York.

I remember being in the ER telling the doctor lies of how much pain I was in. I mean I really spilled it on him, manipulating him into getting me some good stuff for pain. When the doctor went off to get me a shot for my exaggerated pain, I got up to use the bathroom. As I had on my white hospital gown, limping like I was in pain, I saw an inmate from the local jail. There he was cuffed to the bed in an orange jumpsuit waiting for the doctor. He looked at me as he was thinking how lucky I was to have my own freedom. There were two police officers next to him and I wasn't sure if it was my mind playing tricks on me due to my guilt. It seemed they were looking at me with serious eyes as if they knew

I was committing a crime in plain sight with my false report to the ER to obtain narcotics.

I kept seeing *"Stop"* signs and *"Wrong Way"* signs as I thought about getting high but I didn't want to hear it. *"Do Not Enter"* signs as I would cross the threshold into a hospital parking lot. They just always popped out at the right moment of my thoughts. All synchronicity flows throughout the immeasurable universe and if I would have gave in to it I wouldn't be in the mess I made for myself. For many years I have known about a spiritual power that guides me but I chose not to take heed to the warnings I had been given. I had a calling, a purpose in life, but I put it on hold for my own selfish needs and sickness. The obsession of the mind and the power of addiction!

Now about an hour before I got arrested, the ironic part of this whole situation was I phoned in my last refill for my fake prescription on my way to make a deliver to another prison!

There I was… again… driving around a different prison fence staring at the buildings they house inmates in. A huge gray water tower that feeds the prison stood tall. I was able to see part of the yard where there were a lot of convicts just doing whatever they do. My spirit kept telling me this was not good and I should forget the last of the medicine. But my obsessed mind just told me to shut up and get them and that I would be just fine. I got the sensation of how I would feel later on. Seeing myself lounging on the couch, watching television and feeling good motivated me even more to go get the chemicals that altered my brain.

I made my delivery to the prison docks where inmates unloaded my truck. They were nice guys all dressed in the same green prison outfits. As I waited, I felt cold air blow on my face while I looked out at the bleak sky that was over and around the prison. My mind battling itself, stealing all my energy made me feel weak. Anxiety ran through me as I just wanted to get this over with. I truly hated every time I had to go to the pharmacy to pick up the pills! I always got shaky and nervous driving out of town, crossing state lines, hoping I come back. I would do nothing but drive stiff, palms sweaty, rushing myself there and back.

The truck was unloaded and I was ready to get out of there. I felt a sudden sadness within my spirit and all I wanted at that moment was to go home to Xanadoo. I suddenly started missing her.

I got back in the truck and it was off to the drugstore to commit yet another felony on company time without much thought to the signs. My demon of addiction was too powerful feeding me lies that it's ok the whole time I rushed to the pharmacy! So I made a delivery to a prison and ended up in one within an hour's time!

So there I was in a police station removed from society with a questionable future all for those little white pills that gave me a quick brain high. I started to come to grips as the officer sat down with me and asked if there were any more prescriptions out there. I of course said no.

He looked down at his papers. "So we contacted the other pharmacy and we were told you used a fake accent pretending you were the prescribing physician to phone in a refill for Hydrocodone and Soma."

"Yes I did," I said. "I used to be an actor."

"Would you mind showing me?"

I gave a quick impression of me using a fake accent as if I were a foreign medical doctor using the phony name that was meant for me.

He leaned back in his chair and said to another officer. "You see this? We have an actor in the house!"

He laughed for a moment then leaned forward and began to read off my charges. Maybe I shouldn't have done that I thought. There I went trying to show off my talents that I once used in a different part of my life. I didn't take the time to think that my acting talents meant nothing in that matter. I had so many gifts but they had all gone to waste for well over a decade!

Ok, let's get down to brass tax. There were two counts of forgery, three counts of acquisition of a controlled substance by fraud and two counts of receiving stolen property. They had charged me twice for the same crime of writing my own prescription, which was interesting, because I felt like I was getting a buy one get one free deal. The question of how could they have charged me with receiving stolen property when it was me who stole them stood out in my mind. I received nothing! I took them myself. Because it was from another state they called it "receiving stolen property", which really didn't make any sense. But I was in no position to question the criminal complaint! They

10

had brought me to a holding cell where I was to wait to see a judge to set my bail.

I found the waiting was the worst. There I was locked in a holding cell not knowing what was going to happen to me. What will Xanadoo think? Will I lose the love of my life? Will I have to go back to my old life in Baltimore City? The life she rescued me from. Is my life as I know it really over? That worrisome sick feeling stayed continuous as my mind kept thinking of all sorts of horrible things.

After a short wait, while they processed my paper work, I was brought to see the magistrate judge. They sat me into a small room almost like a mini courtroom and I waited. I overheard the arresting officer tell the judge my prior record. No it didn't sound good for me at all!

Prior arrests:

Possession of cocaine, Broward County Florida, 2002.

Resisting arrest, Broward County Florida, 2004.

Theft under $100, Ann Arundel County Maryland, 2005.

Possession with the intent to deliver a controlled substance, Baltimore County Maryland, 2007.

And now adding color to my record, Prescription Fraud, 2013!

The judge and the cop came in while I sat handcuffed. The judge said the only thing going for me was that I had a full time job. I wanted to say, not anymore! I knew I'd be fired for sure! The bail was set at $25,000!

Next I was brought over to the county jail and reality began to set in. I was able to make a five-minute phone call at intake. I called Xanadoo and she was happy to hear from me but that would soon change once I told her what happened.

I said in emotional pain. "Honey... Listen... I'm in jail."

"What?" After a short pause of shock, I remember hearing her crying softly. She said in sorrow with a sniffle, "I'm not going to see my honey tonight?"

Heartbreaking words that ran through my mind over and over again! After a brief explanation of what I did to get arrested, I told her the bail amount but said all that was needed was 10%, $2,500 and gave her some numbers of bail bondsman's. It was a very stressful, scary and emotional call for us both! I held on to the phone in silence for I couldn't let her go...

The woman correctional officer gave me a look that my time was up.

I said in misery, "I have to go now."

We said our heartfelt goodbyes. Once I hung up with her I sat down, as the woman CO took my info and went through my personal belongings. My thoughts were racing so fast and hard, I couldn't get an emotional grip! She pulled out of my wallet a picture of my sweet Xanadoo.

She said, "I can tell you're very emotional right now." She showed me the picture and asked. "Would you like to hold on to this?

"Yes." I said with a slight feeling of hope.

That was so nice that she allowed me to hold on to it, I thought as she handed it to me. As I looked down at it, all I could do was break down in tears! Her bright blue eyes and her glowing smile just made me sink. She was so beautiful to me and I was not able to go home to her.

"Oh my Goo... how sorry I am for this." I whispered.

I missed her like hell and I just wanted to go home!

Once they processed me they brought me up to a single cell and told me to hang out in there for a little while.

Those CO's lied to me!

I thought I was to stay in that holding cell with a bed for a few minutes while they go see what block I was to go to. I had no idea I would be in that hellish jail cell all night! They had placed me in isolation due to my highly emotional state a passing CO told me an hour ago. How could I not be emotional? I'm incarcerated and I do not know what will happen to me. The life I had left behind me was an intense one. I thought those horrible days after I lost my mother were over but I was wrong because there I was... again!

After a miserable night in isolation, which felt like a lifetime, I knew my Goo was doing everything possible to bail me out. My first night couldn't have been more sickening! Around 5pm yesterday was when they served me a tray of slop I could not eat. After they took that unsettling meal away, I decided to lie down and try to sleep. I lay there under the covers with the light from above beaming down on me twenty-four hours a day. There was a slight buzz coming from the rather large cell light. It never went off! There were no windows, nothing to look at, nothing to read or watch and nothing to do but lay there with my thoughts…

Every last twisted one of them!

I tossed and turned, ached, feeling restless and what felt like a whole night had past, I got up and went to the cell door to try and get someone's attention. I had to know what time it was. I caught the attention of a female CO and asked. She told me it was nine twenty.

I asked, "AM?"

She said, "no, PM."

My eyes widened and I was like my God! Only four hours had past! Time couldn't be crueler as it dragged on.

Some time later… I believed… it was finally a new day because there was a new shift and one of the CO's had told me I would be bailed out shortly. Thank God I thought! But instead of coming to terms with my arrest the only thing I could think of was going home and getting high on the painkillers I had there and where I could get more.

I waited and waited and thought geeezzz… how long does it take to post bond?

The isolation door opened and in came a guard who handed me a piece of paper with a surcharge on it and told me I was unable to make bail. Apparently, since I was from out of state, I was declared a flight risk and the only way I could get out was if my Goo would post the full $25,000! I knew that was impossible!

I sat there in disbelief and without words. I was frozen! Oh my God! Please! I just wanted to go home!

More time dragged then I was brought to go see the nurse the whole time feeling sick and terrified! I had begun to detox from the pills I was taking on a daily basis and just wanted relief. The nurse checked my vitals and I had to tell her what drugs I was taking. There wasn't much she could do for withdrawals. She told me they would give me some Vistaril, basically like Benadryl, to help with anxiety and some kind of nausea medication. That wasn't enough for what I was coming off of.

I was brought back to the isolation chamber and wondered how long I would have to wait in that pit of hell? As I lay there on the uncomfortable jail bed, I began to daydream. If only I had powers! Powers to get up and kick the cell door right off its hinges, having it smash quickly into the concrete wall! Powers to throw lighting from my hands against anyone who would try and stop me from walking the hell out of there. I imagined three guards rushing at me and I raise my hand and a punch of lighting streams out knocking them into the wall!

Or perhaps it would be easier to just vanish from there and teleport myself home at the speed of thought. I envisioned vaporizing out of there and instantaneously reappear next to Xanadoo to wipe her tears away...

But I knew I couldn't do any of that. Sucks that I couldn't so I just trailed off fantasying of super natural ways to get myself out of that nightmare. It helped me cope.

Once again the cell door opened and the CO told me I had a visitor. Who was here to see me? Was it my Goo? I was brought down to the visit room and there was the same cop who busted me looking really pissed off.

He came in and the first thing he said was, "you lied to me!"

"About what?" I asked feeling nervous.

"You told me you only took two prescription sheets and that there were no more!" He had some papers in his hand and showed me. "Look! We found the other drugs you forged over the past two months! You're a liar and a criminal!"

"I'm sorry!" I cried. "I was scared! I have an addiction. I'm not a criminal!"

He began to read me my rights… Again?

I felt like saying, I'm already in jail in a degrading green and white jumpsuit and you're reading me my rights again?

He said in a nasty tone. "I'm charging you with eight more forgery charges and eight more receiving stolen property charges."

"I guess I'm going to prison!" I said feeling sorry for myself.

He stood there for a moment looking a little bad for me. "Not necessarily." He said as he overlooked me like he felt a little bad for me.

He left and the whole time as they brought me back to my cell I was lost for words. I knew I was ruined! I was locked back in that dreadful cell and laid down on the bed. All I wanted to do was go home and forget this horrible reality but I couldn't. I had been banished from my life and had to wait and see what would become of me. I had to figure out who I became. How could I get my old self back? There was a time when I was a person who was once sober and successful. My God! I have lived so many lives and had survived many storms. Did I know when I was a child that I would turn into a man with this terrible darkness inside me?

I think of back to when I was as an infant. I envision being outside my body staring down at myself as a baby. I would look intently at my newborn blue eyes and I wondered would that baby know he would grow up to be incarcerated, entwined with a grim disease of the mind and spirit? All that innocence I had would slowly be stripped away to some of the brutal realities of existence and the mind. What had happened to me down this extraordinary twisted life I have led was the question I had to find. How did I end up in isolation locked away from everything at the age of thirty-nine?

I desperately needed to find peace! Only a few days had past since that awful day of my banishment from society. They moved me out of that nightmare isolation cell, which felt like a lifetime of losing my mind. My own personal hell. I was already imprisoned in the insanity of my own construct. How could they just toss someone who already has emotion distress into a cell like that? The only thing that kept me somewhat sane, was holding on to the little hope I had, but even that was hard when I felt like I was treated like a disease by the system. They put me on the

17

intake block or what's also known as the block they put you if you're a troublemaker, badass or a nuisance.

My withdrawals from all those pills were getting worse so I masturbated a lot to get relief temporarily. I must have taken care of myself five or six times being in that isolation tank! It was a way to cool my body of the aches and discomfort from detoxing. I needed to get a serge of pleasure that would cloak over the misery I was feeling! It was a way of releasing pleasing chemicals from my brain throughout my entire nervous system. I felt that chemical would slow and calm down my over active nerves that were firing hysterically all over my body, especially my restless burning legs. The orgasm itself rushes through my nervous system like a shot of ecstasy! The lingering effects of the orgasm gave me about 15 to 20 minutes of deliverance... somewhat. The discomfort was so bad, the pleasure coating did only so much and only for so long. I had exhausted my sex drive after a while.

They called my name for my preliminary hearing to see where my fortune may lay. I was placed into shackles around my ankles and they strapped a heavy belt around me and set my hands in cuffs that were attached to the belt in the front. Really now! Where the hell was I going to go I thought? It was very uncomfortable and a pain in the ass to walk! They walked me outside from the jail to the courthouse, which was next door. I was walking on slushy snow wearing only socks and jailhouse flip-flops. I looked up at the cloudy sky and felt the cold breeze blow on my face. It felt so good to be outside for only a moment then the moment was gone.

Xanadoo was there waiting for me and I was so ashamed being cuffed and shackled like some kind of murderer! I was brought down to the lower part of the courthouse and there she was sitting in a chair. She didn't deserve to have a man like me. I was a freaking disgrace I thought as they sat me down next to her. She looked so beautiful, so loving and so kind as she was so happy to see me. We weren't allowed to kiss or touch each other, which really burned me up because who the hell were they to take away my free will because I had a sickness?

My public defender sat down with us and reviewed the charges I was arrested on. He talked and acted like a weasel on crack in a suit and tie. He wore jewelry and a couple of rings. He seemed liked a hurried man and wore heavy cologne. I wasn't sure about this guy. I sat there knowing that the arresting officer who paid me that surprising visit was coming at me with more charges! Much more, which made me very unsettled!

I asked, "will I go to prison?"

My public defender better known as the Weasel said. "I don't know."

I saw my arresting officer go into the witness room with the assistant district attorney who looked like she was straight out of the 1980's! She had long curly hair and seemed vicious, mean like a pit bull unleashed! She was defiantly in charge. This didn't look good I thought when I saw the DA walk out and there sat the officer looking really angry after telling her his side of my crimes. My public defender and the DA went around the corner to have a chat about my case.

"I want to put this guy away!"

That's what I swore I just heard the DA say!

I told my Xanadoo but she said that's not true and that perhaps I was hearing things due to my fear. Why would she want to put me away? I haven't killed anyone or did anything unforgivable. The Weasel came back and brought Xanadoo and I into a small conference room. He began to lay it all down for us and I was nervous as hell! As he was writing something down, I kept hearing his wrist jewelry clank on the table.

He said, "ok we got two counts of forgery, which are felonies in the second degree. Looks like you're up to seven counts of procure drug by fraud, which are un-graded felonies. Eight counts of violations of the controlled substance, drug, device and cosmetic act that go along with the forgery charges. They are also un-graded felonies, which is the lowest level of a felony. And seven counts of receiving stolen property, which are misdemeanors."

Holy shit I remember thinking! It appears in the Commonwealth of Pennsylvania when you get a felony it comes with more felonies! How the hell could they charge me more than once for the same freaking crime? Apparently it was a felony to commit a felony!

"Why are they charging me with all that?" I asked. "All I did was forge a few script's because I simply needed pain medicine."

"In the Commonwealth there are other laws that come into play."

"For basically one crime?"

He rolled his eyes in frustration. "Look… You stole quite a few prescription sheets, forged a doctors name and obtained controlled substances."

I paused for a moment then asked. "Will I go to prison?"

"Uh, ya might," he said in a harsh weasel like tone.

"I just needed medicine for myself. I need help. I can't go to prison!"

The Weasel snapped at me. "Well you shouldn't have done what you did!"

What the hell kind of man was this I thought? There was no need for him to be annoyed with me; he's meant to be my lawyer! He was supposed to be on my side, especially since I'm crying out for help. But how could he when this was his life? Case after case…it just never ended for this guy! I was just another criminal case to him. Another idiot who fucked up one too many times on the streets and had to be corrected. He took out a piece of paper and wrote down all my charges.

He said, "ok, we are going to drop everything except three counts of violation of the controlled substance act, which is also known as obtaining a controlled substance by fraud. Which are ungraded felonies. Will you be willing to plea to this?"

"I don't know. I am not even sure how all this works."

"Well, I'll give you some time to think about it. Next time we talk you just let me know."

I asked with great fear. "How much time does this hold?"

"Well," he said, "the maximum penalty is five years each."

I jumped and cried. "Fifteen years?!"

"Don't worry, that is not what you will be getting. It's just the max the state can go." He took in a breath. "Look, I'm not the judge. I do not know what he will do. If he wakes up in the morning and likes his bacon and eggs then it is good, if he doesn't… well…" he shrugged his shoulders. "I'll tell ya though, I have seen a man from New York once get 3 years for a drug charge."

"I became addicted to the pills. I'm not hurting anyone but myself, struggling with a disorder. I shouldn't go to prison for it."

"Yeah, yeah," he said. He moved his hands out hearing the clank of his heavy watch knock on the table. "Listen, everyone in here is a drug addict!"

Xanadoo jumped in and said. "Everyone?"

The weasel looked to her and said. "At least 95 percent. Much of my cases are drug charges, mostly nonviolent and simple possession."

I said, "doesn't sound right when you look at the big picture. There's millions of people out there struggling and you throw them in prison? We need criminal reform. The war on drugs has failed!"

Xanadoo jumped in. "Sounds stupid locking people up over drugs when most just need help, not jail and treated like a criminal."

The Weasel stood up and said, "it does flood the jails and keeps me busy but I don't make the laws."

I looked at my Goo and she looked very sad and was just as scared as I was. What will happen to me now? This lawyer sucked I thought! He was my hope? A weasel that talked and acted likes he was on crack? I knew I was doomed! I badly needed shelter from the coming storm but in my mind there was none!

Once we were all wrapped up, my arresting officer came and began to walk me back to the pits. My Goo walked along my side and I didn't know what to do. I was helpless now.

I said to Xanadoo. "Don't worry honey. We will get through this together."

She smiled and said. "I know we will."

She had to go her own way to freedom, waving with sad eyes, while she walked down the exit hallway and I was led back to the pits of my own hell. I tried to make the officer feel bad by the way I told my Goo goodbye in a sad tone but he didn't care. I even apologized to him about lying on the way back but he didn't seem to care much about that either. I wasn't a criminal or a bad person. I just was suffering with an inner demon. It was ridiculous to make someone a common criminal over nonviolent drug offenses. A crime to put a mind-altering substance in our own bodies, to experience different types of pleasures was wrong? It's a personal choice for some, an illness to others and it shouldn't be criminalized and demonized.

The United States started this stupid war with President Nixon declaring drugs public enemy number 1 back in 1970. Meanwhile Nixon was a corrupt politician who got involved in a scandal as people were being arrested more and more for drugs. In the past decades the war on drugs cost the US over a trillion dollars, have ruined millions of lives, caused mass incarceration and has killed countless. The war on drugs causes more harm than good. Drugs will be consumed no matter what the cost. During prohibition, substances get stronger, making more overdoses and health problems. The homicide rate has gone up dramatically. The problem is there will always be a demand as long as addiction remains active.

Senseless raids, breaking down doors, pointless deaths, and so much madness! All for what? Because some people want to get high? The use of mind-altering substances and herbs has been used throughout the sands of time. It will continue going on as spiritual, recreational and medical uses. Turning a persons life upside down and ripped out of society for altering their own minds wasn't the answer. It's the ancient addiction that's been around for millennia that should be addressed, not ruining lives by throwing someone in jail with a criminal record that will affect the future of getting work or education! All that time, money and resources wasted when it could have went toward treatment and more research.

All the dominos that surrounded my world were all going down one by one at an alarming rate! I am going to lose everything and there was nothing I could do. I knew I was screwed! It was time for a re-appraisal of my entire life and find the answers to how I ended up at that point in time.

When I got back to my cell I had a new cellmate. A young man around 26 trying to find his way in life. He got caught up in drugs and the wrong people, which landed him back in jail on a probation violation. But what seemed different about him was he looked like a kind person. I had a sense for those things. He spoke well and was clean cut. It is such a shame to see good people be misled. He didn't belong there anymore than I did. Jails become a revolving door when all they do is make a criminal out of an addict.

There was madness on the block. The television was up loud in the day room and everyone on the block was making a racket! My new cellmate handed me a book called *"Live Before You Die"*. I breezed through it and read something that stood out.

"God does not reveal his plan for us over night. It comes little by little, like a slowly blooming flower."

I thought of where I was at that time. Where did my life go? What's coming next? Where I felt I was in that moment was the beginning of a long road for my mind. The waiting killed me and I wanted to get over the finish line of this mess. What I saw ahead was having patients and let time slowly reveal what's next. I knew in my spirit it would be all right.

There was this one guy who was on the phone in the day room and all of a sudden he starts yelling at his wife and mother.

"Fuck you bitch!" He was talking to his wife at the time. "I swear when I come home I am going to slap the shit out of you!" Then he began talking to his mother. "Fuck you mom! No one is talking to you!"

My mother was dead and I would have given anything to be home with my Goo and there that guy was verbally abusing his mother and wife when he gets out soon! I could see why he was in jail. Just what was it that made that guy so bitter in life?

They called for us to take it all in for lock down. I remember thinking I needed peace, sanctuary, and a way to deal with this terrible situation and find a way to cope. I jumped up on to my bunk and lay down. The only thing on that block that gave me some peace was one of the inmates who sang. He would sing songs in a low tone and I would close my eyes and try to ignore the fact that I was in jail as I fell into the melody. From time to time I would hear a radio playing in the distance and I heard Human League while it was quiet. It was the song *"Human"*.

"I'm only human… of flesh and blood I'm made… Human… born to make mistakes."

As I listened it felt somewhat comforting. It brought back a few good memories of when I was a growing up that gave me a short time of peace. I knew I was only human but the mistake I had made was one that I may never forget! I was restless, ashamed, I felt like I wanted to die. I began to think of ways to kill myself. Yeah, I thought, I could wrap my sheet around my neck and hang myself. Couldn't do it anyway because my new cellmate was there. I didn't want him yelling for someone as I would just want to die in peace. Plus they would throw me right into suicide watch and I didn't want that! I couldn't take it anymore so I grabbed a pen and paper and began to write a letter.

Dear Xanadoo,

26

First I wanted to say how sorry I truly am for all this! This isn't me! I still think of how we first met in person after falling in love with you over the phone in our long distance relationship. I remember walking off the bus at the bus station after a 12 hour ride from Baltimore to Erie PA. You were so beautiful and you said my name in happiness! What I wouldn't give to hold you again! We have made it so far and been through more than anything any of us had been with before. My hands are shaky. It's hard to write. There are a lot of dumb asses in here and I keep mostly to myself. I'm gonna tell you what it's like in here.

Ok... Around 5 am we are awakened for head count. It's so stupid! We all have to stand like a bunch of goons! Some CO's make me climb down from the top bunk I'm on just to stand and by the time I get down, they will be gone! So it's like, hello! I have a bad back and can't be climbing up and down the hard metal. They can see me just fine when I sit up on my bunk. Then I lay down until 6 am when we eat chow. A pathetic little bowl of cereal, skim milk and toast with spray on butter. Every freaking day we eat the same thing for breakfast! I miss eggs and bacon! Then we lay back down and around 7 am the cell door opens. It's screeches while opening then a loud clank when it stops! Then the mop buckets come out and cleaning takes place. I don't bother because I am too sick to care. Then it quiets down and around 9 am the television comes on. Slowly some of the guys get up and calmly go out into the dayroom to watch it. I have been too sick, scared, having stomach pains, emotional pain, feeling stupid wondering what will happen to me. I miss you and the baba's (Our cats and dogs) so much! Around 11 am we all go back into our cells and they lock us in. Clank again! Lunch is served around noon. We get the same shit every day for lunch too! Soup and a sandwich. It's either one thin slice of meat on bread or a peanut butter and jelly sandwich. The soup is mostly nasty. One soup we get, they toss everything into. We call it garbage disposal soup! It looks like something you would find in a stop drain in the kitchen sink! Uh yeah, it's real shitty! The rest of the day drags! I lay in my bed all afternoon then around 5 pm we eat dinner. Some of the dinners aren't bad. I lay back down again with all the noise and loud voices and banging on the tables! I am close to losing my mind! I must have masturbated at least 20 times since I have been locked up! What is wrong with me? Why every time I withdraw from drugs and land in jail I get overly sexual and feel the need to jerk it? I am so sorry again my Goo! I can feel the pain I caused you and my mother. When I overheard that prick curse out his wife and mother it gave me an appreciation for what I have. I know the real me is still alive somewhere in here. I promise I will do what it takes to get it right if I ever get the hell out of this nightmare! Please don't leave me! I love you!

The Peace of my Youth

I felt it as a baby, a mysterious entity watching over me. I wasn't sure if it was good or evil, I just knew it was real. Without explanation I could strangely remember being in my crib, when we used to live in the Bronx, that entity gazing at me with no words. It was something I could not see or touch. I had a thirsty naked feeling as I felt its presence, which I couldn't explain. Like I was exposed naked before heaven and I strangely thirsted for cold, clear, refreshingly pure water. I was innocent and new to the world with a mysterious guardian that seemed to silently watch over me.

I was the youngest of three brought into humanity in the dead of winter, late January of 1974. Those memories of myself as a baby remain a puzzle, as they are barely visual. My first clear memory was when I was eighteen months old or so. We had just moved out to Long Island to our first house. It was a beautiful early June morning and my mother held me in her arms as she sat on the red deck of the above ground pool feeding me baby food. Not knowing why but I enjoyed the smooth tasty baby food. I had known no other taste yet. The day was mild on my skin and I could see the sugar maple tree in full bloom with its green leaves gently blowing in the breeze. It felt like a new dawn, a new beginning of a warm season. The first time I breathed in the late spring, entering early summer air was a heavenly new sense of the seasons that change.

As the time moved on my memories became more vivid. Back then everything seemed much brighter, as I became more self aware to life around me. Clearly I remember walking around our backyard noticing the glistening sunlight reflect off of the bushes and hemlock trees that surrounded our entire backyard. I noticed every blade of grass, the way the sun shined down on them and the shadows the trees gave. I was in awe as I looked around at the beauty that encircled me. This became my first wondrous playground and sanctuary.

What I didn't know in my precious little world was how much my mother was suffering. She got married at twenty-four to my father and life for her then was fresh and new. They were a fun couple with good friends that just lived carefree. Drinking and smoking cigarettes was the cool thing to do back then and they had plenty of pictures of their early life to see that young people do what young people will do no matter what decade. It's just not something you think much about because we only know our parents as our parents and never as teenagers who once did some wild things.

However, my father was an alcoholic and I guess my mother didn't really notice it until after she married him. My father was real romantic when he proposed to her my mother had later told me when I got older.

Sitting in his car, parked, he said out of the blue. "Hey? Ya wanna get hitched?"

No getting a ring and asking her to marry her on bend and knee on a special day. My mother accepted his rather disappointing proposal and thus began what would be my family back in the mid 1960's. My oldest brother, Richard, was born a year after my parents wed. They had another child named Scott but the doctors said he was sick and could not identify what was wrong with him. Baby Scott died at only four months old. Thee worse, most heartbreaking thing that can ever happen to a mother! That was something she could never let go of! My father didn't show much compassion and only drank more. I was sure he grieved but in his own way. He just escaped into the bottle.

I remember my mother told me after the death of baby Scott she saw some strange spirit that stood in the back of our old Bronx apartment. There it was swaying about like white robes in a slow breeze. My mother had felt great fear and grabbed my oldest brother Richard and ran out of there. She never saw it again and had no idea what it was. Could it have been my would have been brother Scott trying to tell her all is well or was it some other kind of being warning her of what was to come? Was it the same entity that had been watching over me?

They had conceived another son a year later. My brother Chris was born next into our growing family. My mother told me she had to have another child after baby Scott died. The weird thing was that baby Chris, my other older brother, at the time, had the same symptoms as baby Scott. It was that mysterious sickness the doctors couldn't figure out. All that was going on was a mother's nightmare. My brother Chris had gotten better later on and turned out ok. My father had worked nights at the New York City Transit Authority. He was a chronic alcoholic and was an absentee father and husband. But he did make a good living and they got by.

I was never planned my mother told me. I was an accident that was brought into the world five years later. I was a breech baby. Apparently I had missed that last turn in the womb and my mother had told me I walked out. I also had the same sickness as baby Scott and Chris. Could it have had something to do my father's drunken sperm? Just strange not knowing what the hell that sickness or virus was and why my brother and I made it but not baby Scott? I guess I would never know.

I was able to feel some of my father's memories. When he wasn't working, he would be down in the basement den, watching his television and even though no one ever actually saw him drinking, we all knew what he was doing. All those old TV shows like All in the Family, Happy Days, Welcome back Kotter, Sanford and Son were some of the shows he would watch in the late 1970's. To me those opening themes always brought me back and in a strange way I was able to live my fathers darkness in my mind.

When he wasn't isolating in his own prison he would always be consumed with fixing things around the house. He could fix everything and anything. With no schooling he could fix cars, electric, plumping, taking care of our pool and more. It was a great shame he let the alcohol take him over because he was such a smart man! Those were the gifts my father had that were not passed down to me unfortunately. Instead he passed down the disease of addiction. Its structured in our DNA, weaved into our minds, a horrible disease.

I was very afraid and intimidated by him and would stay away as much as I could. He just never seemed approachable or happy. When he wasn't down in the den, on a bright sunny day, I would go down there with no lights on and the red curtains we had would create a dim eerie reddish glow from the daylight. It was intensely haunting and I was fascinated by the way it looked. It was as though I was lost in a calm nightmarish daydream that I was not afraid of.

I often explored the entire house I lived in when I was alone. Having that realization that this is where I actually live and no lights on with the daylight coming in the house, I saw it in a daunting way. It felt like I was aware that I was aware looking out of my own eyes and feeling the home I lived in at that point in time. It was the foundation and safe zone of my childhood where I had comfort. I would see the dust particles float as rays of sunlight shone in. I was actually alive, a conscience, a being with a spirit, a soul. I was just one of many many souls and lives out there yet I only knew my own world, as if its the only one in the entire universe. It drove me crazy that I was conscious on the planet I live in. I couldn't understand the meaning of life as I try to reach God.

As I grew older I became a bit of a loner for my part. I was happy being by myself and would walk around my backyard just admiring the nature around me and feeling the energy. We had an above ground pool with a perfect size backyard. There were the two sycamore trees at the front of the backyard, that sugar maple I remember as a baby off the side of the pool. Two big trees that stood behind the pool by the back of the yard. And all the surrounding hemlocks, fur trees and bushes gave me my own wonderland and privacy.

I was my own best friend. During the seasons I would become aware of a lot of little things. Springtime I would enjoy looking at the trees and bushes and notice every day how the buds on the bare trees would slowly turn into tiny flowers and grow into leaves. I loved the smell of April rains and the sunny warmer days of May where I could breath in the scent of flora. I admired greatly when all the trees were in full bloom and the warmth of summer. I studied every tree around me when fall would arrive and watched each passing day as the foliage slowly change colors and the days got shorter. I was in tuned to the circle of seasons and grew intensely mesmerized by the death of summer. The way the autumn leaves fell and gathered on the ground and blew in the draftiness of the shifting winds captivated me. The smell of the fallen leaves everywhere and cooler weather felt so refreshing. I loved the dead of winter with the bare trees and the cold air. It was excitingly haunting to see the bare trees against the bleak wintry overcast sky. I became very in touch with nature as the globe kept spinning and revolving around the sun year after year.

As time went on I began to hold more memories and became conscious of something outside of my own reality. I just didn't know what it was as the reality of my childhood came into play. New things were about to enter my life.

I had become well known through my school years for my eccentric and unusual behavior. I was introduced to the group of children I would enviably grow up with in nursery school when I was around 5 years old.

I began kindergarten in September of 1979. I remember feeling nervous and weird the moment my mother brought me to elementary school. I didn't know what to expect or what was to happen. I had that anxious moment of walking into the school feeling alone with my backpack on, holding my lunch pail. I knew no one and I had no idea what to do or say.

After some time I got more comfortable in the school routine, made a couple of friends and became more myself. I became labeled a weirdo due to my obsession with cheese. The lunch my mother had packed for me had sandwiches and I would pick the cheese off and lay it on my desk until it became warm and then peel it off the desk and eat it.

Cheese was one of my very first addictions that I could remember. I would play with it by mashing it up into balls or small pieces and ate it in out of the ordinary ways. I couldn't just eat it like normal people. I would bask in the taste! Let it melt on the roof of my mouth and tongue it around. It was smooth, salty and delicious. I rebelled from fruit and would toss the bananas my mother gave me in my desk where it would become unfit for human consumption. They would turn brown, sometimes started growing mold spoors and it grossed out the entire class.

The 1980's rolled in and I realized I wasn't the fastest learner when it came to dumb stuff I didn't feel the need to gain knowledge of! In first grade the teacher would give us our assignments and I was always the last one finished. I got bored easily and got frustrated with schoolwork that I felt I would have no use for or didn't want to understand. Just about every freaking day once all my classmates were done with their schoolwork, there I was still working on mine, always being the last one to finish. The teacher would gather everyone up to the front of the class and completely humiliate me.

As I tried to hurry my schoolwork, she would say loud. "Who's done?"

My classmates would say all together. "Everyone!"

The teacher continued with, "except for?"

The whole class would shout out my name!

There I was, as this went on day after day feeling completely brainless and weak. What the hell was wrong with me I used to think? I hated those moments when the teacher, an adult woman who was supposed to be there to help everyone, have the whole class get up and make a fool of me when I was simply struggling with the work I could care less about.

One day the assignment that was handed out was something I was interested in. Something I could really get into. Well that day I became the first one finished and I was sure that I surprised the hell out of everyone! I remember the teacher announced my success and the whole class applauded me as I got to play with the toys they had for those who finished their work. I showed them I thought!

Second grade I was very hyper and was sent to the principal's office often. I just could not keep still so they put me on Ritalin! At the time I really didn't understand why, I just knew I had to take it. An amphetamine, speed, that would calm me down and help me focus. Rather ironic for a stimulant to work different in a young growing brain.

Third grade I was well known for smuggling in a playboy magazine that got the attention of a lot of my fellow male classmates! I thought it to be cool if I had one and showed it to a couple of kids but the moron I told not to tell anyone spread the word real quick! Before I knew it I was sitting in the cafeteria when I saw a long line of kids coming my way. That caught the attention of the teacher and it was not good. The magazine was confiscated and I was sent to the principal's office yet again!

My mother had brought me to see a psych doctor to talk things out. I didn't have a whole lot to say instead I used to play head games with the doctor. I guess I was rebelling being there.

Later on my mother had told me that the doctor said that she would lose me emotionally.

The doctor's exact words: "Your son seems to have a lot of issues. I'm sorry to tell you this... You will lose your son emotionally when he gets older."

My mother and I were very close and we had laughed at the diagnosis! Who the hell was he we thought! Would that doctor have hit the nail on the head with his findings on my future mental outlook, was my thinking.

Halfway through fourth grade they had found an answer to some of my issues. I was told I had a learning disability with hyper activity. The school I was going to at the time didn't really deal with that type of situation so they sent me to another school. I was sent way out to the freaking goonies and was placed in a class with other emotionally disturbed children. Being torn away from the classmates I got to know was tough on me. I needed awareness from the other crazies so I went into the bathroom and took a shit on the bathroom floor. Even then I wasn't really sure why I did that. I probably just wanted attention. Perhaps it was a cry for help. "Get me the hell out of this school! Please mother, I just want to be normal!" My mother was contacted yet again about my sick antics. The teacher had told my mother that in all the years she had been a teacher she never saw anything like that and didn't know what to do with me. I actually out weirded the weirdo's in that crazy class!

Fifth grade I was sent back to my original elementary school but placed in a special education class, which they only had for fifth graders. Once again I was surrounded with unstable kids. I remember one day I saw my father drive by the school on the way home and he got pulled over by a police officer.

The attention was brought to me, as someone in my class said, "isn't that your dad?"

They had arrested my father for drunk driving in the middle of the day and I was ashamed. Good one dad I thought! It wasn't bad enough that I already had an unusual rep in that school but now you add that and yeah, I felt like the biggest loser in my school! One of my classmates I had became good friends with. His name was Brice and he came from a really messed up family! He was reckless, tough and a troublemaker. We went around after school and caused all sorts of shenanigans! My mother did not approve of me hanging out with him.

In my fifth grade class the teacher would separate the class into two sides. There was a good side and a bad side. I had a bit of hard time wondering if I was good or bad. One week I would be on the good side and another week I would do something stupid and placed on the bad side. I wanted to be a good kid but I was also attracted to the bad side, which gave me pleasure.

Being in touch with nature my friend and I had volunteered our time at this beautiful 135-acre park. We worked with the rangers, taking care of all the animals, geese and chickens. That park was my sanctuary. My best friend Ralph and I would go there every weekend first thing in the morning. My mother would give me some money so I could get a bacon egg and cheese on a kaiser roll along with Nestles Quick Chocolate Milk! I had intensely become addicted to those! Every Saturday throughout the mid 80's, it was breakfast at the park and a beautiful childhood day in the sunshine of my life.

Winters we enjoyed those inside the warm nature center that had a musky smell with education of nature. The ceiling was vaulted and made of wood. There were stuffed seagulls, owls and other small animals. There were large tanks with turtles, frogs and fish. Early spring, we would have breakfast by the big red garage that was old and had chipped paint. We would sit with one of the park workers named Chris and make maple syrup that was boiled in a large metal pot on a fire pit. Late February into March, we went around and tapped the maple trees and hung an empty milk container to collect gallons of it. The smell of the wood burning and smoke rising with the aroma of the tap from the maple trees was so invigorating! I felt that time of year when every thing is still cold and bare trees against those gray cloudy days. That soon the days will get warmer and the sun will come out as the trees and bushes bloom being reborn. It felt like that there was no end to the days I was living.

It didn't matter if it was summer or winter; we loved being there all year round! I took a lot of time to myself to explore the woods and went on my own little adventures. Many trails led different ways into the woods that I knew like the back of my hand. Admiring the hills, walking with God in my heart and a strong connection to nature. I continued to notice every patch of sunlight that shined on the leaves, ground, grass and bushes that was all around me. It was so bright and beautiful and it lifted my spirit so much! Thank God my mother had moved us out to Long Island otherwise I would have never known such beauty!

When I was alone I lingered in the wonders of that magnificent place but I was also attracted to causing trouble. My friends and I would go to the edge of the park and throw rocks at all the cars that would pass on the side road. It gave us a rush of excitement hitting passing cars then running off into the woods to hide! The houses that were near by we would also toss rocks at and waited for the noise it made when it hit. One after another that knocking sound would give us a thrill. Those terrible things we did were a part of us and we didn't realize the problems it caused the people we had terrorized. We never once thought, hey, what if that were us? Would we like it?

I had a problem with stealing candy and stuff. Sugar and candy was another addiction that developed. There was something about going into a store and lifting as much candy I could then go outside and just totally wrap myself in the flavors and sweetness it brought me. I took handfuls of candy at once, unlike normal people who take a couple. It gave me a great high as my eyes closed, mouth watering as I savored every second in deep enjoyment. My taste buds sent messages to my brain and in return releases many natural chemicals stashed in the brain sending out an intense endorphin rush! Like a body orgasm stretched out, watered down, yet still feels so incredible within the body, lasting longer through the duration of eating it and the calming, satisfied feeling that mildly lingers afterwards.

I found peace in music. This was an amazing connection that kept me in touch with my mind and spirit. I'd lay in my bed and could create my own world as I listened to music with my headphones. But something strange was around me. I remember I had moments where I lay in my bed at night and felt like stone. My whole body felt stiff, solid, thick and heavy. I'd be half awake and with my eyes closed I could see a never-ending blackness before me. Behind me felt like an unseen wall and in the distance stood a figure. I never could make who or what it was but sometimes it would be far in the blackened distance and other times it would be right in my face staring continuously at me.

Feeling like I was stuck between a rock and a hard place, I would become paralyzed staring back at this thing with no words, which in a strange way felt like I was staring at myself. I couldn't quite make out a face and never understood why it was so close one night then gone in the emptiness of that outlandish realm beyond my own reality. It was like I was trapped in a sphere of nothingness with a being that was watching me with my back against an invisible wall. It would be pressing into me, face to face, then vanish off into the infinite, mysterious, obscure space before me. Other nights, being fully awake, I was aware of that strange entity I felt as a baby gazing over me yet again. There I was alone in my bedroom feeling completely naked with an abnormal thirst I could not explain. There were no words to clarify that phenomenon and I knew it wasn't part of the real world.

Sixth grade I was sent to yet another school because of my stupid learning disability! There I had met a girl who developed a crush on me. It was a nice feeling because most of the girls of my class thought I was whacked. The feelings I started to notice about the opposite sex ran deep. So deep in fact that I ran away from it and the girl who liked me. The emotions were too great.

Seventh grade I went to another school and I was tired of it! I got involved with some real hoodlum punk asses and got into trouble for tearing someone's bike apart. I had begged my mother to please get me back into my school district with my generation I grew up with.

In eighth grade my mother had gotten me back to my own school zone and reconnected with those I was away from. I had to go to a special class. It was there where I met my new teacher who became a little like a father figure to me. I helped him with the animals he had during seventh period. Mainly mice, a gecko, and a couple of bullfrogs, which we would feed baby mice to. I found it fascinating how a frog will eat anything that moves, have it in its mouth and slowly swallow it. They'd even eat each other. They are stupid like that. We had a great connection and he always rewarded me with a Coke. He always took me down to the teachers lounge to go to the vending machine. Just the thought of it made me excited!

One day he didn't have any change for my soda fix and I freaked!

I remember saying. "But I need a Coke!"

"Did you hear yourself?" He looked down at me in concern and said. "You need?"

At the time I didn't think much of it. I didn't take heed to my growing addiction and obsession. All I wanted then was the sweet bubbly taste of a Coca Cola Classic!

In the springtime of that year I saw something that really got my attention. I was playing around with this girl my fat friend Bill at the time introduced me to. It was when I saw her sister walk out of the house to the edge of their yard and asked if she needed anything from the store. There she was with her long dirty blonde hair, pretty face and an astonishing young sexy body!

I remember raising my head in awe and said to myself. "Who is that?"

Deep within me a great passion developed. It started when my fat friend Billy and a girl he started dating were sitting on small couch in the spare bedroom of that pretty girls house. Her and I were sitting next to each other on another small couch. Fat Billy came up with Truth or Dare for all of us to play. As we played, truth was asked the first few times as we delayed the dares. I was so attracted to that 14-year-old girl sitting next to me. Her hair fell over her shoulders and her blue eyes looked intensely at me. I felt her youthfulness, innocence and the aura coming off of her and the sensation felt miraculous as I took all of her essence into me. It was something I never felt before.

The dare came for us…

She said in a sweet tone. "I dare you to kiss me."

That moment when my heart dropped and my body tingled in excitement. Those eyes of hers stared wide and striking into mine. With our eyes closed and for the first time I felt her lips touch mine. A soft amazing kiss as our lips pressed to each other's, slowly kissing and breathing in one another's breath over and over again.

When we were just cuddling together, I often looked up to her bedroom and wonder if we would some day make love. All sorts of sexual fantasies began to develop in my mind. The kiss goodbyes in the mild weather I will forever remember. I had lost track of other things in my life and was with her almost every day. I got to know her and we dated for about a month until my inner spirit overloaded and I ran away.

Experiencing her kiss's and a developing relationship with a female overwhelmed me! A strange type of insecurity formed and I had just stopped calling her and didn't answer the phone when she was trying to call me to avoid her. Each day that passed, it bothered me within but my fear kept me away from that beautiful girl.

Many new feelings came over me that was new and exciting! I started masturbating a lot in admiration of women and it became an obsession. I absolutely loved women like a fine painting, which to me was like a true work of art. I had a hard time mentally and emotionally containing myself so many days and nights, I would fantasize, making love to them in my mind. I had become addicted to masturbation and humans of the female variety!

When I was thirteen it was my oldest brothers 21st birthday in June. He got my friend and I a 4 pack of wine coolers as the sun was close to setting. Later into the evening as the party in our backyard was on, I started blacking out and back in again after my 4th wine cooler. My awareness became blind and my brain was working for my addiction controlling my body. I came to thinking to myself, "More!" I remember grabbing a pitcher of beer and downing it. It wasn't me!

I came to again behind my pool throwing up with my friend who was also vomiting from being so wasted… went black… Came to passing my mother in the kitchen trying to act normal… blacked out… Came back to sitting on my bed with just the hallway light beaming in, throwing up on the floor on my bedroom, as my brothers got a kick out of it… Passed out.

My mother wasn't too happy about it the next day and I had the worst hangover for my 8th grade finals. Dry heaves and feeling like shit. For my first time with alcohol, it was a miracle I didn't die as much as I drank. I never gave it a second thought at the time how I lost complete control. It was like something dark inside me was reaching out to try and poison me.

All through ninth grade I regretted running away from my first love and whenever I saw her in school I was too unconfident to approach her. It caused me to believe she didn't even like me anymore. I'd see her in the hallway looking so beautiful, yet I just could not say anything, as we passed by like we were just another face in the crowd. We'd sometimes look at each other as we walked by but with no words. I often heard on the radio a beautiful sad love song in a strange connection to my thoughts whenever I was dreaming about being in love again with her.

Brenda K. Starr sang, *"I still believe… someday you and me…we'll find ourselves in love again."*

The song hit me right in the heart. I felt the words, the powerful melody go right through my soul. My body would tingle and pleasing sensations ran through me. It was mystical yet I couldn't pick up on the deeper meaning of synchronicity. All I knew was I was still in love.

In the beginning of August of 1989, six weeks before tenth grade, I had an idea to get her attention without actually calling her myself. My fat friend Billy use to make tons of prank phone calls to her, harassing her at one point. I think he was upset with her because her friend dumped fat Billy and thought she was the reason why. I would actually watch him call my ex-girlfriend and breathe in the phone, whisper crazy words and especially loved to fart and burp on the phone then hang up. I was never really sure why he kept doing it and why I just watched getting a kick out of it. Its been a while since he did that so I thought I could use it as an in to have her call me. My fear overthrew me to call her on my own. Always the hard way, I couldn't just call her myself. I made a few prank calls and sure enough she called me asking for Billy's number. We began talking and she told me she thought I didn't like her. I guess it's only natural since I ran away. But I felt more connected and we had made plans to meet again.

My plan had worked and we got back together without me running away. I remember riding my bike with my friend Ralph to meet her once again. It felt so good seeing her beautiful face in the warmth of late summer. I was back where I left off a year and a half ago. Only this time I was ready to dive into love. We had kissed again and it still felt like the first time. We spent the rest of the summer together and got to know each other. The smell of the late summer nights after we would kiss goodbye was wondrous. I would ride my bike back home as the mild air felt good on my skin. The sound of the crickets that passed as I rode my bike constantly thinking about her. Watching the streetlights come on, as the sky grew darker. I never felt anything as powerful as what I was feeling at that moment.

As we went into tenth grade, I fell deep in love and a new obsession was born. She was my first kiss, my first girlfriend, and my first time making love. Basically she was my first of everything with the opposite sex. We had lost our virginity to one another on a mid September evening. Her parents went out and her and I were alone on a Saturday night. We were passionately kissing on her bed in the dark of her bedroom when she had taken off her panties and slowly guided me in. My heart had sunk in that moment and it became a night I would never forget. I became numb because of my anxiety and was trying to focus on that once in a lifetime moment. The way it felt to be inside her and as we were connected passionately, moving our bodies together was something I had fantasized so much about and it was actually happening.

She was so stunning to me and it was so amazing to make love to her over and over, which was fresh to me! A deeper relation developed and after school the first thing we'd do was have great sex. Hands completely all over each other passionately kissing as we breathed in each other's essences. Falling asleep as I lay on top of her after I had an orgasm.

She was on birth control after her parents found out we were having sex. We didn't have to use condoms and I could cum inside her, which we both loved. I would hold it still as I blew and she felt it splatter all inside feeling warm and squishy. It was an amazing teenage dream! It was the best thing her parents could do putting her on birth control. It was a good thing they understood we were at that age and would find a way to do it anyway. We had all natural sex together and it felt warm, wet and wondrous, with the smell of our bodies, breath and hair! Our naked bodies sweating as we made love, feeling the silk like sensation from our sweat. It was like I could feel her body in more slippery soaked detail. We did different positions, on the bed, in the woods, on the bathroom toilet… and so much more.

Her parents sometimes made her leave her door open when they were home. I think they knew we snuck in the bathroom because we'd rattle the toilet. We had explored each other sexually and just could not get enough! We were both natural lovers and really knew how to have amazing sex! I was so good at everything sexual she even asked me if I was really a virgin. I assured her she was the only one I had ever been with and I wondered where that gift of being able to create great love to a woman came from. I never had done that before yet I knew instinctively what to do. A new addiction was emerging. We were both passionate and hypersexual. A highly intense sexual experience combined with true love.

I had found out my parents wanted to sell our house and move down to Florida after my tenth grade. I wasn't old enough to stay behind but my older brothers were. How would this work out? How will I be with my love? I had told her and she was saddened by it but we both didn't seem to worry much. There was still months ahead before the move will happen. I was hoping and praying we would never sell that house I grew up in.

Time rolled on, we shared the Holidays together and celebrated a new year right into a new decade. An alter ego had awoken, which took me over. It was a strange whisk of emotions stirred by insanity. I would talk her into acting out pretend rape fantasies. It was thrilling when I would go outside her bedroom door then in a strange twisted force of the imagination, I would pretend I was about to rape her.

She'd lie on her bed and when I opened the door and walked in, she would sit up and say in a pretend scared way, "Who are you?" I would rush up to her and pin her down on the bed and forced my way to kiss her as she tightened her lips and moved her head side to side, kicking her legs as she tried to fight me off. I would lock my legs around hers keeping her from moving. I would touch her all over and lift up her shirt then yank off her panties and ease it in. By the time I was deep inside of her and getting into it, she would instantly stop acting like she was a rape victim and really get in motion with me and moaned in ecstasy.

Sometimes intrusive thought would arise and sometimes I would pretend she was my sister while we made love.

What the hell were these perverted thoughts? Where were they coming from? It was almost like I was attacking myself with my love as the victim, pouring out disturbing energy around that teenage girl who was in love with me, who just wanted to be a teenage girl in love for the first time and always remember it. At the time we always wanted to be together… forever.

"Forever your girl" by Paula Abdul had been released on the radio and she made it our song. The lyrics were expressing how she had felt for me. *"Baby just remember I gave you my heart, ain't no one gonna tear us apart."*

We were so in love, no one could tear us apart… except me. I allowed the influence of fat Billy to consume me so we started prank phone calling her again. It was a thrill, a rush, and a serious sickness. For some reason I wanted to play the psycho boyfriend in what I often pretended was a movie of my life. With a combination of being artistic and deeply in touch with the power of my mind, I allowed it to take over. The fact that I was moving tore me apart and I had fear of her hurting me, leaving me for someone else.

Picking up the payphone, putting it to my ear and pressing 0 making a collect cal gave me a thrill as I pretended I was in a movie. I was like the villain of the story in my mind. Billy had a smart idea by connecting a stretched out paper clip and sticking one end in a tiny hole in the base of the payphone then putting the other side into the speaker of the phone receiver. It overrode the telephone and allowed us to make free calls.

Seeing payphones as I rode around in a car or riding my bike passing them began to become a new obsession. It became such an addiction I would even sometimes stop at a payphone when I rode my bike to her house. I would make a quick stop and use the trick Billy showed me to make a free prank call. But nothing was more twisted like the sick mind games I laid on my first love. The constant prank calls, telling her off the wall stories that freaked her out and my aggressive manner. I had begun to frighten her.

Her and her family had gone out of town for the day and I broke into her house. I went up to her bedroom and turned all of her fifty dolls heads to face the door so when she walked in her room they'd all be looking ghostly at her. I remember standing in the doorway making sure every single doll was staring right at me.

The night before, we were kissing and petting. I saw one of her dolls in arms reach looking away. I silently moved my arm and turned the dolls head facing us. After we stopped being intimate, she turned around and jumped!

She said nervous. "That doll wasn't looking at me before. Did you do that?"

I put a seed of fear in her head. "No… I noticed it was looking the other way too. Maybe it's a ghost."

I thought doing that with all of her dolls would be a thrill seeing how scared she got from the one doll. Later on that day, she had called me and told me what happened. She told me when she came home that day she totally lost all control in fear! She told me she screamed and panicked!

"Oh my God when I walked in all my dolls were staring at me!" She cried over the phone. "What's going on?"

In my sick mind I smiled knowing my trick had worked as I played out the whole scene in my head. I convinced her it was a bad spirit of some sort and that I had nothing to do with it. She believed me.

I wanted attention so bad I used to cut myself and told her I had a bike accident. I really began to become an enemy of myself where I would punch myself in the face a lot. Maybe it was my inner demon but I got great pleasure when I would physically beat the shit out of myself! I became destructive in so many other ways. I would tear tree limbs off and break it over the trees trunk. I would get off by climbing trees during a lighting storm. I had an amazing fascination with lighting and windstorms! It was destruction at its best I thought. I was getting in touch with my inner god as I felt the power.

My brothers and I made pipe bombs and we would blow stuff up giving me mad amusement. My friends and I would go around with bb guns and just shot the shit out of whatever we wanted to destroy! We blew up mailboxes with M-80's and we would go around and kick down garbage cans. Fire became another crazed obsession and I got off on watching flames consume whatever I lit up! I even lit myself on fire by spraying butane on my clothes and lighting it up. I got my friends into exploring underground drain sumps and the tunnels that were in them. Large concrete pipes that drained rainwater from the streets above. We were able to crawl around in them. It was something many people couldn't believe we did.

Little did I know that the end of my childhood was drawing near. My parents had sold the house, which I did not want! How dare they I thought! I hated the fact of moving so much that I took a baseball bat to the *"For Sale"* sign for our house I didn't want to leave.

In mid May the most painful experiences happened all at once! My first love had broken up with me and I only had a month before we moved. We were down in her den during the beginning of a thunderstorm. I looked out the window and the sky grew darker, the wind began to pick up and we could hear thunder in the distance. There were no lights on in her den and the room had gone strangely dim from the storm and heavy clouds. She was sitting on the couch as I was standing up before her.

She said in a sad voice, "I think we should break up."

"I don't!" I appealed feeling my heart slowly break.

I looked intently at her and in that moment lightning lit up the room and I didn't even blink! The thunder rolled as I stayed locked in her eyes as she stared back at me in fear in our moment of silence. Like it was me who made the lightning strike in that moment of my despair. It was if the weather was in sync with my emotions! A lightning strike the moment our break up became real, the true moment I lost her. How was the weather in sync with my feelings?

I sat beside her and asked for one last kiss. We leaned into each other and kissed softly for a moment as we heard the rain begin to fall. A moment I didn't want to ever end. It still felt so good to kiss her but once we stopped the feeling left.

I peered into her eyes and whispered, "goodbye."

She whispered back, "goodbye."

I walked outside as the rain fell and the sky kept lighting up with rolling thunder rumbling. I was numb at first but later that night I unloaded heartbroken tears knowing it was really over.

She began to date someone else and being that I loved her so deeply to the point of obsession and insanity, my hurt ran deep to the point of lunacy! I began to stalk her and really went off the deep end with the prank phone calls. I went from payphone to payphone making collect calls using crazy names like Billy Goat Gruff and Fighting Horse!

There I was on the other end of the line in a phone booth, as her or her parents would answer the phone. The recording would announce. *"You have a collect call from, 'FIGHTING HORSE!'"*

I couldn't image what they were going through but I kept doing it like an idiot! I truly ran a mental muck on the entire family. I made false threats to her and became totally fixated with bringing her serious emotional turmoil. My friend and I who had a car and a PA system would go by her house at night and I would speak into the mic announcing I was outside her window. I saw her looking out of her bedroom window pushing the curtains back.

She had a look on her face like she was thinking in a hurtful and frightened way," why are you doing this to me?"

I did it for a while one night until her father came running out after us with a Billy Club. That was our cue to leave. Why was I doing this would cross my mind from time to time. I guess I was being selfish and vengeful and the fact that I was moving made it worse. It gave my dark half power and excitement. In a way it was like my inner demons and psychosis opposed the strong love I had for her, which made me lash out in the opposite way of how I really felt. The deeper I loved the more immoral my alter ego became. Like two sides battling it out and my first love got caught in the crossfire! Even still with all my thrilling retaliation, there was no way of explaining the hurt I was feeling! It killed me that I lost her and she was with someone else and there was nothing I could do about it.

We were just in love, happy and exploring each other. Where did it go and what have I done? And to top it off I was being ripped out of my childhood to move to a place I have never been and knew no one!

As it got closer to moving and being done with school, I would watch music videos on MTV in my room that would soon be empty. The song *"I Remember You"* by Skid Row came on that I loved. With a homeless man in the video walking around, looking at old photos of his lost love, a fright came into me. I just lost my love and I'm moving with an unknown future… will that be me one day?

The lyrics hit me so hard. *"Remember yesterday… walking hand and hand… love letters in the sand… I remember you."*

The clips of the dirty homeless man showed him walking around a big city in the dead of winter remembering his first love. For some reason, I really felt what that would be like. I felt the cold, the pain and the memories of my first love experience that was over. I looked around my room and knew that was it. All that I knew and grew up with was gone just like that.

We packed every thing up in June, my brother's got their own place and since I was only 16 at the time had to move to Florida with my parents. I didn't know what I was going to do carrying the sting of the loss of my first love and losing my youth. The 1980's were over and it was 1990. A new decade where I would have to learn how to survive that pain, the growing battle in my mind and to start completely over somewhere else. .

As it was just my father and I driving down to Florida I was thinking of everything and everyone I knew and loved. I couldn't grasp the concept of time when all I wanted to do was go back. I missed my home, my friends, and my hometown. My heart ached for my first and how will I ever get by was all I thought. Just then on the radio a song by Ozzy Osborne was playing called *"Goodbye to Romance."*

The lyrics sang to me. *"I said hey… goodbye to romance yeah…Goodbye to friends and to you… Goodbye to all the past… I guess that we'll meet… we'll meet in the end."*

That was it. I was leaving it all behind and tried to look ahead as I saw the trees and scenery pass me by on the interstate south. I supposed that in the end we will all meet again. But for the time being I had a long road ahead.

My Time In An Irregular Cell Block

The intake block I was on only had visits on Tuesday when my Goo would be working. I desperately needed to see Xanadoo so I wrote to the Warden and begged to have me moved to another block for more than one reason. I couldn't take it there and I needed Saturday's visiting day, the day Xanadoo could see me.

I was moved upstairs to D block and as soon as I walked in I saw a window at the end of the block that brought in more light and a more opened feeling. Ah, one step closer to freedom I thought. I went to the cell they told me was my resting quarters. There was a guy in his mid 30's, with a mustache, on the top bunk lying there.

The first thing he said was. "Don't mind me if you happen to see me crying. I am a blubbering baby. This is my first time in jail. My name is Wayne. Wayne Johns."

I introduced myself and looked out of my cell window at the bleak dreary winter day outside. It was March and still cold outside. The trees around were all bare and the sky was cloudy with snow on the ground. How badly I wanted to be out there! Wayne had asked me why I was in jail and I briefly told him the story. It was when I asked him of his crime was when it got interesting.

He explained. "I'm accused of sexually assaulting my sixteen year old step daughter. She told my wife that I forced my hand down her pants and took a picture of her vagina but that's not true! Now I'm going to lose everything!"

I remember thinking my God! That's not good. Did he really do it or not?

He continued, "uh, you do know you are on the sex offenders block, right?"

"What the hell am I doing on this block?" I said in shock. "I'm not a sex offender."

"Did you want weekend visits?"

"Yeah."

"That's why." He got up off his bunk and gathered himself. "Come on. Let's go out into the day room, you should get to know everyone."

I noticed everyone was out in the small dayroom talking and watching TV. Except there was one creepy looking young guy with whacked out hair and a strange look on his face, locked in a cell staring out of the small square cell window. I asked Wayne what the hell his story was. I was told he was accused of biting the nipples of an older woman. He was charged with 'Indecent Sexual Assault.' Apparently he did not play well with others and had to be locked down at all times. The only time they turned him loose was when everyone got locked down for about an hour. They gave him only one hour to have the dayroom to himself and watch whatever he wanted on the television. They called him Stooper and he looked like he was missing a few screws.

I met another guy in his late twenties named the Penguin because he looked like one. The Penguin was in for sexually assaulting his own sister! It kinda got weird there after I heard that for a moment. Then there was a thin older man who was mostly bald with a big bushy beard. I asked what his deal was and Wayne told me he was known as the Bearded Molester. He snuck into a ten-year-old girl's bedroom and went down on her against her will. I cringed at the thought of such a sickening thing! How could anyone do that to a little girl?

I excused myself and got on the phone immediately and called Xanadoo. I hated using those jail phones but I had no choice! She answered in her sweet voice.

I quickly said, "you're not going to believe this! I am on the sex offenders block!"

"What?" She said in shock.

"Yup!" Feeling bad for myself I said, "I guess I'm no better than a freaking rapist!"

My inner adversary was coming out and started to put a beating on me as Xanadoo tried to talk positive to uplift me but I wasn't hearing her... I was hearing my inner demon.

"You loser! You are as bad as a sexual deviate! You belong in jail! You belong incarcerated forever! You don't deserve to be in society ever again!"

As I tried to talk to Xanadoo, I noticed such immaturity in that place. Constant loud chatter, senseless dribble and crude jargon were all I heard! They were banging on the metal tables, laughing and joking like being there was one big party to them.

I told Xanadoo exactly what was going on at that moment with all the madness! It was hard to hear what she was saying over those idiots! I looked out of the big window and fantasized about being a god again. If I had powers I could run, break through that window, land on the ground and blast home to my Goo. I wanted to rip the phone out of the wall and scream so loud that it would shatter all the solid glass windows around this block!

I couldn't talk on the phone due to all the noise. Xanadoo gave me all her heart through words to make me feel better. It was always sad having to hang up.

When I got off the phone, I just crept in my cell and lay on my bunk. I started thinking of what I would have been doing at that time had I not been arrested. It was mid afternoon on a work day and I would have been at my job working. I would have probably been on the road, making a delivery, listening to music, sipping a soda at that moment. Counting down the time til I went home but instead I was in jail. I closed my eyes and asked God to please help me out of this mess I got myself into! I couldn't take it anymore so I took out a piece of paper and expressed my emotions.

Greetings Goo,

I thought I'd write you again. The thought of losing you is killing me. I don't know what will happen to me. Some of the guys say I may go to prison, some say I'll only do some county time, like 6 months or so. I hope so! I cannot believe how amazing you are! First you accepted me for who I was and never judged me for being a drug addict. Being homeless at one point and the way I used to live. I survived so much in my days but I don't think I could survive losing you! I miss playing footies with you so I lay in my bunk and play footies with myself pretending it is with you. I miss when we are on the couch and I rubbed your booty and you give me that cute smile. I miss holding your breast and putting my hand between your legs. It would be a real tragedy if I lost you! I keep thinking of a no Goo future.

Let's say I do go to prison and later on when I get out assuming Pittsburgh is the nearest city. I see myself homeless again like I was in Baltimore. Picture a gray miserable winters day and I come across the bus station I had my lay over when I used to visit you. Imagine a sad song playing as I stand outside of the bus station remembering those beautiful sunny summer days we had when I came to spend time with you when we first met. I can see myself dying there from a drug overdose. I would end up in a dark ally, lifeless, dead forever. Why the hell do I dwell on such morbid thoughts that haven't even happened? I'm sorry! I am venting my sick mind right now!

I want to work on myself but I am too sick and too weak to begin my spiritual journey. I have been beating myself up over this stupid mistake I've made! I went to a NA meeting and as I sat there with the feelings of self-pity and defeat there was a booklet, the cover was slightly lifted. It read, "We suggest you give yourself a break." I wondered if that was a sign. I asked God, what are you saying now? After the meeting I see one of the guys with a pamphlet in his jumpsuit saying, "More will be revealed." I felt a little better after seeing that but once I got back to the block I started to feel that black hole within me being locked up and detoxing off drugs and feeling anxious! No hope, no desire, not seeing the light at the end of the tunnel! Tomorrow is my arraignment and I am nervous! Let's try to turn this into something good. I have never loved anyone as much as I love you! Remember that!

It was the day of my arraignment and I wasn't alone. Wayne was also called down for his as well which made me feel better. There I was in cuffs and shackles sitting next to Wayne waiting for the judge. Xanadoo was there sitting behind me. I'd turn around every now and then and smile as she smiled back giving me hope.

The judge came out and we all had to stand even though we were all in chains as if he was some kind of royalty.

Ridiculous traditional court system nonsense. He's just a man in a robe judging our crimes of man-made laws. When it was my time to approach the judge for my plea I got up feeling all twisted inside. When I accepted my plea for the three counts of obtaining a controlled substance by fraud the judge put the fear in me. He read off all three one by one stating that each can hold a maximum of five years! What could I do? Fifteen years was way too much time for my crimes. I was told not to worry, that was not the time I would get by everyone, including the weasel! It was just a maximum amount the state can bestow on someone, which I felt was rather harsh. Once that was all said and done I took one last look at Xanadoo before they took me back to the pits. She was so beautiful and I missed her so much! Fuck! Frustration broke out. I just wanted to go home!

Once Wayne and I got back to the block there was a new guy who was around 27 years old. One inmate was giving him a hard time over his offense. Turns out that new guy had been texting what he thought was a 14 year old girl but was actually a 50 year old women who was setting him up. He was texting her sexual messages and had made plans to meet her at a motel. He was expecting to meet a 14-year-old girl when he showed up at the hotel room but instead he met a bunch of cops! Once we knew the story we called him Sexter for his texting of what he thought was an underage female's sexual thoughts! They nailed that guy for attempted statutory rape of a minor.

There was this one goon who kept talking and talking. I overheard him say, "I don't mind being in jail! I'm used to it."

I don't mind being in jail? I'm used to it? I minded being there! I was not ok with that! There was another younger guy around 20 watching the television and this young girl was on acting out her part in the movie she was in. That guy watching it puts his one hand up and slaps it with the other.

He said, "shut up bitch and suck my dick!"

Where the hell am I? What's wrong with these guys? Stooper was in his cell luring inmates over and showing him his dick through the cell window. Apparently Stooper really got a kick out of freaking people out! I understood why he had to be locked down at all times. I heard someone farting and laughing at it like a goon!

I remember saying to myself. "I am an addict and I need help. This isn't helping!"

I couldn't take much more of that! I got on the phone with Xanadoo and I told her about the lunacy that was going on. She wasn't happy so I asked what was wrong.

She began to yell, "I'm tired of all this! I deserve so much better than this! I'm alone, doing everything by myself! Why did you do that stupid thing with the pills?"

"I don't know. Please…"

"No!" She cut me off. "I'm stuck here cleaning up the mess you made!"

I tried to calm her down but nothing worked. She was beginning to get to me. It was bad enough I was feeling more guilt than anyone in here but now she was screaming at me for something I could not change. I didn't know what to do with all the chaos going on all around and Xanadoo yelling at me. With no defense, I just yelled back and hung up the phone in anger!

I went into my cell and started to sink in depression! That was it for me. I was going to lose everything! I looked out of my cell window and saw people walking, cars going by, and life still moving on, as I was behind the walls of not only that jail but also the walls of my mind. The earth would keep spinning, the birds would keep flying, and the seasons would continue to change. Life would not stop for me. The world kept going despite my banishment.

My inner enemy had raised its vile head yet again. He spoke sickly soundless words in my head. "She's gone now!" I was convincing myself that I would go to prison and the love that I had would be gone. I began to envision myself doing my time then being released from prison much later on down the line. I would end up on the city streets again with nowhere to go, no one to go home to. An all to familiar feeling. The sky would be gray and cold outside with newspapers blowing at my feet with the city functioning around me. Holding my long black overcoat closed as I walk in the busy city.

I would duck into a dark ally and sink to the ground. Old memories would arise of Xanadoo and I happily in love with a heartbreaking feeling in my chest that those days were long gone. I fucked it up again and now it's too late! I see myself pop a huge amount of pills and close my eyes. I felt myself falling, losing grip with reality. I was not God's forgotten child but deeply detached and alone in my own personal hell.

I struggled to stand up but something was not right as I got to my feet. I would turn around and see myself still sitting on the ground icy and dead! Pale lifeless eyes that stare eerily back at me. What is this? I can't be dead! I keep looking at my pasty face and the wind would blow my hair but my body lay stiff. My dead eyes pierced hauntingly right through me. There is no one in that body anymore. I see myself holding a picture of Xanadoo, my lost love, as I sat there frozen solid with my eyes wide opened. Anger arises in me and I wanted to kick in my own head!

"You idiot!" I yelled. "Why did you choose pills over her? You were given so many chances! You could have been so happy with her but now your dead!"

Was there no way to escape this nightmare? Please God! Help me! I do not want to end up that way!

I came back to the realization that I'm fucked on that jail bunk. I felt a strong urge to attack myself so I started punching myself in the face! White flashes I saw, as I would slam my knuckles on my face. It was physical pain that actually felt good.

At that moment Wayne walked in.

"What the hell are you doing?" He asked in shock.

"I'm beating the shit out of myself, ok!"

He sat down on the metal toilet we share when we are locked in this horrid cell together.

He said, "I know you had a fight with your girl. But you haven't lost her. For some reason I feel this is your last chance in life. You haven't lost everything." He paused for a moment then continued. "I lost everything! I lost my job forever, my wife is divorcing me and I am not allowed to even see or call my own children! My wife got a PFA and I can't even write them or talk to them on the phone!"

"PFA?" I asked.

"Protection From Abuse and I never even touched them! All because my stepdaughter told everyone I forced myself on her, which I didn't! Now my own family has turned their backs on me. I'm looking at prison time and I never ever been in trouble with the law! I have nothing! Nothing!" He shouted. He took a breath and continued. "My family and I used to go to church every week. I prayed all the time and kept a relationship with God. But we fell away from God and started to drink and we sank into lust and a lot of bad things. Now look at me! God saw what I was doing and knocked me to my knees! You still have a chance. You haven't lost everything like I have."

He was right I thought. I only had a fight with Xanadoo not a break up. Why did I keep attacking myself like that? I had a small sense of hope and if I were to make things right I had to call Goo back and tell her how sorry I was and that I love her.

A new day had come and I made peace with my Xanadoo. She was just feeling overwhelmed over all that was going on and I couldn't blame her. Because of my mistake and addiction, someone else gets affected and it wasn't fair. She still loved me and wasn't leaving me. It was late March and my court date to be sentenced was less than a month away and I received some good news. I was on my jail bed when Wayne stood on the toilet looking out of the window. The sun appeared as the clouds parted and I developed a sense of hope.

He looked down at me and said, "I have a feeling you will be going home on your court date next month."

It was a moment of bliss as if God was saying everything would be all right...

Ironically a few hours later I was called down to see the probation officer to have my investigation to see if I will make probation. I knew I had a prior record that would make it a bad thing to go to court with. I knew they would use my record against me and I would go to prison for sure. Some kind of spiritual energy was there because he could not find my prior record. I asked what that meant and he told me since he could not find anything I would be going home on my court date in a month.

I raised a smile and felt so happy! I had to call Xanadoo right then and there and tell her the great news! The probation officer allowed me to use the phone briefly. She was overjoyed! After telling Xanadoo the good news I had to hang up.

The probation officer explained. "Ok since we cannot use your prior record that means you have a gravity score of 0. This is good because in the guidelines with your offense means you probably won't get any jail time. You will more than likely get two years of probation for each offense."

"Six years of probation?" I asked.

"Yes. However if you don't get into any trouble they will drop the last two years. This is just my guess don't forget. The judge could say different but I doubt it in your case."

The probation officer brought me great hope and he even bought me a Pepsi, which tasted so good since I got used to that nasty jail food! Oh, it was bubbly and sweet just like when I was a kid.

Once we got done with that amazing information I was taken back up to the block. I went right into my cell and saw Wayne.

"Well?" He asked.

"You were right. They could not find my prior record and he told me that I will be going home on my court date next month!"

"I told you! As soon as the sun came out and shined on me I felt it. God told me to tell you that you will be ok and you will be going home! Congrats buddy!"

As I basked in my joyfulness I noticed they had brought in a new guy to the block. He was around 35 with wild hair. Dark energy loomed off of him that I sensed. He had a crazy looking smirk like he didn't have a care in the world. He looked pure evil. I asked Wayne what his story was.

Wayne said, "That's Satan in the flesh! He raped his eight-year-old daughter and you want to know the worst part? He did it because he was curious! He continued to molest her and have sex with her to his delight."

"But to do it because you're curious?"

"I know its crazy. Its just what I was told!"

That new creepy guy was much worse than the Penguin and even the Bearded Molester! The only thing I could think of at the time was thank God I was going home!

It was well into April and my sentencing court day was a week away. Xanadoo came to visit me every Saturday. She always made sure I had money on my commissary so I could order snacks and other things I needed. Seeing her behind that plate glass was terrible but I assured her I would be home soon. Even though I was told I was going home on my court date I felt as if I had nothing to look forward to. Perhaps it was my lingering withdrawals from the pills. Maybe it was the shame I had felt and that I ruined a good job. I was beginning to dread being on D block in county jail surrounded by lunatics. I got to know many of them and wondered what makes a grown man do those terrible things to children. Everyone I talked to in there told the same story. They were either beaten and or molested as children themselves. They were troubled men who never really grew up due to their childhood scars.

Wayne was crying on his bunk looking out of the cell window searching for his soon to be ex-wife to drive by. Just sitting there waiting only to see her face even for a moment. He was completely alone and that made me a little more grateful to have my Goo!

Stooper was sentenced to 1 to 2 years in state prison. They still had him locked down while he awaited the bus to take him down state. He could have avoided prison time and got county time but because he was such a nuisance they kicked him out of county jail and wanted the state to deal with his twisted tomfoolery. Really now! How the hell does someone get kicked out of county jail?

They sent the Penguin home. I wished him all the best and hoped he got the help he needed. The Bearded Molester was going over his court papers and studying law books in the hopes that he could not go to prison for his perverse crime. I had asked the Bearded Molester what would happen if he went to prison. He calmly told me that he would simply read and maybe become a lawyer. He was a thirty-nine year old man and he didn't seem to have much shame about where he was going or what he did. He was facing at least 5 to 10 years in prison and it wasn't good with his sex crime to be in prison.

Sexter had his own fears of going to prison. He was scared and told me how sorry he was for what he had done. He wasn't a bad person I thought, just a little lost in life. He cried a lot and kept saying, "I'm not a bad person! I just made a mistake! I don't want to go prison!" He was facing 1 to 2 years. My Goo told me to be the light in there and that's what I was becoming. Many of those men on that block respected me and opened up to me.

When I told Xanadoo how the guys were telling me their story as if they felt comfort in me it did not surprise her at all. She said it was one of the qualities that made her fall in love with me. She told me I was a real person and there wasn't many like that in the world. I was rare, talented, artistic, eccentric and caring yet I had a sickness that nearly killed me many times over. God must have saved my life plentiful times for a reason. I needed to figure out what that was.

Satan, the one who raped his 8-year-old daughter, who I called The Evil One, was facing 3 to 6 years. He didn't seem to have much of a problem with that; at least he didn't show it. There were times when he tried to call his wife but she would never accept his calls. I would see him come out of his cell, dial the phone, wait and then hang up every time. That was sad. He, like Wayne, was also abandoned because of his crimes. The Evil One paced a lot in his cell and for kicks and giggles he continuously farted in a bottle, capped it, then would mossy on up to someone and turn it loose in their face! I was so ready to get the hell out of there! But something within my spirit was wrong. Most of the time I would isolate and fall into a depression. I was going home, why was I feeling that way? I had seven days to go and I should have been happy but I wasn't.

I received a letter from the probation office stating my report. The cover letter read: "Please review the following and make sure all the information is correct."

Ok, I thought.

I read the first page and it had my name, address, birthday and my charges. I turned the page and there was my prior record!

What? Wait... What!

I was told my record could not be found! Well I knew that would raise my gravity score and could result in prison time. I read the sentencing guidelines on the docket. I had three counts of Acquisition of a controlled substance by fraud. The first count held a standard range of 6-16 months in jail. I read the second count and that held a range of 30 – 30 months! Oh my God! Seriously? This has to be a mistake. I read the last one and it held a range of 18 – 24 months! This added up to a total of 54 months minimum in prison! I didn't even want to know what the maximum was!

"What the fuck!" I shouted out. "That's 4 ½ to 9 years!"

Wayne came in and asked what was wrong. I showed him the paperwork and he tried to justify it.

"Maybe it's a mistake," he tried telling me.

I kicked the metal toilet and felt there was no hope at all! How the hell do I go from going home on my court date to 4 ½ to 9 years in prison?

I ran out to the phone and called Xanadoo! I frantically told her what the docket had read.

"What!" She said in shock and sadness. "I thought you were getting out? Now this!"

I told her to call the probation officer immediately and have him come up to see me right away! I hung up with her and I paced around in fear! How could this happen to me I wondered? The guys there tried to calm me down and give me hope that it was a mistake but I knew it wasn't. I knew there was something wrong.

The probation officer came up to see me and I asked what the hell was the deal with the docket. He explained he had found my prior record and since the pill count was high on the painkillers I forged it became aggravated and it raised the range! Like scratching a wound, aggravating it, making it worse, except this was to the law. He advised me to get in touch with my public defender. I would have to contact the Weasel as soon as possible but it was too late that Friday! Of all days! The weekend will be torture! This kind of timing always seems to happen to me. Always falls on a weekend or a holiday! Like some sort of cursed deja vu! It was all over for me!

I went over the situation with The Bearded Molester and Wayne because they had documents on the laws. The Bearded Molester had a matrix chart that showed the ranges of every crime. I developed severe OCD as I looked at the crimes that fit my range. The time I was facing was up there with involuntary manslaughter, kidnapping, homicide by vehicle, sexual assault and arson!

I called Xanadoo and in tears telling her to forget me and find someone else. She said she would not forget me and would never let me go. She was willing to stick it out with me until the end.

"Why are you staying with me? I asked. "I'm done!"

"No your not!" She assured me. "I'm sure they made some kind of mistake. That's too harsh for what you did. You don't deserve that."

"The time I am facing is up there with crimes like kidnapping and involuntary manslaughter!"

"What?" She said in shock.

"Yeah… I'm up there on the felon list! I don't want to go to prison, I don't belong in there!"

"Maybe you're meant to go to prison not only to get yourself better but to help someone who might be scared. You are the light! Remember that."

At that moment I had a premonition. I envisioned a young man in his mid twenties, skinny, and afraid. It would be his first time in jail and we would bond and aid each other through the nightmare of being incarcerated. Maybe I would be helping someone who needed my guidance and by helping him it would help me too. Still I didn't want to go to prison, especially for 4 ½ to 9 years minimum! Judge could go higher if he wanted to. I talked to Xanadoo until my time ran out then went into my cell to wallow in self-pity. I'm going to lose my Goo I knew it!

We met online through music when I lived in Baltimore. We e-mailed each other everyday and opened up to one another. I was having some issues and out of the blue she called me at my work on the first day of spring. She had told me she got the number from information and I was surprised. From that moment on we became close and fell in love. I took her everywhere emotionally, on the city streets of Baltimore, on my cell phone. Now if I lost her and were to go back to Baltimore when I get out of prison, I would be reminded of her great love with every step I would take on those streets. The bus stops, the library I went to, all the places we had beautiful moments on the phone before we physically met. Every step would be a heartbreaking reminder of what I once had. She deserved so much more than what I could give. I could no longer do this to her. I had to let her go because I loved her so much. This was my mistake not hers and she didn't deserve to suffer anymore. At that dark moment I felt like Jesus Christ on the cross. Oh God, why have you forsaken me?

A New Lane Of Memories

It was ridiculously hot and steamy in what would be my new home in the summer of 1990. South Florida was much different than Long Island. The trees were different, the air smelt different, everything around me was all new. No hills, flat, swampy... It felt like a whole new atmosphere! There I was in our new home that was just built. That smell of new carpet and wood cabinets encased the entire house. We had a lake in the backyard and were having a pool and hot tub put in.

I had my own room with brand new furniture but none of that mattered. I wanted to go back to Long Island! An eerie sense of what was real and what was unknown fell upon me. I developed a funny and strange feeling when I looked around the Florida environment. What I felt was a separation of my childhood into something that would become my older years. Remembering the way Long Island felt, cooler, comforting, the memories, and the friends I knew was all gone. I felt in my spirit the times I was living on Long Island and all that surrounded my world was a part of me. It would be a piece of my life that would forever remain in my heart.

When I looked around my new home I thought to myself. "What is this place? Nothing looks familiar! Where am I?" There were many weird and wonderful feelings to know & feel, that I grew up in one place then moved to a totally new place where there were no memories at all. It was if I were staring at a blank mass of nothingness that would become the construct of my unwritten future.

In my new neighborhood, houses were still being built, there was still construction and I would take walks and survey that nonconforming reality that had been hellishly brought upon me. There was no grass yet on some of the lots and dead weeds dirt by the lake. Strange bugs would make noises and jump out as I walked by. I'd look at the homes that weren't complete yet and sneak inside. As I looked around those unlived homes it was an unusual feeling to know that there were no memories present. Soon there would be people moving in and bring life to that empty unfinished home.

My destructiveness still lay with in my character. I hated my parents for moving me to that swampy part of the country away from everything I once knew! I carried the pain of losing my first love every single day. No matter what… I just could not shake the sorrow! For each passing day, it was a cruel and lonely summer.

There were so many lightening storms, which I loved. Pounding thunder and frequent lightening with heavy rainfalls would sweep in from the everglades. The heat would warm the marshy wetlands and water would rise creating strong thunderstorms. Later in the afternoons, the clouds would build and the sound of distant thunder would begin to rumble. The lightning would strike and the thunder would thrash! The rain would begin to pour, as every thing around grew darker. It also was exactly how I felt inside.

I began punching holes into the walls of those unlived homes for kicks to relieve the stress of that lost, hurt, and scared time in my life! I would unload my fists into the walls causing major damage all around the house, then run back into the soupy heat of South Florida. I was a partly cloudy, hot and humid day with afternoon thunderstorms emotionally.

I tried to be more accepting to my surrounds and would put on music to help me escape. There was an interesting synchronicity to the time in my life because even the radio was cruel! It felt like someone or something was talking to me constantly reminding me of where I was in that place and time. I kept hearing a lot of the same songs and they spoke to me always in sync with my thoughts and feelings. I couldn't escape it! Wilson Philips just came out in 1990 and *"Hold On"* was their first hit.

"Don't you know, things will change, things will go your way if you hold on for one more day... Yeah, I know there is pain

but if you hold on for one more day you'll break free from the chains."

I felt a glimmer of hope every time I heard that song like something was telling me to hold on.

Phil Collins sang a powerful reminder of my first love! *"Do You Remember"* came out right when she broke up with me and I remember sitting in my old room listening to it over and over again!

The words that really hit me was, *"The way you looked and told me. It's a look I know I'll never forget."*

That moment when she told me we should break up and then the lightning that flashed at that instant I will never forget! Something was trying to tell me that I was not alone in dealing with heartache or I was intensely in touch with the weather. I fell deep into the lyrics and levitated my mind to a happier time in my life but it still hurt!

Rod Stewart sang, *"My Heart Can't Tell You No"* which was another influential reminder of my lost love.

It felt like it never ended!

Rod sang telling me I wasn't alone. *"When the one you love is in love with someone else. Don't you know its torture... I mean it's a living hell."*

Just thinking about her being with another guy made me sick! I would torture myself with vivid thoughts of them kissing and having sex over and over. I constantly fantasized him being inside her! Making love to her like I use to. She was still on the pill and it killed me even more knowing that guy wasn't wearing a condom and could cum inside her. For some reason I was very sensitive to another guy inside my first love all naturally. I really was in my own living hell! I have never felt pain like that ever before. I was still in love with her and I couldn't stop dwelling on those visuals and that I will never have her again. I remember but now its over.

Many other songs played on the radio as well and it kept those remembrances with me. I began to recognize what I had was gone. I took much of my childhood for granted especially my first love experience! How it was new and we could not get enough of one another then time turned it upside down. What was once a happy loving time became obsession and chaos. How do we fall in love only to be heart broken? Just like the words from that Wilson Philips song *"Hold On"* that truly spoke to me

"You got no one to blame for your unhappiness. You got yourself into your own mess."

I really did create the mess I was in emotionally. Maybe the heartache was inevitable because nothing lasts forever and I was moving. It would not have worked anyway. Still, I had made it so much worse with my thoughtless twisted behavior. I started to grasp what a fool I had been! I began to see the pain I put on that teenage girl who once loved me. Oh God! I completely and utterly regretted doing what I had done to her so badly I couldn't stop thinking about it. The guilt started to really fall on me more and more as I remained locked in my own prison in my mind. I scared and hurt that poor girl emotionally what I did. Why! Why did I do that? What was I thinking? Where the hell did that come from? I tried to understand my actions but I couldn't get it. I never felt sorrow like that before. I began to breakdown as I remembered all the cruel and bad things I had done as if it were me it was happening to. It hit me hard that I had destroyed something beautiful! What have I done?

Time rolled on and I got through a very sad, angry, confused and lonely summer. The regret I had for harming my first grew even more and I kept beating myself up over what I had done. I could still not let go of any of the feeling I had for her and my stupidness!

"Oh God! Why did I do that? I'm so sorry!" Kept repeating in my head.

But I was in no place to call her. She wanted to never ever hear from me again. And to make things worse, I had to start over in yet another school. Something I had become all too familiar with in my past. When my parents took me to that new school it was in a different lower class, mostly black neighborhood. It wasn't that I was prejudice; it was that I came from an all white school and it was a whole other culture I didn't know of nor understood. Since our new house was built, there were no school zones in place yet, so I had to go to a school outside of what should have been a zoned district, which didn't make any sense. It was a brand new horror I would have to endure as if what I was going through wasn't enough! Being there was a shock blended perfectly with my already existing dismay and heartache!

My mother told me I had to make lemonade out of lemons and that's what I did. I began meeting new people. For some reason the smoking section kids gravitated to me. The smoking section of the school was filled with acid freaks, potheads, troublemakers, D students and girls who pretty much were an easy lay. At the side of the school, under a canopy next to the side road is where we would hang out. Across the way there were run down apartments that people lived in. Everyone would have their cigarettes and outspoken clothes. Getting to know them little by little, they all came from broken homes and lived in low-income houses and apartments. I couldn't quite understand why I hung around that crowd but it intrigued me.

I met my first friend Key who sat next to me in social studies. He also hung out in the smoking section and seemed like trouble. He was from Ireland and didn't know the 50 states. Since I was good at that I told him helping out on the test we were given. Hey, it was a whole new world for me so I took kindly to just about anyone. There were so many girls that loved my New York accent and thought I was cute! It was new to me because I was labeled weird back on Long Island but those new girls knew nothing of my weirdness or my sickness. It was a chance to start over with who I was and begin a new reputation.

Later on in October of 1991, Key had set me up with a pretty girl named Alyssa and an unexpected compulsive sexual relationship developed! She became my girlfriend and sex was always on the menu! Anytime, anywhere, anyway I desired. It became a new addiction! She streamed of femininity with long soft blonde hair. She had a delicate personal scent that totally intoxicated me. Her body was soft to the touch and penetrating her felt like warm silk, which made me shake. It became a dangerously intriguing form of unprotected sex that I could not deny. For some reason I had it deep down in my spirit that she would not get pregnant. At the time I wasn't sure if it was intuition, my sixth sense or just plain recklessness.

I still had to take special education classes and that was when I met a black student filmmaker. His name was Flip and he sat behind me in class and talked about a film he wanted to make, which intrigued me. I began to change in a good way. I started to dress cleaner with dress pants and button down shirts. I had grown my hair long, down to my shoulders and it felt great! I began to write my first novel about my first love experience, which was a good release of the pain I had carried since the move to Florida. It was also a good way to keep reliving it in my mind. I still wasn't over my first and leaving my childhood behind.

I got involved in television production, journalism, drama, theater and I worked with Flip as his assistant director for our first student film to be entered into the South Florida Black Film Festival. I raised my grade point average from a 2.0 to a 3.7. I was getting mostly A's on my report card. I couldn't quite understand how I was so smart yet had a learning disability. I had developed to be very powerful in that school with my reputation and style. That ghetto neighborhood where the school was that I was petrified about at first, I came to know really well and could walk around in without fear. It was a new lifestyle I was learning and on the film crew I was the only white person, which didn't bother me. I had become one with everything and everyone around me. It all was an affirmation of my growing moral being.

I had become a great success! The films Flip and I did won first place in the Black Film Festival. I had graduated from high school and continued to write my first novel about my first love experience. Something Alyssa hated. I had done some emotional harm to her. I had talked about my first love so many times Alyssa got very envious and hurt.

She had asked me one day. "If your first wanted you back… would you leave me and go back to her?"

I had foolishly said, "I would go back with her."

I was stupid telling her that if I had a choice I would go back with my first love and leave Alyssa. I thought being honest was the right thing but it broke her heart. I still couldn't let go! I was still obsessed and in love with my first.

The relationship Alyssa and I had developed into either fighting or fucking. We had a lot of wonderful moments and loved each other. I was reaching inside her to bring out her best. I took her places around Florida that she never been to. We had happy moments but there was something wrong. I had a problem talking about my past and she had a childish temper. She wouldn't always listen to reason and I must have been blind and obsessed with talking about my first too much. We would have our arguments and she often would storm out of my house and walk to her friends. I most of the time just let her go. She would always come back.

When we would be driving around a song by Richard Marx played often on the radio called *"Keep Coming Back to You"* like it was meant just for us.

The lyrics sang with a smooth jazzy sound. *"You know just how to hurt me and how to take all the pain away."*

We both had a way of doing that to each other. We would fight then make up over and over again.

The song continued as her and I listened. *"I don't know why… I… keep coming back to you…"*

It was strange but we both knew those lyrics rang true but we were deep in passion. I didn't want to leave but as this continued, I became more confused, more angry… Frustrated! Though the sex was great, she drove me insane, and once I reached the end of my rope I had to end it with her. I had broken up with her exactly a year later in October 1992. It was ironic the timing but I couldn't take it anymore. I did wrong, she did wrong… we just couldn't keep it together.

We remained friends and from that point on we never had a single argument again, which was strange. She admired me greatly because I had become a positive influence in her life. Her parents were cold to her and she had little guidance. Many days I had taken her out of the world she knew and showed her another side to life. One filled with beauty and love. I found her inner talent in photography and got her started on getting a degree. I hadn't realized I had been so caring and compassionate to her yet so cruel. She dedicated the song *"The Wind Beneath My Wings"* by Bette Midler to me. The lyrics she pointed out were, *"Did you ever know you are my hero."* Alyssa had shown me that I can make a difference in someone's life and I felt euphorically euphoric about that! I didn't know I was or could be the wind beneath anybody's wings.

I found my creative side awakening more and more. I got into photography as well and became in touch with the southern nature of Florida, capturing its beauty. No one saw Florida like I did. When people think Florida they automatically assume warm sunny skies and palm trees all year round, which was mostly true. However, I noticed a different side of Florida. The summers were rather brutal but the winters would bring in refreshingly cooler air from the north. When a cold front moved over the peninsular it would usher in drier, cooler and crisp air that was so rejuvenating! I admired when the sun would set and the horizon was deep orange and blue, the temperature would begin to drop and bring in the outside aroma of the north.

The further inland away from the ocean the cooler it got. My friends and I took many journeys out to the Everglades, which at night spoke a wondrous and marshy accent. It was a blend of peaty tropical air mixed with the smell of fireplaces and that cold air that I remembered back home on Long Island. Unfortunately the cold snaps would not last long but I always watched the Weather Channel in search for the next one to come.

The beaches were beautiful with the sea breeze that rolled in off the ocean. Many times when a hurricane was brewing near it would create intense waves that I would jump into and fight. In an attempt to relieve my inner tension, I would fight those strong waves without mercy! As the huge wave came at me, I'd dive into it, do flips into the wave, jump and punch through the strong waters. It had become an addiction and a huge rush to have the ocean totally kick my ass every which way! Though I was always defeated by that side of Mother Nature, I never backed down and the more superior the wave the more I would charge into battle with it.

One cool evening Key and I were cruising the Fort Lauderdale strip in search of females in the hopes to get laid. There were two girls that noticed us. One was young and cute and the other was a little older, heavy and unattractive. We had pulled over to talk to them and they invited us up to their hotel room. Let the games begin I thought. It turned out the younger cuter one liked Key and before I knew it they were engaging in a sexual romp on the floor. The other girl and I lay on the hotel bed as my friend and that girl went at it. She was coming on to me big time but I just couldn't do anything with her like that. Instead we talked and talked and talked. I opened up to her about the strange way I see life. She read my palm and told me I had a great spirit and an exceptional life was ahead of me.

We spoke in depth of how there was more to life than what we see. There were no such things as coincidences and that we are all connected in many ways. I had realized that synchronicity was real and chance meetings of certain people can deliver answers we subconsciously seek. While Key had mindless sex, my mind was evolving and a door was being opened that would never close. It was a doorway to my newfound spirituality that would grow and grow. I found myself on a path to find God and to understand what life was all about. It still felt weird to see myself there at that point in time when all I knew at one point was growing up on Long Island. I was 18 years old and time was carrying me on to new adventures and could not be stopped!

Time had rolled on into March of 1993. I was 19 and I had met a sweet girl named Amanda who I saw great beauty inside and out. She was a senior in high school who was close to graduating. She was classy, adorable and charismatic to my soul. She had long wavy brown hair, dark blue eyes and an outgoing personality. It was a relationship that developed into a charmingly formed young adult love. I was shy at first because I didn't think a girl like that could like me. It started out as a blind date and we would all hang out at places and friend's houses getting to know each other. I remember studying Amanda and felt something strong for her but couldn't get the strength to talk more to her.

The night I drove her home, I felt insecure again. Scared of rejection. When I pulled up to her house I turned to her and went blank.

I stuttered, "I… umm… would you… umm…"

Amanda couldn't hold back and giggled at me. I put on a sad face.

She said in a sweet voice. "No, I'm not laughing at you. You're trying to ask me out and I think it's cute."

The weeks past and we were in love. I couldn't stop thinking about her whenever I wasn't around her. One night when Key and all of us had a sleep over at a friends place. Amanda couldn't stay and I remember she left her purse behind and I held on to it all night. I was so sentimental. As the love grew, I developed wondrous sense for her features. I learned every curve of her face, the way she kissed, that beautiful feeling holding hands. The recognition of every part of her body was new to me. I never had felt a love like that before. I just knew that being around her made me strong, happy and more grown up. I wasn't making the same mistakes with my first love and Alyssa, which I still had regretted. I had learned the hard way not to make those mistakes but instead I was making all new ones!

Alyssa and I still were friends and she had wanted me back since we broke up. She would come on to me a lot and I would have to resist until one foolish night… I was over Alyssa's house just her and I and temptation was at its best. There she was looking all too inviting on the couch. I gave in to my sexual addiction for Alyssa and as I was deep into the invigorating sex I remember saying to myself, "What are you doing? What about Amanda? You finally found love again and you're doing this?"

I told myself to shut up and continued until I had that orgasmic release then the guilt poured into me!

You fool I thought! I sat up and Alyssa sat beside me as I broke down and cried. The guilt was so great I couldn't stop crying. Alyssa had stayed next to me but I couldn't image what she was feeling. She looked as though she was sad with me. Well

I guess I was a cheater and that new addiction of free sex took over! A normal person would think, hey, this is wrong. I made a bad choice and I could not allow myself to do such a dreadful thing ever again.

Instead I continued with Alyssa in our sex-fueled connection. We became friends with benefits while I was in love with another. What took me over even more was since I already cheated before what's it going to hurt to do it with another female? My quest for liberated sex had gotten the best of me and I slept with a couple of other young women. It got strangely easier to do that despicable act the more I did it. I had adapted to the emotional pain.

I couldn't defy one cute female's wonderful words one night while my friends and I all were hanging out at a table by the swimming pool of Key's complex. It was our weekend spot to just sit around and congregate and bullshit. Everyone was engaged in conversation while she stared intently at me. It looked like she was in thought and her long brown hair sat over her shoulders and her chin resting on her hands. I looked up at her across the table during that warm South Florida muggy night. There was a moment of silence and that pretty teenage girl leaned forward still looking at me.

"I'd fuck you!" She said out of the blue.

I said in a surprised way. "Wow! You just say whatever your thinking."

She giggled a little and Key gave me that look like, "Do it bro."

The only response I could muster together was… "Umm… Okay. Let's do this!"

As I continued to toss my dick on the crap table, I had no regard to the one I was supposed to be in love with. How could I be cheating if I were in love? It was a selfish way to live my late teenage years since my younger years had been filled with rejection. Girls actually found me attractive and wanted me sexually, which I never had before. I had become fascinated intently with the opposite sex more than ever and gave into the lust that stirred within my loins! If God was testing me I undeniably was failing!

I got myself a good driving job that gave me the time to be alone while I worked. It also gave me the chance to admire more of Florida. Those cool misty mornings that would turn into mild sunny days. Seeing the blue skies above and the puffy clouds. Admiring the South Florida trees, lakes and ponds. I had the best and longest delivery run with my job that went north. I got to see the ocean, downtown West Palm Beach, the subtropical countryside, and the airport, which I loved seeing the planes. Even with all its wonder Florida still didn't feel like home. It was flat and I was growing weary of the year round green and sunshine. I wanted seasonal change, hills and snow!

Ever since that night with that girl, my mind had still remained opened to the spiritual realm that was in contact with the physical realm. I became more in tuned with music and began noticing the meaning of songs I grew up with. Having the opportunity to drive and listen to music was very therapeutic. A song called *"Lunatic Fringe"* by Red Rider came on the radio one sunny day on the road. As I listened to the words it gave me a story in my head about the way I battle myself.

I envisioned destructive and creative ways my alter ego and I would have it out. I would picture my dark side driving along side of me trying to blow my tires out and I'd light up a stick of dynamite and toss it into his car and watch as it explodes or my other half would blow out my tires as I wrecked. We'd fight each other having superhuman strength and skills throwing one another through brick walls and off tall buildings. We'd rip each other apart but were always all right being immortal in my mind. Like two gods battling it out in a supernatural way. I even envisioned us just talking like we were friends then sucker punch him or he'd sucker punch me. When my other half wasn't around, I'd visualize my search for my other half with the words from that Red Rider song playing.

"Lunatic Fringe... I know you're out there. You're in hiding..."

I would develop an entire story line on me verses myself.

The lyrics sang on. *"This is opened season... but you won't get too far."*

Those words would sing from the radio and I felt it was opened season on the devil that was part of my own spirit. It was an exciting way to have an immortal war with good and evil in my own mind.

As I tuned deeper into the radio another song would come on that would give me a feeling I never felt. Songs that totally brought me back in time giving me a beautiful sense of how things used to be throughout my childhood to where I was in time then. One after the other songs from the 70's and 80's played in a strange sequence as if God was giving me remembrances of the special times I had growing up. I could see in my mind and feel in my spirit all the memories I had as the music played on. I had never felt anything like it.

I gathered new meaning to music and noticed I was able to relate to the lyrics more now that I was growing older. It amazed me to no end how a melody and vocals can deliver clear memories and the feelings I had at times past. From that point in time music became the gateway to my memorabilia. Another interesting phenomenon music gave me was noticing the synchronicity of life around me. It was like everything could flow to the beat of songs. The dreamy and psychedelic kind of music such as Pink Floyd led me to notice the sway of the trees, clouds above drifting by and a strong sense of something Divine and mystical functioning around me. Music was strongly connected to my mind and soul and I was tapping deeper into my own essence. I found that side of life to be eccentrically beautiful and prominent.

Within everything that surrounds us there is a balance and since I was in touch with my godly side, the dark mischievous spirit was always lurking. I was listening to this eerily eerie song on a trip up to central Florida with Amanda right before sunrise. We were going to Universal Studios in Orlando. We had decided to leave early to meet her parents there and have a full day of fun. It was still dark out and I knew a brand new day was coming.

What I felt was a demonic force with a skull and blackened eyes. It was an intensely evil being watching me out of the shadows of the remaining night. It was almost like instead of the sun to rise it would be a cursed dark skull to rise and loom over me. I knew it was no hallucination, just a vision in my head but a message of something in the distance to come like a revelation in my mind. It was an invading sinister spirit that was punching a hole into my world. Or perhaps what ever this thing was, it was awakening within me. Instead of having fear of that new sickly sense, I began writing a new novel. It would be based on living through darkness in ones mind. Darkness had become something I had become greatly interested in.

I continued to become more developed with my artistic side and got a talent agent to see if I could get involved in movies. I felt the need to express my acting side since I was so good at it. I had gotten a few jobs working as an extra and it was interesting to actually see how movies are made. I was a growing person trying to make it in the world. However, since my friends smoked a lot of marijuana, I began to wonder what it was all about. I had always been the good one in my circle of friends, the responsible one. I was even more mature than my older brothers who drank and partied a lot.

One night my friends Key and Ian had rolled a joint and I just had to try it. I smoked and smoked until I flew right out of my earthly mind. I had a weird and wonderful sense of self-awareness that I never experienced before. An imaginary force field surrounded my reality and gave me the power to look at myself from within, as if I were standing outside of myself. Cannabis had opened so many more new doors in my mind.

Was I really looking out of the eyes that were in my head? Were the sounds I was hearing real? How was I able to see and hear things? The body became a fascination to me and I tried to analyze its functions. I felt my heart beating pumping blood through out my entire body. I have lungs that take in oxygen and deliver it to my brain. My brain was a living lump of tissue but it held the core of my consciousness. Like a light bulb that illuminates when electricity runs into it, our consciousness, our mentality, our spirit and soul does the same thing to the brain. What were these silent words that I could not actually hear in my head I thought repeatedly? I know I am saying it and understanding my own communication but it boggled my own mind to fully understand the concept of that phenomenon. I was holding a conversation in my mind but there was no sound at all. Only thoughts. Streaming thoughts.

It was the same thing when it came to my imagination. I could picture something in my mind. A memory or a thought but it was something I couldn't see physically. When I closed my eyes, all I saw was the back of my eyelids, yet I was able to visualize anything I wanted. All those things were something I could not see, hear, smell, taste or touch. What I had found was a new fascination with the power of the mind. I could feel my nervous system and envisioned the whole function like an electrical system. My brain sends messages to parts of the body I wish to move. I had realized I was in charge with the vessel I was living inside of. It was all a part of the mechanics and technicalities of the physical realm.

Cannabis really helped me notice nature at a deeper level and would study the beauty it had. I tried to translate the night and figure out the stars and the universe. I noticed that when I looked out into the night, when the moon was sitting in the sky, I saw the cosmos as it stood. It appeared three-dimensional and I noticed the distance between the moon and all the stars that were visible. All these appealing visions of the way the sun spins, spewing out enormous amounts of gas, fire, heat and radiation. The planets that orbit the sun at different speeds all under the powerful spell of our great star. All the billions of stars that spiral in our galaxy and the billions of galaxies existing in harmony throughout the universe. How could all this be I intently wondered?

Old memories struck me differently and I broke down all I had been through and felt happiness for the good and great remorse for the stupid things I had done. With music, I could hear every instrument and fully understand the meaning and apply it to my world. Marijuana was simply a plant broke down to be smoked but it enlightened my psyche deeply! It was a new way to see the grand spiritual side of my own existence and all that was around me. It had become so intense I could not be around others because it shut out what was normal in the every day world. It held me in the deep corners of my way of thinking.

With all the wonderful ways pot elevated my mind and spirit there was a not so fun side that often affected me. Paranoia! I had to drive my friends to get something to eat because we developed a severe case of the munchies after our smoke fest. There we were totally stoned in the drive through of Checkers waiting for our food to come. The girl in the drive through window had been waiting for me to give her money and for that moment it felt as if she was staring at me like she knew I was high! The moment felt like it was dragging on and on with her staring at me like she's thinking, "I know what you did!"

Finally when she went to get our food, I noticed a window on the other side. Checkers had two drive through windows on both sides and for some reason when I looked inside the drive through window to the other side; I thought it was a mirror.

There I was staring at what I thought was myself but something wasn't right. I was looking at myself but my reflection wasn't looking back at me. It appeared to have a life of its own, it seemed, as the person I thought was me did his own thing, his own movements as I remained still, confused at what the hell was going on there. This is strange I thought. Suddenly the passenger in the car at the other side snatched the bag from the driver. I thought it was my friend Ian next to me and I flinched and looked seeing no bag and Ian just sitting there in the passenger seat of my car. What the hell I thought? Was I losing it?

Of course I told them what I just saw and they played into it.

Key said, "you better watch out. They know you're high. They are calling the cops right now."

"Good God man!" I said frantically. "We have to get the hell outta here! Quick! Go before they get here!"

They laughed at me and Key said, "uh dude? First off, you're driving and we were only messing with you. You were looking at the people on the other side of the drive through ya dumb ass! There was no mirror."

I didn't know what to believe so I just tried to forget that crazy occurrence!

When I got home my father was still up and being high like I was I didn't want him to know about it so I rushed into the bathroom and locked the door! I heard my father yelling something. I remained quiet and hoped he wasn't talking to me.

My father was yelling, "awe come on! Why are you doing this? Get out of there right now!"

I stared at myself in the mirror and said to myself. "Oh shit! What do I do now? Wooh God! I'm fucked!"

Paranoia ran deep throughout my entire body! I took deep breaths and tried to come to terms that I had been caught while I was high but how could he possibly know? I slowly opened the bathroom door and peaked out to see if he was still there. I crept out and tried to tip toe into my room but there he was all of a sudden. I turned and saw that the whole time he was talking to our dog! All that fear for nothing. With a sense of relief I went into my bedroom and locked the door to hide from the rest of that weird night!

It was 1995 and I had turned 21. Amanda and I broke up and found it best to stay friends. It had been another form of rejection. What have I done this time I wondered? She had no idea of how many times I had cheated and it was best that she didn't know. It hurt but I understood that it really wasn't working out. Boys to Men had a hit song that came out during my new heartache that was always in sync with my thoughts. It was called *"On Bended Knee"* and it spoke to me immensely!

The lyrics that spoke to my heart sang this sad tune. *"Can we go back to the days our love was strong? Can you tell me how a perfect love goes wrong? Can somebody tell me how to get things back the way they used to be? Oh God give me the reason, I'm down on bended knee."*

I came to the realization I had taken another love in my life for granted. The love we had was a perfect love and I couldn't figure out how such a perfect love goes wrong. We were always together and couldn't imagine life without one another. Amanda had given her virginity to me and I thought we would end up married. The loving moments we shared were over. How does it happen I thought? How do we fall in love expecting to be together forever but disconnect later on?

When we first dated we loved everything about each other. Later on as the relationship grew we talked about moving in together. When her parents went out of town for a week, Amanda gave me the key to her house and I wore in around my neck as the key lay on my chest. It felt at the time like we were a young couple living together. Like that was our house together and we could sleep in the same big bed in her parents master bedroom. I spent the nights we had alone together and would get up for work the next morning. I would kiss her goodbye and told her I would be home later. I couldn't wait to get back home to her! We ate together, talked, laughed, cuddled watching television and made love. It was the age of the beepers and we use to beep each other codes when we weren't together and when I was at work. 143 were I Love You or I Miss You. I loved when I got a beep from her like that to help get me through the day until I saw her again. We traveled together and shared so many beautiful moments.

The disconnection started when she started not wanting to have sex, which was part of the reason I strayed more, but still no excuse. We started to get annoyed at a lot of little things about one another. We became detached sexually and lost that loving feeling we once had over some time. I guess we just fell out of love and I may never understand why that happens when the love seemed so perfect.

I found it easier to move on from a broken heart because I had been through it before. What doesn't kill you really does make you stronger. The pain I experienced with my first love made me a stronger person in the long run. However the remorse I had for the way I treated my first still stayed with me all those years. I tried to apologize but she said I screwed her up so bad that she didn't want to hear it. She had told me I gave her nightmares for months and she even had breathing problems due to anxiety. I could not believe I scarred the girl that much! It was something I would have to accept though it was not easy. I often fantasized about sending my present consciousness into my younger self and change what I had done. Relive it with the knowledge I had learned and the love in my heart. Reconstruct the whole experience but I couldn't. Even to just simply heal her pain I caused. I just wanted her forgiveness and to see the person I had become. Not the psycho I was when I was 16!

I had received a phone call from my old friend Flip whom I did the student films with. He moved out to Los Angeles to pursue his directing career. We talked about the new and exciting possibilities that we could both have if I were to move out there with him. I had nothing holding me back and I wasn't crazy about Florida. I felt it was time for a daring new challenge to find the artist within me. California was a wild and attractive place with a different lifestyle and culture. I became intrigued by the notion to drive across the country and explore new territories! I could move there and really chase my acting and writing career! I sensed my soul mate was out there somewhere and was hoping that I would meet her there. I felt in my heart I would find her one day. I envisioned a beautiful, eccentric artistic woman with long brown hair and deep blue eyes. Such a loving woman in her heart I felt. I knew she was out there but was nowhere in sight. I had thought Amanda was my soul mate but something wasn't right in my spirit. She's still out there! I knew it! Maybe I will find her in California!

Flip and I talked it over and when I announced it to my mother she seemed saddened that her baby son was moving. My father however was all for that idea because he wanted to make my room into his.

I still worked as a driver but I needed to make money fast! I got a second job delivering pizzas in the hopes I can make money as quick as possible. I worked… and worked… and worked… and when the time was drawing near I realized I had saved $2,500! Would it be enough I wondered? One way or another I had to go to California and nothing was going to stop me!

An amazing gift God had sprung on me for this new adventure was $10,000 in e-bonds I didn't know about. My grandmother had set aside those bonds for my brothers and I years ago to give us when we got older. I found that to be a miraculous blessing and I knew the time was right to move out west. I was so grateful to my grandmother for doing that and there were no words to express! Strange synchronicity that had occurred made me feel it was meant to be. Flip flew in, I picked him up and he slept over.

The next morning we got things all packed up and ready to journey across our great country. The look in my mother's eyes broke my heart because we were so close I knew we were going to dreadfully miss each other. Part of me didn't want to go and I knew part of my mother didn't want me to go but this was something I had to do. Like a baby bird that grows up will one day fly the nest to go his own way, I also had to fly the nest my mother had made so wonderful for me. I had said goodbye to all my friends and would stay in touch. My parents had bought me a brand new mustang not to long ago. It was another blessing for me, a head start in my life. It was red, sporty and all ready to go. I hugged my mother with tears then set forth on to the California experience.

The Consequence Handed Down

I lay dead inside knowing that my dreams have been murdered by a nightmarish reality. As the psycho babble when on out in the day room, I remained isolated in my cell. Thoughts of suicide crossed my mind so many times but I did not have the nerve to do such a thing. I knew that if I were to kill myself I would carry a great sadness with me and my soul would not be able rest. I would remain trapped in my own personal hell reliving the pain and regret of my stupid mistakes and bring about true darkness.

My name was called and I slimed out of my cell and went downstairs to the visiting room. There was the Weasel with his papers ready to tell me what may occur. I sat down in fear and waited for the Weasel to talk to me.

He said, "well, it appears you are looking at a significant amount of time."

It was two days before my court date and he came to tell me that?

The Weasel continued, "I talked to the DA and she has her heels dug into the three felonies. However, if I can talk her down to a lesser pill count we can go to a much lower range of time. I can't guarantee 6 months in county jail. I think there is no way to get around prison time but it won't be nearly as much as you're facing now."

In high hopes I said, "but I could still not go to prison right?"

"I don't know. I'll talk to the DA and I will let you know."

As he gathered his papers I drifted off for a moment staring at the empty spot my Goo once sat when she last visited me. I looked through the plated glass and remember seeing her but not being able to touch her. Being in that horrifying situation made me feel a deep distressing sense of her loneliness having to go back home alone when we were always together. Walking into an empty house without me there. Since I use to do all the cooking she had to make dinner herself and she couldn't cook. She was only able to make TV dinners in the microwave and eat alone. We would always eat together and watch TV. I felt her pain as she slept on the couch because she couldn't bear to sleep in our bed without me. That was true love and I felt the heartbreak in us both. I thanked the Weasel and was taken back up to the pits.

As I staggered back to my cell and flopped on my jail bed, I started thinking about my Xanadoo all alone and me being trapped in that shit hole. I reached down and pulled out the lyrics

Goo had sent me of Elton John's *"I Guess That's Why They Call it the Blues."*

I read the first lyrics. *"Don't wish it away. Don't look at it like it's forever."*

Xanadoo wrote next to it, *"Because it's not!"*

I kept reading the lyrics. *"Between you and me I could honestly say that things can only get better."*

Xanadoo wrote next to those lyrics, *"And they will!"*

Continuing the lyrics… *"And while I'm away dust out the demons inside and it won't be long before you and me run to the place in our hearts where we hide."*

Xanadoo wrote *"So true!"*

Back to the lyrics… *"And I guess that's why they call it the blues. Time on my hands could be time spent with you."*

She wrote next to that, *"And we will have that time again!"*

I had nothing but time on my hands being exiled from everyday life. I guess it wasn't forever but it felt that way. Was I really away to dust out my demons? All I knew was that I wanted to run home back to Xanadoo! I got up and looked out of my cell window. There I was watching life still functioning without me. Cars drove by, people walking on the sidewalks living out their lives. The trees were beginning to bloom in the springtime that was going on without me. Clouds drifted by allowing the sun to peak in and out casting shadows on the ground that faded in and out.

I had written two letters to the judge in hopes that he would go easy on me. Xanadoo also wrote a beautiful letter along with our friends stating my character and that I was not a menace to society. I was facing a fight for myself and I wondered if there was hope? As I thought of that I looked down and saw a newspaper and there were words in bold letters that read: *"Fight to finish!"*

I gained a sense of optimism realizing it wasn't over just yet. The Bearded Molester, The Evil One, Sexter, Wayne and a few others had absolutely no one in their corner. Basically they have been cast aside and left to fend for themselves in the madness of being caged. I still had Xanadoo and she was not going to leave me!

Just as I thought that the Weasel had come up to see me stating that he got the DA to agree on a lesser charge, though I still was facing three felonies, but they weren't a total of 4-½ to 9 years minimum! There was hope yet! I immediately ran to the phone and told Xanadoo the news.

It was the day before my sentencing and I was getting nervous. There was a lot of negative energy looming all around me. I felt something bad was in the air. There was this guy named Tony who had a bad habit of running his mouth. He always had something stupid to say and he was getting on Wayne's last nerve. Wayne got up and stepped in front of Tony and they started to argue!

Wayne said loudly. "I am getting so sick of you running your mouth!"

Tony came back with, "just get out of my face!"

"No!" Wayne stood his ground. "I'm sick of you!"

"You better get out of my face while you still can!"

I was thinking, geez, here we go! They started pushing each other and a few other's came to try and calm them down. By then it was too late, Wayne and Tony started choking each other then fell on the ground wrestling, yelling curse words! The guards should be running in any moment to take them to the hole I thought but there was no one. Wayne got Tony in a strong headlock and was choking the life out of him! Good God! He's going to kill him! Tony was turning red as he gasped for air!

I shouted, "Wayne! Let him go! You're killing him!"

It took three of us to pull Wayne off Tony and while we tried to talked to Wayne to calm down, Tony was on his knees holding his neck and chest. It took Tony about fifteen minutes to gather himself and crawl into his cell. I had Wayne come into our cell to try and reason with him but he was unstable.

"You almost killed him Wayne!" I said.

"So what! Someone that ugly and ignorant doesn't deserve to live!"

"Yeah, then you'd be charged with murder and you will never see your kids again."

He pounded on the wall and shouted. "I need a cigarette! It would be worth it to go to prison just so I can smoke a fucking cigarette!"

"You'd take a mans life just so you can smoke a cigarette?"

"Damn right!"

"Think about your kids! Even if they charge you with indecent assault on your step daughter at least you know it will only be 2 ½ years minimum, not life!"

He started to cool down then he turned to look out of the cell window. He wiped a tear away and I knew it was because he had lost his wife and could not see his kids for at least three years due to the PFA. It wasn't Tony that made him so angry like that. It was all the pain he had been carrying since his arrest and the loss of his family. It just so happened to all spill out on Tony. Tony just triggered the madness within Wayne.

He looked at me and said, "thank you. I'm sorry."

"Why don't you write to the governor and senators like I told you? Look at me, I wrote to the judge and I know it will make a difference. You need some help in here and this place has no help at all! Make that difference Wayne."

He smiled and I handed him some paper and a pen. An amazing thing happened. He began to write! There I was feeling so good knowing that my words had given him hope. Xanadoo kept telling me to be the light and I knew what she meant. I believe that God is the source of all light, love and hope and all that still shines down in the world. God gave me a great gift to guide people and I have done a lot of that throughout my life. I always seemed to have that encouraging spirit to ease the pain someone bears alone. It often hits me to see how delicate we as humans can be in this world that can be cruel at times. I understood that there were people like me that shed the light and bring them hope! And there were people like Xanadoo who remind me of that. It was the synchronicity and sense of balance I felt that makes our world go round.

It was the end of April and the day finally arrived. It was time to find out once and for all my fate. There I was sitting in chains before the judge along side a few other inmates awaiting their fate as well. Xanadoo sat behind me in the courtroom and I was in hopes of a good future because I saw outside that the sunrays making its way out. It shined into the courtroom making it appear like a good sign of things to come. In a strange way, I remembered Xanadoo's encouraging words if I were to go to prison.

"Maybe you are there to help someone who is scared. You are the light."

That image of the young man came to mind again. I felt his fear within my spirit and he would need me for his first time in prison.

As I sat in anticipation for my sentence, court began and I knew the moment would be coming! Oh God! Please help me through this! I had all sorts of sickening thoughts through my incarceration. I fantasized many real losers that would be a poison to society before the judge and he would go easy on them turning them loose back into the community to cause more evils.

Self-pity consumed me and I would envision the judge saying to me, "I can see you are a good person and you just made a mistake. You are not a menace or troublemaker and have been a great asset to the community. It is in your best interest that you get proper help, not prison time, because I know you will do well for yourself later on. No one should go to prison for having the disease of addiction. However, I am going to make an example out of you! I sentence you to 10 to 20 years in prison and may God have mercy on your soul!"

At that moment I would faint and bang my head on the podium that was before me and collapse on the floor. I would be brought to the hospital and fall deep in a coma for months! The doctors would tell the judge I was not fit for prison but the judge would not care!

"I don't care how much good he will do or that he is in a coma! He must be locked up!"

I snapped back to reality and told myself to get a grip! Stupid thinking!

They began calling names and the first person to be called up was a thin guy around 25 years old named Andy Woodward. He approached the judge with his arms stiff by his side, shaking like he was completely paranoid of his near future, standing on that line of doom or freedom. He had short brown hair and looked frail and broken. There he was shaking slightly as the DA and public defender argued their sides of his story. Apparently he was in a sexual relationship with an underage girl and it did not look good for him. The judge spoke harsh words stating that he showed no remorse in his lustful act and had done nothing to better himself. This guy is doomed I thought!

The judge handed down a short prison term, which was a little over a year then took him away. I remember thinking "geez, I am in for it!" I could always just drop dead before the court. That would show em'!

My name was called and the sunlight that was shining in faded away as my heart began to palpitate. I turned to look at Xanadoo and she gave me a smile of hope. Standing before the judge, the Weasel argued my side of the crimes I committed. He told the judge that I was addicted to the pills and that some county time and probation with a drug program would be the best thing for me. Didn't sound convincing to me. The DA got her say in. She went off on me stating that I had a nice scam going and that I could also be a drug dealer! I was thinking oh please! I was using them not selling! This was it I thought, I'm going to prison! It was my karma of bad choices biting me in the ass!

I had a moment to say something and I sincerely spoke out saying that I was not a drug dealer and I do not belong in prison. I expressed that I really was a good person with a sickness, not a criminal. My only hope was that the judge had read all of my character letters and go easy on me. The judge did mention those letters in the next moment.

He looked right at me and stated, "it seems you are well respected in the community and have friends… its a shame you didn't utilize your support group of friends sooner."

Reality took a turn for the worst as he handed down my consequence for my foolish decision and reckless behavior.

He said, "I'm going to go with the minimum. You will be confined in a state correctional facility for 18 to 36 months. 6 months each for three counts of obtaining a controlled substance by fraud."

My heart sank and my body shivered with fear! My God! What was happening I frantically thought? That was it. They took a hold of me to take me back to the pits and before I went, I turned and saw Xanadoo. There she was looking terribly saddened by my dreadfully written short-term future, which felt like a lifetime.

I felt like falling on the floor and beg them to please not take me away from my Goo! I felt like shouting to the courts the song by Chicago, *"Love me tomorrow"*.

"She loves me! And that's all I need to know. She's part of my life, just a part I won't let go."

I knew that I could not do that. I stayed locked with Xanadoo peering in her eyes how sorry I truly was for what had happened. I turned face forward and with the weight of another heartache, I tried to come to terms with what was in store for me. I would be taken back to the pits and await the horrifying moment when they would take me to the penitentiary.

It was the very next day and I was before Xanadoo separated by the plate glass in the visiting room. I had my hands over my face in extreme shame for my outcome.

I got myself together and said into the phone receiver. "I'm going to prison. I understand if you want to find someone else."

She put her hand on the glass and told me to put mine where hers was on my side. I placed my hand and felt the glass and it hurt that I couldn't actually touch her! She stared into my eyes with immense love. She moved her hand away and pulled out some papers. She smiled and put the first piece of paper to the glass.

It read in big letters, *"Remember that…"*

She took it away and placed the second one on the glass and it read, *"You are not dead!"*

The next paper she put up said, *"God is not done with you yet!"*

Encouraging words she was able to tell me without speaking. How could someone have that much love and hope!

She put another against the glass that read, *"See this as an opportunity to help someone else!"*

I immediately thought of that young guy Andy who was sentenced before me to a short prison term. They had placed him on the same block I was on. He had been classified as a sex offender since he had sex with an underage female.

The next paper she put up read, *"They are scared also…"* I thought of Wayne and Sexter and how frightened they were to go to prison. I felt in that moment that I really wasn't alone in that lurid nightmare.

She continued to smile at me and showed me the next page that read, *"I love you!"*

116

She took that away and replaced it with one that read, *"I will wait for you!"*

The last one she showed me read, *"I will never leave you!"*

I was so touched that a tear ran down my face.

I said, "how can you want to wait for me? I really screwed up!"

"You are a good person who is pure of heart." She said. "So what if you made a mistake. I don't feel you should go to prison for it but it is what it is."

"I have to tell you something." I hesitated for a moment. "The day I got arrested I was planning on doing a hospital run to get more pain killers. It was one of many hospitals I used to secretly go too often when you were at work. I remember those roads to get there and back was so hilly and windy and I saw myself killing someone or myself. Can you imagine if I killed someone and the cops found out I used a fake name to get pills and a life was taken because I was irresponsible? I would have done some serious time!"

"That's what I mean. I hate to say this but I am glad you got arrested. God saw you were on the wrong track and stepped in to save yourself! Thank God you're not dead! You could have killed yourself then it would be all over! I don't know what I would do if you died!"

"He must have saved me for a reason. I'm not sure what that is yet."

"It's to be the light." She smiled. "You have saved me in a lot of ways and I know you will help others."

"Like that guy Andy?"

She said in sadness, "I saw him outside of the courthouse before you got sentenced. He was coming off so many drugs that he collapsed before he went in."

"I know, he told me. I got to know him in the pits. You know what's interesting about all that? Remember when you said a while back that I am supposed to help someone who would be scared through this?"

She nodded.

I continued, "Andy was exactly the same guy I saw in my vision! I pictured him before I even met him and now here he is. How do you explain that?"

"It's part of your gift from God!"

"No, I mean, what the hell is that? How can I see things coming?"

"I really don't know. It's a gift."

I continued on. "He is a good guy, just a little lost in life."

She smiled and said, "did you read all the songs I mailed you?"

"Yes! The lyrics are really helpful in this horrible time!"

I looked intensely at her and tried to figure out who this woman was. Why was she sticking with me through all this? There was a time when we both had no idea that we even existed and there we were in love even with a plate glass and the system keeping us apart. I thought of one of the songs she sent me. It was called *"For The First Time"* by The Script. The words that captured my attention in our darkened time spoke true.

Xanadoo had highlighted parts of the song. *"And we don't know how, how we got into this mess. Is it God's test? Someone help us because we are doing our best... Oh these times are hard, yeah, they're making us crazy. Don't give up on me baby."*

She wrote next to those encouraging words *"I won't!"*

It couldn't be a more perfect song for her to send me. What I was experiencing had to be a test from the Divine. Not just for me but also for the true love Xanadoo and I shared. That inner glow, the light within my spirit, which was buried under all the darkness I held on to for so long began to grow again. It was an amazing feeling I started to be aware of for the first time in a long time. I really wasn't dead! I was alive with a hopeful future that I can write for myself. It was the beginning of the spiritual journey I had to endure. It was a moment of knowing everything would be all right.

What began to sadden me was soon the visits that were getting me by every week would be over with. There would be no more Xanadoo sitting where she was and me so happy to see her. I know the day would be coming soon that I will be taken far away and then what?

I asked, "what's going to happen when I am taken down state? What if it is six hours away?"

She replied in a positive tone. "We will work through it. It's not forever."

Our time was up and I had to be taken back to the pits. We placed our hands on the glass one last time and repeated the words "I love you!"

It was interesting because I knew I was incarcerated and going to prison but the love between Xanadoo and I was strong! So strong that the guard who escorted me always smiled and was pleased to see us. Our love even made the guys on the block smile. Our love really spread its way into everything and everyone that surrounded us. I got on the elevator and waved to Xanadoo as long as I could before the door completely closed.

It was well into May, nearly four weeks since my decree from the judge. I was sitting by the big window looking outside into freedom. It was a beautiful spring day and I was locked up in the pits of my own hell! The trees that I was able to see were nearly in full bloom and I was powerless to smell and touch the wonders of nature. Xanadoo and I have been fighting on and off over the misery that has been going on. She was just as scared as I was and she was dealing with being alone and taking care of things. Before I came into her life, she had never been alone and was having a hard time coping with that reality. I was supposed to come into her life to make her feel loved and desired but I had failed! What was killing us the most was wondering when in the hell they would take me down state to prison? It would be a sneak attack I have heard. They do not tell us when they will come and rip us out of these pits to put us into the states pits of hell!

Bastards I thought! I made a mistake to get medicine to feed the addiction. I don't belong in prison being treated like a common criminal! I filed for a motion for reconsideration in the hopes the judge would change his ruling. Xanadoo and I wrote more letters and got copies of my medical records to prove I had pain issues. I had been called down once more to the courtroom. There I was with Xanadoo behind me in the courtroom yet again before the judge. The Weasel stated a weak speech that I would do better with a short county time and a rehab program but the DA once again took a bite out of my ass! She debated that I belong in prison and that I did not like my condemnation. I felt like saying, damn right I don't! I remember the judge saying that he did not make the laws and he went as low as he could go on his judgment.

The only good thing that came from all that was he announced that he believed I was not a drug dealer and that I obtained the meds for myself. That made Xanadoo and I feel better because in no way was I ever a drug dealer! At least we tried.

Sitting in that moment, as the idiocy of the block went on, I had before me a song that Goo sent me. James Taylor's *"Fire and Rain"*.

Goo highlighted the lyrics that read, *"Won't you look down upon me, Jesus, you've got to help me make a stand. You've just got to see me through another day."*

Goo wrote next to that last part *"He will!"*

I continued to read on. *"My body's aching and my time is at hand and I won't make it any other way. Oh, I've seen fire and I've seen rain. I've seen sunny days that I thought would never end. I've seen lonely times when I could not find a friend, but I always thought I'd see you again."*

Xanadoo filled her own words saying with all her heart, *"You always will see me my sweet! I love you!"*

Those lyrics truly spoke to me in that time of need. It was exactly how I felt. It was like Xanadoo knew exactly what song to send me that would be in sync with how I was feeling. Oh Jesus, I do ask that you help me through this! I really am aching and the time is drawing near to be brought down to a whole new world I have never lived before. In all my life I have seen fire and I have seen rain along with sunny days and lonely times. I had found a friend in God, myself and in Xanadoo. Still, with all that, I was unrelenting battling myself.

Andy sat down next to me and asked how I was feeling.

I said, "just wondering when they will take us down state."

He answered back, "I don't know. This waiting sucks!"

"How are you feeling? Still ill from the methadone withdrawals?"

"Yeah. This place is so stupid! I told them I was in a methadone clinic and I can't just stop taking it! What kind of system is this?"

"It is stupid! They didn't do anything for me either when I told them I was on pain meds. They need to start treating addiction as a disease, not a crime!"

Andy looked at me. "You know I don't understand why I am going to prison for having sex with a girl who was under 18? It was consensual. She even wrote to the judge saying we had feelings for each other. The state creates a law making someone under 18 unable to make their own decisions! Its human nature damn it! Not a terrible act of evil! She was 16 and I was 23!"

"I know. Look at Elvis! He was in his twenties when he was with Priscilla and she was 14!"

"The crazy thing is now she is 18 and of age the stupid law requires because they think someone under 18 can't make their own decisions! Like they don't know what they are doing. Now my life is all screwed up for having feelings for someone who was 6 years younger than me!"

I thought for a minute that I didn't necessarily condone what he did but in a way it was true. It was human nature and in some cases age can be only a number. My first love and I were 15 years old when we first made love and we knew what we were doing. There are so many underage people having sex willingly now days. I could understand if the girl was 12 and he was 40 and it was done unwillingly, that is rape! Andy was a very talented artist and musician and now his talents would go to waste. He has written a few songs that stressed the way he felt, which I thought had a great deal of raw emotion. His art works consist of mostly demons and skulls that showed he was in touch with his dark side. We all have a dark side to us but he found a way to express it creatively.

Andy continued, "I had a rough life to begin with! I was beaten at a young age! Then I became addicted to drugs to cope! I was a victim once! Where was the law then?"

I thought of Wayne when he told me he had been sexually assaulted and abused at a young age. He was a victim as well and no one helped him. So it was all right, it seemed, that their abusers got away with messing up their lives. I heard the same story being on the sex offender's block. Everyone who was a sex offender had been molested or abused at one point. Then they grew up not right mentally and have to live with a sickness. It was like a double-edged sword. Those men who were abused were left with scares and tend to only have desires for children because they are children themselves! They never grew up from something like that. Stuck. However, if they experienced that type of torture as a child why would they do it to another? Perhaps they grew up thinking that is ok to do since it happened to them. I wasn't sure what the answer was. I was thankful to God for never being treated like that as a child. I have enough of my own troubles.

It was getting close to lock down so I got up to call Xanadoo one last time. I held the phone thinking of the day they would take me away.

"Hi honey," she said in a low tone.

I said in worry she was not in good spirits. "Hi. Are you ok?"

"No! I can't do this anymore! I am having a hard time being alone. I need you here with me!"

"I know! I am sorry for all this."

"Why did you have to do that? All for a stupid pill and now you are going to prison!"

"I'm sorry!"

"I don't know what I am supposed to do now! You're not here anymore, I'm alone dealing with the mess you made, the bills to pay, the animals to take care of!" She yelled.

"I said I was sorry!" I said getting frustrated.

"I deserve better than this! I work hard! I'm a good person. I don't need this in my life!"

"Then go find someone else!" I snapped.

"I deserve someone to take care of me! You were really dumb to do what you did!"

My time was getting close, they were about to lock us down for the night and I didn't want to be fighting again with Xanadoo. There she was going off on me for my incarceration. I didn't know what to say because it was my entire fault. I saw the guard come in to have us all go into our cells for lock down.

I spoke into the phone with desperateness, "I have to go. Please don't leave me. I need you!"

Xanadoo sighed and said. "What do you want me to do?"

"Please don't leave me! I love you!"

A CO said loud to me. "Hang up and take it in."

I expressed my feelings once more to her then had to hang up the phone. Fear built within me. Is she going to leave me? I am going to end up all alone again in a big city, lost to the world with nowhere to go? I was leaning on the edge of madness! Being locked up in a nutty block, losing my Goo, my freedom gone, everything was stripped away and there was nothing I could do about it! And on top of it all I was going to be taken to a place I heard horror stories about! Oh God! Please see me through another day!

I lay in my bed the next morning with my eyes wide opened. I wasn't sure what time it was but I felt in my spirit my time was coming. It was still dark outside and I prayed that I would not be taken away yet. Please God; allow me to stay another week here in familiar territory. As I closed my eyes to block out my reality, my cell door clanked opened! I jumped out of my bed and rushed out into the day room. There were two guards walking in and I knew it was time!

One guard called my name and said loud. "Pack it up! You're going to state."

My heart sank! The last thing I said to Xanadoo was *"please don't leave me"* as she seemed unsure of our future. They told Andy to it pack up and at least I wasn't alone in that wretched situation. I nervously gathered my stuff and as Andy got his stuff together, it was our time to go. The guys all lined up to say their goodbyes. I gave Wayne a hug goodbye and he thanked me for influencing him to write to the right people. He was finally going to get the help he needed and I was glad I helped him do that. My words really got him going on those letters and he finally got a response from the state rep. I wished him the best as he was continuing to fight his case in court. Sexter shook my hand and thanked me for all the advice I gave him. He told me if it weren't for me, he would have been a real mess. I helped to ease his circumstances and if I was able to face prison then so would he.

There was the Bearded Molester and I just waved bye to him. I knew he would have some serious issues from the other inmates when he gets down state for his nauseating offense! I really had nothing to say to The Evil One. He was another that would have to really pay for his disgusting foul acts! We said our goodbyes to the rest of the block who wished us luck.

After we left the block, Andy and I were brought down to a holding cell. We sat in anticipation of the next stage of our dreadful nightmare. I sat and wondered, wasn't all the punishment I put on myself enough? I put myself through more hell than anything the state could put me through. Couldn't I tell the judge, hey, I kicked my own ass on the matter at hand! Losing my job, my freedom, and my mind! Being contained in a whacked block and having a window where I could look out of knowing everything is out of my reach! The torture, the madness I have felt through my time in that zoo! I felt I had suffered just about enough! Doesn't that count for something? In the real world it doesn't matter how much pain one brings upon ones self, or that you lost everything, they want to make sure you pay on their terms!

There would be no more visits from Xanadoo every week! I would not be able to call her any time of the day. Once again, the life I came accustomed to was removed from me and now I was off to another outlandish site of agony! What lies ahead would be unknown to me and only God knew what was in store.

The California Experience

"Was this really happening?" I remember thinking. Flip and I were heading north on I-75, passing through Valdosta Georgia. It was mid November of 1995 and for the first time in five years, I was seeing the trees around me changing colors. We were right on the border of the sub-tropics and the temperate zone where the trees transform through all four seasons. Something I missed since I moved to south Florida. It was late in the day and the sun was bright orange, getting low in the western sky. The sun shinned blissfully on the beautiful orange and yellow leaves that were all around us. I wanted this trip to last so we decided to take a longer route up to I-20, into Atlanta, then head west. I looked before me and saw the long shadows stretch across the highway from the setting sun and the rolling hills that lie in the distance. I was in complete awe from this new experience.

What will become of me when I get to California? Will I be a star? I always wanted to become somebody important and often pretended my life was a movie and I was the main character. Would I meet that someone special out there? For some reason I had this notion I would meet a beautiful eccentric woman named Sarah. I wasn't sure if it was another premonition or just a fantasy. For some reason the name Sarah always allured me.

I asked Flip, "how is it out in Cali?"

He said, "it's a whole other world!"

"Do you think we will make it?"

"You and I are partners for life. We are going to blow up Cali!" He looked at me with a smile. "Yo, I want you to check this out."

He pulled out a cassette tape and put in my player. Was this going to be some crazy ghetto rap music I wondered? Slowly a peaceful organ intro began to fill my ears. A beautiful sounding voice began to sing and I was instantly intrigued.

She sang, *"Listen as the wind blows… from across the great divide. Voices trapped in yearning… memories trapped in time. The night is my companion. The solitude my guide… would I spend forever here and not be satisfied."*

Those lyrics were something I could truly relate to. The melody was new and refreshing, serene and calming to the soul. Music had made some changes since the 80's. It was 1995 and music had many new sounds. Nirvana alone had changed rock music in a big way in the early 90's, now there was this wondrous sound from an unknown artist.

"Who is this?" I asked.

"Her name is Sarah McLachlan. This song is called Possession."

I couldn't help but be in tuned to that harmony, which really got to my spiritual side. Song after song I became mesmerized by her brand new anthology of symphony.

Before we knew it we saw the tall buildings of Atlanta, Georgia. We cruised into downtown and the bright lights and the big city life amazed me. It was time we got a hotel.

The next morning we tooled around Atlanta for a short while. I had paid for the hotel room and even bought Flip a $100 necklace from the Underground Mall we went to. That was a very interesting experience. Never been to an underground mall. We got back on the interstate and headed west on I-20. Was I being taken advantage of I wondered? I hadn't told Flip about the $10,000 my grandmother had given me. Even though Flip had broken out of the ghetto to create great black films, he had told me many stories of his string of crimes when he lived back home in the dumps of South Florida. They say you can take a man out of the ghetto but you can't always take the ghetto out of the man. Flip showed his appreciation for my generous ways many times and always said we would be partners for life. Still I was a little concerned about what I was doing going all the way to California.

When he lived in Florida, I remember he used to sell crack cocaine. Me being the curious type wanted to know what that was like. So I went with him one night as he sold crack in the projects.

It was scary yet enticing to be there and witness that side of life. Business was good because many crack heads would come to him for their fix. One guy was so desperate he gave Flip some weed in exchange for some crack. Flip told me stories that he owned a gun at one point and he confided in me that he did shoot someone once, nearly killing him! Now he wants to take his experiences and make more films.

We rode freely on the expressway as we were well into Alabama. Seeing the city of Birmingham, I just had to veer off and explore. We had no map; no exact way to get to our destination, all we knew was what we were doing was a true venture through our country. We drove through northern Louisiana then into Texas. The day was winding down and we headed into Dallas off the beaten path we were on. I remember when we got out of the car, a cold front had passed through and the air was refreshing and cold. Ahhh... how I missed the change of seasons! I smelled that delicate scent of snow and with the clouds and chill on the breeze, I began to have old feeling of being home on Long Island.

As we continued into the next day, I noticed everything around me change from green to desert. We were well into Texas and there were less trees and it was like I was in a desolate land of nowhere. As that day went on, the sun once again began to get low in the sky. What I saw at the end of that day was the orange glow of the setting sun painting the desert mountaintops. I was wordless as the beauty just struck me hard! I was in a state of bliss. We stayed over in El Paso and once again I had paid for the hotel. I began to worry that I was being taken advantage of but I had to continue on with my journey. I knew it was too late to turn back. The fact that I received that money from my grandmother unknowingly and that I was going no matter what intrigued me. Why that money was placed in my path at the point in my life made me realize that the trip out west was something I had to go through. There was something waiting for me out there and God made it possible for me to venture to find it. Once again it was synchronicity well balanced in my life.

We traveled through New Mexico into Arizona and landed in Phoenix. By that time my loins were speaking to me. I paid for another hotel room and asked Flip if he would mind if I ordered me an escort to have sex with. What would he care I thought. So we flipped through the phone book to find one. I made the call and asked for an escort who was open minded. By saying "opened minded," meant opened for sex. After I made the call, I went out to get some ice and as I was thinking about the sex I was going to have with a complete stranger, I banged my head off a light fixture. I knew what I was doing was wrong and I felt in my spirit me banging my head was God. It was like He was slapping me on the back of the head saying, "what are you doing?"

Once the escort came to our room and Flip left, in no way was she going to have sex with me.

She said, "not for $150!"

I wasn't going to spend that kind of money just for her to dance naked in front of me without touching her. I wanted the whole package! I ran and got Flip then apologized to the girl and sent her on her way after she kept $50 for the trouble. Flip tried to make some more calls and made sure they understood that I wanted sex. I told him to forget it. I knew God was watching over me and my guess was what had happened was a sign from the great Divine!

We got back on the road the next morning, which would be our last day we would be traveling. We entered California and I was getting restless. I wanted to get to Los Angeles in a hurry. We had been traveling for days and even though I was enjoying it, I wanted to get my future started. The desert began to turn green again and sure enough we had arrived. I saw the high rises of Los Angeles and was in high spirits. We made it! Would I be a new man I wondered? Had that journey across the states changed me? We got to Flip's apartment and I called my mother. She was excited to hear from me but sadness was in her voice. For that moment, I felt far away from home. A strange sadness overcame me and I became home sick. I knew I could not go home now. I knew it was too late; I was in a place that was new and foreign yet again. I would have to learn how to reestablish myself in a brand new place.

I gave in and told Flip about my $10,000 my grandmother gave me. I had cashed in the e-bonds and opened a checking account. We went on the hunt for a two-bedroom apartment and being Southern California, we found one in the valley, Van Nuys, just north of Hollywood. Flip being a broke ass artist struggling in the pits of Hollywood, I offered to pay the security deposit and first months rent. A total of $2,000. It was a nice two-bedroom, two bath apartment and Flip being the way he was wanted the master bedroom. He told me he would pay a little more for the rent when he gets paid at his part time job.

I needed an escape so Flip and I took a ride to downtown Los Angeles to find me a hooker. I wanted sex bad and we found two hookers about 18 years old. So young I thought to be selling themselves but being in the over sexed state of mind I didn't ask any questions. I wasn't being stupid.

I was told it would be $100 for some sex but I hesitated. Could I really do this I thought? I took too long to decide and they walked away because there was a cop patrolling. Ugh I thought! "Now what?" kept plaguing my mind. We went back to the apartment and Flip's younger brother was there. He had been with Flip for a little trying to get his career going but wasn't making it.

I asked, "got any weed?"

"Awe hell yeah! I'll take you to go get some," he said.

So I went on a new adventure to a not so nice part of the area. He knocked on the door of this house. I saw a black man look out the window. The guy opened the door and we walked inside. The place reeked of pot and there were about three Jamaicans asking who the hell I was. Flip's brother told them I was cool and we needed some weed. I was led over to a table where there were two candy bowls full of dime bags of fresh green wonderful marijuana! I had the pleasure of choosing any sac I wanted! Nice I thought! We got a couple of pouches and headed back to the apartment.

I dropped off Flip's brother and arrived back at the apartment. It was a typical Cali place with a garage to park the car behind a metal gate that opened with a remote. The front entrance also had a security gate. I walked around the courtyard and there was a swimming pool that was surrounded by the rest of the apartments. There were pretty bushes and a few palm trees that were kept nice. There was a laundry room to do a wash. I had met the manager who was an old crazy cat lady who Flip and I called Crazy ol Girl. She was really nice but a bit off her rocker who had about 30 cats. A real crazy cat lady! I went up to my apartment and rolled a joint. I blazed up and inhaled the intense smoke of that Southern California weed. People seemed more laid back when it came to cannabis there and I even heard talks of the state legalizing medical marijuana. From my understanding it has always been a medicine and I knew a lot of people could benefit from it. For me it was always a spiritual medicine.

I got really high on the stuff and started to set up my room. I got really creative on weed but I was limited. My room consisted of my computer, which I set up on the floor, a lamp and a mattress. Being in that weird state of mind from the weed, I felt strange becoming righteous in my mind. I remember thinking this isn't my home. Where the hell am I? I became frozen in that moment and I knew something positive had to be done otherwise I would have constant bad mind trips. I knew it was time to get the show on the road. It was a brand new life I was starting and I had to gather as many resources as possible to build a successful career in Hollywood.

I went to the gym 3 times a week to work out and build myself. I was eating a lot and making an effort to get in better shape. Little by little I was starting to put on good weight by lifting weights building my muscles. I found a talent agent and dropped $500 on 500 headshots and an acting course. When I was in the office with the agent I looked on the wall and saw so many headshots of other hopefuls. Breaking into the business could be harder than I had thought! Since there were loads of movies being made I was offered to do some extra work. Nothing special, just background acting. It was something to go on the set of those movies.

I had to be there around 6 am and hung out in a tent where they had breakfast for all of what they called the *"Talents."* We waited until they needed us and then we all went on the set and did what they needed us to do. It was time consuming and at some points boring. I was surrounded with an assortment of models and wanna be stars.

The next day I got another extra gig for a Power Rangers episode. It was a baseball scene and we had to sit in the bleachers and cheer on the game. There was a pretty girl that was sitting below me and I started a conversation with her. We talked casually and I thought of asking her out. She seemed to have liked me. We were on the scene for over eight hours and were finally told it was a wrap. That girl went down and I followed thinking of ways to ask her out. I was very insecure and afraid of rejection but she seemed into me when we were talking. There she was talking with her girlfriends and I slowly approached her.

I stuttered, "uh… I want… umm…"

She looked at me like I was bothering her. "Yes? What is it?"

"Would… would you like to go out sometime?"

She smiled and said, "uh, no. I don't think so."

She turned away from me and continued to talk with her friends. Was there something wrong with me or were the girls in the business all bitches? Was I in search of love or was just looking to get laid?

Flip and I went out to a nightclub in the hopes I could meet someone. There I was sitting at a table with Flip watching all the pretty girls dancing. Flip told me I would have to get up and mingle if I really wanted to find a girl. I didn't have it in me to do it so I just sat there. If I wasn't feeling bad enough already, this attractive girl comes to our table and sits next to Flip.

She says to him, "you look bored. What's your name?"

Was I the invisible man I thought? I was sitting right there, kind of bored myself, but no one was asking me that question. Flip got up and had some fun with her as I sat alone beating myself up. My inner enemy was telling me, you're a loser and that's why no one wants to talk to you. I pondered that pathetic thought for a moment then had a revelation. It had dawned on me. I wasn't a loser. I wasn't unattractive. I was merely giving off a weak vibe of my own positive liveliness. The sort of self-confidence that makes a person shine and have people gravitate to. I was sitting there feeling low and women were able to pick up on that. A person can really become invisible if they allow the negative feelings to consume the spirit. It becomes a block on many different levels with intrusive thoughts that never shut up sometimes!

Flip and I went to a few more nightclubs but I had no luck whatsoever. For some reason I could not raise my energy high enough to attract a female. I had given up on finding someone and had my computer hooked up to a new thing called the Internet. America Online was brand new and rather expensive. It was roughly $2.95 an hour but I didn't care. I found myself smoking a lot of weed and going into chat rooms online. I continued to work on my novel when I wasn't on the Internet.

The nights began to call me and I started to stay up all night, high, watching old re-runs of sitcoms and Bugs Bunny cartoons. Night after night I sank into a personal life of flashbacks of my childhood. I bought myself a bong that I smoked cannabis out of and sat on the floor watching cartons, eating bacon and eggs, a childhood favorite my mother made me. It was like I was being pulled right into my past and the cannabis made me feel like I was almost there. I felt more connected to my youth in a way I never experienced before.

We had no couch, no furniture, or anything. All we had in the living room was a television that was placed on a milk crate. My money was slowly dwindling but I tried not to worry. I could always get a job I thought. I would be just fine.

I had it in me to explore my new home so I went on many drives around the area. I cruised through Beverly Hills and admired the big beautiful homes. I had a strong desire to live that kind of life and felt hopeful of it. I voyaged my way to Venice Beach, which was filled with a lot of people. I remember getting out of my car and walking on the beach. The Pacific Ocean was different from the Atlantic. There were cliffs and high hills all along the inner coast. The cool sea breeze hit my body with a refreshing sense of peace. There were people on bikes, roller blades and a couple of guys lounging around playing their guitars. In some ways I felt like an outsider. It was as if I didn't belong there and I was just a person who was passing through.

I toured my way into Hollywood and saw a lot of classy coffee houses and ritzy stores. I was hoping to see some celebrity's but had no luck. I got out of my car and tried to look cool with my hair styled back and my sunglasses on. I wanted to stand out there but being in a place like Hollywood, everyone wanted to stand out. Were all these people for real I wondered? It felt like I was just another artist in a land of many artists trying to make it in the realm of entertainment.

I walked on the sidewalk of fame seeing all the names of the stars that did make it. Would my name ever end up here I thought? In some ways, I felt that Hollywood could be a revolting bitch goddess! So much competition to deal with and torturous hours on the set kept feeding into my mind. Not to mention the other disgusting parts of Hollywood. Sleazy porn, scams and just plain emptiness. Some people fall victim to the depths of this place. Suck you dry and slide down a slippery slope into darkness and madness. Some people end up homeless, on drugs, in jail, hurt or dead! Some come to commit suicide! Many vivid intrusive thoughts were beginning to build up. I began to doubt myself.

It was another clear and cool day in Southern California and I wanted an escape. So I fired up a joint and headed towards the San Gabriel Mountains for a spiritual experience that marijuana gave me. In the distance I could see the mountaintops covered with snow, something I haven't seen since my last winter of 1990 on Long Island. I had great sense of direction and found the road that led into the mountains without a map. I journeyed up the windy hill and just drove until I saw little patches of snow. It was blissful and just what I needed. I drove through a tunnel then into a park that was covered in snow. I got out into the cold air and took in the breath taking in scenery that was all around me. I felt like I was the only one there and nothing could hurt me. I had my camera with me and took some wondrous pictures then I saw the rest of the mountain that went upward to the partly cloudy sky.

Something in me was inspired to climb to the very top so I went to the base and looked at the steepness before me. I ventured on and I climbed and climbed. I had to pull myself up on some small trees but I kept going as dirt and rocks crumbled down. The clouds covered the sun and I was out of breath and tired. I was about halfway up the mountain. I looked down and thought it was too late to turn back. I looked up and thought how the hell am I going to get to the top? I pretended the mountain was my life and I would have to reach the top in order to be successful. Come on, I thought! You can do this! I used all my strength and carried on, pulling myself up and up taking short breaks. It was a battle I knew I had to win.

I finally reached the top and when I pulled myself over the last hurdle, I was on top of the mountain. Suddenly the clouds parted and the sun shined all around me. The snow that was on the bushes next to me glistened like diamonds. I looked forward and to my amazement I saw the tops of the mountains that seemed to go on forever. At that moment I wasn't under the influence of the marijuana anymore and felt a new high I have never had before. I felt close to God and my energy soured! There I was on top of the world filled with silence and ecstasy. I could observe for miles and not one soul or the madness of the world could bother me. There was no other place I would want to be in that corner of my existence. I captured that astonishing moment with my camera. I put the camera down and continued to stare out into the beauty of the world.

I said, "dear God. I am finding myself to be getting lost. What is my life for? Is this where I am meant to be?"

The wind blew slightly and I felt a loving spirit move me deep inside my soul. I wasn't cold. I wasn't afraid anymore. I was lifted and wanted to fly off that mountain and ascend into the mystery of life!

Time moved on and I found myself back to where I was before the mountain top experience. I was dealing with my demons again. I had made many pit stops at the Jamaican's to buy more weed. Though cannabis always heightened my spirituality, there was an underlying issue going on. Something else was holding me back. My hunger for the touch and feel for a woman grew increasingly harder to resist every day! I was way to shy to go out and meet someone so I went to an adult store to maybe buy a porno to watch. There I was looking around in the den of the devil, searching for something, anything that would give me satisfaction. I saw in one of the aisle quite a few blow up dolls for sale. The box had a beautiful picture of a sexy woman in lingerie. Hmmm… perhaps this could ease my suffering a bit, I thought, and then I saw the price. $130! I wasn't about to pay that much for a blow up doll! So I looked to see the cashier who was busy with another customer.

The place I was in had a backdoor, so I grabbed the blow up doll box and held it in my hands, hesitant to what I wanted to do. I looked up and saw one of those big round security mirrors and saw myself in a weird way.

"What the hell are you about to do?" My reflection asked me.

Why not I thought… just walk out with it? I slowly made my move and out the back door I went. I got in my car and drove off with my heart pounding beneath my chest. I can't believe I just stole a blow up doll! My inner demon told me I really needed some serious help! Well at least I would have something to keep me company on those lonely nights at the apartment. I knew I had reached a new low.

I was right about one thing. You can take the man out of the ghetto but you can't take the ghetto out of the man. Flip told me of a place he wanted to rob to get some extra cash. I foolishly went with him to gain yet a new experience. We drove in his hoopty ride into a neighborhood where mostly college students lived. Since Flip was taking some courses in a community college, he had known a few people. Apparently, he knew the people we were about to rob because after he parked the car he knew exactly where to go. We hopped a fence and got to the backdoor of a nice house where no one was home. He must have planned this in the knowledge that they would not be home. It felt scary and exciting standing outside in the night. Only the back door light was on shedding some light. It was rather quiet around us.

He broke the glass of the door and made his way in. There I was in the dark as Flip scurried around finding things to take. I went to the front door to look out and to my surprise it was unlocked. I told Flip there was no need to have to break and enter through the backdoor. We could have used the front door. Only me this would happen to!

I began to get nervous standing in a strange place in a city where I knew no one and had no memories. I had a moment of feeling alone. Completely alone. It was a strange moment of total isolation from existence captured in a void. I couldn't stand it any longer so I tried to find Flip. I called his name and thought, oh my God! Where is he? I was relieved he had gone to go load up his car with the stuff he wanted and came back. I knew what we were doing wasn't right but for some reason I was led into that crime. I grabbed a radio and a few other things and we ran ourselves the hell out of there. Never mind me stealing a blow up doll. I just committed a burglary! Yet again, I had reached a new low.

A couple of months had past and it was March of 1996. I had done a few more gigs. Nothing special, I played an extra in two commercials and sat in a live audience during the filming of a sit-com. It was interesting to see the "Laugh" sign light up for everyone to make noise as if what they were saying was actually funny. There wasn't much on the show that I found even mildly humorous. I felt like a goon being told when to laugh at non-sense that wasn't even worth a chuckle. But being Hollywood there were dues to be paid and that was one of them. I found myself losing grip with reality and my hope to become someone in the business was fading. I never felt I was of this world and it just may not be destined to be anything in that part of life. I was smoking pot every night and staying up until the crack of dawn reliving my childhood in comfort. I slept most of the day away and when I would slime out of bed, I went right to the floor of the living room with a pillow and put on the television and got lost in my past again. I just had a lazy, sleepy feeling I could not shake.

There are consequences for everything we do and being that I was letting myself become a sloth, I discovered something devastating. I had in my head a song by Sarah McLachlan called *"Hold On"*.

The lyrics kept repeating *"Hold on… Hold on to yourself for this is gonna hurt like hell."*

For some reason, whenever I was writing my novel listening to that tape, that song always stood out as if it were trying to tell me something. I felt it in my spirit something was wrong, especially since those lyrics always called out to me. I would get mad every time it played because I didn't want to believe something bad was going to happen.

"Nothings wrong! Shut up!" I would shout.

It was like a premonition I didn't want to face but was coming no matter what. It was inevitable.

I had opened some mail from my bank and found a few cancelled checks that I did not write out. I saw the checks I had written for my half of the rent but those other checks looked like Flip's handwriting that he written for his half of the rent. My heart sank when I saw that $300 had been withdrawn from my bank, knowing I would never take that much out at once! In my sleepy stupor, I remember Flip would open my bedroom door and not really say anything. I noticed he went on the shelf where I kept my checkbook and ATM card. I didn't think much of it thinking he may have been getting something he needed. I never would have thought he would have been robbing me!

I realized that if I wasn't so aloof and foolish to have wallowed in the deadly sin of being a sloth, Flip might not have taken advantage of me. What have I done? I became sick to my stomach and felt really alone and scared. I thought Flip was my friend. There were many days where Flip would confide in me about his life and his dreams. He opened up to me in ways he never did with anyone and said I was his best friend. I was so easy to talk to and he said he always felt better talking to me about his concerns. It was a gift I always knew I had but this time I was duped!

I called my mother and she was in shock of what I had to tell her about Flip. I was so far from home and knew I could not stay there any longer. My mother was sympathetic and told me I always had a place with her back in Florida. My father, however, was not too pleased about my situation. I called my ex-girlfriend Amanda and she had missed me so much and said the words that struck my heart, "Come home." What could I do? I would have to leave as soon as possible but without Flip knowing. I would have to make my move when he went to school.

I had a major pity party for myself and just sat in my bedroom in deep emotional pain. Flip had come home and opened my door to talk.

I gave him a sad look and said, "I found out what you were doing. You stole my checks and wrote out your half of the rent with my money? Also you helped yourself to $300? How could you?"

Flip simply said, "I can do that."

I yelled. "No you can't do that!"

"I'm sorry." Flip had a sorry look, "I really am but I needed the money."

"You could have asked me."

I didn't want to talk to him anymore so I told him I needed to be alone. I really wanted to hit the bong and get high for a spiritual mind journey but I was too depressed over what was happening. Also the weed may enhance the negative state of mind I was in making it worse giving me a horrible mind trip. You can do that huh Flip? Well guess what? You can have the apartment all to yourself and deal with the rent. What I can do is pack up when you're at school tomorrow morning and leave your sorry ass to get evicted when there is no one to help you. The night lingered on and I was wondering how I would fall asleep over how I was feeling. I lay in my bed waiting for the next morning to arrive.

The *"Hold On"* song kept playing in my mind singing, *"So now you're sleeping peaceful. Lie awake and pray and you'll be strong tomorrow and we'll see another day and we will praise it."*

To my surprise I found myself drifting off peacefully...

I had awoken the next morning around 6 am with a strong sense of hopefulness. I felt renewed and strangely inspired! How did I fall asleep so easily last night I wondered? It was as if an angel waved her hand over me and put me to rest knowing the next day I would have a long drive ahead of me. Maybe I should stay I thought since I felt so good. As I heard Flip getting ready for school I knew I could not stay there anymore. I peaked under my bedroom door and saw him walk past then out the door. It was my time to hurry! I gathered all my stuff and loaded up my car. I went back up to the apartment to make sure I had everything. I went into Flip's room and saw the computer he had stolen and the

147

other things that did not belong to him. I wanted revenge on what he did. I felt like taking a baseball bat and smashing everything in his room!

In my heart I knew rage and vengeance wasn't the answer. I already had committed enough sin and crimes during my time in Cali. It was madness what I had experienced but it was also a miracle I did not get arrested for my crimes. I knew it could have been so much worse. Being in the Los Angeles County Jail would have been a real nightmare and I thank God he spared me of that. I prayed that I would make it home safely. I had rolled myself five joints to make it across the country for the next 5 days. It was perfect. Ironically I had just enough without having to make another stop at the Jamaicans for more weed. I knew I would have been too nervous to do that! The Divine and synchronicity were with me on that venture. I told Crazy Ol Girl, the manager, what had happened and how sorry I was to have to leave. She was sorry but was unable to give me back the security deposit I gave her since I had to break the rent agreement. Still she was such a sweetheart giving me a hug and wishing me the best.

I left that apartment behind without Flip knowing. Ha I thought! I could not wait for him to come to the empty apartment and find I was gone! I left my bedroom window opened so when he opens the door all he will get is an eerie sense of emptiness with a breeze that would make the curtains wave around hauntingly. I took nothing we had stolen from that house and left my blow up doll deflated behind. I really should have stapled the thing to Flip's door but I didn't. I had no use for it anymore and I did not want to take any of my regrets with me back home. It felt good to leave that place and everything in it. I was getting lost there and wanted to go home.

I had stopped at the bank and closed my account. I had $1,450 left of the $12,500 I had when I first left Florida. I drove out of LA and headed east on Interstate 10. The road was wide open and what I needed. The next few days on the road were to be my own. Ironically I heard on the radio Jackson Browne singing, *"Running On Empty"*.

He sang, *"'69 I was twenty one and I called the road my own. I don't know when that road turned onto the road I'm on. Running on – Running on empty – Running on – Running blind – Running on – Running into the sun but I'm running behind."*

I turned up the radio and just cruised feeling free again. I began to think how did I end up on this road? Was I running on empty? Was I beginning to fall behind in my life? I lost a lot of money; a friend betrayed me and I could not make it in Hollywood. I was traveling across the country by myself not sure what my future held.

The song continued, *"Looking out at the road rushing under my wheels. I don't know how to tell you how crazy this life feels."*

That song truly spoke to me because my life so far had been so crazy and there I was on the road incased in my own world. The song ended and I put in Sarah McLachlan. The song I had going was called, *"Good Enough"*. The lyrics spoke to me as I felt a long way from home.

149

"Here your glass is empty. It's a hell of a long way home. Why don't you let me take you. It's no good to go alone."

I felt there was an angel beside me. Some kind of guide and protector. I wasn't alone in where I was in that place of time. I thought of what Flip did and how I trusted him and how I opened up to him.

The lyrics continued, *"I never would have opened up but you seemed so real to me."*

I knew there was something guiding me then. How could those lyrics be talking to me in sync with my thoughts and how I was feeling? Someone or something knew exactly how I was feeling and was comforting me from the unknown. The sky was perfectly clear, not a cloud in sight. The sky displayed a serene blue and the road ahead of me was inviting. Everything that encircled me was calm and slowly turning into the vast desert land. I knew I would make it home safe and everything would be all right. I knew Divinity would be with me the whole way. In that moment of serenity, I could not hold any more anger towards Flip. I was able to let go and forgive him, which gave me an astounding feeling of being totally free from all my own sins.

Torn Away

Andy and I were shackled and had a heavy belt wrapped around our waists with our hands cuffed before us. We were in the back of a van that was split down the middle with a metal wall and a screened window to see the others on the other side. There were four others taking the great ride down state. Two on one side and me and Andy on the other. I was looking out of the back window in sadness as I was taken further and further from home. There was this little punk around 19 who had caused all sorts of trouble in the county. His name was Dean but we called him Little Bastard. He had all sorts of charges and didn't cooperate with authority. They had him in the hole during his county stay until he got his sentence. He had stuffed his jump suit in the toilet and flushed it over and over. He single handedly caused a huge mess. There was water and shit everywhere! He tore up the mattress he was supposed to sleep on and cursed out the guards, threatening them. They couldn't control him and ended up kicking him out of the county jail, sending him down state, taking away all of his county time he served. So the six months he was there did not even count towards his sentence of 1 to 5 years. If the moron had just behaved better, he would have gotten county time and avoided prison. I do not see him getting out on his minimum of 1 year. The state will most likely deny him parole and give him every last bit of his of his 5 years!

He was running his mouth the whole ride down. He started talking to Andy and I and asked what we were in for. I told him my charges and he laughed!

"Holy shit!" He said. "That is funny as fuck yo! Writing your own drugs! Very smart!"

I said, "yeah, after I got caught."

He immediately started calling me Doc since I was my own medical doctor. Andy made a huge mistake by telling Little Bastard his charge of Statutory. Where we were going, anyone with a sex crime with an underage female was not good! Even if it was consensual and there were not many years between them. Like in Andy's case where he was 23 and she was 16. Even though Andy told his crime, the four of us just talked among ourselves. Asking questions about what its like in prison. Little Bastard couldn't stop talking. He said that he was nervous going down state, especially being so young, that that was his way to deal with the anxiety. I mostly gazed out the window admiring the highway and all the trees that were lush and green. That was my

152

way of dealing with all this. The van rattled and squeaked as we traveled south to Pittsburgh. I surprisingly just wanted to get there.

We finally arrived at the prison after a three-hour ride, where they would process us and stuff us in a horrible lockdown for a few days. Everyone on the van was uneasy but thanks to my Goo for sending me the info on that prison, I knew what to expect. Kind of... At least I had the image of what the prison looked like. It made it easier to know I was at the right place. Xanadoo's mental picture stayed with me, I really missed her so much! They drove us into a huge garage like space then closed the big door to secure us. We were taken out of the van and all led inside. I couldn't believe where I was. I couldn't believe I was actually in a prison! Buzzing lights were over our heads; the sounds of walkie-talkies were all we heard. We all went into a room where there were a few cells.

"Ok! Listen up!" A sergeant said forcefully. "We are going to unlock you one at a time. Then we are going to process you. Cooperate and all this will go quick."

One at a time they removed our chains then were told to take a bagged lunch, a milk and were placed in a holding cell. An uncomfortable concrete bench encircled the cell and there was a metal toilet in the corner. So basically if someone had to shit it would have to be done in front of everyone. I looked around the cell seeing a solid wall of brick squares and a vent above. I looked intently as the vent blew out air as small pieces of fuzz and dust that stuck to it fluttered. It was a cruel reminder that I really was banished from open-air, living outside those walls. There was a stink I could not identify. Like stale paint mixed with festering ass! I wasn't that hungry but I knew I had to eat. How the hell could anyone eat with a stink like that, which was so persistent, it was like a constant punch in the face!

I opened my bag and pulled out two pieces of bread, a small cup of peanut butter, jelly, and a plastic spoon. Ah geez I thought. Not the best meal but what could I do? We all ate and waited for them to call our names.

Another county must of brought more inmates because there was another group of criminals that were unleashed and placed in the holding cell with us. I remember thinking; I hope there are no more because I can't stand to be in a cell that's over crowded. They called Andy's name and he went out to see the officer in charge of processing. I remember overhearing Little Bastard talk about Andy's charge to everyone. He was really making him look worse than what actually happened. A few of the guys were getting pissed and talking shit about my friend. I didn't say anything because I didn't want any problems.

They called my name next and I went out into a small office where there was a middle-aged woman behind a desk. She didn't look too happy at all in her job. I could read in her eyes that she had grown weary of dealing with inmate after inmate. It was as if she turned off her emotions. I couldn't blame her. I wouldn't want her job. She asked me questions about my charges and how long my sentence was. She typed it into the computer then brought me out to quickly be finger printed. I tried to smile and say a few nice words showing her that not all of us prisoners were bad people. And to my surprise, I saw a smile grow on her face.

I had to go back into the holding cell and Andy didn't look happy at all.

"What's wrong?" I asked low.

He whispered, "everyone is making fun of me. They keep talking about my charge."

"Try not to let it bother you. This will be over soon."

But would it be over soon I wondered to myself? Time dragged on and another group from another county were put into the cell making it more jammed up! There was a black guy in his mid 20's, dressed nicely, sitting next to me. He must have been bailed out and went to back to court to be sentenced. Apparently, dressing nice does nothing to impress the judge. So I always wondered, why wear a suit and tie? Everyone that was brought down state was dressed in their street clothes when they got arrested. I was in my dirty work clothes I was arrested in.

He said to me, "hey man. My name is James. What's up?"

I introduced myself and said. "Not too much."

"Been here long?"

"A couple of hours now. What are you in for?" I had to ask.

One guy that came on the van with me looked at me and shook his head. "You really shouldn't be asking those questions."

I thought why not? I wasn't there to judge anyone.

James smiled and said. "Put it to you like this. I'm here because I needed to take care of my family but went about it the wrong way."

Burglary came to my mind. I have heard stories of people having to rob someone else just to survive. Or perhaps he was in for dealing drugs. I knew whatever it was, it wasn't right but sometimes struggling people get backed into a corner and do what they must do to make ends meet.

Time kept dragging and it was dinnertime. We all got a plastic tray and a drink. I opened it and to my surprise it was real chicken and rice. I remember biting into it and how good it tasted! The county had real shitty food. I heard some inmates say they'd rather do a year in state prison than 6 months in the county jail. The county was definitely not the place to do long term jail time. I was close to losing my mind being in that county zoo!

I continued to sit on the hard concrete bench, getting restless, feeling a bit trapped by the walls that surrounded me and the chatter between everyone that was going on. I was a little sick to my stomach and my back began to ache. All the noises in that place from the CO's squawking walkie-talkie radios to unruly inmates talking loud were getting to me. What the hell is taking so damn long I thought? It was dreadful being in a holding cell so long like that!

They had called out a few guys and got them ready to be quarantined. I was so ready to lie down! I looked out of the cell door and saw it was close to seven o'clock in the evening. Seven o'clock? Geez! We got here around 11 in the morning, I remember thinking! What the hell was going on? Finally Andy got called out and soon enough was placed in a white jumpsuit. They called me next and I went into a room to have my photo taken. It was an awful mug shot to identify me as state property and to have the reminder I was no longer a citizen of the free world. I was then told to strip down to my bare ass. I stood there for a moment and thought, what?

The sergeant said, "don't worry. I have been doing this for a long time. I have to see naked men all the freaking time. Its my job."

What choice did I have so I took off all my clothes and was exposed before that strange man.

The sergeant said, as I was completely naked. "Ok, move your hands through your hair." I did then he continued. "Push your ears forward." I just followed whatever he told me to do. "Now hold out your hands... Lift up your arms... Now lift your dick... lift your balls... turn around and lift your feet one at a time... now bend over, spread your cheeks and cough."

My God! What the hell was this all about I thought? I just came from county jail! Like I would be hiding something up my ass or under my balls! How humiliating! Next I was given a white jumpsuit then back to the holding cell. There was Andy looking scared. I told him to hang on and that everything will be all right. We went to see the nurse to answer a few health questions. I remember breaking down when I told the nurse about my Goo and how much I missed her. She was sweet and sympathetic about it and told me my time will go quick. Finally we were brought upstairs to a wing that looked like a hospital. It was all us newbies that had to be quarantined before we can move on to the next level of torture in that grisly place. We were given a bag with a blanket, sheets, pillow and hygiene products.

"Anyone need to make a phone call?" Asked one of the Correctional Officers.

I told the CO I needed to make one and he took me to a phone on the wall and told me I had fifteen minutes. I had to call Xanadoo and tell her about the agony I was in. I dialed her number and luckily she answered. I had to wait until the recording told her that she had a collect call from and inmate at the prison I was at. As if I needed to hear that!

"Hi Goo!" I said happily.

"Hi!" She shouted in happiness. "Oh my God! Are you ok?"

"Yeah, I'm ok." I paused in sadness. "I'm in hell now."

"I am so sorry I yelled at you last night!" She said in a heartfelt way. "I didn't know they were going to take you away from me like this so soon. I got a phone call from the county telling me to pick up some of your stuff you couldn't take with you. It was so sad for me!" She whimpered. "I just want you to know that I love you so much and I will never leave you! I love you even more now!"

Her words filled me with hope again. I loved my Goo so much and wished so badly that I could just go home but I couldn't! I was damned to that ailing reality for a while! I didn't have much time so I gave her my inmate number and the address to the prison

I was in and that I would only be there for a couple of weeks. Then it would be off to the classification prison that was even further away!

We talked until my fifteen minutes were up and told her I would call as soon as I could. I hung up the phone, deeply missing her. At least I knew I still had my Goo. I told the CO I was done and he led me to my cell. I was hoping they would put me with Andy. He needed me as bad as I needed him.

Once he opened the cell, there was Andy looking scared and frail. As soon as I walked inside the cell he rushed and hugged me! I embraced him as tight as he embraced me! We were both connected in the nightmare we were going through, giving each other the support we desperately needed.

He said happily, "I prayed they would put you with me! I do not trust anyone else but you. You are my only friend in here!"

I said in return, "I was praying the same thing. See how Divinity and Mysticism works?"

I could tell that Andy was as relieved as I was to be in the same cell. With his crime it would not be good to be put in a cell with the wrong guy! Thankfully the spirit of the Divine was with us in our time of need. There was a desk to write on and cabinets to store our stuff. The place was new and I could still smell the fresh paint on the walls. The cell was big with one bed against the back wall, which Andy took and another against the sidewall. The toilet was in the opposite corner. We had a lot of space for just the two of us. Thank God we were together and that holding cell nightmare that dragged downstairs was over. We were exhausted and crashed wondering what the next day would bring.

Two days had passed and the quarantine wing became a zoo! Inmates were being rowdy and loud, cross talking from cell to cell. By that time, Little Bastard had single handedly spread word of Andy's charge, which he made it sound so much worse and everyone was ganging up on him! It was total madness as the guys were threatening Andy, calling him all sorts of names.

Little Bastard said, "hey Chester molester? How ya doing in there?"

Bastard seemed really cool at first but I saw how people could do a 180 on a dime! I could tell the little shit was trying to gain popularity by putting someone else down. Make that person look bad to take the focus off just how ugly Bastard was inside. He seemed like more than just a product of bad upbringing. He was a natural asshole. I had told Andy not to give into their ignorance but after a couple of nights, he blew and began yelling back.

Another inmate shouted. "Hey Andy in cell 116? I'm going to beat your ass when they move us to the other block!"

Andy shouted. "I was beaten and whipped when I was a kid! You think you're going to scare me?"

Andy had showed me the whip scars on his back and I felt so bad for him! There was no reason a young boy had to go through such torment. He didn't belong in prison.

Another inmate said. "Hey? What about the other dude that's in there with Chester? Is he a toucher too?"

Little Bastard said. "No way! That's Doc! He's cool as shit yo!" He laughed. "He wrote out some scripts for himself!"

Clearly they were talking about me. The guys were laughing a little and asked me a few questions about it. Though I was relieved not to be in Andy's shoes, I wasn't sure what to do about the matter at hand. The CO came around with a resident inmate in brown clothes to pass out our blues to be moved. They give all new inmates blue jeans and long sleeve buttoned down shirts until they place us in a home prison. Then they would give us browns once all of us were classified and in a home prison. They went from cell to cell handing out all the clothes. Once he came to our cell I told the CO what was going on with Andy. The CO told us to hold on and left for a moment.

I said, "Andy. I hate to say this but you may have to stay here or go into protective custody. I don't want nothing bad happening to you."

He nodded and the CO and a Captain arrived at our cell. Andy explained to the Captain his situation and the Captain was actually really nice.

The Captain said, "OK. You can stay here until they're ready to transfer you to a home prison. We will take care of you."

I got my blue garments and put them on. I looked at Andy with a sad face and put my hand on his shoulder.

I said, "you will be just fine here. We will see each other again, I assure you."

"I hope so," he said. "You're my only friend here!"

I smiled and gave him a hug. The cell door opened and as some of the other inmates were going by, one inmate stopped and looked into the cell at Andy.

He said in a harsh tone. "You little pussy! If you were out here I'd beat your ass you fucking toucher!"

He passed and I stepped out giving Andy one last smile. I moved on where everyone was lined up. I couldn't understand why they were calling Andy a toucher or a molester. He was 23 and had consensual sex with a 16-year-old female a couple of years ago. To me a toucher is someone who puts their hands on an innocent little girl against their will. Telling them lies with their evil sickness, like the Bearded Molester and countless others. Many of the men in here are fathers that have teenage daughters and they get filled with rage when an older man has sex with them. So I can understand where they are coming from but was it really necessary to have to hurt someone over? At least I knew Andy was safe and I was going to miss him. But I felt in my spirit I would see him again.

We all had to grab a bag of new sheets, a blanket and a pair of state issued boots. We followed the CO outside and I saw a large concrete yard that was surrounded by barb wired fence. There were a lot of inmates in browns hanging out and smoking. Some were playing basketball and others were sitting down talking. They gave us a look knowing we were new inmates in our blues. I began to grow panicky and a few scary thoughts ran through my mind. What if they were looking at us to pick out someone to be their bitch? Another scare came to me when I saw the actual prison in the distance. It was long, high up and creepy! It was old, all brick and had tall arched windows with huge bars. It looked like an old haunted insane asylum!

We entered into the old dungeon and once we got to our destination we sat down on some metal picnic tables. I looked around that daunting place and saw there were five levels, or five tiers above us. There were ghostly cells in a long row from the bottom level to the top level. The ceiling was high and opened, there was a railing along each tier and I wondered how many inmates in the past had been thrown off and died. I could hear the screams of those inmates and feel the impact when they landed on the concrete floor!

So much pain and misery!

I had heard the prison was built in the late 1800's and I wondered how many ghosts were lurking around. Across from the tiers, the windows were soaring, big and aged badly, letting in daylight. I felt like I was inside an old abandoned warehouse that was condemned. Voices echoed all over the place since the demoralizing place I was in was so vast. There must have been 50 or more cells, mostly with two inmates on this block. There was a smell that was musty and tainted. I tried to play it cool like I had done prison time before but deep down inside I was nervous. I picked up on a conversation between two black dudes around the same age as Andy, who were part of the jerks who were threatening Andy for his crime back in quarantine.

One said, "hey yo, remember that one little bitch that lived up the street?"

The other replied, "you mean that 15 year old lil whore?"

"I had that bitch suckin'my dick yo! I turned that bitch around and laid my dick all over that ass!"

That was interesting because they were along with the others ragging on Andy yet they did the same damn thing! It was no surprise that there were many other guys in their twenties who slept with under aged girls. It seemed that it was all right for them but not for someone who got arrested for it.

The CO started calling out names and telling us where to cell up. I wondered who my new celli would be and at that moment they called some younger spanish guy and me. We got a level cell and didn't have to go up to the higher levels, though I wanted to so I could look out of the windows to have a small sense of freedom. All I'm going to see is the wall! We walked into this dingy cell that was the size of a walk in closet! About 10' X 10'. There were nasty bunk beds to the left, a small desk to the right and a porcelain toilet in the corner. Basically we could write, sleep and use the toilet at the same time, it was that small. I introduced myself to my new cellmate. His name was C and he was 23 years old with a 3 to 6 year sentence for assault and burglary. He was a laid back guy luckily. We had no television, no music, nothing to read but the inmate handbook, which I already knew cover to cover due to severe boredom!

Time moved so slow and I found myself losing my mind! Our routine consisted of waking up to a CO yelling into the intercom that was wired throughout the entire block, which sounded like distorted COM chatter. No one could understand what the hell he was saying but we knew that it was chow time. Most of the time I didn't bother getting up for breakfast. I was feeling to ill to eat so when C left, I turned off the cell light and lay in my own misery. The rust color light from the block shined through the bars that was above the chamber door giving that wall an eerily glow, which made it appear more like a hellish nightmare. I couldn't sleep of course and I felt like total shit! Then we'd all lined up for shower time before and luckily we had individual showers to use. Two levels of metal box showers with a metal door. Then we were locked down all morning, getting an hour of block time every other day.

Lunchtime I forced myself to go eat and when we walked outside there was barbwire fences all around us with a long tall concrete wall that encircled the prison.

Everyone lined up in the chow hall, which was very intimidating to me. I felt as if everyone was watching me. There was this one big brawny looking guy with a bald head, a mustache and goatee who walked beside me.

He looked intensely at me and asked in a harsh tone. "Hey buddy! What are you in here for?"

I looked at him and said, "forging prescriptions."

He said calmly, "oh… alright man."

I figured to ask, "got a cigarette?"

"Sorry buddy, I don't," he said as he trailed off in search and destroy mode.

My guess was he was looking for someone with a sex crime to give a hard time. Thank God I was not in the place of a sex offender! I am not the fighting type and would have a hard time dealing with the nonsense those bullies gave.

After we ate lunch we were given an hour of yard time that was through a fence with that wall around us. There was absolutely nothing to look at because of that stupid 12-foot wall! I had begun to socialize some and found that many other inmates felt the same way I did. The wonderful aroma of tobacco filled the air and I started to crave a cigarette. Luckily someone had passed me a rolled up cigarette and as I inhaled the first drag in over three months, I had a wonderful feeling. I missed the flavor of tobacco!

When yard time was over we had to go back into the pits! I had heard there was an older man who was labeled a molester and Little Bastard along with that big brawny bastard and a couple of others were threatening him. The guy appeared lost, afraid as he was making his way back into the pits with the crowd. He was dorky looking and wore glasses. As we all were going inside the dungeon, Little Bastard, who was before me punched the guy dead in his face, knocking his glasses off!

"Fucking toucher!" Little Bastard said loud.

What was his problem I wondered? The kid was only 19 and had a horrible attitude! The guy picked up his glasses and carried on pretending that nothing happened.

Once I got back into my cell the afternoons felt like an eternity. I tried sleeping but I had a hard time, feeling fidgety and ailing in physical and emotional pain. I had no watch to know what time it was and it was a long time before we went to eat dinner. I got up and went to the cell door and stared out at the empty block. I heard in the distance of the outside world a freight train blowing its horn. The sound of the train rumbled slightly as it was passing by. I heard the sounds of geese. They were the lucky ones to be able to roam around freely.

There were rays of sunshine, which peered through those towering windows. I watched as the patch of sunlight slowly over a course of time moved across the cracks of the hard dark gray floor. I knew once the sun spot got past a certain hole or crack in the floor it was close to dinnertime. Little by little... millimeter... by... millimeter, the sun patch was painstakingly moving in such slow motion it felt like it wasn't moving at all. I was highly focused on the sunlight to make its way to my freedom from that chamber of torture. It was torture waiting just to be let out for a small about of time... Finally the doors would all snap unlocked with loud clanks all through the block then we all walk to the chow hall to eat then be locked down for the rest of the night.

There I stood slowly losing it trying to understand why I was there. Cause and effect was the true origin of my despair. The suffering I was facing was my life gone wrong! If I had made a different choice I would not be in that cell away from home and my Goo. At the same time I was dealing with an addiction that drove me to break the law of man and to fall in sin against the great Divine. I was aware of what I was doing but there was a force beyond my own power that enslaved me. I knew it was time to evolve from my current mindset and spirituality and grow from that nightmare that I was trapped inside of. I saw there were many writings on the walls. I looked on the chipped paint of the wall to my left and saw something sickening.

Someone wrote, *"This is where men are made and boys are raped."*

Another writing said, *"White Boyz Rumble!"*

Someone had drawn a couple of swastikas on the cell door. Oh this was ridiculous I thought so I grabbed a pen and began to write my own words.

I wrote *"God"* in a few places.

Then I thought of Xanadoo and smiled.

I wrote *"Love"* in a few more spots to try and bring hope to the obscurity I was in. I couldn't allow the negative characteristics of prison bring me down. I started to feel a bit inspired so I sat down at the small metal desk and wrote Xanadoo a letter.

Dearest Goo,

It is now June 3rd, 105 days that I have been incarcerated. It has been 3 ½ months so far. Can you believe that? I was thinking about how to look at my time away so it won't seem so bad. First look at how fast my time went in the county. At first it seemed like forever but it's in the past now. Also, think of how fast our lives have gone by. Our childhood growing up is long gone. Our teens and twenties are but a distant memory. I think of all the times in my life that were rough are over now. When I was in jail in Florida and Maryland, it zipped on by. The years I had to take care of my mother, when my darkness settled in are long since past. My time when I was homeless is over. Even looking back when we first met over four years ago!

I met this guy who I call Uncle Bob. He told me my time is nothing, small time, a short bid. He said I could make it hard time or easy time, meaning if I stress or over worry it will make it harder than it has to be. He said I will be home before I know it. I want the change. I do not want to be on pills ever again. Uncle Bob, however, says he wants to get out if he makes parole, skip out on parole and move to another state so he can get drunk and high. He is in his early fifties and has no will to better himself. I do not want to end up like that! I have seen my future if I went back to drugs. I would end up in a city alley dead from an overdose in the dead of winter. That is a scary vision I never want to live!

I have broken down my sentence along with the good time I am eligible for. That early release incentive program the judge gave me. I asked around and I would have to do only 75 % of my minimum of 18 months as long as I do my programs and do not get any write ups. This is what I am predicting: First we will have to cross the Summer Bridge. I see myself being sent to the classification prison in a week. I see myself being there until August then I will be placed in a home prison. Some say I could be at the classification prison for three months or longer but I sense my time there will be short. Then it will be September and we will be crossing into the Autumn Bridge. I see myself involved in a program or a routine by October. Then we will move into November and December, which will be the Holiday Bridge. It will be a new year and we will enter the Winter Bridge that will take us into the springtime, a New Beginning. It will be April and I will be home! I want to be home with you so bad right now! Always remember our love is strong and Uncle Bob said a prison experience could either make or break a relationship. I feel it will make us even better! Remember we may be feeling sorrow now but soon our sorrow will turn into joy. Say it with me my Goo... We may feel sorrow now but soon our sorrow will turn into joy! I will forever love you!

The Return Home

It was March of 1996 and the five days I spent on the road was so amazing! I took the southern route on Interstate 10 the whole way. I was on the spiritual journey of my life. It was just God, myself and I. As I drove through the desert, the days were clear and carried me to the inner peace I sincerely needed. Once I passed through Arizona and New Mexico, I entered Texas and stopped to rest in Fort Stockton, on the western side of Texas. Traveling on the road came so naturally to me. I felt at ease having no map to guide me. I relied on my sense of direction and the spiritual sense that guided me. I drove with the heightened senses being on cannabis, from sunrise to sunset and had the spirit of my music with me the whole way. So many songs spoke to me as I felt like I was floating in my own bubble with the clear blue skies around me. I found myself driving just under the speed limit and more focused of everything around me.

I continued on and found that Texas was the longest state to ride through. Even after a full days worth of traveling I ended up in Houston on the east side of the state. It was so beautiful seeing when the day was close to ending. I would look in my rearview mirror and see the sun setting. I admired when I'd see it sink under bridges as I passed by giving me a painting of comfort.

I felt completely safe in my own world with my windows rolled up and the fresh aroma of marijuana would linger giving a spiritual high I couldn't explain. I was able to see the trees sway as the wind moved across the land, especially when the breeze was in sync to the songs I was deeply in touch with. The sunshine gleaming on the highway before me was serene feeling like I was close to heaven. Music spoke softly to me like an angel whispering in my ear telling me all is well, constantly in sync with my thoughts. I tried hard to focus on how that works and where it comes from. It was no coincidence because it happens all the time. I couldn't escape it!

I drove through New Orleans, Mississippi, Mobile Alabama and finally into the sunshine state of Florida. Driving across the country was like going through so many different worlds. From the frantic lunacy of Los Angeles, through the vast wastelands of the desert. All those little towns I would stop to get gas and eat were dry and dusty. I felt like "The Lone Traveler" passing through seeing the local folk as I enjoyed a good meal sitting at the counter at a desert dinner. I felt free and light inside and just took everything in. I got back on the interstate and headed east, sky beautifully blue and the sun lit up my surroundings. I journeyed into the cities of the south and how the desert scenery changed into a sub-tropical marshy land, with more trees, grass and a musky moist smell.

Once I got into south Florida everything still looked the same but the way I felt was different. I had experienced something not many get the opportunity to do. I took the chance to venture out and change my life but it did not work out. I wondered what would have happened if I had stayed there and ran out of money? Would I have ended up on the streets of LA lost in a world of drugs and darkness? Thank God I found out what Flip was doing before it was too late!

I was back home at last! My mother was so happy to see me back but my father was upset that I had lost most of my money. He had told me I would have to find a job right away and start paying some rent.

Before I got serious on a job I had to see my old friends again. The first person I saw was my ex-girlfriend Alyssa. She had been through quite a few hard times with men and had two children from two different guys. I knew she still wanted me back but having children turned me away and I found it best to be friends… with benefits. Alyssa and I still engaged in unprotected sex and I still felt in my spirit that everything would be all right somehow. It was a very strange gift I had but couldn't quite understand. Like an intuition that somehow guided me. I was

173

always able to sense I would be ok when I started to worry about having an STD or AIDS. I would get really OCD and over think making myself believe I have a disease! I couldn't get it to shut up but then I get a calming sensation that I was just fine and I always was. It felt like a sigh of relief in my chest with a happy feeling and an inner glow. That's how I knew something was reaching out to me, getting inside of me like the Guiding Spirit. Almost like heaven pouring pleasing emotions and love into my soul to let me know I was ok. Even with our sexual relationship, she looked up to me and felt safe in confiding in me all of her problems.

I saw Amanda next and she looked so gorgeous! She had grown into a spirited youthful woman. She was happy that I was back and we started to fall in love all over again. There we were at her friend's salon and her friend asked if we were getting back together. Amanda smiled and blushed and I knew we were back together. I had gained about 30 lbs of good weight and I looked so much better within the few months I was out west. Interesting how I put on the weight from when I got there all the way til I got back. I got bigger in that few month timeline between the times I left home to the time I got back. I remember going to the gym, lifting weights and putting myself on the scale. I kept seeing it slowly go up from 140, 146, 159 to 170 lbs. I had worked out a lot out there and went from being a skinny kid to a bulkier young man within those few months out west.

Maybe it was all the Fat Burgers I ate! Fat Burger was a California favorite of mine along with In and Out Burger. Never had that before. I knew it was one of the many good things that

174

came from that journey out west. I was happy and free and felt so good with myself. That's what Amanda noticed right away with me. That I matured and was even more handsome than before looking more like a man. When I first laid eyes on her I saw the look in her eyes when she laid eyes on me walking through that door. She gleamed and ran up to hug me like she missed me. When we talked I noticed how she was becoming a young woman and how she looked more beautiful than ever. I couldn't believe being away only for a few months could change people like that. I continued to hit the gym and work out and eat healthy.

I saw my old friends from high school and went right back to cruising around, smoking marijuana for my spiritual experiences and living life. I had applied for a few jobs and I finally landed one at a gas station. It was a graveyard shift that I would have to work from 10 PM until 6 AM. As I got into a new routine back home, I started to become very attached to the nights again. Unlike those California nights smoking weed and watching old reruns and cartoons, I went out into the hours of darkness a lot. I loved the sense of knowing I was completely alone for those hours I worked. I would go outside to eat on a break and listen to the crickets and the melody the night would bring. Dark all around me as the big bright lights of the gas station canopy beamed down, buzzing with bugs flying all around them. Night insects looking for the light… that always fascinated me. They looked like little souls trying to get into heaven.

There wasn't much to do during my shift so I became aware of a local chat line. I never took into consideration the .99

cents a minute rate. So I went into the back room for a few hours during the dead of night and would be on the phone and would create all sorts of crazy voices and characters. They gave an option to create a short profile of yourself and I made up several names and accents. I started to become comfortable with what I was doing and I started smoking weed to see what it would be like during my phone sessions and drinking beer. I learned a trick in which when someone accidentally pushes a six pack of beer off the back of the shelf, the gas station would write it off. So I would take a six-pack, smash a couple of bottles and drink the rest. I wrote it up in my report as, *"Customer damaged alcoholic beverages."*

There I was, drunk and stoned in the back room on company time, racking up a tremendous phone bill with my shenanigans. Amanda would sometimes come and see me and when I told her what I was doing she couldn't believe it. I was beginning to make all sorts of mistakes since I had returned home. Alyssa often came by my house and I couldn't resist the sex we had. Once again I had cheated on Amanda! As if I didn't learn the first time around! My desire for sex had begun to overtake me and there was no way I could escape it! I started calling a few of those 900 sex lines at work and instead of having mindless phone sex, I would question them why they do what they do.

I should have been asking myself why I was doing what I was doing. Being on cannabis, reaching my higher self, I didn't like what I was becoming. I always became very righteous when I used cannabis like that. It touched my godly side and it was scaring me. I had become reckless in how I was living and never worried about the consequences. I was in too deep with those phone calls and met a few females on the chat line. I found myself getting into phone sex with those women and on company time. There I was getting paid by the hour and I was masturbating as some strange female spoke dirty words to me. Luckily there was a garbage can next to me and I had good aim. I was getting out of hand and continued to steal beer and smoked too much of the wild flower as I ran up the company's telephone tab. I just couldn't stop!

I didn't realize just how fast time can move and before I knew it, six months had past. It was September and I was paying my parents $100 a month for rent and things was getting rocky with Amanda and I. We were starting to become detached again. Despite what we were feeling we kept trying to make it work because we still loved each other.

I should have seen what came next. I received a phone call from my boss and he began to question the phone bill and my work ethics.

He said, "uh, yeah... I got quite a few monthly statements for the phone that adds up to over $30,000! Were you making calls during your shift to a local chat line and some sex hotlines?"

"Well sir, I uh..." I stuttered.

"We know it was you man!" He jumped in. "Don't deny it!"

"Why didn't you say anything the first month when you first noticed it?"

"Because we weren't sure who it was."

"For six months?"

"Uh, yeah. For six months you were racking up, on average, a $5,000 phone bill! We had to be sure it was you. You're sick, you know? You need help! You're fired man! They are going to prosecute you man!"

Those words scared the hell out of me! How could I do what I was doing and think nothing would have come from it? How could it happen? For six consecutive months this went on! How the hell would I explain this to my parents? I remember telling my mother and she was highly disappointed. My father, however, said it would be my responsibility to deal with whatever happens. He would not bail me out of that one! My mother didn't need to know what I had allowed to happen. She had multiple sclerosis and it was beginning to get worse. She began using a cane to walk and on some occasions she had to use a walker. She became very fatigued for the most part and was unable to drive. She had waited all her years, dealing with my fathers drinking and holding the family together to get the car of her dreams.

She finally gets the Cadillac she dreamed about and she wasn't able to drive it. It was something that really made my mom upset and depressed. Good one God! Felt like a curse to me for sacrificing herself. My father had long since been sober because back before we moved to Florida the doctors told him he would have to stop drinking otherwise he would die. He was the same emotionally unavailable man but sober. He had all sorts of health problems including severe liver damage and bloating of his stomach. The doctors told him approximately 80% of his liver was destroyed and that he may need a liver transplant. I knew in my heart he wasn't a bad man. He took my mother on a few vacations and took care of her needs with the MS she was dealing with.

He cooked for my mother and me and when we were having spaghetti he would make thin spaghetti. I told him I really wanted angel hair pasta but he always gave me a hard time.

He would say, "ah, I'm not making both! Just eat what I make will ya."

The funny thing was even after he complained and swore he wouldn't make it, he still did without any more words. I would see him in the kitchen with two pots of bowling water cooking the pastas. There was one for my angel hair and the other with regular pasta. Despite not being a good father figure, I still saw the good in him.

Something was not right with Amanda and me still. For some reason we became sexually detached again and we got annoyed with each other over nonsense. It was time yet again for another breakup. Why didn't it work I kept thinking? We had the perfect love when we first met and now that we are mature we still can't be with each other. We found it best not to be in a relationship so we became friends again. I knew my true soul mate was out there. I began to imagine a beautiful woman with brown hair and blue eyes again. I sensed her being artistic and eccentric in her ways. I felt in my heart her loving ways. I also sensed a dirty side to her. She would be a sexual woman and that notion intrigued me because it almost felt like I knew what making love to her would be like. I like a good girl with a bad and dirty side and I felt that in her. I knew the one was out there, I just wasn't sure where. Just in that moment I heard on the radio a song by The Eagles called *"One of These Nights."*

It sang to my soul, *"I've been searching for the daughter of the devil himself... I've been searching for an angel in white. I've been waiting for a woman whose a little of both and I can feel her but she's nowhere in sight."*

That song always plays when I was thinking about my soul mate. I felt the spirit of love talking to me, that she really is out there somewhere. I just wanted to find her! I really could feel her but she is nowhere in sight of the near future of my life. I kept working on my novel and wanted to get back into the swing of things. I was paranoid every day I went to check the mail in anticipation of a letter that would summon me to court for the $30,000 phone bill from my previous job. Day after day I checked the mail hoping and praying nothing would come for me like that. To my surprise I received my last paycheck from my old job at the station. My old boss told me I would never get my last paycheck that they would keep it due to the outrageous tab I ran up. He said in all his days never has he seen anything so fucked up as what I did for those six months. Congratulations! I broke a company record of worst employee ever.

I had to give thanks to the Lord because Divinity had spared me any legal action that should have been put on me. I gave thanks every day that nothing bad happened to me. It was a close call but I turned out all right. How I kept wondering? I couldn't figure out why they never came after me. It truly was a miracle nothing came about that terrible mishap of mine! I knew deep down in my spirit that it was going to be ok. I had that feeling in my chest of relief when I use to over think about it. How I could always sense those things I still didn't know. That remained a mystery but it was amazing.

I got myself a talent agent so I could do more movies there in Florida. I got a gig for an extra in the movie *"Wild Things"* and got to meet Kevin Bacon. He was a down to earth guy and was really cool. It was a four-day excursion and many hours were put into the scene. The pressure to get the film done had us work an 18-hour day! Delays happened and we had to stay longer. The Production Assistant had to go out and get McDonalds for everyone as we continued into the night. I started thinking about all those hours actors put in to making movies. I got impatient easily and loved getting in my car at the end of the day and going home. Carrying that around weighed on my confidents along with my acting career. How would I ever make it if I hated being on the set for a long time? Still, I kept going with it. I was mostly seeing the glamorous part of being an actor and not all the work that goes into the entertainment business.

My agent got me an audition for a stand in for Kevin Bacon.

My agent told me. "Congrats, this is it, you're on your way!"

However, I didn't really get that excited. When I was interviewed I had a good feeling I would get the job.

The woman interviewing me asked, "are you willing to cut and dye your hair?

I hesitated and looked away then said, "um... I don't like dying my hair."

She gave me a strange look and I could tell they didn't want to hear that. I corrected myself and said I would but it was too late. They wanted someone who was more secure in themselves and willing to alter their selves for the part. I knew I had screwed that opportunity up. Just another stupid regret I won't forget!

I auditioned for a local play called *"Bye Bye Birdie"*. I got a small part as a bartender and the rehearsals were fun. I learned what it was like to work with the cast and crew of a play. We became like a close-knit family.

After months of rehearsal it was about an hour before show time and the guy who played Hugo, a vital part of the play, skipped out on everyone. He had some sort of issues and just left without warning. Me being the next of that age group, I had to take on the part. I did a quick rehearsal and when the lights went on and the audience was ready for us, we proceeded. No matter what I learned the show must go on! I did the part with a few mistakes but nothing anyone would notice. The biggest mistake I noticed was when the lead girl sang to me and after I had to run off in happiness.

I bounced on the stage and said, "oh the only one my girl loves... the one and only person my girl really loves... that girl is me!"

I remember bouncing off stage left and thought, "That girl is me?" I hope no one heard that. It didn't really matter in the end because everyone was so grateful that I stepped in because without me stepping in the show would have been canceled. I felt great that I saved the play and that the show did go on.

I landed a driver job delivering radioactive medicine to local hospitals. It wasn't a bad job but my concern for the radioactive medicine made me wonder if I would become a mutant. The thought of rolling around in the radioactive stuff so I could obtain superpowers. That would have been so cool. My boss at the time told me I had no worries, that I was safe driving with it and had a bit of an attraction for me. We actually went to the gym together and became friends. He had finally told me he was gay but I didn't have a problem with that. Just as long as he knew where I stood in my sexuality. I loved women too much and was in search of one at the time. Being single weighed on me a lot!

My older brother Chris, who I nicknamed Screwface, had moved down from Long Island to live with us. Apparently he had broken up with his fiancé and was struggling in his finances. He moved into the spare bedroom and had to readjust to a new location just like I did. It was good having my brother living with us. It was much better having our own rooms. Not much about him changed though. Still the same ol semi unemotional older brother of mine. He still drank beer quite often and seemed to be stuck in it like my father but not to the severity he brought it to. I was in my bedroom watching television and my father came into my room.

He said, "you have to come out in the kitchen with us now."

I said, "not now. I will eat later."

Since my father didn't know how to really communicate, he got frantic and spilled out the words... "You have to! It's important!"

For my father to respond like that meant it was serious. I went out and there was my mother, Screwface and my father. I sat down and waited to hear what was going on. The time had finally come after all those years. My father told us that he had to go in for a liver transplant and wasn't sure what the outcome would be. It was serious now.

My father had gone into the hospital to have the surgery and my mother's multiple sclerosis became worse. There was a lot of stress on all of us as the doctors told us my father had complications after the transplant. First he had an aneurysm on his spleen and they had to take him in for emergency surgery. As if that wasn't bad enough he developed another aneurysm on his brain, which was another shock! The medical team had to open his skull and remove it. There was so much going on with my father they had to take him to Miami to continue his treatment.

My mother was suffering more and more with her MS and we had to get her a wheelchair. All the stress, I believe, had made her worse.

My oldest brother Rich had to come down due to my father's condition. There we all were, my mother, Rich, Screwface and me watching as my father was a wreck. He was on his hospital bed with his left leg constantly jumping. His head was partially shaved from the surgery on his skull. He could only mumble and I could see in his eyes that he was sorry for the way he lived his life as a drunk and absentee father. He struggled to point up and it seemed he was trying to say, "I want to got home." He was trying to tell us he was sorry and wanted to go home to heaven.

He stretched out his shaking hand and slowly waved for me to go over to him. He was desperately trying to tell me something but I could not understand what he was saying. The liver transplant and complications severely messed my father up. I looked into my fathers blue eyes and saw he was trying to ask for forgiveness. The nurse gave him a pen and paper and he tried to write out what he wanted to tell me but his hands were so shaky he couldn't even write. Alcohol had bestowed a terrible outcome for him and I felt in my spirit that, even though he wasn't a good father, I could forgive him. I never could hate my father and it felt good.

My father wanted to tell my brothers something but he still could not get the words due to his ailments. He was in much pain and the nurse had to come in to give him more morphine. My mother and my two brothers left the room when visitation was over and there I was alone for a brief moment with my father. I looked into his scared blue eyes one last time and felt great sorrow. I could tell he knew he was on his deathbed and that he truly was regretful for the way he lived his life. A tear developed in my eye and that cry ball feeling in my throat arose. I could not hate my father for how he was.

I said to him as he looked attentively into my eyes. "I forgive you dad and I love you."

That was the very first time I ever told my father I loved him. It was a moment of letting go of any resentment I had for the man. I felt lifted and free. My brothers held nothing against my father and were able to forgive as well. I knew my father could now go in peace knowing that none of his children hated him. My mother, however, still held on to the resentment.

It was the end of February 1997 and my father had passed away. It was time my family and I returned back to our old home in New York. My mother took a plane up with Rich and Screwface and I drove, separately. I felt the drive alone would do me good and it was my father who taught me how to drive on the interstate. When we moved to Florida, I had rode down with him and I was just learning to drive at the time. We didn't say too much on the way down but I felt the connection of him and the road. I had learned that I got my sense of direction from my father. As I was cruising up Interstate 95, I remembered my father taking me to different restaurants and telling me a few of his stories when he was a kid. At that moment I heard on the radio Eric Clapton singing, *"My Father's Eyes"*.

"Where do I find the words to say? How do I teach him? What do we play? Bit by bit, I've realized that's when I need them, that's when I need my fathers eyes."

It was very ironic that song was playing at that time and the parallel connection, despite our emotional distant, that I felt between my father and I.

The viewing of my father after he died was a little unsettling. He was bloated, pale, and you could see the surgery scar from when they opened his skull. As I looked down at my father, I thought of the demon of alcohol and what it did to him. He looked like a dead Frankenstein. It was not easy to see the man my father once was turn into the corpse he became after his battle with liquor. It truly was a sickening display of what drinking can do to a person. Now that he was gone it would be up to Screwface and me to take care of my mother. Thank God she still received my father's pension and disability. My mother was set for life thanks to my father's good job. One of the main reasons why she stayed with him.

It was the first time my family and I were all together in the Bronx, where we as a family, all originated from. My parents had a plot where my brother Scott was buried. It was a cold day in the Bronx and we all stood around as they lowered my father into the ground next to baby Scott.

Now, I knew my father's half of the family was a little off but when we saw his parents, my grandparents, showing up looking ragged, no one could believe it. My grandfather had on dirty sweat pants and a heavy sweatshirt with work boots. My grandmother wore an old housedress with a winter coat over it. They didn't even seem upset by their own son's death! They say it is tragic for parents to lose their child before they do but not in this case.

My grandmother said to my mother in her shrilly voice, "Oh, you lost a good friend."

My mother was speechless and I was baffled for a moment. Oh you lost a good friend? I remember thinking; this is your son and my mother's husband, not friend. The only one who was decent was my father's twisted, burnt out younger brother, my Uncle Corey. He had on a suit and tie but was asking around if anyone had any weed. Was this a funeral I thought or a freak show? No wonder my father fell heavy into booze and was emotionally unavailable! He had no guidance and apparently not much love shown to him.

After the funeral I drove back to my hometown on Long Island. I toured the place I grew up and noticed things were different. I repeatedly wondered what my life would have been like if I never moved. I felt it would have been a rather bleak reality and I would have existed just floating around in a fog. Though I missed home, I was glad I moved, otherwise I would have not experienced what I had so far. I stopped at my old house and saw they had made some changes. I badly wanted to go up to the door and knock telling them who I was so I could see my old house. I was too scared to since a friend told me not to because the owner wasn't a nice person.

The last time I was on the Island was when I was 18 years old, about 5 years ago. I remember I was staying with my brother Rich and I was tooling around on his bike traveling down memory lane. On the way back to his apartment, I rode the bike through a shortcut and ran into some troublemakers. I was behind a shopping plaza and it was at night and apparently, I was trespassing on some gang's turf. Three dudes stood before me as I had stopped my bike. My heart began to race and I was scared because I was out numbered and trapped. I felt I was about to get my ass beat bad and my bike taken away.

"What's up punk?" One said in a mean tone.

I said nervously, "I used to live here. I was just reminiscing. You know, riding around remembering old times."

It was in that moment after I spoke, I heard a familiar voice say my name. To my surprise it was my old friend Brice I knew back in school, the one who I used to cause all sorts of havoc with. I was so relieved to see him and I thanked God it was his gang I had intruded on, otherwise, who knows what would have happened. That was a miracle in itself! He told the guys that I was cool and I fell into a conversation with good ol Brice. He was older, lost in a world of the streets and drugs.

After a long chat and catching up I was about to head back to my brothers apartment. Brice had given me his number and told me to call him so we could hang out before I went back home. I never did call him and I had regretted doing so because I had

189

found out later on that he had died. He had a fatal motorcycle accident and lost his life at the young age of 18. It was probably not too long after the last time I saw him that he endured his untimely death. Even though he was gone his memory would live on in my mind. That was the first time I had known an old friend to pass away. It was weird that at one point we were kids causing trouble and that those days were over and he was laid to rest in the ground. There was no more life, no more consciousness left in his body just like my father. Time had taken them from my reality and I knew I could never go back to relive old memories with either of them.

As I kept driving arriving around I passed by my first love's old house and yet another regret still lingered with me. For years I had been beating myself up over how I hurt her. I had ruined my first love experience and there was no going back with the mind fuck I put her through. I had to make it right and tried to call her in the past but she didn't want anything to do with me. She had been holding a grudge for such a long time. I could no longer hold in my regret, I knew I had to try one more time. I was staying at my childhood friend's house and I called her. Her sister answered and told me to go to hell, but once I truly poured out my heart in sorrow, she told me she would have my first love call me. Sure enough, my first love did call me back and was standoffish at first.

She said, "Are you ready to come to terms with what you've done?"

I told her that's all I ever wanted. I needed for her to see the man I became not the nut job I used to be but she was not comfortable seeing me face to face.

She explained. "You realize you gave me nightmares for a long time. I had panic attacks because of you! I think its best we just talk on the phone."

I said in sorrow, "I can't begin to tell you how sorry I am."

"You use to pretend I was your sister!"

"I actually said that out loud?"

"Yes. And a lot of other sick shit! Not to mention all the prank phone calls, the stalking, the threats... I couldn't sleep because of you! Never in all my life have I ever been through anything like that!"

I explained to her that my father had passed away and I was in town and I had to make amends. Once I told her why I believe I did what I did and how sorry I really was she became more talkative in a good way. She had reminded me of all the bad things I did and how it felt. In those moments I started feeling what I put her through. The fear, the emotional pain, the torture and the heartbreak. It made me cringe how stupid I was!

I explained. "You were my first kiss, my first love, my first time making love... my first of everything! It doesn't justify but I was overwhelmed. I was always different and saw things different being artistic and eccentric. I didn't have a father figure in my life. A dad to talk to about stuff and bond with. My mind wanted me to believe I was in a movie and I was the bad guy. I allowed my inner demons to hurt the one I loved. For some reason the love

I felt for you overloaded me. An obsession grew and I was moving... I... I'm just so sorry. It wasn't the real me."

She told me she was sorry to hear about my father passing away and we had moved on to other things to talk about. We talked for an hour and a half and I felt so good inside that I was able to tell her the man I became in Florida. Everything I had accomplished and where I wanted to go in my future. The people I have helped and inspired and those I want to inspire. Things began to feel different with us in those moments.

She explained to me that after the pain I caused her she had more crap in her life. It wasn't easy for her after I left but she had finally met the right man and was happy in her life. That's all I ever wanted for her. Though she didn't say she forgave me, I was just happy to connect with her, show her I grew up and I regretted ever doing what I did to her. I got to say what I've been wanting to say for years to her. What took me over back then scared me because I still can't understand what really made me destroy my first love experience. When it was the end of our conversation, we finally got to say goodbye on good terms. I had gained closure on a terrible mistake I made with that once in a lifetime first love phenomenon. I had returned home not only for my father's funeral or to see my old hometown again but to make that wrong right with my first.

I had made one last stop by my old home and remembered all those times my father was around. I saw all the trees we had in the yard that were all bare against the gray overcast sky. It was cold out and for a moment I could feel my father's spirit as I gazed into the past. We never really talked and I wish I had known him better. There were so many things I wanted to tell him but I couldn't. At that moment as I sat in my car the radio spoke to me.

"I wasn't there that morning... When my father passed away... I didn't get to tell him all the things I had to say..."

It was an old 80's song from Mike and the Mechanics called *"The Living Years"* and it brought back so many old memories.

I turned up the radio a little and listened. *"I just wish I could have told him... In the living years... say it loud... say it clear... you can listen... as well as you hear. Its too late... when we die..."*

Those words held true remembering that I wasn't there the morning my father died. I wished I was there holding his hand as he passed on. To let his soul know he had been forgiven but I wasn't there to do that. None of us were there and he died alone. The song reminded me to appreciate those I love. To say the things I wish to say while they are alive because it really is too late when we die. My mother was getting worse with her MS and I knew it was going to be my time to take care of her. She was the best mother anyone could ask for. She never once let my brothers or me down. We always had the things we needed, there were always Christmas presents under the tree and we, especially me, always had her to talk to about anything. I remember thinking it was time to return home to Florida and continue on in these living years.

\

Further Away From Home

We were called out of our miserable cells around 4 in the morning. It had been two long weeks and we were finally being sent to the classification prison. It was well into May, beautiful spring that I was missing! As everyone lined up, there were a few guys I knew from the yard. This one guy named Rick had a rolled up cigarette and lit it up while we waited for the CO. He passed it to me and Ahhh! I couldn't wait to get into a routine, to order commissary and a radio. Most of all, I wanted to see my Goo! It had been nearly four months since I last touched her. I knew it would be a glorious day when she visits me and runs into my arms! I just couldn't wait to see her again.

We were all called and followed the CO back to that terrible holding cell they had us in when we first got there. I sat down on the edge of the hard seat and felt like I was being stuffed into a corner. There were quite a few guys in the cell and it was cramped. As I looked out of the cell door, I saw them bringing in a few other inmates to be transferred. There was Little Bastard in an orange jumpsuit. Turned out they had learned that he punched that guy a little while back. They had taken him and that big brawny looking bastard to the hole for misconduct. So Little Bastard came from the hole in the county and ended up in the hole there in state. He's going from the hole presently to directly into the hole at the classification prison. Way to go there Little Bastard!

They put him in a separate cell, and then I saw Andy! He was still in the white jump suit they had us wear in quarantine. He saw me and smiled and I asked if he was ok. He nodded and they put him into another cell. Looks like we will be taking the great ride on the prison bus together. I hoped they would put him into the same cell when we get there. We waited and waited...

Time was dragging on and I was getting restless sitting in that overcrowded cell. The guys along the benches were sleeping with their heads leaning back against the wall. There was one guy crunched up on the floor with his blue shirt over his head. Another guy was pacing back and forth and was getting fed up with all the waiting.

He went to the cell door and said loud, "Hey yo? Yo CO?"

The CO came to the door. "What's up?"

"What's going on? When are we getting on the stupid bus already?"

The CO said, "Could be another hour or so."

"Why the hell do they get us up at 4 in the morning just so we can wait for hours?"

The CO nodded and said, "Why indeed."

The CO stepped away with a smirk and the guy was standing there, still wondering why we were there so early if they did not take us for three or four hours. Apparently that smart-ass reply didn't quite answer our question. I peaked out and saw that it was almost 7 o'clock in the morning. I tried to put my head back and close my eyes but it was no use. I couldn't sleep. I wanted the hell out of that place already! Intrusive thoughts began to enter my mind. What if my Goo gets into a fatal accident on the way to see me? Scary visualizations plagued my mind as I envisioned her all mangled up in a car wreck. She would be screaming out as her body would be split in two and her intestines hanging out as blood was splattered every where.

I clinched my fists and opened my eyes.

It was atrocious to keep entertaining such twisted thoughts but they kept coming into my head! Leave me alone I thought but I couldn't do it. Would I be raped when I get to my home prison? Would someone come at me with a blade and slice me up, disfiguring me for life? I would be trapped in a cell and a couple of big inmates would be kicking me with their boots breaking my nose many times over! Kicking in my eye sockets embedding my eyeballs into my brain literally! They would continue by breaking my jaw then grab it and tug and tug until they rip the damn thing completely off, leaving me a blood soaked gory mess on the floor twitching. My dark half kept whispering to me that I would suffer and die in prison.

"Listen up!" A CO yelled. "We are going to get you out and ready to be transferred."

Oh thank God I thought! I couldn't take that sickly stream of thoughts any more! I must remember those are not my thoughts and I can control them but it wasn't easy, especially being in prison so far away from home. I suppose it was easy to have crazy thoughts being contained. We were all placed in another white jumpsuit then they placed shackles around our ankles. They strapped on that heavy tan belt, locked and cuffed our hands in front of us. They made sure we weren't going anywhere; they even put a small lock on the chains that were around us! They placed a small black box between our wrists making it hard to move our hands freely. It was truly uncomfortable and humiliating to be confined so tightly.

One by one we were brought outside to the bus. It was a beautiful, mild, late spring morning with the rising sun casting long shadows and the smell of the mist welcoming a new day. I hear birds chirping and the sound of distant cars on the roads. The sky was clear blue and a slight cool breeze blew reminding me of what I lost. The world continued to move on without me, as I was in chains being taken further away from home. I got on the bus, which reminded me of the Greyhound bus I used to take when I first began visiting Xanadoo. As I sat down on the hard wood seat, I was reminded that it was no Greyhound bus. It was a prison bus and they sure as hell didn't make it comfortable. Really now, they couldn't put some cushions on the rows of seats? I luckily got a window seat so I could look out at the road and the scenery.

I saw Andy coming towards me and there was an empty spot behind my seat. He sat down and I turned around to greet him. He looked forward and motioned his head for me to look. I turned and I saw them bring on board Little Bastard in his orange jumpsuit. They had to put him and a few others that came out of the hole in a cage that was in the front of the bus.

I turned to Andy and said, "he's not going to make it."

"He's a dumb ass, plain and simple!" Andy said and laughed.

"So what did they do with you after I was sent over to the other block?"

"I stayed in that cell for the whole two weeks! It was really boring and I couldn't wait to get the hell out of there!"

I nodded and the CO's were ready to depart. There was one CO that went around the bus to make sure everything was secure looking under the bus with a large mirror. They had locked the gate that was in the front of the bus and started it up. The engine rumbled a little and shook the bus. Another CO walked to the rear of the bus with a shotgun and got into a small space in the back of the bus. I heard the click of him pumping the shotgun to make sure it was ready in case someone tries to escape. I turned to Andy who also heard it and he looked a bit nervous over it. How the hell could anyone escape the way they secured us? Somehow, every so often, someone figures out how.

The bus was loaded and it slowly pulled out of the penitentiary and onto the road. I looked at the warehouses and businesses that were around and saw some workers showing up to start a new day. I saw some people going into stores to do some early morning shopping. I observed the passing cars and the people in them that had their freedom going on with their lives. The sun was a little higher in the sky and made everything around us look bright and new and there we were locked down. I remember thinking, how did this part of life happen? I knew it wasn't something God intended for us, but there was that dark force that led us mortals into our own personal hell. To me being incarcerated was like my own prison that I had walked into and could not get out of. Why did I listen to that fiend of addiction when it told me I would be ok if I forged those scripts? Why didn't I heed to the signs my angel was giving me? It was clear as day but I thought I could get away with what I was doing. For a little while at least. So instead of being able to go to work, make a living and go home to my Goo, I was trapped in restraints on a prison bus leaving what life I had behind.

Andy had an old friend named Woody, ironically who was on the great ride with us. They were engaged in their own conversation, which was good, because I needed my own time. I looked out of the window and noticed we were on the Pennsylvania Turnpike heading east. I knew it was going to be a long ride but I felt good. Being on the road always made me feel free even though I was in chains. I gazed out and saw endless fields and meadows. There were breathtaking flowers and long grass as we rode on. I could visualize Xanadoo and I walking in those fields, as I would pick flowers for her. We would bask in the beauty that was all around us as we held hands.

I saw in the distance a few houses with huge backyards. I pretended Xanadoo and I were lying out in the sun completely free of the weight of the world. As I looked at a passing car slowly riding past the prison bus, I remembered how her and I traveled together. I pretended for a moment her and I were driving jointly as the reality I was in didn't exist. I knew it wasn't over with us and we would be together again! Even though I was not physically with her, she was with me in my agony of confinement. I had to take her with me on that journey I was banished inside of in my heart and my mind. I was searching for heaven in my hell. The CO's had some music playing and I suddenly heard through the speakers a new song by Carrie Underwood called *"See You Again"*.

She sang, *"I will see you again, whoa... This is not where it ends. I will carry you with me, oh... 'Til I see you again."*

As that beautiful song played on, I smiled as I looked out at the sun-drenched day, knowing that where I was surely wasn't the end. I would see her again! It was exactly the song I needed to hear in that moment. That's what I was doing in that horrible situation. I was carrying my true love with me until I see her again. I wasn't alone and I knew the good Lord had given me someone to help me through where I was going and the song to remind me of that.

We finally arrived at the classification penal complex near Harrisburg. The site was huge with long high barbwire fences. It was a sickening sight and what's more was that I was five hours away from home. We were out in the middle of the state near the capital. What really stood out for me on the ride was seeing the signs on the turnpike. When the interstate split there was a large sign for **Baltimore, Maryland.** My stomach turned at the thought of being that close to the city I got rescued from. The city I nearly died in. Was that a sign that I may lose Xanadoo and end up back on the streets of Baltimore City? I was feeling good on the prison bus for the most part until I saw those signs realizing how close I was to my old hellish life literally. Then my mind shifted gears into a negative state feeding me bad thoughts.

We were all led inside, our chains removed and were all put inside a holding cell. We had to take off the white jumpsuits and turn them into a big basket then we were all left in our boxers and t-shirts while we waited. I remember thinking, not this again and why are we in our underwear? There was an elderly man who looked like a sick old drunk. As I sat quietly, the guys began to make fun of him because his penis was sticking out, through a big opening on his boxers, on display for everyone to see. He didn't seem like he knew what was going on and I felt sorry for him. I looked down to make sure I wasn't making the same mistake that strange man was making. I didn't need my dick hanging out either.

Time moved on slowly as it usually does in matters like being contained. We were called one by one to get our blues and get dressed.

When we went out of the cell, we were directed to grab our boxes that were brought with us from the other penitentiary. I didn't have much, just some letters from Goo and some pictures. We were processed into their asinine system then we all went outside carrying our boxes. The CO's weren't very nice and treated all of us like we were the scum of the earth. In two by two formation we followed the CO through the prison, which was rather large and a little overwhelming. It was similar to a college campus only no one could leave and we were incased in barbwire fences being monitored by cameras that watched our every move. It was hot and the sun beat down on me as I began to sweat.

We were taken to a new building, where I heard would be our home for about a week. It was the medical block for all the new commits and we would have to take a few silly tests and be locked down until we were placed into another block. We placed our boxes down and were told to stand still and keep quiet until further instructed. There were about 30 of us new inmates and they put us in the holding tank, which looked like a waiting room to see the doctor. There were rows of chairs and I noticed it was way more comfortable than that other prison. Woody, Andy and I all sat together and waited for whatever came next.

There was this young, thin CO in his mid twenties or so who came into the tank and gave us all a dirty look. I could tell he was going to be a problem so I nick named him Junior.

202

"Listen up!" He shouted. "We're not here to kiss your ass! You will all remain seated and quiet until you are called to see the counselors. I don't want to hear any bullshit or have problems otherwise I will put you in the hole and take away your meals! This isn't the county anymore. The funs over gentleman!"

I looked at Andy and thought, the funs over? The fun never began so what the hell was Junior talking about? Some of the inmates began to laugh at the way that young CO came in and tried to act tough.

One inmate said, "I would beat the piss out of that little peckerwood if I ever saw him on the streets."

What came to my mind was that Junior was only a man and strip him of his uniform and he would be no better than any of us. I remember thinking that it was against the law to take away any of our meals while we're in the Department Of Corrections, so Junior can quit his bellyaching and give up the act!

It was time to eat and everyone was called out to grab a bag. Once Andy and I got our bags we sat back down in the tank. I opened the bag and realized the rumors were true. The stories I was told in the county about the joke that was the meals during that part of the prison intake process. Two slices of bread, a cup of peanut butter and jelly, a stick of celery and a bag of raisins! That wasn't a meal and we would have to endure the same crap everyday. We were to be in the tank awaiting the rubbish they called the classification period.

Time went on and we saw a couple of counselors to tell us what level we were. There was level two, which was minimum security and came with fewer restrictions. Level three was the middle of the road and level four that was meant for higher security inmates. Then there was level five which basically was RHU, Restrictive Housing Unit, or better known as the hole or the bucket. Andy and I were both a level two thank God! His friend Woody, however, was a level three. Woody had a 2 to 4 year sentence from an aggravated assault charge. Since he already had a record they sent him to state prison for his crime. I was Andy's spiritual guide and friend but I told him I could not get into a fight if the other inmates ever started up with him. He understood that getting into any kind of fight or trouble would ruin my chances to make parole and go home to Xanadoo. Woody was tough and I felt God always sends in a protector and he was Andy's. There was one guy from the other prison who gave Andy a hard time about his charges. He was with us in the group that was taken on the prison bus. As usual he was saying digs to Andy. Woody leaned over and stared him down.

"Got a problem?" Woody asked.

"No man." The jerk said. "I don't have a problem. Your buddy might."

"If you want to go right now, we can." Woody stated firmly. "I got nothing to lose. Leave him alone, ok!"

The jerk just turned away and didn't speak anymore. Thank God because I didn't want any problems for Andy. He was just a guy trying to do his time.

Junior came back in and said his little speech again. He added, "All you new commits better understand that I don't play around. I will take your meals away and put you in the hole in a minute! You all will be going upstairs soon so keep quiet and wait until you are called."

I hated that term "New Commit!" I remember thinking, I didn't commit to this! I understand they use that term when someone has been confined but to me I saw the word as "commitment." I have made commitments to women, jobs and even drugs. But I never thought I would have to be committed to a freaking place like the Department Of Corrections! I felt myself becoming angry that I was being held against my own will. That I was taken away from my Goo and my life! Unfortunately, I didn't have much of a choice and tried to go with the flow. Andy and I were called in to see the nurse. We had to get a TB test, which I always hated! They stick a needle under your skin and put some kind of crap in ya. It bulged and became itchy. Next they had to draw some blood to check our levels and other things.

Once we had our stats done we were finally able to go upstairs. It looked like a new, clean prison dayroom. Two levels of cells were on both sides with showers at the end. We all sat around at these metal tables then were told if we wanted to make a phone call to come up to the desk and sign up with the CO in charge. Andy and I signed up and when it was his turn, he got on the phone, but had no luck getting through. The bitch of where we were was that the CO's really were a bunch of jack offs! The CO only allowed everyone exactly three minutes to make our calls. Since Andy couldn't get through, the CO yelled that his time was up and to sit the hell back down.

I got on the phone and rushed to dial Xanadoo's number but there was no answer. I hung up and called back again, frantically trying to rush, as I knew the jack off was timing me. Finally I got through and had to wait for that stupid recording to tell her I was calling from a correctional facility. As if she already didn't know. I felt like saying, oh shut up! You're sucking up my time with my call.

She shouted in happiness, "Hi honey! How are you?"

That's when the bastard yelled, "Hey, you there? Times up buddy. Let's go!"

I said to him, "But I just got through!"

"Three minutes is all you get. Hang up now!"

What a piece of shit I thought! I had to briefly tell Goo that I was all right and that I would call her as soon as I could. I hung up feeling highly frustrated. Really now! Who does this I thought? Why bother even giving us a phone call? How the hell can anyone be rushed to make a call to their loved ones? It took over a minute just to dial and get through the recording jargon. Ugh!

Once I sat back down with Andy, we had to grab our boxes and see what cell we would be in. I got my box and sat down, then Andy grabbed his and sat back down with me. God had granted another blessing on us because we were once again celled up. We may have been in a shitty predicament but at least we would be in each other's company during the remainder of time on that medical block. We had a strong bond and it truly made the situation much easier to deal with.

It was the next day and we were all called out and had to wait in the tank yet again. It was bread, peanut butter, jelly, raisins and a celery stick again for lunch. If being in that holding tank wasn't punishment enough the food was!

Finally we were all called into a room, which was like a classroom in high school. There were those old school desks I remember with plastic chairs. We all sat down and I felt as if I were back in school again, only this time I wasn't going anywhere but back to a cell. The counselor got up from her desk and stood before everyone.

She said, "ok, we will be handing out your IQ tests. Fill them out to the best of your knowledge. These are to determine your IQ scores. There are no wrong or right answers. If there is any talking, looking at each other's test or any horseplay you will be dismissed and taken back to your cell and you will return tomorrow to make it up. Please gentlemen, if you want to make this go smooth, just follow the rules and you will be done."

There were two inmates with browns on passing out our tests. They were lucky enough to have a prison job in the education department. The classification prison was also a home prison for some. I hoped I would not get placed there as my home prison! I needed to be closer to home so Xanadoo could visit me and not have to drive five hours to do it! After the inmates handed out pencils we were told to begin. I opened my test and saw a few silly questions. There were four squares with four different choices to make in one question.

"Which picture does not belong?" was one of the questions.

There was one picture of a baby holding a spoon, another of that same baby holding a baby bottle, the third was the infant holding a pacifier and the last picture was the toddler holding a wrench. I remember asking myself, are they serious? I checked off the tot with the wrench because... well, didn't look right to me! The next question was the same concept. Check off the picture that wasn't correct. There was a man sawing a tree branch and he was cutting a limb as he sat on the outside of the branch, instead on the inside, so just the branch falls off. I thought well if this dumb ass were to saw the branch he was sitting on, he would fall down with it. Come on now! No one is that stupid I thought. I checked off that picture.

There were four pictures of a dog and I was to choose what didn't fit again. As soon as I saw the picture of that dog wearing sneakers on his back paws I checked it off immediately. What are all these crazy questions they are asking me I thought? I heard a few guys laughing and mocking the test.

I overheard someone say out loud, "This shits crazy yo!"

I wasn't alone on how dumb those questions really were. I just carried on with the silly tests they were putting on us. I didn't have much of a choice.

The next day we were brought down to a room with rows of computers. The next set of tests we had to endure was a TABE test. That determined our grade level and to see if we would need further education. Luckily I scored high and knew I would not have to take anything for that. The test that was set up next was a drug and alcohol evaluation. I ran through the questions and realized it was almost as crazy as the IQ tests.

One question asked, *"Were you so high you had to miss days of work?"*

I could say that no, I wasn't *sooo* high I missed work. I was high on the job on several occasions but that's not what the test had asked me.

"Were you so high it was causing problems at home?"

No, I was fine in my relationship with Goo for the most part. There were a few drug related mishaps but certainly nothing that broke us apart.

"Were you so high or drunk you found yourself waking up in strange places not remembering how you got there?"

Oh my God No! If they had asked these questions back when I was really bad, I certainly would be answering much different. That was many years ago and my drug use became more controlled, though I knew, I was still an addict.

"Do you feel you need a treatment program? Not at all? Moderately? Very much so? Definitely?"

I put down moderately because I knew I had an addiction, but I have done programs before and it didn't do much good. I mean, why bother asking that question when chances are people are going to put "not at all" down for the answer, unless they wanted the help.

Once all the testing was over with, Andy and I were mostly in our cell as the days dragged on. It had been about seven days since we have been on that block. It was so quiet I could hear a pin drop. The rules in that phase were we had to remain quiet, submit or it was the hole. That wasn't anyone's home block. We were just passing through. I had moments when Andy was sleeping that I was far off in a distant world completely alone. I would stare out into the empty dayroom with no movement what so ever and felt I wasn't real. It was as if I was banished to a strange fate to endure with no life around me. It was a creepy moment where I felt lost beyond space and time.

We were starting to get restless and I knew I wanted to move to the next block so I could call Xanadoo and have some yard time. Andy had been drawing really cool pictures of demons, skulls and psycho jesters. He was a talented artist and every time he showed me one of his twisted drawings I would say, "Sick!" But my version of *"sick'* meant how *delightfully twisted!* That gave him the idea to call his work *"Sick Prison Art"*.

There were those days I would look out of the window and see the rain falling and felt far from home. The raindrops would plummet down splashing into little puddles that I could not touch. I saw in the far distance the edge of the Appalachian Mountains that was calming to my soul. Close by I would notice the fences that kept us all prisoners in that corner of the world and some of the other blocks. There were those geese that freely wondered around within the fences. Why geese would actually be free on the prison grounds was beyond me. They didn't know any better and if they did know, I was sure they would fly the hell out of there! I know I would.

I began to fantasize that I had powers. I imagined I had the strength to plow my way through the concrete wall. Both hands and BOOM! Blowing the wall everywhere as I stood looking at freedom. Jumping out of the high window, I would land on my feet and I would launch myself up and fly home to Goo!

I would often close my eyes and make a wish and when I opened them I would be home again. No matter how hard I tried though I would open them back to the nightmare I was in. Clearly, there really was no way out of the mess I got myself into.

I was trapped in that enclosed space and there wasn't much to do. Being locked down was driving us to the edge of sanity! Andy had told me he really wanted to make a difference in his life and quit using drugs. We shared moments at the metal table with two stools where we ate. I'd glance out the window as Andy and I talked. I felt I had given him some good advice but I knew it would be hard for him when he got out because his friends and family all did drugs. Where else was he going to go? I have the love of my soul mate, but Andy had no one and I'm still struggling to get it right! Where he lived it would be all around him. The temptations would be too great. He grew up in that environment and will have to go back. I'm older and wiser and I was still struggling to get it right. Addiction is a very allusive, sneaky and powerful mental obsession, a weakness to our spirits.

Our time was drawing near and I knew we would be moved soon. Andy and I were sitting at the table talking about how old being in that cell was getting and wanted OUT! Suddenly the lights went on all over the block. We went up to the cell gate and looked out the window to see what was going on. There were two inmates, block workers, going around pulling name tags off the cell doors, which meant we were going to be placed somewhere else. Another block where we would have phone calls and yard time and wait to be sent to a home prison.

Anticipation began to arise as the inmates in browns came to our door and pulled only one of our names. I wasn't sure which one of us would be going.

Andy asked, "Who do you think is going?"

"I don't know," shrugging my shoulders. "Looks like we are going to be separated again."

Andy sat on the bed and put his head down. He said nervously, "I'm scared."

"Just do not tell anyone your crime. If anyone asks, just say aggravated assault. You nearly beat a man to death. Be cool, makes some friends... you'll be ok, you'll see."

Andy walked back over to the cell door and looked out again. I wonder when and where they will be taking one of us and who it is? Just waiting to find out is killing me!"

I walked back to the door, peering out of the window.

I said, "soon I'm sure. But the waiting sucks. Who's going, who's not. Being in prison is more than doing time, screwing up ones life... its madness! Having to deal with personal and spiritual emotions, anxiety, fear of the unknown, anger, regret... and so on."

Finally at that moment our cell door began to slide open. The anticipation was so great, even the cell door sliding opened felt like a lifetime! I stepped out into the insanity as everyone celled up was beginning to come out. I discovered they were only moving, not all but most of the others and me but not Andy. I turned to him and knew he was not happy and neither was I. We were being separated yet again.

"What the hell is this bullshit?" Andy said bitterly.

"I don't know... I guess they have us moving to different parts of this prison."

Andy took in a deep breath and said to me. "Thanks to you man... You helped me get through this."

I smiled and said, "it helped us both.

As the block got noisier, inmates were pouring out of the cells with their possessions and hurrying down the stairs into the dayroom. The floor vibrated a little and we could hear the stomp of their feet hitting the metal stairs. Through our opened cell door a CO was yelling for everyone to get in line. What once was a quiet, peaceful block when we were locked down became a zoo! That week had past on by and now it was another phase to deal with. I packed up my stuff feeling rushed and a bit anxious.

"I wonder where we go from here?" Andy asked in confusion.

I assured Andy that he will be just fine and to think positive. I told him this hell we were in would be over before we knew it. I had my stuff all packed and I gave Andy a hug. I knew I would miss him. We shared so many memories of our past and

213

acted out scenes of our favorite movies to pass the time. We both talked about some of our favorite music and even wrote a couple of songs sharing that cell together. He was what I needed to get through that part of the prison experience and I was what he needed. The great Divine Power was at work and I was grateful to have had Andy as a cellmate. I backed away and gave him one last look of assurance. Once again he looked scared and fragile but I knew he would be just fine. It was time for me to move on and get the classification period over with.

\

Duality

Life can truly be unfair at times. My father had passed away and a week later Rich and his wife had their first baby girl brought into the world in early March 1997. My father said before he was a mess that he wanted to see his grandchildren before he died. It was a strange way of how the circle of life keeps going around and around. He was once born into this world and now he was leaving. I didn't cry at my father's funeral and Screwface didn't understand.

He said, "I drove to the Bronx, saw daddy dead, went to Long Island for a few days, then drove back like I didn't miss a beat."

It was hard for me to cry over a man I had only a few good memories with. My only regret was that I didn't get to know my father the way I wanted to. Now he was gone and it would be up to Screwface and me to take full care of my mother's worsening condition.

I didn't give what fully entailed into being a caregiver into much consideration. My mother was in a motorized scooter but remained independent and insisted she do as much as she could, otherwise she would feel useless, only existing. The only thing Screwface and I really did was help her in and out of bed and cook the meals like my father used to.

Later on in September, I landed a great new job as a driver, where I would deliver wave runners and motorcycles. I worked six days a week and got to travel all over the entire state of Florida. I continued to go to the gym with my gay ex-boss who became a good friend. I got another small part in another theater production called "Cinderella". I also had a part given to me by my agent for a Coke commercial down in Miami.

I was on a roll with my dreams and I still was working on my novel. I felt so alive in the theater production, always laughing and feeling high-spirited! Those awesome days on my new job, I would do an overnight delivery run up to the panhandle of Florida and it was like a spiritual getaway for me. I was able to ride on the wave runners in the ocean, flying high off the waves! It was such a rush! I was completely lifted on high!

Amanda had met what became her new boyfriend Mike and when I met him it was an instant click. He was a musician and it inspired me to get my musical talent in order. Since I was making good money and had no real bills to pay, I began buying musical equipment.

I had an eight-track recorder to lay down tracks, a beautiful black double cut away electric guitar. It was a Kramer Sustainer and I could hold a note forever if I wanted to when I flipped the switch. I purchased some effects processors and a rather expensive Yamaha keyboard. I had gotten a bass guitar with a few other things and Amanda, Mike and I would lay tracks down creating our own harmony. I was so into making music, I would create my own songs and lay down each instrument myself. I continued to rock on with all my amazing talents but there was that enticing influence that called me. I had tried cocaine for the first time and found that it was powerful! I was over my friend Key's house and he had some and I thought, why not, so I engaged in a few lines.

I had begun buying my own cocaine and when I would watch a porno it made the women really stand out as if I could touch them and feel them. I became highly sensual on the drug and along with my hyper sex drive, it became a dual passion that I could not resist. The first time I masturbated on cocaine, I felt the orgasm was much more intense!   I was offered ecstasy one day so I tried it. The drug slowly consumed my body with tingles, sensitivity to everything with a powerful sense of love for everyone. I took an E pill one night and took a bath and found that I could not get out. The water felt like warm silk all over my body and it was so alluring that I kept filling the tub with more and more hot water, replacing the old water that got cool. Before I knew it there was sunlight coming in through the window and my mother questioning me why I was taking a bath at 7 in the morning.

My friend Key made a lot of money at his job and always had hundreds on him. We would hang out at the tiki bar near Fort Lauderdale, on the beach at night. He would have me run up to a nightclub where he knew a drug dealer for me to buy us some drugs. The place was dim, with flashing lights and loud music. People were engaging on a Saturday night, drinking and having fun. I remember handing the guy Key's money and I would go right into the bathroom stall and do up a good line of cocaine. It seemed alluring for some reason to snort the cocaine in a bathroom stall of a nightclub. The bathroom itself was a little dirty, with toilet paper on the floor and the smell of urinals. The lighting was low and captivating. How could I be so attracted and comfortable doing drugs in stall?

Once I got back to the tiki bar, Key along with some friends would roll hard on the X. I found that drinking alcohol enhanced the effect of those drugs and could drink like a fish! I felt so free, sexual, in love with the world. I remember, I was so high, I took off all my clothes and swam naked in the ocean at night. The water was all over my body and I was one with everything feeling so superior. The black sky around me with the tiki bar and beach hotels shining some light. I felt light like air as the ocean swayed and I could hear the sound of the waves. I remember turning into the ocean and looking at the darkness. It felt mysterious, exciting, scary and unknown. My creativity and artistic side combined with my eccentricities made me feel drugs differently than others.

I had become undone in what life I had in my talents and began too obsess over those effects of drugs. I couldn't just take the drugs and enjoy them; I had to learn up on them. Where they come from, how it affects the brain, etc... I studied everything and became addicted to a new way of life. I found myself facing darkness and being lured into it. For some reason I was attracted to darkness and wanted to explore it deeply. Nighttime was when my energy came out so I started to align myself to the dark hours. I used to walk all hours of night in my neighborhood and saw all the houses that I past. I peered into the homes and noticed there were numerous lives just existing. What problems do some of these people have I remember thinking. Some were watching television and others were eating a late dinner. Some were reading and every so often I would walk past a house where there were some people arguing. It was like I can feel the life and memories in those homes. I would feel comfort with those watching TV and the light flickered with each scene from where I walked past. Anger or feeling the tension in some homes. The emptiness when those homeowners weren't there and the houses that were dark. These were some strange feelings I couldn't understand. How was I able to read homes people lived in? Feel as if I knew those houses lives as if I lived there.

I would smoke myself a joint and be lifted into that spiritual mindset cannabis always put me in. Being in that state of mind really got me more in touch with that strange gift of sensing all those homes. At the end of my street, I climbed over a fence into a small park and listened to the calming sounds the night brought. I was falling into myself and was intrigued by my spiritual journeys. I would continue on through some woods and wound up at a construction site. They were building up the area I was living in and from the rust color lights that came off the nearby Florida Turnpike, the construction site looked like a post apocalypse war zone.

I would walk around the half built houses and felt there were no reminiscences there. There was no grass, just light brown dirt on all the properties and within the entire sub division. They were empty, bare, unfinished homes before time would create its life memories. Soon families will start their lives as time moves on. Then people move and new people move in beginning their lives there. Before we all know it, a 100 plus years will pass on by and many generations would have lived in those homes. It felt almost haunting being there in the midst of night in what felt like an unknown realm far away from the every day world.

I would run up onto the dirt mounds the bulldozers made and look all around me.
The sky was black above me, no life around me, I felt like a god of the night. I would wear all black and from the way the grounds looked I often pretended that the end of the world had already happened and I was left to guide the lost as an immortal. What was interesting to me was when someone would be walking his or her dog in that area, or a car may have driven by, no one ever saw me. I was like a ghost in the night. I felt protected by God on high and wondered if how I felt on that dirt mound would be something the Lord would call me to do. Would I be a guide in

the great Revelation? Would I be a god helping those who have lost their way in the shadows? I wasn't sure where my life was going but I knew I was deep in duality of my existence. There was the productive and positive side of me doing all the great things in the entertainment world and there was the dark side of me rising. The drugs had gotten a hold on me but I felt I would be all right.

My mother's ailment of her sickening disease of multiple sclerosis was still on a slow downward spiral. She was struggling more and more to do the things she was used to doing. Even with her persisting struggles she still made it a point to come see me perform at the theater for the play Cinderella. Screwface would load her up in our handicapped van we had to buy and took her to see me. She was really proud of me for living my dream. When I would write into the night in my room, I would print out what I wrote and read it to her.

I would sit in front of her while she sat in her chair and share with her my gift of words. She always loved what I wrote and would tell me if there was something not right. I knew she would not patronize me. She told me I had a real gift and to never give up on it. I got involved in a writers group meeting that was held once a week at a local bookstore. I would sit in a group with other writers and share my work and have it critiqued. It was a great way to get my work out there and to see what others thought of it. My job continued to take me all over the state of Florida. I was driving down to Key West and once I got there I unloaded the wave runners. I had the awesome perk of being able to ride the wave runners yet again. What a rush! The drive back was incredible. There I was as I was cruising over the islands with the radio going and free from all worries. I remember when I got on to the main land, I was driving up on the Turnpike and the sun was low in the sky, creating a magnificent orange glow against the clouds. It looked like the sky was on fire but in a brilliant way like a painting.

I was feeling so alive and I truly wanted to get my career going. At that moment I heard Jon Parr on the radio.

"I can see a new horizon underneath the blazing sky. I'll be where the eagle's flyin' higher and higher. Gonna be a man in motion. All I need is a pair of wheels. Take me where the future's lyin'... Saint Elmo's fire."

The song was speaking deeply to me as I saw the road ahead of me going by faster and faster.

The song kept rocking on... *"Just once in his life a man has his time. And my time is now... and I'm comin' alive! I can hear the music playin.' I can see the banners fly. Feel like you're back again and hope riding high..."*

I took a moment to look out at that blazing sky right as the lyrics sang, *"I can feel Saint Elmo's Fire burning in me."*

I felt in my spirit inspiration was being brought down to me from heaven. That guide was still beside me, speaking to me through music but I really wasn't aware of it that often. I just felt the connection between the Divine and my soul. My passions were burning deep within me but my dark side was slowly moving in.

I had to find an answer to what my life meant to me so I continued on my spiritual journeys at night. I would roam free and talk to God to find an answer in my life. I asked Him why my mother had to suffer so much but couldn't get the response I was looking for. I asked meditated and pray to either take my mother home or give her a cure since she was getting worse. I carried on with my life as I usually did and landed a gig as a ball boy for the movie "Any Given Sunday". It was great to be on the set again and I was able to meet Al Pacino. He was laid back and tossed the football around with us nobody's. Once again my mother was proud that I went forward with my dreams.

I worked on the set for four days and had hurt my back. Unfortunately I had to leave the set and return home. My friend Key had some Percocets and had given me a few. I remember sitting down in front of my computer to write, I had taken one Percocet and ate a bowl of cereal. There I was typing my words onto the screen when all of a sudden the painkiller crashed down on me. My head sank and my body felt lifted. At that moment I wanted to just put my head back and enjoy the high I was feeling! I took another Percocet and decided to lie on my bed and watch some television with no lights on. Once the other pain pill kicked in I did not move. I had a smile on my face for no real reason and I felt like I was floating on cushy clouds that held all of my weight. It was similar to a lingering body orgasm with a calming effect.

It was brilliant, the semi-synthetic opiate that ran through my veins, unleashing wonderful chemicals in my brain all over my body. It had given me the kind of high that I was looking for. I could just kick back and enjoy a free flowing internal radiance and warming sensation within my body. I had to understand that medicine so I began doing research online about it. As I discovered the main ingredient in Percocet was oxycodone, I started looking more into it. I came across the opium poppy plant, where the natural occurring drugs morphine and codeine came from. Heroin is processed from opium making it two and a half times stronger than morphine. I learned that oxycodone was synthesized from codeine and thebain, another natural occurring alkaloid, straight from the opium poppy. Just as heroin is made from morphine.

I immediately ordered some opium poppies seeds online to grow for myself. Nature's medicine. The medicine of the gods. The flowers were spectacular as I looked at pictures. A week after the flowers fall off, the poppy pod begins to ooze opium milk. It's been on the planet as far as we can remember. I couldn't help but wonder how it was discovered. I wished I were able to teleport back in time and witness history. All of history unharmed.

Why not, I thought, nurture my own opium plants and make a wondrous tea out of it and smoke it. An amazing gift from Mother Nature. I got high just thinking about getting high and growing that miraculous plant. I got some cannabis seeds from Key and started my own little garden out in my back patio. I had gained a fascination with all sorts of plants that I grew, which included roses, jasmine, marijuana and opium. I was obsessed with the growing part and made sure I was out there every day watering them all and taking care of them. The marijuana grew easily but I had a hard time with the opium. I researched that a place like Florida, with the strong sun and hot weather was hard to grow since poppies liked cooler wetter weather when they begin to grow then warmer, drier weather. I tried growing it in the winter since it was cooler but still no luck. I wasn't about to give up so I just kept trying over and over again.

My mother helped me get a brand new mustang. It was April1998 and I needed a new car since my old mustang was developing problems. I got the top of the line Mustang, a six cylinder and was fully loaded. Black leather interior and candy apple red exterior. The feel of a brand new car was so exciting! I loved driving it!

Key and I went every Friday to the sportsman night at Moroso Race Track up in Palm Beach County. It was another intriguing form of a rush that I loved. My addiction was completely warped and I went off racing all the time. I loved the speed of racing my Mustang in the quarter mile. I loved the way I sank in my seat and made the tires squeal and the smell of burnt rubber! There was where I met up with an old friend. Her name was Sherry and she had been involved with our old friend Ian on and off for many years.

Sherry and I got close and started dating. She was spiritual in a different way. She was more into scientology but open minded to the many possibilities of the universe. We would talk for hours and I took her on my nighttime expeditions. There we were walking in my neighborhood looking up at the sky trying to

225

find an answer. Once we got to the fence she told me she had a strong fear of fences. She did not want to climb because of her phobia. I took her hand and showed her it wasn't that bad. I climbed the fence first and then she struggled to climb it. She was halfway over it and began to cry. I encouraged her not to let the fear consume her. I rooted her on and told her anything was possible. She made it over the fence and she hugged me.

"No one has ever helped me with that! Thank you!" She gratefully said.

I took her onto the construction site and showed her all the houses being built with the dirt properties. The rust color light from the turnpike shone down across the area like a dying sun, casting long shadows behind the houses.

I asked, "what do you see?"

"It looks like a post war apocalypse! This is really weird!"

Sherry was the only person I took on those night walks. I knew I needed to share what I saw with someone who was in touch with their spirituality as I was. The thing about Sherry and I was we never once had a single fight, which was a bit odd. We always got along and I wondered if that was an issue. How could it be? Not fighting was good! The sex we had was intense and for the first time in a long time it was like making love again only I wasn't sure. Was I in love or in love with the idea of being in love? Her ex-boyfriend wasn't a good person to her and Sherry swore she would never ever go back to him. She told me I was so good to her that she would be foolish to leave.

We shared moments of synchronicity and the strange way the Divine talks to us. Like the time she took me on the expressway to drive up a high bridge that veered off the main part of Interstate 95. Reaching the top we saw all of downtown Miami. Beautiful buildings stood, many lit up with colored neon lights. The night sky lay behind and a full moon above as the song *"One Headlight"* by the Wallflowers played as we drove in her car with actually one headlight working. Other songs played that were in sync but what did it all mean? What was it really telling me?

I remember sneaking her in my room after my mother went to bed and we must have been speaking too loud. Suddenly we heard the clicking of my mother's motor scooter and Sherry had to run into the spare bedroom and hide. My mother peeked in my room and questioned me who was there. I assured her it was no one and that I was working on a song with my music.

She said suspiciously, "oh yeah? Let me hear what you're working on then."

I calmly got my electric guitar and started playin her a tune I made up then and there. For about twenty minutes I played and I knew Sherry was under the bed in the spare bedroom. I had to play it cool so my mother would go back to bed and not know I had snuck her in. Finally my mother went back to bed and I got Sherry out from the spare bedroom. She didn't seem too happy and said she had to go. I snuck her back outside and saw her drive away.

Days went by and I didn't hear from her. I called but she was never home. Had I done something wrong I wondered? We were dating for four months and it seemed everything was going great but I had found out that she went back to Ian.

I was hurt all over again and confused. How could someone say they were happy and would never go back to her ex-boyfriend who treated her bad? I carried the pain with me and as I was at work driving down I-95 on a delivery, I remembered asking myself why am I allowing her to hurt me? We were only together for a short time and if I could get over my first love and the love I had with Amanda, I could surely get over Sherry. At that moment the pain went away and it never bothered me there after. I still had some anger towards Sherry but I didn't allow the heartache to stay with me. I had to keep on living my life and take care of my mother.

Acid became another new drug I got into. Key along with a few of our friends would drop LSD and I thought it was time I gave it a try. Though my psychotic friends would drop a ten strip of acid, I wasn't going to take that much. We all dropped the acid and tooled around on a drive. We went out to the Everglades and the acid had kicked in on me. There we were deep in the Everglades parked in a dark spot. We all saw some people with their headlights on, tossing things at the alligators and to me it seemed like we stumbled onto some kind of crazy cult. I became paranoid, as everyone wanted to know what was going on there. Words became abnormal to me as I tried to listen to what those people were saying.

"We better get the hell out of here!" I said panicky.

Key said, "they're not making sense. I thought I heard one of them say they were almost out of ladyfingers. I think they are feeding them body parts. We may be killed and fed to the alligators!"

What the hell was going on I franticly thought? The acid had shifted gears on me, as I suddenly felt a strong sense of peace. Tapping into the earth for energy, I felt brave enough to mosey over to the crazies that were having a picnic with the reptiles. I figured the gators weren't afraid so why should I be. I was the most frightened over those people but the first to go up to them and start a conversation. I found out it was all right and they were just regular folks feeding the gators some ladyfinger cookies. There we were tripping on acid in the middle of the night, in the swampland, feeding the gators cookies.

We went to the bowling ally and it was Rock n' Bowl night. They had the lights swaying, flashing and the music jamming! I remember walking off to find a bowling ball and as I was walking, I wondered where the hell I was. What is this place I thought? Panic ran though me again as I felt detached from my friends. I felt like I was deep in a wild realm of noise and flashing lights. I could not find my way back! Things seem to be moving very slow and the walk back seemed like a lifetime. It was a moment of being all alone amid the lunatics that were tossing balls down a long isle. Voices seemed strange and nothing made any sense. What seemed like hours were only a few minutes and I had found my friends. They were bowling, tripping and having a blast not knowing of my strange experience. If one hit of acid does this,

I couldn't bear taking ten hits like everyone else. I knew I was the only one of my friends that had to stay in control. I had always been the responsible one but that seemed to be fading away.

Time moved on and Screwface had to move out with his girlfriend. My mother couldn't stand his drinking and his rushing her in her handicapped condition. Perhaps my brother couldn't deal with seeing our mother go down hill. Things kept changing and though Amanda, Mike and I were making great music, they started to back off some. They got married at Amanda's house. Nothing fancy, just a small wedding with close friends. I went of course and was very happy for her. I couldn't go by myself so I took an ecstasy pill and rolled at her wedding, which wasn't like me. Rolling on ecstasy at my ex-love's wedding? Really? My friend Key got married and I felt as if everyone around me was moving on, as I remained stuck. I was smoking pot more and started drinking beer every single night.

I kept on with my novel and was close to finishing it. I wanted to continue with my acting career but something was holding me back. I began to dread getting up in the morning and was angry having to leave my comfortable bed. I had to make sure my mother was safely out of bed and had her coffee and donut ready before I left for work. I was still happy once I was making my delivery runs but couldn't wait for the night to come, to be alone, get high and drunk. To really dive deep in the spiritual pond of my mind. I went to my writers group meeting but found myself getting restless because I had a six-pack of beer waiting for me. I began to leave the group earlier and earlier. Once I put my mother to bed at night, I shut off all the lights in my room and lit candles. I sat down to try and finish my novel. I had smoked some cannabis for that spiritual lift and cracked open a beer.

There I was in front of the computer with no lights on feeling comforted. I played a Sarah McLachlan song called *"Back Door Man"*. The beat was smooth and the song was peaceful. I swore it felt like someone was speaking to me through the music.

"Now the angry morning is the early signs of warning. You must face alone the plans you make. Decisions they will try to break."

I became hypnotized in her song and tried to understand the meaning.

"All of your life you lived in a world as pure as Eden's sixth day. Now all you've been allowed is taken away. They will not let you be so proud. And you have felt the fear growing inside. Protest follows far and wide. They'll see how long it will take 'till you fall from so much denied. Your soul it aches relentless for the fear they will never guess... So unfair that they can make you feel so small and the fear you know is real."

I tried to shake off the weirdness of that moment but I couldn't. I was getting angry waking up every morning and felt it was an early sign of warning of the darkness to come. All my years I did have a pure life, protected by the angels above and the sheltering of my mother. The fear was beginning to grow inside me, sensing something evil lurking around my spirit. Are those demons trying to make me fall and take away my calling in life?

The fear within me was so real I was starting to breakdown. The next song that played was called *"Shelter"*.

"Give them shelter from the coming storm."

What's going on here Lord? Who's talking to me? Was it too late for me to avoid the coming storm? It was like standing in the middle of nowhere feeling the wind pick up and blow in my face. The sight of threatening clouds in the distant rolling in as the thunder shook my soul and the fear of an unknown darkness coming that could not be stopped.

I kept on working at my job but my boss was getting tired of my shenanigans. I was always late, beating up the old work truck and my latest prank where I was playing bumper cars with another employee with the good work truck. I had lost a credit card once before and took too long on a few runs. I was called in the manager's office and was told I was fired. I didn't think much of it until I got home and told my mother. She couldn't believe it and was disappointed in me. I tried to gather myself to find out what was next but all I kept seeing was a long dark tunnel.

Amanda and Mike had moved to Ohio and I was left with all that music equipment and no one to rock out with. It was a time I started to feel all alone. My mother was suffering, Screwhead had moved out and on with his life. Key got his own place with his new wife. Everything around me had fallen apart and I just allowed the darkness to slowly consume me. I had pulled out my back again and this time my mother felt responsible since I had to lift her in and out of bed. She told me to call her doctor and tell them that she would need pain medication even though they would be for me. She had me lie and tell them my mother was in a lot of pain and needed something fast. I got a happy feeling when the nurse called me back and told me they were phoning in some Vicodin. Excellent, I thought as the sun shone bright outside then a cloud passed over and cast a shadow dimming the house.

I had begun to slow up on my writing and after I put my mother to bed I would pop one Vicodin and drink a few beers. The beer enhanced the pain pill in a good way and I became hooked. It made that inner glow and the pleasure coating in my body much more intense! I started to watch old reruns on television and became so lonely that I created a female version of myself online. I felt I couldn't get a girlfriend in my sickened condition so why not become one. I created a female account pretending I was like what my soul mate would be with a mix of me. Actually sitting there I felt my feminine side. It was interesting to see what women actually go through with men. 9 out of 10 guys online were pure pigs and I understood what it was like to be a woman. At least how they dealt with men for the most part. It also gave me a great idea for a new novel.

I would go out and buy a six-pack of beer, smoke a joint and pop a Vicodin to numb my pain. I would try to put some music together with my little recording studio but was feeling very little inspiration. I had felt abandoned that everyone had moved on and there I was getting lost having to take care of my mother. My writing stopped and my mother had asked me time and again why I stopped writing. It was sad for me to hear her tell me she missed me reading what I used to write to her. Her words kept repeating in my mind not to give up on my gift but I just could not go on anymore. I developed a new addiction within myself of being wrapped up all warm and snug in my drugs, alcohol and my past. I thought back of what that doctor had told my mother when I was a child.

"You are going to lose your son emotionally."

It seemed that he knew what would become of someone like me. I was falling off the grid fast but I didn't seem to care. It was the beginning of 1999 and I just wanted to fall away and be dead to the world.

The Summer Bridge

The summer had begun and we all lined up to be dispensed to different blocks. We all followed the CO until we got to a T in the walkway. There was a long stretch of blocks that were separated alphabetically.

The CO yelled at us. "Now the blocks are all labeled with the letter you were assigned to. If you do not know you're ABC's then you are a dumbass! Now find your block and have a nice day!"

I began walking with my box in the direction of the block I was meant to go to. That CO was almost as big of an asshole as the one who assigned me. I forgot my towel back in my old cell with Andy and he called me an idiot. If that wasn't bad enough he told me to say, "I am an idiot" out loud. I felt like saying, "Ok, you're an idiot!" I didn't want any issues so I just repeated his stupid words knowing I wasn't an idiot. Those CO's had the power to mess up our committed stay. I didn't want to end up in the bucket for mouthing off so I bit my tongue.

I entered the block I was told to go to along with a few other new commits. The block had two levels with cells stretched along both tiers making me feel intimidated. There was a Sergeant at the desk with a CO beside him. We were told to have a seat at the tables in the dayroom and gave us a list of rules for the block. No one bothered to really take the time to read it. I glanced at it and didn't care too much for their silly rules. I was just here to do my time and go home. The Sergeant laid it down for us that any problems and we will end up in the hole. Just go with it and cause no trouble was basically the speech he was giving us. We would only be able to make one call every four days. There were only three phones on the block and they had us sign up on our designated day.

Every four days?! That's maddening!

I was informed which cell I would be in and as I began walking in that direction, I wondered who my new cellmate would be. Hopefully someone nice and someone I could get along with.

I entered my cell and there was an older gentleman sitting at the desk reading his bible. I smiled in relief and told him it was good to see a friendly face. He introduced himself as Dale and that he has been there for a few months, waiting to go to his home prison. I got along with Dale right away and I had set up my bunk then sat down and had a chat with him.

Dale stated, "I've never been in trouble in my entire life! I'm 60 years old and I had been accused of something I did not do!"

I asked, "what for?"

"My lawyers advised me not to tell anyone of my charge or how long I have."

"Oh… Well I am here for forging scripts. It was something stupid I know."

Dale insisted I not tell anyone of my charges. It was nobody's business he told me but I really wasn't shy about admitting my mistake. Dale had been married for over 40 years to the same woman and was a born again Christian. He was a minister at his church and was from out of state. Dale and his wife were visiting and apparently something bad had happened. He was accused of a terrible crime and had a warrant sent for his arrest. The police, where he lived in North Carolina, had to go to his house and arrest him and then they extradited him back to Pennsylvania to be charged for his mysterious crime. He had spent over two years in county jail fighting his case in which he had spent over $40,000 on lawyers! My God! That was a lot of money to spend and he was still doing time in prison. It gnawed my mind of what he did and how someone who was a minister and never in trouble with the law ended up in prison at his age? Sounded to me like whatever it was had to be some kind of violent sex crime my intuition was telling me. I wasn't about to get into Dales business, though I was curious. I had enough guilt over my silly charges and was getting home sick and missing my Goo!

It was chow time and once our cell doors opened, we had to stand outside of our cells and wait to be told to go eat. We had to go in order and I stuck by Dale's side since I was new and a bit nervous. We walked in a long line out into the summer heat and bright sunshine. I noticed all the other blocks around as we all walked between barbwire fences. There was a stop gate that we had to get buzzed in. We got to the chow hall and the line was ridiculously long. He told me we would only have five minutes to eat and I couldn't believe it. I looked around me and saw all the inmates that were eating with a lot of thunderous talking. Who were all these men? There were so many faces I saw knowing each and every one of them committed some sort of crime to end up in prison. They were men with families, children and I was sure they all had some kind of life going before they got arrested. What was all of this I thought? Was it real what I was going through? How did I end up in that penitentiary on the chow line waiting to eat shitty prison food? As we made our way to the front I heard loud talking from everyone. The smell around me reminded me of being in high school waiting on the lunch line.

Dale and I got our tray of some sort of chicken patty, rice and green beans. The patty looked like a stale hockey puck and I wasn't looking forward to eating it. I grabbed a drink and sat down with Dale. I began to shovel my meal in my mouth as I saw the CO's walking around telling each table to wrap it up and leave. It was terrible to have to be rushed to eat like that. I took a sip of the drink I had and nearly spit it out! What the hell is this I thought? I couldn't identify the flavor of whatever that drink was. It was a strange color and tasted bitter as well as bland.

"What the hell is this?" I asked Dale.

Dale shrugged his shoulders.

Another guy at our table had said. "It's the bullshit they feed us! My advice is when you buy commissary, get your own drink mix and sneak the shit in."

"Does it get any better?" I asked in hopes.

"Sometimes, but don't count on it."

The food was pretty bad and as I looked around the chow hall I saw most of the inmates making that yuck face. The food was so bad I saw the yuck faces spread throughout the chow hall like a virus! I wanted to chuck the chicken patty across the room but I knew I couldn't. I found it best to just devour the crap and try not to taste what I was eating. I saw another inmate take a sip of his drink and he spewed it out!

He said sickened. "What the fuck?"

I overheard many others complain about the food.

Someone said loud. "I can't take this shit no more son!"

Another said, "I just want to go home!"

I heard someone a few tables away say. "This food is cruel and unusual punishment! I'm never coming back to prison again! They finally broke me! I learned my lesson!"

The CO made his way down our section and told us to move out. Luckily we were done eating so we all lined up with our empty trays and tossed out whatever was left. We headed back to our block with our tummies completely devastated!

Anymore of that nasty food and my stomach was going to jump out and beat the crap out of me! I knew I had to order as much commissary as possible as soon as possible!

Once we got back to our cells it was our section of the block's turn to shower. Apparently we were allowed to shower every other day. We had to be undressed with a towel wrapped around us and ready to rush in and out. Dale and I removed everything but our boxers and waited for them to open our cell door. We just waited by the door, cold, half naked and trapped.

Once the doors opened we went out to where everyone had to line up with soap in hand. There were only eight showers for a hundred men to use, which was why they rushed us. Some of the guys had soap and shampoo already on them. It was a trick for them once they got in, all they had to do was rinse off. What the hell is this about I thought? We only got three minutes to shower? As if waiting on that line wasn't bad enough, we had to rush a shower every other day! There I was on that line with my towel around me waiting my turn with half naked men before me! The guy ahead of me had two small round scars as if someone had shot him in the back. I thank God that never happened to me!

As the inmates before me went into the shower, the sergeant yelled. "Soap on!"

Huh I thought? Soap on? What the hell was going on?

A minute later he yelled out. "Soap off!"

After about another minute he yelled loud. "Get out!" He made sure the group before me got out and then shouted. "Next group take it in!"

What a way to take a shower I thought. By the time I made it in, I hurried to get off my boxers and rushed under the water.

I heard him shout again… "Soap on!"

I scrubbed fast and rinsed off! I had realized in that moment how much I really missed home and to be able to take a bath in peace instead of this bullshit.

I heard him bellow. "Soap off!"

I'm going! I'm going, I remember thinking! I was finally done and began to dry myself off as fast as I could and that's when he told us to get the hell out and for the next group to take it in. I felt like I was in the military by the way he ordered us to get in and out. This was no way to live I thought. It was insanity at its best and I almost felt like I was in a mental hospital for scoundrels, deviates and lost souls. I hightailed it back to my cell and got dressed thinking of what a degrading experience that was! What a freaking nightmare!

It was the next day and I had signed up to make my call to Xanadoo. It was about 9 in the morning and there I was at the cell door waiting for them to call me. I so badly needed to call her and let her know all the craziness that's been going on. I was wishing they would hurry and call me because I had a pass to see a drug counselor at 9:30. Time ticked away and it was getting close and they still weren't calling me for my call. I saw all the phones were in use and I was hoping that I was next. A CO came down from the station bubble and confirmed something on his radio.

He yelled, "OK! Everyone take it in! Lock down!"

"What?" I snapped.

Dale was coming back from his bible study and my door popped opened. I rushed over to the CO!

"I have a pass to go see the counselor." I said.

He retorted, "I don't care what your pass says. You need to take it in!"

"I didn't get to make my phone call and it is important. Will I be able to make my call later?"

"Probably not. We are locked down now and not sure for how long."

I walked away feeling sick not being able to call my Goo. Stupid lockdowns! I went back in my cell and closed the cell door in despair.

Dale said comforting, "don't let it bother you. When I first got here I didn't talk to my wife for over a month."

"I just hate these lockdowns! I am not a part of their stupid issues!"

"It is what it is. There are some books on the shelf if you want to read. We may not be getting out for a day or two."

I sifted through the line of books and saw one called *"Enjoying Where You Are On The Way To Where You Are Going."* It was a spiritual book by Joyce Meyer. I went by the window with the book in my hand and looked out the window. It was a beautiful sunny summer day and there I was locked down. I saw the bees that were flying from flower to flower in the grass area between our block and the block next to us. I saw the birds hopping around searching for something to eat. I sighed in sadness then jumped up on my bunk and began reading. The book spoke all about finding happiness within ourselves if we believe.

Dale didn't seem to feel well and went over to the toilet.

"Are you ok?" I asked.

"I don't think so. I think I am going to be sick. Bare with me please."

Dale began to throw up and it wasn't pleasant to hear the gross sounds when someone is heaving. I found it hard to read while my cellmate was hunched over the metal bowl in our cell. He slowly got up and flushed the toilet. It was then I looked out of the cell and saw a bunch of CO's putting on rubber gloves. What the hell is this I thought? Apparently it was a shakedown. They went from cell to cell having the inmates come out with only their boxers and t-shirts on in handcuffs. They were searching the cells and tossing out mostly extra fruits and other contraband.

They made it to our cell and Dale and I had to strip one at a time and show we had nothing on us. Once the humiliating strip search was over we put on our boxers and t-shirts on. We had to back up to the door and put our hands out of the slot on the door so they could cuff us.

We were removed from the cell and placed standing face first against the wall as they searched through our cell. This is so stupid I thought. The nonsense that went on in the prison world was outrageously absurd. Really now? Who does this I thought again? As I stood there I tried to define the word "nonsense" in my mind over what was going on. Nonsense, baloney, idiotic, asinine, hooey, hogwash, stupid stuff, bullshit! All those words

243

applied to the situation I was facing as I looked at the wall before me. They got done wasting their time because Dale and I were just two men trying to do our time. Dale and I went back into our cell and got dressed.

They continued to search the rest of the cells and I had a feeling we would be locked down for a while. Dale still wasn't feeling very well so I jumped back on my bed and he started vomiting again. I felt terrible for the man. I went back down to see if someone was walking around to alert them of Dale's condition. A Sergeant walk by and I had told him what was going on. He looked down at Dale.

Dale looked up at him and said, "I'm not well!"

The Sergeant simply said, "you'll be eating soon."

He walked away uncaringly. What a jackass I thought.

Dale said, "don't worry, I'll be all right."

Dale got up and went to lie down. I continued reading the book and something stood out for me.

The book read: *"Keep your mind filled with happy, glad thoughts, and, as you trust God, He will take care of your problems."*

Dale got back up and continued to be sick as I tried to pretend it wasn't happening. The title seemed to have an interesting message for me. Enjoying where you are on the way to where you are going seemed easier said than done. Where I was at that particular moment was a classification penitentiary waiting for them to classify me. Where I was going next would be my home prison where I'd be until I make parole... if I make parole I thought frantically. I had no idea where they would place me but I had great fear it would be far away. I needed to be close to home so Xanadoo could visit me. I would never forgive myself if I was placed on the other end of the state and she got into a fatal accident driving hours just for me.

There were so many know it alls I had met so far being there and some say they place you close to home. Others said they take everyone from the west side of the state and place them on the east side and vice versa. How the hell can someone recover or have therapy if they place us far from home? Ironically the prison handbook encouraged visits from families and loved ones to support the inmates in the hopes they will be rehabilitated. It gave us hope and joy knowing we had those visits and I knew I felt detached from everything being far away from my true love.

The truth of the matter, I felt, was that the system really didn't care too much for us criminals and could put us away and toss the key. According to them we are the scum of the earth. We were men who made bad choices or had a bad upbringing and only knew survival. I had lived many days on the streets and knew many types of people who were troubled. Every story was similar and they all had some type of dysfunction that landed them where they were. My problem was that everything that went wrong in my life and most of the pain I endured was self-inflicted. I had become a product of my own undoing and it was time to fix that problem. I knew I deserved better!

Dale had gotten back up to puke some more and I was trying to be happy like the book I was reading told me. How was I able to find joy in myself when I was locked down away from Xanadoo? I was unable to call her because of the stupid shakedown. Those rushed showers and meals in the chow hall were a constant reminder of where I was. I had to wait a while before my commissary would come. I had no radio and no television, still. I was home sick and had nothing but my twisted thoughts. I wanted to be happy but found it hard with all that was going on and my cellmate constantly vomiting. I knew I had to trust God because there was no way I was going through all that for nothing. I felt in my spirit something good could come out of that horrible situation.

A month had past and I was out in the yard. It was all concrete with a basketball hoop and a few metal bars to work out. I was sitting near the fence gazing out at freedom. Outside the fence was a big tree that stood full of branches and leaves that swayed in the breeze. Behind it was a huge field where I could sometimes see the deer roam. The yard there was terrible and rather boring. Each block had its own little concrete yard that was separated by more fencing in a long row. There were so many prisoners that were playing basketball, handball, gambling with cards, but mostly just sitting under the hot sun, waiting to go to their home prison. I had been classified and was offered to go to boot camp. I turned it down because I knew that wasn't for me. I was way too light hearted to be in that kind of environment. Even though I had a drug charge, I was not recommended for any drug programs due to my low-test scores. What worried me was where

I would go in my final destination of a home jail, where I would spend time until parole or until I max out. I was told they could put me any where in the state. I tried to not let it bother me, but found that hard since I thought of Goo all the time, visiting me, having to travel long distances.

I had gotten to know quite a few of the guys who were waiting as I was to be classified. There was Hillbilly Bob, who had been in and out of prison since the late 70's! He really didn't say what for but he always maxed out his time because he hates parole. He told us that he had written the parole board each time he was incarcerated and told them to "Shove parole up their ass!" To be sure he didn't make parole, he made copies and sent one to each parole office in the entire state. His parole had been denied many times over due to "Negative Attitude".

There were three elderly men who seemed so nice and didn't belong in prison. Mark, who was 65, a Christian, was there for some kind of sex offense. He was given a 15 - 30 year condemnation for a crime he would not tell me much about. Another mysterious sex crime like my cellmate. It really made me wonder.

Bill, who was 61, received a 5 – 10 year stretch. Apparently his granddaughter was online looking up some porn and came across some underage sex sites. Since it was his computer, and the fact that his granddaughter was underage, he had to take responsibility for it. He had never been in trouble with the law and this was his first summer away from his family.

Unless there was more Bill didn't tell me, I found that highly unfair! But God only knows what really happened.

There was Rudy, who was a shocking 88 years old, in addition to being married to a 32-year-old woman! He also was accused of a sex crime, which he would not elaborate on, at 88 years old, looking at the rest of his life in prison.

All were Christians, in one form or another, and I couldn't understand why so many Christians were accused of those crazy sex felonies? Have they been suppressed that much in their belief that the beast within came out? Holding in all that desire growing up, having a belief pushed on them, scaring the hell out of them. They probably didn't get to experience the sweet things I did with females as a teenager and into my twenties. Being married to one woman all their lives could have also created a root cause of why they lashed out in a sexual way. I wasn't there to judge so I just acted casual with everyone.

There was Jess who was around 40 years old. He was there for burglary of his own house. I couldn't understand how someone gets arrested for robbing their own home. He had explained that his ex-wife was living there and he broke in to get some of his old things and got caught. Apparently his ex-wife had a restraining order against him and was ordered to not be in a certain distant.

I met a guy who I called "The Long Hair" due to his heavy metal long hairstyle. He was 30 years old and had been in and out of prison both state and federal, mostly for gun and drug charges. Not your ordinary small time guy, this guy had trunk loads of guns and pounds of drugs! The Long Hair had told me I certainly was not a person who belonged in prison.

"What are you doing here?" He had asked me when we first met.

He told me I was a spectacular guy and I would do fine there. He always told me to watch my company since, yet again, the sex offenders seemed to have gravitated to me. I was a bit of a social butterfly and got along with just about everyone but I didn't want to always be around them because that falls on me. Other inmates may think I was a toucher to. I didn't need that! I was just too nice to be mean to anyone.

I tried to get involved with what the penal complex had to offer. I began to go to Sunday services and attended bible studies a couple of times a week. It was good to get out of the cell and see what God may have had to tell me. In no way was I a Christian, or had a certain religion, but I believed in living life the way Jesus did. I was spiritual along with believing I could be the change the world needed and if we all worked on that concept the world would be a better place. There really wouldn't be much need for that prison nonsense and the madness that came with being human! But like all humans, I was not perfect and tried to be the best I could even though I was flawed.

I met this fat guy named Big John who I called Fat Body. He weighted close to 400lbs and all he thought about was Eat! When he would lay on his back in the yard, his stomach was so fat that if you tapped it it would sway like the ocean. Since he didn't have much money for commissary, he made deals with too many of the wrong guys. He had owed someone a honey bun for a long time and Fat Body, one day in the yard, had returned a honey bun to someone else. The other guy he owed didn't take to kindly to that.

"Where's my honey bun you fat bastard?" He asked Fat Body.

Before he could answer the guy started beating Fat Body up! They both ended up in the hole over a honey bun. A honey bun! I had overheard others say they would risk going to the bucket over a .28-cent soup. The mentality in prison was so grossly pessimistic, so incredibly tainted that often guys went to the hole over stupid stuff that won't matter latter on.

"Fuck that shit! I'll go to the hole if I have to. That fucker owes me a soup and it's been two weeks now…" was a common saying there.

There were names like The Negotiator, Old G, Train Wreck, Flavor and Pee Wee. The guys called me Doc due to my crime. The sun beat down on me in that overheated concrete yard and I hated being stuck there. I often fantasized they would call my name and tell me to pack it up, that I was going home. I pretended I would see Xanadoo walking in the yard rushing up to hug and kiss me. She would take my hand and tell me, "Let's Go Home!" I was still home sick and Xanadoo said she would be visiting me in a week. I couldn't wait to see her again!

I continued to sit and stare out into the open land that was taunting me. Freedom was only a hop and a jump over that tall fence with tons of barbwire. Escape wasn't on my to do list and if someone were to try and escape, it would be an automatic 5 years or so added on. Young Beam sat down next to me and shared a cigarette. He was only 20 years old and was sentenced to a 1 to 2 year stint for having sex with an underage female around 15 or so. Once again the law had gotten a young male for doing what was normal, human nature. It was consensual sex, not rape, and I felt he didn't belong there. Really now, the kid looked like he was 15 himself! I sat along side the gang I got to know but I knew it would be soon that we would be separated. Where I was certainly wasn't the place to get too close to anyone because it was only a temporary stop for us.

So many guys are in and out of that place so fast. The prison system was way overcrowded, which in a way, was good for me. I was told they want to get someone like me, with my petty crime, in and out of the system and I surely welcomed that! I just went with the flow the best I could until what was next would arrive.

It was a great day because my Goo was there to see me! Before I could go out into the visiting room, I had to get completely naked, run my hands through my hair, and raise my hands and arms up in front of the CO. I had to lift my penis and balls then turn around, bend over and cough as I spread my cheeks. I had to do a humiliating strip search and change into a brown jump suit. The idea was so nothing went out and nothing came back in. Really now! What am I going to smuggle out? Luckily I had learned the routine a few days before when my brother Rich came to see me.

I went out to the visiting room and told the CO I was ready for my visit. I waited and realized I had not seen my Goo face to face in months! I hadn't touched her in so long and I couldn't wait to be close to her again.

I looked up and saw Xanadoo walk in across the room looking sad and lost. The moment she laid eyes on me she started to cry and run in my direction. It was something out of a love story when the one you truly love comes running so happy to see you. In that moment, as she was coming toward me, I felt the love I hadn't felt in a long time. It was pure bliss and I had felt hope within me again. The CO had told her not to be running and she slowed down and landed in my arms. She cried like I never seen her cry before. She was breathing heavy and couldn't control her tears.

She said over her sniffle. "You don't know how long I waited to hold you like this!"

I knew what she meant, as I smelled her hair and ran my hands down her back. I had forgotten how good it was to feel her against my body. She looked up and I looked into her striking big blue eyes. I leaned in and we kissed for a moment, which felt like there was no one else around us. For that moment in time, I had forgotten I was in prison and was free back in my loves arms! I had about four or five good hours to spend with Xanadoo and I hoped it would last. We took a seat and she held my hand tightly.

She said, "you don't know how hard it has been without you at home! I just miss you so much! I got lost a couple times coming here but thank God I found it. I had to come see you!"

"How long did it take you to get here?" I asked.

"Well, I got lost so about 8 hours or so. I was so scared driving here but I knew that I needed to visit you. How is everything?" She looked intently at me. "Anyone bothering you?"

I smiled and assured her that I was fine. I said, "no worries Goo. Have you been getting my letters?"

"Yes! I love getting them!" She spoke happily. "They are getting me through this. You want something to eat or drink?"

"You don't know how gross the food is here! I want a cheeseburger so bad!"

She got up and went to the vending machines. I had to remain where I was. Inmates in the classification prison weren't allowed to go to the vending machines for whatever stupid reason. She looked so incredibly gorgeous as she faced away from me in the distance with her long brown hair that flowed down her back. In that moment I wondered why someone like her drove all this way just to see me? She was a successful person and never been in trouble in her life. She lived a clean and sober life... so why did she choose me? I couldn't understand why she didn't leave me once I got arrested.

She sat back down with some snacks and a Coke. I opened the soda and it tasted so good! As I drank down the cold sweet bubbly Coca-Cola, it reminded me of being young again. All those days being high made me forget the little things in life.

I asked, "why are you doing all this for me?"

She smiled and said, "I wasn't going to leave you in here. You didn't kill anyone ya know. You have an addiction and you needed help. I love you and believe in you. It's not forever."

"I just want to thank you for everything. I was able to get my commissary and I even got myself a radio. I know money is tight but you never once let me down since I had been here. I'm so sorry you have to put money you need on my books here."

"You need to have things. I'm happy to do it for you. How are the guards treating you?"

"Some of them are real jack offs! I'm like, we may be guilty of our crimes but some of these CO's are guilty of being assholes!"

She laughed! I looked around to make sure no one was looking. I snuck in a kiss even though we weren't supposed to. We were allowed a kiss and a hug upon arrival of our visit then again when our visit leaves. It had been way too long since I was able to touch and kiss the Goo. I kept sneaking kisses and touching her where I shouldn't have been. It was so nice to be able to do that again. She was enjoying it as she giggled each time I touched her. The CO at the desk called me up and I looked at Xanadoo in concern. I went up to the desk where the CO was.

He asked, "what are you doing?"

I said knowing he must have seen us. "What do you mean?"

"You see those cameras in the ceiling?" He pointed up and around.

I looked around and saw quite a few cameras watching our every move. I should have known better. I looked back at the CO in sorrow.

He said, "why don't you two sit over there so I can see you and make sure you behave yourself. I understand you are happy to see your loved one but there are rules and I don't want to terminate your visit early. If I catch you again, I will terminate your visit."

I said in relief. "Thank you for understanding. We will behave ourselves."

I tuned around and waved Xanadoo over to me. I told her we had to move our seating and told her what the CO had told me. We sat down at the seats closer to the CO's desk, like he requested and simply held hands, which we were allowed to do.

Xanadoo said, "it's so stupid that we can't kiss!"

"I know. But this is prison and we shouldn't forget that."

"Thank God he didn't terminate our visit! I would have been so upset if that happened! So tell me what's been going on."

I continued, "Rich came to see me a few days ago and he is approaching 50 years old already! I am starting to see that dash in my life. The dash we see on a tombstone that spans our life between birth and death. The time line that carries us through our existence has stretched far enough for me to see it like a long road. My oldest brother is starting to age and I wondered what the hell happened to the time? We were all growing up on Long Island and now he has a family that is growing up so fast! I will be 40 soon and feel I haven't done enough in my life. I don't feel I have much time left. Remember I always felt I will die at 50 and I see the timeline in my life is well past the halfway mark. Both of my brothers are successful and I fell off the grid so many times in my years! Now I am in prison! It seems the storms in my days never end and this time the storm that hit my life again is the worst of them all!"

"You have done a lot in your life ya know." She smiled and touched my arm. "You should be proud of what you have done. You took care of your mother. You did movies and plays. You published a novel. You were in a band playing the bass. You made it through so many things that I would never have been able to do. I don't know how your handling being in prison. I know I couldn't deal with it! It's not forever you know. We will get through this!"

At that moment we overheard on the radio they had on by the CO's desk, a new song by Gary Allan called *"Every Storm Runs Out Of Rain"*.

Xanadoo held my hand as the words spoke through the radio. "*So hold your head up and tell yourself that there's something more. Walk out that door… Go find a new rose, don't be afraid of the thorns… 'Cause we all have thorns. Just put your feet up to the edge, put your face to the wind. And when you fall back down, keep rememberin'… Every storm runs, runs out of rain. Just like every dark night turns into day. Every heartache will fade away. Just like every storm runs… run out of rain.*"

It was a moment of knowing everything would be all right. That inner glow rose up within my spirit again and for the first time in a long time I felt buoyant. It was true; every dark time in my life did turn into brighter days. All those heartaches I endured in my past I got over. As for the storm that I was in, I knew it would run out of pain. I had my Goo and she still loved me and that made a huge difference in the cyclone I was going through. Even though the time in prison felt like a lifetime, I knew it would soon pass and I could get myself back again.

The Periodical Midnight

It was well into the new century, a new millennium had begun and I was entwined into the darkness of my world. It was spring of 2001 and I was into a routine where I would put my mother to bed, go into my room and lose myself in mind-bending substances all night. Seeing my mother suffer with her M.S. had put a beating on me emotionally. I was sitting on my cozy comfy cushiony chair, my feet propped up on a footstool, watching TV with no lights on. To my right was my computer where I would later on fool around on AOL; connect with the outside world via technology, instead of working on my novel. I was high off a handful of painkillers, drinking my tenth beer. I was numb and higher than I had ever been in my life.

There I was sitting in the dark with the eerie glow off the television flickering around me... bent, high and twisted, watching old reruns, movies and chatting on the internet throughout the entire night.

I was getting a large amount of high dose Vicodin, which was Hydrocodone, a groovy painkiller from my mother's doctor. When I first started getting those from her doctor, I only took one a day. Then one became two over time... two became four... I needed more! In addition, I obtained my own doctor and was getting another high quantity of even better, stronger painkillers, Percocet, which was Oxycodone, plus Valium.

I was mixing Vicodin High Potency with Percocet. I found mixing a twelve pack of beer with Valium and the painkillers made a great cocktail. I felt relaxed, that inner glow in my chest and a warm comfy feeling ran through me. It was 2 in the morning on a dark Sunday night into early Monday morning and while most of the world was asleep, I was up deep into the hours of darkness, insanely shattered! Sunday evenings were my favorite since the TV shows I enjoyed the most came on during primetime television. I would celebrate with more than usual pill popping and lots of cold beer. I would get myself a New York style pizza with extra cheese and kick back in my darkened room until it was time to put my mother to bed.

When Sunday evening became early Monday morning, I would put on the channel that went off the air at 2 AM. I wondered who does that? Was there anyone else out there on the same mental frequency as I was on?

There I was waiting as the announcement said, *"This concludes our broadcast day."*

The station would go off the air and I was left with the color bar on the screen and a loud piercing *beeeeeeep*...

I would stare into the stripes of colors and let the shrilly noise carry me to a distant world of oblivion.

I often wondered what was behind that color bar and why that noise seemed to hypnotize me in a weird and wonderful way? I felt something was lurking in that abnormal plane of existence. Was it that entity I felt as a child or was it a demon? It felt like a dark shadow watching me, gazing into my mind and soul. Whatever that thing was, I felt it knew my thoughts and my desires. I had that funny feeling of madness stirring in my core, as I felt paralyzed in what became my life. I wanted to peel opened the curtain and expose that thing. I wanted to get up and change the channel but it was not easy when all I sensed that was on the television was a color bar.

The station wouldn't come back on the air until later that morning and I was wondering when I would come back to existence. I felt like my life had gone off the air of the world of the living, as the color bar tried to reach me like a prism of an outlying guiding light. The radiance of God had fallen further and further from my spirit and all that was left was a fading distorted beacon. I would later on around 4 or 5 in the morning shut everything down, lay in bed and try to sleep...

A faded daylight would creep through the closed blinds and between 8 and 10 in the morning would start out with my mother banging on the wall to alert me she needed to get out of bed. I would slowly slime out of bed feeling angry and meander with no emotion into her room. With no words, I would pull her out of bed and place her into the motorized scooter. I would guide her into the bathroom where I would pull her off and on to the toilet. We had a system of changing her adult diaper, though degrading, it had to be done. I made sure she was ok to clean herself up then I would get her coffee and donut ready in the kitchen.

Once that was all set, I'd come back in and get her off the toilet then carefully pull up her new and clean adult diaper. My mother was just as depressed as I was but I was dealing with it much differently.

I drifted back to my room with the blinds shut making it look dreary and grim all around my messy room and sloppy bed. I would pop a couple of Fioricets with Codeine that my mother's neurologist had given her because I had told them she was having migraines. It was a barbiturate combined with a mild narcotic painkiller meant for bad tension headaches. I was taking them to help me die in my mind as I fell back into my bed on those out of the ordinarily weird mornings.

Half asleep, I began losing grip within existence and what was my spiritual demise. I wasn't sure if I was dreaming or not but I felt someone or something crawling under my covers touching me and saying my name. I became paralyzed and no matter how hard I tried, I could not break free. My bizarre mind's eye and dreams bled into each other and I had an eerie mental delusion I was walking outside my old elementary school.

Clearly, I visualized the creepy way the extended part of the school looked. There was brown wood siding with undressed windows and short black metal stairs that were connected to each classroom. It was summer vacation and the classrooms were all abandoned so I went forth to sneak inside. I walked up one of the black metal stairs, opened the stiff metal door and the room had rows of school tables with chairs and gloomy gray all around. I noticed in the front row of the room a male teacher and a boy student doing some studying. They both looked at me with pale dead eyes and blank pasty faces as if they were caught in a world of personal death they couldn't escape. It was a frightening sight as they gazed upon me with there lifeless eyes.

The teacher spoke in a ghostly tone. *"Whooo Arrrre Yoooou?"*

In that moment, I turned and ran as fast as I could but found myself struggling to move! With all my strength, I tried to run but I couldn't! I felt a deep paralyzing sensation fill my entire soul. I started crawling and had to pull myself with my arms but wasn't making much progress, struggling to move. I closed my eyes and tried to escape the shrilly paranormal scene.

I had awoken from that day terror and was full of sweat feeling freaked out! What had become of me, I wondered, as I seeped out of bed around 2 in the afternoon. I went into the bathroom and took out a bottle of Hydrocodone Cough Syrup I had obtained through my mother's doctor along with the 10 mg Vicodin. I had told them she suffered from a bad cough but yet again it was for me. I downed a good amount just to get me moving. I felt a little numb in my face, my legs burned and ached.

I'd sit on the toilet for a while due to the pills slowing down my digestive system and read the TV Guide, which became my guide of the night for television. As I struggled to push out all the toxins and shit, I would gag from anxiety in anticipation for my well being, until the medication gave me just that. I would plan my television night to come then clean up. I would take a shower struggling to balance myself with a saddened face even though the drugs had taken my pain away.

Slowly coming out of the shower I impatiently rushed to dry off. After I put on my going nowhere, loser stay at home clothes, I went out to greet my mother, who sat in the living room, watching television on her scooter... all day... every day. We had been feeding off each other's negative energy for a while. She needed me as much as I needed her. She helped me with my financial requests as I helped her with her physical needs. I did all the shopping, cooking and cleaning and took her places she needed to go. We were always close and I missed the days when she was able to walk and be happy. It was ironic living in the sunshine state of Florida but consumed in bleak grim darkness. Out of all places to be living! I so longed for the cloudy, rainy, cold, dank days up north.

Around 5 PM, I prepared dinner for her and made sure she ate well. It was back to the bathroom for her change then we would just mope around the house. My mom in the living room on her scooter, watching TV and me isolated in my room. We watched the same sitcoms between 6 and 8. I did get her into to some of the super natural shows that came on primetime. One way we stayed connected and bonded. Even though she wasn't into supernatural shows, she watched it because she said nothing else was on. I also knew she watched them to be close to me because after the shows I'd come out and talk about it with her.

I related to some of the characters such as the television show Angel. It was about a vampire with a soul. An immortal who had to live with his dark past for eternity on earth. He was known in his evil days as the demon with the face of an angel. He was good and helped people but the beast remained within him regretting all those he killed before he was cursed with his own soul to feel the pain he caused. It would always be a part of him no matter what. I felt that darkness within my soul like I was part dark and part light. Part good and part evil unable to break away from the past being an immortal in my own mind. Every so often I would see and hear spiritual synchronicity work through those shows. Episodes that spoke to me as I was feeling low and thinking negative thoughts at just the right moments giving me a sense of hope. Like God was still there and I would be safe in the arms of my guiding spirit.

Around 8 pm, it was time to pop pills and drink some beer that I snuck in and hid from my mother. I had a menu filled with optional narcotics and I was able to pick and chose how high I wanted to get. Some nights were a Percocet night, with a side order of Valium, washing it down with several cold beers. Other nights were more laid back and I would pop some Vicodin with just a few beers and perhaps a Xanex. Then there were the weekends where I would just take a few of everything with a twelve pack of beer. I'd put my mother to bed around 11 pm and it was on for me. Chatting on AOL as I watched television with no lights on feeling good, high and in my own world.

Later in the night I would make myself a bacon egg and cheese on a kaiser roll just as I used to get when I was a kid living on Long Island. Feeling empty I often drifted back in time to my childhood. Old wounds and feelings would rise up on me and I would get higher and bask in my past.

I watched so many 1980's infomercials after midnight on the television well into the night. There I would be watching an infomercial on 80's music, completely twisted on drugs and alcohol, as if I were back in time feeling the memories. Each song that had its own reverberation and beat mesmerized me. Every instrument and note that was entwined merged into one symphony, recalling old feelings and reminiscences. The melody of music of my time released chemicals in my brain, which brought me aroused sensations of my formative years. At any given moment I was able to branch off and step into whichever memory I wanted to re-live. The gateway to my memorabilia was wide opened and the emotional journey was awe-inspiring and abundant. Most people my age were moving forward and there I was living backwards!

Every Friday I would go to the video store and rent a porno. It got to the point where the owner knew me by name. I desperately missed a woman's touch and it was the only way to feel connected, somewhat. It seemed that all of my addictions rose up on me and took me over. There was no escaping it. I had died in my mind and became a ghost to the living world. I needed to find out just how many dark twisted nights and weird eerie mornings that had been going on so I began a journal...

April 15th 2001

I felt not so good and gross today! I had a headache even though I took 10 mgs of Hydrocodone. Are all these drugs worth it? I have no energy and I get angry at the slightest things, punching things because shit don't go my way, feeling awful and getting annoyed at that! No exercise, anger towards women. This is a fucked up sickness and I need help! Why is it I haven't put a gun to my head and pulled the trigger yet? I know it could be worse. I could have cancer or MS, what my mother has. No! I just have a self-inflicting disease called addiction, obsession and self-pity. Sooner or later it will come to the point of hell and no more desire to live. I have moments of feeling like I am suffocating. Sick feeling in my head, gross feeling in my stomach. Gurgling and pinching in my intestines. Twisted in the mind. A smell of something dead lingers. A death smell as I feel like dying...? Please God help me!

4-22-01

Tonight I decided to binge on Percocet, beer and weed because the season finales of Buffy and Angel came on. I feel so comfortable and relaxed watching my favorite shows. I can't believe I'm also addicted to television! The funny thing was my mother had a strong craving for ice cream. Is she in touch with my addiction somehow? In touch with my dying spirit? On the bad side I had nothing but liquid poop and tonight I'm drinking more beer. I'm so weak! I drank at least a twelve pack of beer on top of 7 Percocets, 3 Vicodin, 3 Valiums, 1 Xanex, a bowl of weed and about 6 cigarettes. I'm all twisted and its time for me to go nigh nighs now. Good night with a swig of Vodka.

4-25-01

Went to the bar tonight with Key and the gang. Had to buy more Xanex from Andrea. Alcohol, Xanex, Vicodin, Weed, more Alcohol. Running away from the pain!

4-30-01

I'm high on so many painkillers and almost twelve beers since The X-Files began around 9PM. It's 1:30 in the morning now. I feel a lot of anger! I keeep punchinng meself in the faace! Alcohell is evil! I feel such anger and I can't even SpEfLLf...

Spell right! I'm going to go make a bacon egg and cheese on a roll now. I'll be right back.

I'm back. Doing these drugs is like asking Satan to slowly seize my soul. Rip my inner core out of my essence like ripping a skeleton out of a human body! Huh? Where did that visual come from? Yeah, I'm all twisted. The Devil could be writing this for me right now! I have no control! Oh God help me!

5-1-01

I'm stabbing things like my DVD cover. I don't remember doing that. Sooo wasted I shot out the street light outside the house with my air riffle that night I drank a lot. I stuck my 12-gage shotgun in the lake out back and pulled the trigger. The barrel came out looking like a pealed banana! It was something straight out of a Bugs Bunny cartoon. It was a true miracle I didn't blow my hand off! I didn't take the consideration that the water pressure would make it backfire! Someone or something is still watching over me because Key said that should have backfired and blew my hand off and that I was an idiot. I still can't explain how these miracles keep happening. All day I felt not well, slightly sick, gas pains, anxiety and an urge to cry. My body is saying stop! I have been having chest pains. Could be from all the freaking cheese I eat! It feels like heart pain. Maybe it's a heart blockage or just really bad gas. I am suppressing my feelings of being at home taking care of my suffering mother. All those suppressed feelings are recycling in the pits of my mind. I'm closer to hitting rock bottom!

5-3-01

The morning I said goodbye to my mother for my trip to Tampa, the look in her eyes was so sad. I needed to get away for a while. I hated leaving her and having Screwface rush in and out to take care of her. He always is drinking beer and my mother hates that! It's going to be hard when I have to move out and live my own life. We are both comfortable with the way we are living. I am also comfortable with the free life of drugs and isolation. So far this trip is great. I am in Fort Pierce at a cozy and comfy motel. I'm stoned, drinking beer, high on so many painkillers with only the television on. I talked to my oldest brother Rich and he is now back to drinking, as I am worse than ever. He had quit for a while but now he's back. I thought one of us had beaten the curse of addiction my father left us. Now I'm stuck in this motel wondering how any of us will beat the demon of addiction. Some days I see myself dying this way.

5-6-01

I'm working out again and I'm even writing a list of things I need to do. But I am still taking pills with alcohol. I hope this new start will get me off the drugs. I can get a job and get back involved in positive activities like the writers group I used to go to. I had sold most of my music equipment but I still have the guitars. I pray to God and the angels around me that I can find a new happiness soon. I know they can hear me, feel me and see what I am doing. Please forgive me for all I have done. I know I can stop with your help.

P.S. Don't tell the source of darkness, Lucifer, my plans to escape the curse he has put on me to destroy me.

6-12-01

I drugged hard tonight! This habit is hard to break because I feel too smooth, relaxed, free, just fantastic! I'm still

269

working out and I even took yoga. I went swimming and rode my bike feeling good again! Gotta go make some bacon now.

I took mom to the mall today but I was not happy being there. She loves to be taken to TJ Max and just tool around, looking and buying nice things. That makes her happy. But I am too impatient! Rushing her so I can come home and get high! She said she is feeling weaker and that the M.S. is bringing her to her knees! That's how I have been feeling about the drugs and alcohol! I'm watching a TV program about DNA. My DNA has problems! Screwface got a call from our aunt and we found out my uncle through marriage has died. My second cousin, who is only 16, got arrested again. My father's mother, my grandmother is dying. It reminds me how evil my father's side is! My mother's side, however, shows much good but weakness in fighting or defending evil... kinda... I don't know! I feel stuck in the middle, almost in a way like I am not even there. This leads me to think who the hell I really am? Can I get over this or am I stuck with it? I want to write again. Please God give me the strength to write again!

I am so comfortably high! I tried the heroin with plenty of beer! I am taking too much money from my handicapped mother again! Please forgive me. I wanted to change but I guess I am not ready yet. I had snorted one sac of heroin, drank 9 beers, and

270

smoked a bowl of krippy weed. Feeling a bit of a tummy gurgle, better stop the beer. One more please? I can't believe how high I am! I'm so high; I'm higher than high!

6-18-01

Gave mommy a shower with Screwface. I made yummy meatballs with spaghetti for mom and me. I watched "Clean and Sober". I tried to nap but couldn't so I masturbated. Went to Screwface's house and had a few beers on top of 4 Vicodin and a Xanex. Home now... it's 3 am...I drank 3 more beers with 3 more Vicodin. Put mommy to bed then smoked some heroin and took 2 Percocets with a Valium. I'm high watching Nik at Nite. Diff'rent Strokes was on, now I am watching Threes Company lost in my past.

6-22-01

Feeling the emptiness again. I finally accepted I am not a musician... yet I have a great ear and talent for music. Maybe it is my weak will that drains me of going further. I sold my 8-track recorder, effect processors and other stuff except my guitars. I have given up on making any more music.

6-27-01

3:30 am Wednesday morning. I failed twice now trying to make it to the writers group meeting. I smoked some weed on the way there with a tall boy of beer. I knew I wasn't going to make it to the bookstore. I have been taking it way too far with my *mother's money. I spent another $130 to see the dentist just to get more pills! It is now 3:41 in the morning and I just took a swig of 70 proof rum. It seems I have become addicted to the taste of poisonous sweets. Becoming numb again.*

7-20-01

I haven't drank any beers since Monday. It is now Thursday night. Three whole nights with no beer. I did take some painkillers to ease my pain. I'm drinking more water and eating better. Key's wife Angie came over to give me a massage. She has been going to school to become a masseuse and only charges me half price in her personal business. She told me I was the responsible one who helped her through her drug induced days. I was always the clean and sober one, helping others, now she is giving me advice. I watched "Pink Floyd The Wall" the movie and felt my life was like Pink's. He lost his father to the war as I lost my father to his war with alcohol.

These lyrics hit me: "Dad has flown across the ocean... Leaving just a memory... The snap shot in the family album... Daddy what else did you leave for me...? DADDY! WHAT'D YOU LEAVE BEHIND FOR ME...? All in all it was just another brick in the wall."

I feel the same way! He also had a teacher be mean to him like I did when I was in 1ˢᵗ grade. He was mocked for being an artist as I have been before. He had a sheltering mother just like me. Everything bad he went through put more and more bricks in

the wall that he built around him just like I have. I am in
wonderful seclusion here behind my own wall.

8-20-01

Well I finally did it. I went to the ER pretending I had bad
lower back pain. Ironically my cousin was there with his wife.
Her mother had burnt herself by spilling hot water on herself. Her
family comes in and they introduce me and all say hi out loud.
There were two black women whom I didn't know, saying hello to
me in good humor to everyone else saying hi to me. I felt like I
was in the spot light as I was faking an injury to get more pills.
My first visit to the ER had become interesting. The nurse called
me back and when I saw the doctor, a very pretty blonde haired
young woman, I told her my lies of overwhelming pain. She gave
me a wonderful shot of Demerol and turned me loose with a
Vicodin script. It is now 4:15 am and so far I have had a 75 mg
shot of Demerol, 13 beers, 10 Vicodin High Potency, 4 Valium, a
bowl of good weed and about 10 cigarettes. Only God knows why
I am still alive and functioning. Thank you Lord for being there to
watch over my sickening condition!

8-23-01

I did bad today! I took a triple dose of Hydrocodone
Cough Syrup as soon as I got up. I was high and ate some cheese
then had some meatloaf with my mother. I got a lot of gas now
feeling itchy plus my insides feel weird.

9-11-01

The World Trade Towers and the Pentagon had been destroyed this morning! Two hijacked planes crashed into the Twin Towers. I slime out of bed and dosed up like usual and there was a message from my brother, telling me to put on the news. Oh my God I thought when I saw what had happened! It seems the book of Revelation out of the Bible is coming true. All these horrible things are happening all around the world. I think the world needs me but I am lost in my own darkness. God please aid those who are suffering from this tragic day! If this is the beginning of the end, may You, Lord, forgive me of my sins! Please be there for my brothers and their family. Please give my mother a cure or take her home. Please God help me to cry and to be human again.

10-31-01

I was pure evil today! First I went to a different pain specialist as I still go to my current pain-managing doctor who gives me the Percocets. I told him my condition and that I was in a lot of pain. When I asked for some pain meds he said, "No!" I thought, Screw him! I then went to the dentist and had to wait, telling them I had an emergency. She was really nice and gave me a script for some Vicodin ES. Extra Strength! My mother was waiting for me to come home so we can hand out candy to the kids for Halloween but my pills had to come first. I had to wait again to get the script filled and by the time I got home, it was dark. Screwface yelled at me wondering what the hell I was doing,

wasting all that time just for a few pills, knowing I have a bonny
boat load of narcotics in my pig sty of a bedroom. I really oughta
start cleaning my room. I have stuffed so much crap under my bed
that I cannot push anymore under there. It had overflowed under
there with empty beer cans, dirty clothes, and other garbage! Any
hootinadoodle... We had to rush my mother to get dressed then
wheeled her outside to hand out the candy. I have sunk really low.

11-21-01

I just got done watching "Funny Farm." I want that life so
bad! Oh to have a pretty wife, live in the country and be a
successful writer. It hurts me so bad that I can't due to my
problem. I am still stuck in my past and I am doing so many
stupid things!

All right, let's get down to brass tax. Tonight is brought to
you in part by 12 Percocets, 6 Vicodin, 4 Valium, 2 Xanex and 14
beers! I am lost in a strange, lonely, perilous but alluring world.
I keep seeing stop signs when I'm out driving every time I think
about getting high. Music seems to be talking to me. Still a good
combination of drugs and music make the drive feel like a dream.

12-02-01

I feel sick, sore throat, bloated feeling, my intestines are all
twisted because I drank myself stupid again! Gas bubbles inside
me. Terrible aches all over. I have that chest pain again! I'm 27
years old. I shouldn't be feeling like this!

I know I have many gifts. Key's old Rotweiler was chemically insane, kind of like me. No one could go near that dog but me. She would bark and snip at anyone who got close. I was the only one who could play rough with her. Before that, when I delivered office supplies, I opened the gate to a resident and this huge dog came charging at me. I stood still with no fear streaming from me. The dog stopped and sniffed me so I began petting him. The lady who opened the door to her house said, "Oh my God! That is an attack dog! I do not know why he hasn't attacked you. You better get out of there as calmly as you can."

I have always been good with animals but to stop an attack dog like that and to wrestle with an insane Rotweiler? I just want to say Lord is that I still care about the earth and all the animals. My wish for tonight God is to please see me through another day.

1-10-02

Here come the messages from above. I turn the key to my car after leaving Screwface's house in his driveway. A commercial for alcoholism comes on as I forgot the two beers he gave me to take home. I of course went back and got them. The other message came when my mother was cleaning up in the bathroom. I was waiting for her and on the TV they were talking about drug addiction and how people get arrested. They mentioned sometimes people get arrested to save them from complete destruction of themselves. I can't stop and I pray I never go to jail! I have to take care of my mother! Was that a sign? This is a test and I am failing! Will I ever beat this demon? Evil never dies; it always comes back like a never-ending battle. Is there ever-complete freedom? Maybe that's part of the circle of life. We win then we lose.

3-12-02

My mom helped me buy a brand new 2002 Mustang GT. I made it seem my old V-6 Mustang was having problems. I don't deserve it but it is beautiful! Candy red exterior, black leather interior and a V-8 this time! Even with a new car I still feel empty. Gotta go get some more beer now.

6-25-02

I binged a lot of the cocaine last night! I went to the bar and met up with this girl who sold it. I started snorting the cocaine around 9 pm along with some beer and 4 Percocets. After I put my mother to bed I put in a porno and lay on my bed doing line after line. I hit the bottle of rum really hard trying to balance myself out. Before I knew it, I saw it was light outside and there I was on my bed still snorting up lines feeling shaky. I took a total of 14 Vicodin HP, 6 Valium, and a bottle of rum! Even though I saw the daylight I kept binging! It was like I knew a new day had begun and the night was over but I couldn't control myself! I didn't want it to end! By the time I was done it was 11 in the morning! I took a shower shaking and sweating with my heart pounding. I got my mother out of bed and tried to eat some cereal but my throat was closed from all the coke. My nose was all clogged up and I felt like shit! How I survived that night I will never know. It was a miracle I didn't end up in the hospital or dead!

8-9-02

This will be my last entry in this freaking journal! I got arrested last night and had a horrible experience waiting to be bailed out in jail. Last night I wanted to get some coke so I went down to the bar and got a gram. Came home and wanted more for the night. I told my mother I would be right back and that I was going to the store. I went to the bar and there that girl was. I sat next to her and there was a dude on the other side staring her down. We went to her car and I bought another gram. I should have just gone home but no, I wanted to try and get laid! I snorted some coke off her tits and waited to see if I could get into her pants. Suddenly an undercover cop car pulls up next to us and two detectives come out and shine the light on us. We were pulled out and they knew she was a coke dealer. They searched me and luckily they didn't find the gram I had in my side pocket. As I waited I thought of my mother and wanted to go home. They searched me again and found it. He cuffed me immediately and I begged them to please let me go. I had to put my mother to bed but they didn't care. I thought I was going to be sick the whole time I sat in jail. Screwface had to get money from my mother and bail me out. My mother was very disappointed. It is now 3 AM and even after being arrested I still snorted up the coke I had. I took 15 Percocets, 5 Valium and 16 beers! I am so lost! Dying inside! Please God! Help me!

The Mid Summer Transfer

I knew my time was drawing near to check out of that Mickey Mouse hell camp. It was early August and so far another prediction of my prison experience had arrived. I tried to call Xanadoo and the moment I noticed my phone account had been disconnected, I knew I was being transferred to what would become my home prison. The guys I got to know, the ones that were left, said they would really miss me. Jess told me he wasn't as sad when the others got transferred as he was for me having to leave. I guess I had been the light like my Goo said I could be. Even though I was there less than two months, I became close to the gang of new friends. It was 4:30 in the morning and I had given Dale a hug goodbye and wished him luck on beating his case, even though something in me felt he was guilty. I could just sense he did something disgusting, most likely to a little girl. It creped me out some days picturing him doing something sick and evil like that.

I had to sit down in the day room as the CO's waited to have us called over. The biggest fear I had was being sent to the east side of the state, which was way too far from home. Some of the guys told me the buses ran east and other's told me they go west. I needed to go west so I could be close to Xanadoo. I couldn't bear it anymore! I guess I would have to accept the fact that I was going to the furthest prison from home.

My inner swine was all over that fear and told me I didn't deserve to be close to home. My heart was palpitating beneath my chest as the voices in my head told me how doomed I was.

I silently said in my head. "Shut up!"

The sum bitch wouldn't leave me be!

I repeated. "Oh, I can't believe you don't Shut Up!"

We were finally called to be escorted down to where they get us ready for the bus ride. When we all walked outside it was still dark. The air was muggy and there was a stench of skunk all around which reminded me of the aroma of cannabis. Once again I got torn out of a place where I made some friends. I would have to readjust all over again. We got to the block where there were about 20 guys sitting at the tables awaiting their new destination.

I lined up with a few others and awaited their command for us to be seated. I still felt my heart jumping under my chest. I hated not knowing where I was going. I kept trying to reason with myself that everything would be ok but the dark half of me kept placing twisted thoughts in my head.

"Xanadoo is going to die in a car accident and it will be your fault you loser. Way to go! You single handedly wiped out a great successful woman off the planet!"

I would have to find a way to make it work where Goo would only see me every other month or so. There were brown paper bags with names on them lined up on the table and we were told to find our name and have a seat. I sat down where I read my name on the bag that was for me.

The CO announced. "Ok, on your bag will be the home prison you will be going to. Inside the bag you will find the paper work of your property you all have packed up yesterday."

I looked on my bag and saw three letters of the prison I was going to. I wasn't sure of the name so I looked around to see if anyone else had the same thing. I glanced at the others and saw they were all going west. Someone told me the letters was a prison east. I knew it! Why was everyone else going west but me? It wasn't fair damn it! I was so upset I wanted to punch the table and flip it over. My thoughts of being a god arose. I would stand up and blast lighting out of my hands and knock the CO's on their ass! I would lift my hands up and discharge tremendous power of lighting. It would fiercely surge like a wild storm of electricity as everyone would scatter and run for their lives! I would blow the block to shit as the building begins to collapse and debris crumbles all around. I would then teleport the hell outta there in a radiant display!

I came back to my reality when the CO said what the letters I had stood for. My heart sank when I learned it was a prison only an hour away from Xanadoo! For a moment I couldn't believe it! God had granted me a blessing by sending me to the penal complex closest to where I lived! I smiled in such relief I had tingles run through me. All that time I had thought I was going to be hours from home. All that torturous thinking for nothing! My alter ego had nothing to say. I felt he was smiling knowing he had me worry all that time for nothing. The new worry that entered my mind was what kind of penitentiary was it? I asked one of the CO's but he gave me a derogatory response.

"Heard nothing but good things. A fine prison! You'll fit in perfectly." He spoke as he walked on like he knew nothing.

I sat there looking stupid, still wondering what kind of prison it was. We were all moved to the intake section of the prison where we had to remove all our blues and strip naked again. The whole routine search had to be conducted. We were left in our boxers and t-shirts again and were placed in a holding cell where they had a huge pile of white jump suits for the ride. Not this again I thought. Not the best idea to have inmate's press and rush through a pile of jumpsuits for their size. We wanted to get the hell out of there! Everyone scurried through and though it was hard to find the right size for most of us, we all slipped into the jump suits. Mine was a little baggy but what could I do. We lined up by the cell door and the Sergeant came over with a clipboard and started running off names. Once I heard mine, I stepped out and that's when they put the chains on me. Shackles around my

283

legs, a heavy belt around my waist, and my hands in the cuffs attached to it. They had to lock us all up and put the silly black box on us between our wrists.

Like a herd of cattle, we were escorted to the prison bus in their huge garage. One at a time we all had to carefully step up and take a seat. I was in anticipation hoping I would get a window seat again like before. I got on board and saw a window seat opened and took it immediately!

Oh thank God, I thought!

I needed that seat to be able to peer out at what freedom still existed to me. To admire the world around me for the ride. I often wondered about Andy and how he was doing. I had seen him a few times when I went to church and though I couldn't talk to him, we would use signs to let each other know we were doing ok. The bus was loaded and as usual there was always a few from the hole being placed in the cage in the front of the bus. Apparently the hole must have been over crowded because they could not fit everyone in the cages.

There was this tall goofy guy with a funny smile on his face, in an orange jump suit, representing he was straight out of the bucket.

The CO said to him, "as long as you behave yourself, you can sit here and not in the cage."

The name "Happy" came to my mind, because that's what he looked like. He appeared as a happy goofy guy being transferred from one Restrictive Housing Unit, "The Hole", to another. I looked out of the window and saw the CO's running the mirrors under the bus making sure there was nothing suspicious on board. They started the prison bus and a CO with a shotgun went to the back. Once again I heard the cock of the gun. The big security door opened and in ushered the morning sunlight. It gleamed bright, I had to cover my eyes for a moment. We pulled out and it was such a beautiful day and there I was again in chains on a bus to my home reformatory. I had overheard some inmates talking about the place I was en route for and it didn't sound good.

I said to them, "hey, I'm going there. What's that prison like?"

One guy said to me, "yo son, that place is crazy! It is the worst prison in the whole freaking state! It is a maximum security joint and a lot of shit goes down there!"

"What kind of shit?"

"Stabbings, fights, it's just crazy there yo! Even the CO's get stabbed up! Yo son, if your going there I wish you luck! I'm just glad I'm not the one going!"

I turned and looked out of the window at the passing landscape of the summer. I felt a grim feeling rise within me and my heart began to pulsate again! Out of all the prisons in the state, they were sending me to a maximum state facility? What the hell was wrong with the DOC I thought intently? I was a low level inmate with a petty nonviolent crime and a short amount of time! My alter self-image began to put a beating on my mind again! I began thinking the worst and apprehension grew in me. I didn't belong in a place like that! I should have been sent to a low level facility where I could better myself.

I saw myself in a darken cell with a few huge burly inmates. I saw them beating me into submission then gang raping me! A blade would slowly penetrate my inner organs and pain would shoot everywhere in my body. I'd lie on the floor bleeding, as they'd stomp on my skull with their boots making it crack open and have my brain slowly oozes out into a grisly mess!

I stopped thinking for a moment and told myself to get a grip.

"Yeah," I told myself. "Just sit back and enjoy the ride for now."

As I sat looking out into the distant mountains, I couldn't help but continue to worry about where I was going. I had the fear recycling within my being and I couldn't seem to shake it. My enemy was attacking me and I couldn't seem to escape it. I just wanted the power to destroy the enemy once and for all but I couldn't. I felt weak. At that moment the CO's turned up the radio and Pat Benatar was rocking out *"Invincible"*.

"We can't afford to be innocent. Stand up and face the enemy. It's a do or die situation… We will be invincible! And with the power of conviction there is no sacrifice. It's a do or die situation… We will be invincible!"

I felt the angelic guide watching over me delivering another message. I know I must stand and face my enemy. The situation I was in could not be changed. I had to face it head on because I had no other choice. I would have to tap into the power of certainty and move forward knowing I could not give up or give in to the mess I made for myself. I would have to conquer the path

I was on. Still… I worried about where I was going. Frightening thoughts continued to enter my mind and I was getting overwhelmed!

As my fear tormented me, I continued to gaze out of the window, seeing all the beautiful trees, mountains and meadows. The next song that sang through the speakers above me, into my spirit, was from Queensryche. It was a peaceful song called *"Silent Lucidity"*.

The lyrics that spoke to me were, *"I will be watching over you. I am gonna help you see it through. I will protect you in the night. I am smiling next to you in silent lucidity."*

Wow I thought! That song had spoken to me before when I was homeless. I felt Divinity had a great purpose for me and would have a protector be my spiritual guide and protect me from any harm in the physical realm. I felt it like a silent guardian that was with me during that whole incarcerated occurrence.

The music went on pouring into my soul. *"If you open your mind for me you won't rely on open eyes to see. The walls you built within come tumbling down and a new world will begin. Living twice at once you learn you're safe from pain in the dream domain a soul set free to fly. A round trip journey in your head. Master of illusion, can you realize? Your dream's alive, you can be the guide but… I will be watching over you. I am gonna help you see it through. I will protect you in the night. I am smiling next to you…"*

I developed that inner glow in my chest as I looked intently out at the blue sky and the sunlight that shone all around shimmering off the passing countryside. I felt like I was flying alive in a dream in that moment as I saw all the beauty that was just out of my reach. Free from all pain and being reminded that my dream was still alive within me and I could still be the guide to those in need out there. The whole prison experience was nothing more than a round trip spiritual journey connected to my own reality. I remembered it wasn't forever and I would return home and allow the walls that I have built up within me tumble down and be free. All I had to do was open myself to the guide that was with me and know the power that was watching over me was clearly invincible.

We arrived at the halfway point, a penal complex where they distribute us all to our home prison. There were about five buses ahead of us and I figured it would be a little while. Each bus had to pass through the gate, one by one. They close the gate and check to make sure everything is safe then unloads the inmates. I couldn't believe how many inmates had to go through that. Apparently it was an every day thing the system does. Life could be so obscure, so dreadfully impossible to deem existence could be so cruel. All those men being shuffled around, taken away from their home, families and loved ones, only to be placed into an overloaded penitentiary system. What the hell was it all for I often asked myself?

There were a couple of inmates chatting ahead of me and I saw Happy in the front row turning around and trying to get in the conversation. He kept smiling at them in his goofy way and one of the guys looked at him.

He said, "yo dude? Why do you keep looking back at us?"

Happy said, "I was just getting a kick out of what you all were saying."

The guy paused for a couple of seconds. "Why are you here?"

"I broke into a house." Happy replied with a silly smirk.

"Burglary?"

"No. I stole a car."

The guy shook his head and said, "how the hell do you break into a house to steal a car? Was it in the driveway?"

Happy said, "yeah."

"Did you have the keys? Did you know how to get the car going?"

"Yeah."

"Dude!" He says in disbelief. "You just said you broke into a house."

"Huh?"

"What was wrong with what you just said?" The guy shook his head and grumbled. "You told me you are here for a burglary chare. "

"I am."

"How did they catch you?"

Happy took a second then smiled and said, "I totaled the car. I rolled the car down a steep hill and the cops showed up." He continued to have that silly grin on his happy face. He gone on with saying… "They had to help me get out."

"That makes no sense! Do you realize what you're sayin?"

Happy stared blankly…

The guy continued. "What kind of drugs do you do?"

"I don't do drugs."

The guy retorted in shock. "You never did drugs? I find that hard to believe! Yo, you got some issues. I can see why you were in the hole! They probably took one look at you and told you to pack it up. You're going to RHU. You will be going directly to the hole when you get to your home jail. You do know that right?"

Happy replied in a sad tone, "but I don't want to go to the hole."

He laughed a little and said, "you better get used to it son. I can see you doing your entire bid in the bucket. Now do me a favor and turn around and don't talk to me anymore."

I couldn't help but laugh to myself even though I felt bad for Happy. He was just a simple guy trying to fit in but what he said didn't make sense. He stole a car but is in here for a felony B&E… he… uh… hmmm… I don't know.

The buses moved up and it was finally our turn to be let in the gate and for them to check out the bus. One by one we all got off the bus. It was a little difficult stepping down due to the freaking chains they had on our ankles. When we got inside the intake block, I saw there were quite a few cells that had the name of the prisons all over the state above the doors. It was where we had to find our prison and go into that cell and wait. They unchained us and for some reason they couldn't remove the cuffs off a few inmates. The CO's had to get bolt cutters and cut them loose. Wow I thought!

We all stripped down again and had to stand there in our underwear. They announced for us to find our prison above the chamber doors and go inside. I went into the one that had my prison name and waited. They gave us a bagged lunch and as I ate I viewed out of the cell door at all the prisoners that were stuffed in all the cells. All those faces peering out the cell windows, wondering when they would be taken to their home prison. It reminded me of an overstuffed lobster tank waiting to be boiled alive in the system. It was so insane, so asinine to see that part of reality. Was all that madness necessary?

I couldn't get over the fact of all the men's lives just removed from society so the system could hold us hostage for so many petty crimes. Unfortunately there are laws to follow and all of us had broken that. I did believe that many deserved to be locked up but there were many that just did not belong in the chaos of the DOC. Still seeing the rather large number of those men made me realize it was just a waste of life to be there and a damn disgrace. I hated being in a holding cell. There were about seven of us in the cell I was in, the smallest amount thank God, just waiting.

There was this older man around 60 years old standing next to me. He was sitting next to me in silence on the prison bus I remembered. He never spoke a word as I was in my own world, hypnotized, gazing out of the window at the dazzling day.

He looked at me and said, "Don't let what those guys said to you bother you. That prison isn't all that bad. I was there for a while and now I'm going back. It is a bad prison but it is what you make of it. As long as you're cool you won't have any problems. I didn't."

"Thanks. What's your name?" I asked.

"Bill."

I introduced myself and asked. "What are you in for?"

"It's something I rather not talk about here. Basically, I have life in prison."

"You got life?"

"Well, I got seven 10 to 20 year sentences plus a 1-2. I'm 61 years old now. I won't make parole until I'm about 140 years old! Come on now. No one lives that long. So, I made arrangements with the prison to be cremated when I die."

I couldn't believe he got all those stints together! I thought that 70 to 140 years was more than enough. Why bother with the 1-2 year stretch I thought. Just like one man I heard got a life sentence plus a thousand years. Really now! Was the thousand years necessary? I would not know what I would do if I knew I was going to die in prison. To only know that for the rest of my days would be the madness of the DOC. I think I would have to kill myself! I felt sorry for Bill but it gave me a sensation of hope and gratefulness not to have life in prison. I wasn't sure what he did and whatever it was I was sure he had to regret that.

Two CO's came to our cell and told us to get dressed. They gave us white jump suits again. They seemed nice and we were all brought out and chained up all over again. We had to follow them out where I saw a lot of prison buses loading up all the inmates' boxes. There was only one regular van that had windows with a trailer and to my surprise it was en route for my home prison. It was considered the limo version of the penal transportation system. One by one they got us on board then it was back on the road. The seats were cushy and much more comfortable than the hard seats on the bus and again, I got a window seat. The CO's put on the AC and put on some music. I looked out of the window and felt safe within myself.

The backcountry roads were peaceful and I felt myself getting closer to home. I was slowly returning back to the area I knew.

I looked up and read a passing billboard: *"Welcome Back To The Area."*

Wow I thought! Synchronicity was always around me and I still couldn't figure that out. Why? How...? I just smiled knowing it was the Divine welcoming me back to the familiar parts of the land. I tried to not let in my adversary again. I didn't need to hear any more gibberish he had to tell me. I believed in what Bill had told me. It would be what I make of it. I wasn't a bad ass or a troublemaker. I felt good that I was close to home and I couldn't wait to see Goo again. I just leaned back and enjoyed the scenery and the ride. I knew it would be soon that the unknown that lie ahead of me would begin.

There it was as I peered out of the window. I saw a long fence wrapped in barbwire as the van pulled up to the gate. The prison seemed fairly new and the grounds were immense. A wide and long area of green grass was between the fence and the prison. All I saw were a few bay doors and docks with a concrete lot. It was quiet and there wasn't a soul in sight. This must have been shipping and receiving. Apparently for humans too. After they checked the van, we pulled in and they parked by a side door. There was really nothing about that place that seemed intimidating. It seemed to be calm but I was sure that would all change once we got deep into the pits of that structure. We were escorted inside and I noticed the intake block was freshly painted and smelled new. There was a tall wooden counter that was in a huge square where the CO's checked us in. There were several cells that encircled the CO station. They unchained us and while they were unlocking me I wondered why I was at that place.

I asked the CO, "I'm a level two. Why am I maximum security prison?"

He said, "do you live close by?

"Yeah, about an hour north."

"How much time do you have?"

"18 months minimum."

"They must want you close to home, especially with a short timer."

I was freed from those awful manacles and went into a holding cell with the others from the van. I tried to act cool as I wondered what was next. My name was called and I went in to see the nurse first. She had asked me some medical questions and I told her that I was having heart palpitations and would like to get it checked out. I gave her all of my medical history then went back out in the hall. I was called into see the counselor next. I walked inside a small office where there was a man at his desk.

The man said, "how ya doing?"

I sat down and replied, "good."

"Good… I am one of the counselors here. Just going to ask you a few questions." He gathered himself as he typed into his computer. "Are you part of any gangs?"

I smiled and said, "no."

"Do you have a preference of the kind of company you wish to be celled up with?"

"Someone like me," I said.

"Caucasian! Great!" He chuckled.

"That's not really what I meant. I was referring to someone who is laid back and is just here to do their time like me."

"That's ok."

"Is this really a bad prison?"

He stared blankly for a moment. He took a deep breath and said to me. "This is a maximum state prison and yes, there are a lot of problems here. Let me ask you this. Are you a sex offender?

"No."

"That's good." He smiled. "Do you gamble?"

"No."

"And you're not in a gang, so I say you will be ok here. Just mind your own business and don't get involved in the drama that goes on here. Someone like you will probably end up on the honor block where you will have more privileges with other short timers."

"Why do you think I am here?" I had to ask someone else.

"Not really sure. They must of needed some level two's for our outside work program." He typed more into his computer. "Ok, let me ask you this. Are you in fear of being sexually assaulted?"

"Well I wasn't until now."

He laughed then typed in his notes. He looked through his computer and seemed puzzled. He said, "no programs to do?"

"They didn't recommend anything for me."

"Wow. Even with your drug charge huh? I guess that's a good thing." He typed some more into his computer. "Well, we are going to put you in B block. You can get your stuff from the CO's and they will tell you where to go. Good luck!"

I went out to the CO's desk and he told me to go around and get my browns. I walked up to where there was an inmate in browns at a big door. There was a very large room where they had all the prison clothes for us newcomers. He asked me what my size was and I told him. I had to give my name and inmate number for them to burn it on my browns. After a few minutes, he placed down on the counter three brown pants, three brown shirts, a brown spring jacket, a heavy brown coat, a brown winter cap and a brown baseball hat.

"Do you need any whites?" He asked me.

"Sure... Why not." I said remembering the whites I had were old.

He gave me three white boxers and three white t-shirts. I grabbed all my new garments and went to change. As I slipped into that crazy prison costume I couldn't believe all that I was just a freaking number! It felt weird to be dressing up in those silly outfits but what choice did I have? I went back out and was told to grab a pushcart. There was a plastic mattress with my name and number on it and I had to put it on the cart along with my boxes that got transferred over with me. I had a bag of sheets, a blanket and a pillow. Next, I was instructed to head out the doors, down the hallway and out into hysterical nothingness. As I pushed the cart, I felt I was erased off the grid of humanity. I was in a sphere where I sensed I had no name, no purpose and no longer able to live freely. I was property of the state and restrained within the barriers of their confinement.

When I stepped outside into the core of the prison, I took a good look around. There were sidewalks that stretched to all parts of the grounds. A few high fences, along with barbwire, strung across the tops with gates that were checkpoints to stop at. Two high towers occupied a couple of CO's that had a bird's eye view of everything. The prison had separate gray concrete buildings that were the blocks. Long slit vertical style windows were what we had to look out of stretched along on two levels. I pushed my way forward and felt lost. I asked for directions to my block. I was told to pass through the first checkpoint. Simply push the button and they buzz me in.

I did just that and continued forth hearing the gate slam behind me. To my left was the education building and another block that was separate. To my right was a small field of grass and a block that reflected the sunlight. Above me was clear blue sky with a few buzzards flying around. Straight ahead of me encircled from the blocks, a concrete loop with a guard station in the middle that engulfed me as I approached another gate that was opened.

There were four blocks that surrounded me and all of them had another gate to pass through. In the middle was a small hut where the CO's buzzed us in. The gate to my block slowly opened, making that dreadful scraping noise! I felt ill as I entered onto what was the concrete yard. With the exception of the metal gate, the rest of the yard was incased with a tall concrete wall and a layer of barbwire. I was getting sick seeing all that razor wire everywhere I had been. There were some weight machines, tables and two basketball nets. Those long narrow windows looked creepy, as I felt some sinister inmate who wanted to plot my demise was watching me. I approached the door and once again had to be buzzed in. I opened it and pulled my cart into the vestibule. The block was split in two sections. There was the A-side and the B-side. I pushed the buzzer, again, for the A-side and was let in.

Oh God, I thought as I looked around me. There were high ceilings with bright lights beaming down. All around were two tiers of cells and tables in the day room. I saw there was a television with two rows of chairs. It must have been lock down time because no one was out. Everyone was in their chambers and I could faintly hear a few inmates chatting, music being played and even a television. I went up to the CO and he told me which cell to go to. Here we go I thought. Who will be my new cellmate I wondered? The cell door opened and there was a young white guy with an unshaven face and wild hair. He didn't seem to be a threat. I saw on the floor there was a stretch of carpet. He had some towels on the cabinets and pictures of half naked women on the wall. It felt like I had walked into someone's bedroom. He was sitting at the desk drawing as the light from the window beamed in. I gathered my stuff and greeted him.

Luckily he was laid back and even offered me a beer. A beer I thought?

"How do you have beer?" I asked.

He said, "I make it."

"From what?"

"Sugar, yeast, oranges and water. This must be your first time in prison."

"Yes it is. So what's the main yard like?"

"I wouldn't know. I'm on cell restriction for another 30 days."

"Another?"

"Yeah. I got 6 write ups so far since I've been here. They just wrote me up this last time for sleeping during count time. I really couldn't give a shit about it. I'm a deep sleeper and didn't hear them announce count time. So fuck em!"

His name was Todd and he was a country boy in for breaking and entering and burglary. He had six children and wanted to have another. Another? Having another child was something he shouldn't have been thinking about as he told me he had to go back to court for more charges. He had to go on what they call, "writ," which means, even though someone was already sentenced, if more evidence came up later on, they could add more time to their stint. He said he already had 3 - 6 years and could possibly get another 5 years on top of that. I thank God my case was done. My rival raised its vile head again and told me they could find out more about me.

"More of what?" I said in my mind. "Shut up!"

I had about enough of everything I had been through so far. I set my bed up and put my stuff away. Todd quietly continued to work on his drawing while I had to close my eyes. I could only imagine what was next in the depths of despair of what was my new dwelling.

The End Of Innocence

What's this life for was the question I needed to know on that sad day of May 15th 2003. My mother had sacrificed her life dealing with a drunk for a husband who gave no emotional support. She basically raised my brothers and me all by herself, lovingly as our guide, in our living years. Losing baby Scott was something she never could accept but had to live with it. Fighting to get my father's job back after he got fired and holding everything together. If that wasn't bad enough she was stricken with a terrible disease of MS. She was my best friend in this world and she had passed away.

I had walked in her room and there she was unable to speak looking like she was having a stroke. Frantically I called the ambulance and they rushed her to the ER. She went in for emergency surgery for a ruptured appendix and held on for a week in recovery.

In my sick mind, once I knew my mother was safe in the hospital room, I go in the ER myself and tell the same doctor that attended my mother, I had injured my back getting her there. The doctor was sensitive to my pain and gave me a high dose of Percocet. That was pretty low to manipulate a doctor using my mother's suffering making him more sympathetic to my selfish needs.

We had brought her back home after a week in the hospital. After nursing her back to health, she once again couldn't speak and was unable to move. Screwface and I got her to the ER once more and I would never forget hearing the doctors who aided her.

"Ok! Clear... Do it again. Ok... Clear!"

Her heart had stopped and they were trying to resuscitate her as I could faintly hear the sound of that long straining beep that she had flat lined. In my mind I knew she was gone but I didn't want to believe that. Screwface went into the room and came back out crying. I knew there and then she was gone but I needed to hear it.

"What is it?" I tapped his shoulder near in tears. "What happened?"

Over his tears he cried out. "Mommy's dead!"

Crying and more crying was all I could do as I was on the phone with Rich. We didn't have to say much but we cried together even though he was in Maryland.

Being back at the house was a dual emotional roller coaster ride for me. One part of me felt like a weight was lifted. That I knew my mother was no longer suffering and God had granted my prayers of taking her home since there was no cure. The other side of me was overwhelmed that she was really dead. That it was my fault she died. I would stand at her bedroom door seeing the empty bed she was once on and look around. Those dark nights when her television only lit up her room playing old reruns of sitcoms. I would always check on her at night as Nik at Nite was on.

But now, she's gone...

"Mom?" I would say out loud. "Mom? Are you here? Mom I am so sorry I wasn't a better son to you. I should have taken better care of you but I was sick."

All in the time she was born to the time she departed this life would she have held a place of remembrance in this world? A life come and gone in the blink of an eye. Her hand dealt in her existence was to be a nothing more than good mother and she did just that. With devils throwing horrible realities at her along the way, she always held on! I often wondered what was it all for? Both of my parents were dead and I was lost in a world of emotional collapse. Spiritually and mentally I was fading away.

Strange occurrences had happened on the drive up to the Bronx for her burial. It was night and a severe thunderstorm rolled in while I was northbound on I-95 in southern Georgia. During the heavy rain and frequent lightning, my rear drivers' side tire blew out. It startled the hell out of me! I had to pull over on a darkened dead interstate. No lights and no cars passing by. There I was in the dark as lightning periodically lit up the sky, in the pouring rain, rushing to pull the bad tire and put on the spare. Once I was all done the rain stopped… "Now it stops?" I thought.

I was soaked and as I was thinking, I have no idea where to go now.

At that moment, I saw headlights coming up and pulled over behind me. It was two state troopers and they got out asking if I needed help.

I laughed and said, "where were you 10 minutes ago?"

It was too late for any assistance for my Mustang, but they directed me to a town where I could get a hotel room and where a garage was to fix the tire. I remember thinking, couldn't the rain have stopped, then have my tire blow out? Or better yet, not blow out at all? It was a weird synchronicity of the weather being in tuned to how I was feeling. Did my negative emotions blend with the down pouring rain cause my tire to blow out? Was I being delayed for some reason?

The next morning I had brought my car in but the tire size had to be special ordered. I had to wait a few hours and I needed to get to my mother's funeral! Once all was done I hoped back on the interstate and rushed the rest of the way. I got stuck in traffic in Baltimore and then again entering Jersey. I was frustrated and missed my own little world of beer and pills back in my room. I heard on the radio as I thought about my childhood, that was gone, Don Henley sing the song *"The End of Innocence"*.

The lyrics that rang through the speakers hit me. *"Didn't have a care in the world with mommy and daddy standing by."*

I was sheltered and even spoiled by my mother as my father brought in the money. Where I was in that moment of time was alone to take care of myself. I would have to quit the drugs, find a job and settle down. I was too afraid to do that and the lyrics told me, *"This is the end of the innocence."*

Ironically I heard the song a second time as I was nearing the Bronx. I didn't want to hear any of that nonsense. I just wanted to be a free spirit in my ghostly world of nothingness. I didn't want to believe that it was the end of my innocence. I rolled into the cemetery at exactly 2 PM. The eerie part was that it was the precise time the funeral started. I had just made it on time! But why Lord did I have to go through my tire being blown out in that storm and be delayed? Why was I held back only to show up at the funeral at the exact minute it began? I had missed the viewing and perhaps God felt seeing my mother one last time dead was something I wasn't ready to see. Whatever the reason, I was sure it had a good meaning. I just thanked the Great Spirit I made it to the funeral.

We all spent a few days on Long Island, back in my hometown. Revisiting my childhood yet again, I kept hearing that Don Henley song telling me my innocence was over.

"Leave me alone!" I said out loud. "Whoever you are! Whatever you are!"

If that wasn't bad enough, a new song by Evanescence, called "My Immortal" came out. It was all over the radio and of course it related to the great loss of my mother.

"These wounds won't seem to heal. This pain is just too real. There's just too much that time can not erase."

As the soft-spoken song played I became deeply in tuned to the melody. It was a dreamy sound that touched my heart and soul. It was another song I could not escape. It was everywhere reminding me that my mother was really gone and that my innocence was lost, over... finished.

It was well into September of 2003 and we had sold the house and divided up all of our mother's money. My brother's and I all received over $100,000 that our mother had left us. It was a long harsh summer and once the house was sold, I got into a one bedroom apartment just outside of Fort Lauderdale. I was still in the legal system for my possession of cocaine charge. I had to do Drug Court and complete these silly courses and piss in a cup twice a week. Since I would not give up my prescription medication, I could not move up to the next phase of their program. Who the hell did they think they were I thought? Telling me I have to stop taking my medication. I kept testing positive for opiates and benzodiazepines. I had to get approved by their doctor but it took so long, so I kept taking them. Since I had lost my mother's doctor I needed a new source. I continued seeing my own doctor and had her increase my dosage of Percocets and Valium.

I met a few people whom had something called Oxycontin. It was a highly potent form of a time-released Oxycodone. One Oxycontin 80 equaled 16 five-mg Percocets. I was buying a 10 pack almost every day and spending $300 a day on that drug alone. My connections stretched further and I was spending way too much money on a large variety of narcotics. All I would do in my apartment was sleep until noon or so. I was so toxic I could smell the sickness on the sheets as I lay there not wanting to get up. It smelt like a stale bodily secretion of my disease and all the toxins that was coming out of my body yet I was allured by it. I would just take in the smell as the dead daylight shone in the window. Once I mustered the strength to push the stinking covers off my dying head, I'd crush and then eat an Oxy 80 or a handful Percocets. Along with that I would pop a few Valium and take a shower all twisted in my mind! No lights on and the stale light coming in the bathroom window making the bathroom look haunting.

I would take another Oxy 80 and sit on the couch under my comfy blanket and watch "Family Guy" and "The Simpson's". There was nothing like being high, watching crude and funny animated sitcoms as I chained smoked.

I'd have to force my staggering body up and go to those stupid classes the drug court required me to go to. By night I would pop an enormous amount of pills, wash it down with a case of beer, watch television and chain smoke cigarettes. My body became totally tolerant and I must have been taking close to 50 pills a day on top of 24 or more beers! I'd find myself nodding out on the couch and discovered a new burn hole on my blanket the next day. It was a miracle I didn't burn the place down by my cigarette as I blanked out. It was a miracle I was still breathing!

My body continuing to function as the lethal amount of toxins flowed through my veins. Even while I slept with my body slowing down while it rested, nothing jammed me up to completely shut down my organs and have me become brain dead.... Dead period! It was a true miracle I woke up the next day! I was consuming enough drugs and alcohol to kill a horse! A friend's father had died due to an overdose of less than half of what I was taking but that didn't stop me. I heard on the radio another song by Evanescence called *"Bring Me To Life"*.

As I lay comatose to the world I heard the lyrics that spoke to me. *"Wake me up! Wake me up inside. Wake me up inside. Save me from the nothing I've become."*

There was no way I was ever going to wake up from what I had become. In my mind there was no more reason for me to live!

I appeared in court for the umpteenth time but this time I tested positive for cocaine and marijuana on top of what I was already taking. I figured I could splurge a little between urine tests but it caught up to me. The judge had enough of me and it was a moment I couldn't believe.

The judge said, "I gave you ample time to straighten up. You are a drug addict and there's nothing more I can do. You are to be placed within a 90 day in jail drug program!"

Before I could even blink I was cuffed and as they pulled me away I shouted through out the courtroom.

"Wait!" I yelled frantically. "I have my car outside! I have an apartment! I have bills to pay! You can't do this to me!"

I had begged everyone I could to please tell the judge to change the terms. It was too late in the game. The decision had already been made. I had to sign off on all my property and called Screwface to pick up my beautiful Mustang that was sitting in the parking lot. Once I had been brought to one of the psych blocks, I began to feel really ill! The nurse had come by to hand out meds and check on us. I had told her everything I was taking.

She said is shock. "You took all that! In a day? How the hell are you still alive? You should have been dead many times over! Talk about a miracle. Listen... You could have a seizer or worse, die from the withdrawals of everything you've been taking! We better get you to the informatory!"

They never did take me there and I had to deal with the growing illness without any chemical help! It was one thing to detox at home, in the comfort of your own surroundings but to be in a place of hell like county jail made it so much worse! Sweat slowly soaked my shaking body as I felt chills. I had diarrhea every hour, which burned! I had to force myself onto that cold metal toilet and let loose only having a small amount dribble out at a time. I had severe pains in my abdomen, which gave me a continual nauseating sensation. I had no appetite and could not eat for days! My legs were so restless and burned so much I wanted to scream! My body ached and kept jerking and twitching as I felt like I wanted to rip my skin off! It almost was like my skeleton wanted to leap out of my mouth and flee my aching flesh.

I got absolutely no sleep and it became utter torture for me being awake all-day and ALL night in that kind of Agony! I felt the need to masturbate frequently as my sex drive came back with a vengeance. I had realized the drugs took my desires away and it was months since I last had any kind of orgasmic pleasure. Once the drugs were out of my system, I began to feel vibrantly aroused by every vivid sexual thought that came into my mind. I felt my soul was naked and exposed in that realm of emptiness. That overwhelming thirst over took my being. It was that strange feeling I had as a child when I sensed the incomprehensible entity. I could not break free from the soul sickness I had and whatever was watching me again. Once again I felt like stone with my back against the invisible wall as the blackness before me went on for eternity. There was that suspicious being lurking in the distance. When I closed my eyes there it was face-to-face staring at me. It almost felt like I was looking intently at a mirror at my own distorted reflection. No movement, no sounds, no fear, just the unknown spirit and I with fixed eyes on each other, lacking any sort of function. Just completely still.

When they moved me to a regular block, I nearly freaked out by the large amount of inmates and all the madness going on. 55 inmates in a two tear large unit piled up in the dayroom. I couldn't take the sounds of the television and everyone yelling and banging on the tables, which made my teeth grind! There was enough madness in my head. I didn't need any more senselessness outside my sphere of hell! In the haze of my decontaminating brain, I told the nurse I wanted to kill myself so I could go back to the psych block, which was much more at ease.

Instead, the CO's got me out of there, took me to a private room and told me to strip down, put a crazy looking turtle suit on me naked underneath and placed me in suicide watch. It was a 7-cell unit but we didn't sleep in the cells. We had to stay in the dayroom the whole time being able to only use the toilet in the empty cells! If a person didn't want to commit suicide before, being in that place would surely change one's mind after a single night! We had no television, no phone and we had to sleep on mats and cover with a stiff blanket on the floor. They didn't give us sheets or blankets because someone could hang themselves. We were fed what was called "Love Loaf" out of a foam trey with plastic spoons. They didn't give us plastic knives or forks because we may be able to cut ourselves. Like that would do a whole lot of damage!

When I went to use the toilet, I saw an opportunity to smash my head onto a jagged point of metal they had in the cells we used the bathroom in. They were empty bunks without the mattress and the metal frame had a long metal railing that bent down into a sharp point. It was perfect to repeatedly hand bang it and jam my forehead into it over and over again until I die. The thought of doing it, blood splashing out, cutting my flesh and cracking my skull slightly, until I either pass out, die or the CO's rush in and stop me. The thought of having to live with surviving that, with possible brain damage, and or a huge nasty scar for the rest of my life made me think twice. Would be worse than withdrawing doing my jail time. I wasn't going to risk deforming myself over the way I felt and that I was trapped.

The food was everything they normally serve but blended into a paste. I have no idea why they called it love loaf. There was nothing loving about it. It was completely nasty! No one actually ate it but since it was suicide watch, they couldn't give us anything that would jeopardize ourselves. As if we'd hang ourselves with bread or ram a chicken bone down our throats. That's a terrible way to die!

With the thoughts of a painful but somewhat quick death, I felt like someone was squeezing my intestines, my head felt heavy with a dull headache. I felt like I wanted to just depart this life! Right then and there. No banging my head or anything painful. As I lay there suffering, I prayed over and over again for God to please remove the pain or kill me! Dealing with that kind of illness that seemed to never end was torment on my body, mind and soul. The minutes that dragged by felt like hours and hours felt like days. There were moments where it felt like a freight train was running through my skull.

"Please God! Take me out of this world!" I silently screamed in my head!

It was in that moment of spiritual bleakness, I overheard a couple of inmates talking.

"Maybe this is God's way of saving me from myself. After all I was on a dangerous path with everything I was doing. I could have been killed! I guess I need to be here so I can better myself. God doesn't make mistakes and has a good reason to have put me in jail. I truly believe that!"

The words from that song came to mind. *"Wake me up inside. Wake me from the nothing I've become."*

My God! There I was living in a messy apartment with no purpose, just existing. Taking more drugs and mixing it with alcohol than anyone could actually survive from and waking up the next day just to do it all over again. It was complete madness I had been living with for the past five years. All these signs were pointing to Divine Intervention. All in all I missed my mother and lost myself somewhere along the way. I saw that the miracle that had happened was Divinity saving me from myself. Even though the Divine saved me, I still had to live out the consequences of cause and effect. My body and brain had to recover and renew once all the toxins are out. Apparently all sins must be paid for at one point and I was no exception. I really should have been dead a long time ago but for some reason something powerful saved me from what would have been my own self-inflicted death.

It was so hard to know if I were real or not. It had been almost a month and I still wasn't well. After being in suicide watch for that one horrible night, they kept me in a semi psych block and thank God! There were 7 cells, a television hung up high on the wall and 4 round metal tables with 4 round hard metal seats. It had a musky metallic smell as I lay on the upper bunk. I heard some talking but nothing that was madness.

I didn't want to go back to that other overcrowded insane nut block. Ironically, the "semi psych ward" was more laid back and smaller with fewer inmates. The block I was on didn't have any cell doors, just cells with bunk beds. Apparently it was an open block where we can walk in and out of the cells freely. We were allowed to walk out into the dayroom from 7 AM til 10 PM. Fridays and Saturdays we were allowed til 11 PM... Woohoo...

Waiting to get into their stupid drug program felt impossible to deal with. The time I was waiting in jail did not count towards my sentence and I was on the edge. My 90 days haven't even started yet! I was doing dead time. I must have stared at every speck of the cell walls and ceiling. I started to form creatures and other images out of the paint that had been chipped on the walls. Still with no sleep, I thought I was close to having a breakdown. In the course of the nights on my bunk, my legs were still burning and restless and my back hurt. It was frustrating trying to get comfortable on the bed.

I tried playing poker with myself, sitting up Indian style, which felt good. I found some pleasure in sitting with my legs crossed like that. I was able to stretch out some leg muscles and the feeling was similar to a lingering pleasure coating.

I was intensely craving sweets! Like a powerful desire tickling my insides, the appetite for some kind of intoxicating sugar rush to consume me.

Thank God I had money and Screwface had been putting money on my commissary account. I was able to get a few snacks, which I had devoured in my own weird way to tame the fiend within. I was able to get a radio to ease the lunacy in my mind. Ironically in my despair one of the first songs I heard on the radio was *"Brain Damage"* by Pink Floyd.

"The lunatic is in my head. You raise the blade. You make the change. You rearrange me til I'm sane. You lock the door and throw away the key. There's someone in my head but it's not me."

The song was properly placed in my journey at just the right time. The synchronicity was balanced over my existence and insanity was where I lingered. I was no longer sound in a world of madness outside of my walls. Raise the blade Lord and sever my emotional collapse and make that change in my mortality. Take me out of my own undoing and rearrange my life until I am free from darkness. There was someone or something in my head but I wasn't sure who or what it was.

At night I would stand by the opening and stare out in the empty dayroom in hours of darkness. I would see those horrible metal tables and round hard metal seats. I felt like I was the fading god of night since I was the only one awake. I would hear snoring rumble like a concerto and the CO would pop in to walk about checking on us then leave, letting the heavy door slam behind him, with no regard to everyone who was sleeping. Every so often I would hear someone wake up, cough, fart, urinate then flush. Those thunderous vacuum sounds of the jail toilets only added to the tedious world I was living in!

Since there was no door to my dwelling, every freaking morning when the TV went on, it blasted Jerry Springer that funneled into my head like a drill! Along with the experience of coming off those drugs and alcohol, the slightest sound was ear piercing! The fact that I couldn't stand the show made it even worse and I had to put my hands over my ears every time I heard the audience chant *"Jerry! Jerry! Jerry!"* All the madness on that show drove me insane with all the bleeping from the disgusting words they would say and chaos! I enjoyed the peace of the night when it was quiet.

As I stood there looking at a lifeless block with the dim lights above, I wondered what was going to happen to me. How was I going to get through those awful nights and the rest of my time there? In that lonely moment, I heard on my radio Nicolette Larson play a great song called *"Lotta Love"* that reminded me of my childhood.

She sang into my spirit. *"It's gonna take a lotta love... to get us through the night. Its gonna take a lotta love to make this work out right."*

All in that instance, I felt like a child again and I felt hope grow in me. Though I felt alone I really wasn't. There was still a lot of love in me and I knew I could make it through the rest of my nightmare I brought upon myself. I had survived the worst of the withdrawals without any severe issues besides wanting to die. I could have had a seizure or die from the alcohol and the benzodiazepine withdrawals alone. I witnessed my father go into a seizure once from alcohol withdrawals and it was a sickening site. Why didn't I have any seizures from my detoxing? It was a miracle in itself because the amount I was taking I should have dropped dead from shock when I abruptly came off the substances!

Add the brutal opiate withdrawals and it was a grim form of my own personal torment I could not control. Time moved so slow it felt like it wasn't moving at all. It had only been less than a month but it felt like a fucking year! Well, maybe not that long... but pretty damn long.

They finally called me to pack up and moved me to a brand new part of the jail. The CO's said it was the Hilton of the entire detention center. I entered a huge block with two tiers. There was a television, a microwave, cushy rubber couches with a rubber coffee table. In the center were round tables and loose plastic chairs we could actually pull out to sit comfortably. Armrests included! The CO directed me to my cell and it was bigger and even the beds were better. I thought now this is how it should be. Having a sickness like addiction shouldn't have a punishment like that shit hole jail block I was on. The government was learning. I started to feel so much better since I was able to finally begin the 90-day count down. My spirit was finally coming back and I knew I would have to get myself together. After all it was a correctional facility I was in so I needed to correct myself.

I was released in late January of 2004 with a fresh start. The drug program was interesting. We had gathered around 10 AM for a group to study about relapse prevention and how addiction is a real disease. I had learned that the use of drugs was only a symptom. There was much more going on that led me to my downfall. One thing I didn't like in the program was we had to admit we were criminals. I was no criminal but my addiction did cause me to behave in criminal activity. There were daily NA meetings and on occasion we'd work in the kitchen and got fed really good. Though the Great Power had broken the chain of my destructive usage, I really didn't care to be forced into a drug program. I took that bad situation and tried to make something good out of it. I look back on that jail experience as something I needed to go through to save my life. To finally break that fear and daily chain of not having any drugs at all. I experienced for the first time what true detoxing was all about.

Thank God Screwface kept my Mustang at his house for me. Screwface had it cleaned and he took care of it for me. Key, Screwface, along with his wife and my cousin had to clean out my old chaotic apartment and had my stuff stored. He told me he couldn't believe how many pills they found along with an enormous amount of empty beer bottles. There were tons of Taco Bell wrappers with a lot of empty cheese containers scatter around. I had a couple bags of weed and quite a few empty cocaine baggies from those times I thought I could slip the piss tests. The sink was overflowing with dirty dishes accompanied by old decaying food and flies swarming around, which made everyone gag! My bedroom had a death smell. I didn't realize just how sick I had become. Losing my mother really put a heavy toll on my emotional state of being. I remember asking myself, who the hell lives like that?

I still had my life and it felt great to get in my Mustang and ride around in freedom. The slate was cleaned and it was time for me to decide on what I wanted out of life. Living in Florida without my mother had no more meaning for me. I needed to move out of there. I decided to move up to Maryland near my brother Rich and start over. I had to finish Drug Court first. They recommended something called "Aftercare." I got an apartment and began having those cravings again as I would not put to use what I learned in jail from the program. If it wasn't bad enough to have those vivid dreams that I had pills everywhere, reality turned on me and I began to give in.

I went back to my old doctor to see if I could get back on the Percocets and Valium. There I was in the waiting room when she called me into her office. I sat down in the hopes she could give me those wonderful scripts.

She said, "I am sorry but I can no longer prescribe you anymore pain meds."

I responded with, "But I had to take care of something out of state for a few months and I just stopped taking em'. My pain is still there and I really need em'."

She smiled at me as to know I was lying and an addict. I left the office feeling empty. I remember I had to tell the jail that I was on pain meds and who the prescribing doctor was. They must have told her I was in jail and what my charges were. That was probably the reason she had denied me.

There was a pretty young female two doors down from me who took a liking to me. Once again I engaged in free liberal sex. She kept coming over my place and finally I just gave in to her come on. Alyssa also made an appearance at my apartment. By that time she had three children and finally got fixed. It still amazed me she never got pregnant by me. Even though she was currently married, it didn't stop us from fooling around. For thirteen years we had that friends with benefits relationship. I was still someone she looked up to since I was clean again but all that had changed.

A guy named Duffy, who I was in the drug program with in jail, had contacted me. I can't say how he got my number. Perhaps he looked me up. It was nice to see him again and asked me if I could ride him down to Miami. Sure enough I did and we had went into the foul parts of the inner city. I knew what he was doing but my better half was in denial of it. I didn't want to believe I could get caught up in opiates again. He purchased a few sacs of heroin and we drove back making a stop at a Walgreen's Pharmacy parking lot. Ironically it was a pharmacy but we weren't going in there to pick up a prescription. We had our own medication and couldn't wait to get high.

He took out a couple of syringes and a spoon and began to cook up the dope while we sat in the car. I was unsure if I could ever stick a needle into my veins but the curiosity took me over. He did his shot first then I took the other needle and tapped one of my veins. I decided not to wrap my upper arm with anything. I just put the needle into my vein as it was. I didn't feel the need, because, luckily I had good veins. I slowly injected it into myself with Duffy as my guide. He told me once I lay the syringe in, pull back to make sure blood comes flowing in with the brown liquid. That's how I would know I tapped the vein correctly. I did exactly what he said then pushed the hypodermic plunger down turning loose the heroin into my bloodstream.

Suddenly I felt my head tingle and my face flush. An overwhelming sense of a wonderful chemical shifting effect made my body feel coated with natural pleasure! A great deal of endorphins had been released throughout my body as the heroin bonded with my opiate receptors. I began to feel warm and comfy all over and couldn't help but beam. I couldn't believe how high I was. It was an intoxicating rush that no pill has ever given me before.

A new addiction was created and we had made numerous trips back and forth to Miami to get more and more bags of heroin. Shooting up became a new fixation for me and I couldn't stop. I began to get back with some new drug connections and started buying Oxycontin again. I found myself shooting up a whole Oxy 80 into my brain.

Time moved on and I finally completed Drug Court successfully. I lost the desire for sex. That girl two doors down kept showing up at my door but I wasn't spirited for any kind of sexual frolicking. The drugs had robbed me of my sex drive again. I kept delaying my move to Maryland. I tried to stop using myself. I had a 14-day stretch of being off the dope and I was ill all over again and I could not seem to recover. I couldn't bear the withdrawals but fought on every day and night. I knew I needed to get the hell out of there. I went out and got some more pills and began drinking beer again just to function. I had begun packing up my stuff for the move.

It was well into June of 2004 and it was two days before I would actually move. That girl two doors down was knocking on my door. I opened it and she ran in frantically.

I asked, "what's wrong?"

She said out of breath, "I just cut my roommate with a knife. She called the cops. Don't tell them I am here!"

There was a knock on the door, she ran into my bedroom and when I opened it, two cops stood.

"What's going on?" I asked in confusion.

"Where is she?" An officer asked.

I didn't want to betray her trust but I didn't want to go to jail either. Before I could respond they pulled me out and cuffed me. I tried to pull away and resisted the absurdness of that unnecessary detain.

"What are you doing?" I said angrily.

They went in for a moment, then came out, the officers and the girl in cuffs. They brought me down and put me in the back of the cop car. I was fuming! How dare they I thought!

I spoke out with great anxiety. "Why are you arresting me? I didn't do anything! I'm moving in two days for God's sake!"

The arresting officer stated, "You were obstructing and you resisted arrest."

"This is not right! I had no idea why she ran into my apartment! If you had given me the chance I would have told you she was in there. Why are you doing this to me?"

"Sir. If you don't calm down we will have to restrain you further."

"A Life just stops for the law doesn't it? Even for a petty crime like this when you know damn well I will be moving in two days and never be a bother here again! If you really wanted to you could let me go. I had a rough few years as it is! I'm just trying to get myself together."

"That's the alcohol talking. Settle down... Now!"

Bastards I thought! How could they do that to me knowing I was moving? They saw the boxes packed up so they knew. They never gave me the chance to explain a thing. They just pulled me out only to restrain me into their dumb system without a care of my own life! They took away the guns I had. They gave me a receipt and it stated they seized them for safekeeping. Safekeeping I thought? From what? There was no one else at my apartment. The guns weren't going to shoot themselves. Once again I was taken to the county jail and had to call Screwface. My bail was only $100 and told him to take it out of my account.

I was released and took a taxi back to my apartment. I ran up to my place to get the money for my ride and discovered over $100 lying on my bed. That girl must have left it there by mistake. That settles my bail I thought. I went back down and paid the driver. I had those new stupid insignificant charges to deal with. Screw em I thought. I'm moving anyway. I could no longer be held there any longer and wasn't about to allow the system to hold me back over the fact that I never should have been arrested in the first place. I needed a new beginning since I had messed things up so bad there. I wanted to feel the change of seasons and to see hills again. I grew weary of the swampy climate of Florida and the flat lands.

I got myself a U-Haul and loaded it with all my stuff. I had put my Mustang on a trailer to tow up with me. Once I was all cleared out of that place I took a quick ride down to Miami. I had to drive around in the U-haul with my car on the trailer to find someone to get some dope. It was imperative for the excursion I was about to embark on that I do it high, otherwise, I wouldn't enjoy the trip. I saw a black dude sitting on his steps giving me that look. I instantly knew his signal that he was holding. I got out with no fear and approached him. I told him I needed 10 sacs for $100. He only had 9 sacs so I bought him completely out. I got back into the U-Haul and went to say farewell to everyone. It would be sad to say goodbye to everything and everybody.

It had been 14 years since I moved to Florida and I had experienced so many majestic events but also much pandemonium! Little did my 16 year old self back then know he would turn out dire at the age of 30. It seemed like yesterday I just moved to Florida in my heartbroken era. All those memories that spanned through those years flew by. In some ways I couldn't believe I was finally moving out of there.

I had it in my head, while I was caring for my mother, I would be living that way forever. I thought it would never end the way I was going. I was living angry and on a sure path to my ruin. In a strange way, I could not believe she was gone and that time in my life was really over. Living that kind of darkness felt like forever with no hope on any horizon no matter which way I looked. I missed my mother so much it hurt too much to stay there. I would have a brand new start in Maryland and I was excited. I blasted a good dose of heroin into my veins and got on the road completely high. There was no turning back; I was on my way to a whole new continuation of existence.

The Autumn Bridge

It was the beginning of September after Labor Day. In my incarcerated experience the summer bridge had ended. I thought that would be the longest stretch to deal with but it was gone in a blink. Though it wasn't officially autumn, for me the autumn bridge had begun. I found walking to the chow hall, as the heard of us were turned loose outside to eat gave me great fretfulness. I didn't know many people and when I would walk with the entire block, I felt the need to look behind me, thinking someone was going to attack me.

When I take a shower I would be in the stall alone washing up. I would imagine some big bald headed, powerfully built, inmate standing there, unclothed watching me, as I was naked and vulnerable. He would be giving me a crazy smirk, as he would slowly come at me. There was no way I would allow that sick silly son of a bitch to rape me. I would have to fight the bastard first. What the hell was wrong with me? No one was watching me or out to get me. My thoughts were all over the place and giving me moments of the fear.

I put in a sick call because I was jumpy and had continual heart palpitations. Turned out I had an over active thyroid and had to be put on medicine, apparently for the rest of my life. The doctor informed me it was the cause of my heart palpitations and could have been dangerous if I didn't do anything about it. Perhaps it was just anxiety overload making that happen. My mind was creating all sorts of crazy and vivid thoughts. I could not stop thinking!

Next, I went to the see the psychiatrist and he put me on Prozac and Visteril for my mental predicament. I really didn't want to take anything but being in a maximum-security penitentiary can overwhelm a person with great pressure and panic, especially someone like me. I needed something to ease the anxiety and depression I was dealing with. That I believe was the root cause of my heart issue.

I was called down to see the nurse and they had to take more blood to test me for hepatitis C. It was a standard test the prison had to do for everyone. As the nurse drew my blood, old memories of how many times I had stuck my veins with a needle and had unprotected sex came rushing into my mind.

I said trying to remain positive. "If I had Hep C, I would have known by now."

The nurse shattered my optimism by telling me. "Not really. Hep C can remain dormant in the body for up to 10 years.

It's a silent killer. You wouldn't even know you have it. It's sneaky." She shook her head. "It's a real sneaky disease."

I turned away in fear then said. "When will I know the results?"

"If you don't hear anything from us in a week then you're fine. If you are positive we will call you down."

Walking back to the block I began to worry. It wasn't so much me having the terrible liver disease but I knew it was transmittable through sex. I looked up and prayed to God.

"God if You really insist on me to have an ailing virus please give me something that I could not pass on to Xanadoo! Give me cancer or something else that belongs only to me. Not passed to her like Hep C! She doesn't deserve that."

I couldn't bear to think of passing such a sickness to my Goo. I got to my cell and lay down with the fear recycling in my mind over and over again! Todd had told me he had his test and he was negative. Still, I couldn't get the worry out of my head. I was battling my brain in a major guilt stricken struggle. I would imagine Xanadoo younger in her twenties when she was innocent and free. Would that young woman know she would meet a highly disturbed man years later who would be the death of her?

Days went by and we were in another lockdown. Damn this place I thought! Lockdowns could delay my results and I needed to know then and there. Waiting for my results came with a strange form of irony. It seemed that whenever I would have to wait for something important, an oddity of fate always stepped in

328

testing my patience. I peered out of my cell door as the block became empty after the goon squad left. One CO went around to open our slots to feed us and when he disappeared, inmates began to toss things out of their cells and yelling like animals! They were throwing fruit, toilet paper and other things. I swear it felt like feeding time at the zoo! That outburst of madness got us locked down for an additional day.

The next day I was called down to see the doctor and I was in total chaos in my mind. I must be positive for Hep C! What the hell was I going to do I thought? How would I tell Xanadoo when she comes to visit me again? She had been visiting me once a week faithfully and making sure I always had money on my account. She didn't deserve to have that illness I self-inflicted on myself. It was my punishment not hers! I continued to ask Divinity to give me something that would be mine, not infectious to her. As I sat in the waiting room, time moved so slowly...

My chest was tight, my stomach ached and my legs restless. "I needed to know what was going on NOW!" I said out loud. I put my head down and spoke in a low tone. "Oh my God! How am I gonna tell her I have Hep C and she needs to get tested?"

Finally I was called in and sat down with the doctor. I took in a deep breath as she looked through my medical records.

She said, "ok… it seems like…" She shuffled through more of my files for another long moment…

I looked up and thought, "Really?"

She continued. "We got your results for your blood work we had done…" She slowly put on her glasses. "We found you have hyperthyroidism."

I said in relief, "I was already told that. I thought I was here for something else."

"Oh. I'm sorry." She looked through the papers again… "Ah yes. It does appear you were informed about a week ago. I guess we didn't need to have called you down."

I left with a feeling of craziness! I still didn't have the answer whether or not I had Hepatitis C. I was just too scared to even ask the doctor if the results were in.

The next day I was called down yet again. Here we go I thought. Waiting again felt like torture. I was trying to think of ways to tell Goo we were going to die of a hideous liver disease!

I was called back and sat down with a different doctor.

He said, "ok. You have a hyper thyroid and you will need to be put on medicine."

I said in frustration. "This is the third time I have been told I have a hyper thyroid. I'm already taking the medicine they gave me. I have been on it over a week."

He looked at my file again. "Hmmm… Yes you were. I wonder why they put you on the call out list? I'll be sure to inform them so it doesn't happen again."

Once again I was left with no answer because I was too scared again to ask! I figured they might have told me then and there. Was it God testing me or was it Lucifer fucking with my sanity?

"Stop it whoever you are, whatever you are!" I said to myself. "This isn't funny."

A few more days had past and I haven't heard a thing about the test. I was starting to feel in my spirit that I was fine and had no diseases. The fear had slowly declined as the angelic powers eased my apprehension. I felt a sense of relief tingle in my body as I realized it had been over a week and they did not call me down. At least for the Hep C results. The nurse stated if I don't hear anything in a week, I would be fine. After all they can't be calling down every single person who they test otherwise it would be overloaded. Only the ones who were positive would be called back to discuss future alternatives. I thanked God for sparing me of such a curse and that my Goo and I would be just fine. It was a miracle I did not contract any diseases in the madness of my history. I put myself at risk a lot! I was so reckless that I should have been dead many times over. I was tested for other STD's and even AID's in the past and all were negative. I was always too scared to have voluntarily been tested for the only test I never got being Hep C. I guess I let the enemy get the best of me. The only question that remained merciless was did I have any liver damage? Now that new thought I will constantly OCD over! It never ends!

I still didn't know anyone on the block besides my cellmate. I kept mostly to myself. I didn't want to be cooped up there so I had signed up to go to the library. I didn't want to be dormant. I wanted to elevate my mind. The time was 2 pm and those who signed up lined up near the exit. We all get buzzed outside and start walking to the next block. As everyone was walking to the library we were told to wait outside the door for a moment. My guess was it had to be a fight or something stupid. So we all waited…

Suddenly I saw the medical cart rushing up the sidewalk towards us. We were told to step back and they rushed in. Hmmm… maybe someone got stabbed up I thought. We were told to go back to our block and as we slowly walked back, I turned and saw an inmate laid out on the stretcher with blood all over him. His head was leaning back; his face was pale and his eyes opened. His mouth was slightly ajar as they took him to the infirmary. I carried that sickly thought with me back to the cell. I scrambled for possibilities in my mind on what happened. I began scaring the shit out of myself. That guy looked dead! Was he?

A little later on, after the madness in my head subsided, I over heard some guys talking about it. Turned out he tried to kill himself by cutting his legs severing his major arteries. No one knew for sure how he got something in there sharp enough to do that. He wanted to commit suicide because parole board had denied is parole and given him a 6-month hit not being about to go home. He would have to do 6 more months in prison before he would go back to the parole board for another chance at freedom.

Instead of feeling sorry for the guy like I was, my brain attacked me. I was having bad thoughts of me getting a long-term hit from parole and not going home in April. Would I have to do the whole three years? With my good time incentive I was granted, I would only do a little over a year. Thirteen and a half months, 412 days to be exact, including county jail time. My true minimum would be 18 months, which if I didn't have the early release program, would get me out in August of next year. Thank God I was eligible for that. My inner enemy was starting to beat me down, playing out different roles of being denied and never going home.

Ironically at that moment, I was called into see the block counselor. He sat me down and dropped my file on his desk.

"You're up for parole." He stated.

"But I just got here," I said.

"Well not right now. In December you will be seeing the board."

I asked frantically. "What are my chances of making parole?"

He sat down and looked at his computer. "Let's see... you have no write ups. You have a short time with your early release program. You also have institutional support, which means the prison has given you a good recommendation." He looked at me and asked. "Do you have a home plan?"

"Yes I do."

He smiled and said. "Then you should be fine."

I just said the first thing that popped in my head. "What if I get a hit?"

He looked intently at me. "Why would they give you a hit?"

It was a question I couldn't answer. So I said, "I don't know. Sorry, I have bad OCD."

He smiled like he understood how I felt for being in prison for the first time and just wanted to go home.

He said, "you have all aces in your corner. Seriously, I wouldn't worry. They'll take one look at you and the way you speak and have no doubt to grant you parole."

I felt good in that moment. I thanked him and moved forward. Even with all the good things, my brain was becoming overloaded with worries.

Todd's old cellmate had returned from being on writ and I had to move. I celled up with an eccentric white guy with a baldhead and a goatee. I was content with Todd but he had a cell agreement with his old cellmate. My new cellmate went by the name 'The Alchemist.' He was in his mid 30's, a cool guy from California, but stand offish and rather cocky. We didn't talk much at first and he would give me sarcastic digs. I had noticed him before like there was something familiar about the guy. I wasn't sure what it was but he stood out to me when I saw him out in the concrete yard.

We got to talking a little more as the days passed. He was going to have to max out his 1 – 5 year stretch. He had been incarcerated for more than 4 years so far and he was fed up with the parole board. Parole had given him hit after hit for some reason and he had less than a year left. He was in for credit card fraud and from what he had told me, it wasn't his first time in prison. He told me the boards of parole were a bunch of scumbags that would give him a hit for no reason. Hearing that invoked my fear again! The cell he and I were in was in the far corner of the block and it made me nervous. Every time we'd go out to eat I was always the first one back. I had to leave the cell door opened for The Alchemist. I would sit up on the top bunk and fear someone coming in and beating the crap out of me.

I got a job as a block worker. My only job was to help scrub the showers when everyone goes in for lockdown. It was easy and we only worked 5 or 10 minutes and got paid for 6 hours. A whole .19-cents an hour! Sliding my cell door opened, I accidentally bumped this big black guy. I was still lost in a haze of being in prison and the fear that was wrapped around me.

I said to him. "Sorry."

He looked down at me with angry eyes and said. "Sorry? You just bumped me with the door! Where do you think you are?"

"Me?"

"Yeah you! You don't bump someone like that!"

I said I was sorry again and went to clean the showers when I overheard that guy arguing with The Alchemist about it. I was scared because I didn't want any problems so I sucked it up and went back over to them.

I said to him. "Look. I really am sorry. I am not with it and was just coming out to clean the showers. I really didn't see you standing there."

He told me to stand where he was and showed me what I had done with the door.

He bumped me hard with the door and said, "Now tell me, how would you feel?"

"I know." I said as I rubbed my shoulder. "I'm out of it sometimes and I should have been watching what I was doing. From now on I'll be sure to look both ways when leaving my cell."

He smiled.

I asked, "so what's your name?"

"I'm Hollywood." He said in a more relaxed tone. "Hey man, I have been in and out of prison for 20 years. I've seen a lot of shit. You need to always be paying attention. This is prison you're in and the wrong person may have acted differently. I'm not a bad person and just want to get the hell out of here! I don't have much time left."

Hollywood and I pounded fists and began laughing at the mishap. We had moved on to do our block work in peace. I was grateful I was able to stand up and work out my mistake. It was true. I was in a prison, not a picnic and I needed to always be alert to my surroundings. Even The Alchemist told me I had to be careful.

I went out to the main yard when the weather was nice. It was rolling into later September and the weather was cooler and the sun was setting earlier. I was nervous walking around the ¼ mile track that was in an oval shape around the yard. I had music playing with my headphones and my anxiety caused me to feel as if I were stumbling. It felt like all eyes were on me and I stiffened up. There was a baseball field that the track encircled where the inmates were playing baseball. They had basketball courts, weight machines, sac toss, handball court and a volleyball net in a sand patch. There was a deep forest that surrounded the entire prison and it was peaceful to look at outside the razor wired fences. I would sit there during evening yard as I watched the sun slowly go down. I turned away from everything, sitting close to the fence. I would see the sun glow in the amazing way it sets through the trees. It was my sanctuary from the confinements of the DOC.

Being friendly seemed to be dangerous in a place like that. I would often sit in the day room watching the television with a few others. There were two guys that I casually chatted with. They were known around the block as Dookie Stain and Bullet Head. Dookie Stain was a tall goofy guy in his 30's who was soft spoken. Bullet Head was around the same age, shorter, chubbier and had a bald head shaped like a bullet. Allegedly they were sex offenders, which is why they had those names. A lot of the guys on that block didn't like them. As I was talking with Dookie Stain this intimidating skinny guy with a shaved head with a swastika tattooed on the back of his head walked by.

He said to Dookie, "Telling the new guy how you rape little boys?"

Dookie told me he was falsely accused of sexually touching a child and that some of the inmates give him a hard time. He of course didn't do it. It was a story I wasn't sure whether or not to believe anymore. I have heard it many times over by the same type of offenders. I wasn't there to judge anyone but I also wasn't there to make friends. I just wanted to do my time. Bullet Head was also another accused toucher who didn't do it. I was like, whatever. As I was making a deal with Bullet Head

337

to trade some of my tobacco for some cookies that skinny neo-nazi dude came up to me.

He said, "yo, let me holler at ya for a minute."

I sat down with him as he gave me a crazy smirk. He said, "I was going to ask to see some papers but The Alchemist told me you are in here for drugs. I know you're not a pedophile. What you are doing talking with those fucking touchers goes against everything I stand for. You're on my block now and if you are going to continue hanging out with those fuckers, I'm gonna have to do to you what I do to them."

I asked frantically. "What's that?"

"Yo, I'm gonna have to charge you $5 a week to be on my block. If you have a problem with that we can take it to your cell and fight."

"You extort the molesters?"

"Hell ya! They know better to pay me or they will receive a beating!

"Look I'm sorry but I'm not here to judge. I'm not making friends with them. I just wanted to watch the television and they sit there and talk to me. I was just being nice."

"I don't really care. This is prison! Fuck being nice to scum like them! I want $5 a week and if you go to the CO's I will fuck you up!"

I was remaining calm and was trying my best to defuse him. I wasn't about to give that guy $5 of my commissary just to hang out with those guys. I just wanted to make parole and go home, so I made a negotiation with him.

I said, "look, if it really bothers you I will respect what you're saying and not talk to them anymore. I won't even sit over there any more."

He looked around then said, "I'm giving you this one time warning since you are The Alchemist's celli. If I see you talking with those pedophiles I will beat the shit out of you and take all of your commissary. Those fucking child molesters oughta be executed with no mercy! That's how I feel yo!"

I just disregarded his sneering comment and said, "Have you known The Alchemist long?"

"He used to be my cellmate."

"That's cool. What's your name?"

"Dozer."

"Dozer?"

"Yeah. Like I'll roll over you like a bulldozer if you mess with me." He chuckled.

As Dozer and I continued to talk I noticed he lightened up a lot. Before I knew it we were on a totally different subject and actually laughing.

I told him. "I'm a writer."

He said impressed. "We have a writer on the block! Alright!"

Dozer was only 26 and had been in juvenile detention and prison since the age of 12. I could see the evil that was in his eyes. He was a skinhead and was raised to believe that everything gone wrong was the Jews fault. I couldn't believe he was led to believe every single bad thing was because of the Jews. He was a product of a misinformed upbringing being taught Nazism and hatred. Judging and disliking other folk because they're different or don't believe what others believe.

Apparently there are still some out there who don't realize that World War 2 was over and the Nazis lost. Hitler was a monster and must have been filled with pure evil to kill all those poor people who didn't deserve to die. All because of one sick man that gained power as a ruler and dictator with a twisted notion humans should all be the same color and religion. In my eyes we are all human and should it matter what our article of faith was? I did thank God Dozer was a friend of my new cellmate, The Alchemist, otherwise there was no telling what may have happened.

As time moved on things got better. Dozer and I actually became on good terms. There I was in my cell with The Alchemist and Dozer as they were measuring out their huge bin of homemade alcohol also known as hooch. They taped up paper covering the cell window. Putting tape up on the cell window indicated the prisoner was taking a shit and must not to be disturbed. It eluded the authorities from probing around for misconduct behavior or in the case of making hooch.

I had witnessed them use 400 sugar packets, 20 oranges, yeast they had obtained from the kitchen workers and 4 gallons of water. Many of the guys on the block wanted in so they gave them all their oranges from chow. The Alchemist purchased sugar packets also from the kitchen workers. I was a little nervous because I did not want to get caught up in the making of the moonshine. The Alchemist assured me he would take the blame if a CO caught us. He called the hooch his baby and took a few days for it to be made. It had to seethe in a large plastic bag stuffed in a bin. He had to burp it every so often so the bag wouldn't burst.

Dozer and The Alchemist finally grabbed the bin and filtered the booze through a shirt into large container.

The Alchemist asked me. "I know you don't drink but would you like a hit?"

I nodded for just a taste. After all I never had homemade booze. I sipped the cup he had given me and I couldn't believe they made that in only a few days. It tasted like mild tangy orange juice with a pungent sting of the tongue. It wasn't bad at all.

Dozer asked me. "Hey? You want to buy some Oxycontin?"

I said in surprise. "How the hell do you get that in here?"

"Easy yo. I also got weed."

The Alchemist knowing my journey to stay clean said. "Dozer. Leave him alone with that stuff."

I could tell The Alchemist respected me. We even grew closer discussing music and the mind. He believed the Bible was broken down into three parts. Theory, Fact and Fantasy. He believed that the story of Adam and Eve wasn't a literal truth. It was a metaphor of what the world could be if we obeyed God and didn't fall into temptation. It was an illustration how humans fail, to be less than perfect, corrupt. With all the sins in the world humans were unable to function in the world alone. Humans needed Gods help in redemption and peace. Knowing we had a savior gives hope and joy to so many people! The bible is filled with wisdom and inspiration. I found his idea intriguing and never really thought of it that way.

He read a lot of books and always had a dictionary on hand to look up words he didn't know. He had pointed out something about me that I found interesting. He noticed I laid about a lot and was really intellectual in conversation, however, he stated there was a sequence to my walk of life. He noticed I would come across this pocket, a bubble, a block of some sort and it would stop me in my journey. He told me it was something I had a hard time getting around.

Was it a lazy moment in my walk or an obstacle? He had a good theory because whenever I would come into a problem I became weak minded. I got frustrated not wanting to fix the issue. I found myself wallowing in stupid dilemmas and became stagnate and weak. I become aware when I did get the problem resolved, I felt lifted, smart, a better person. I came to the conclusion that I procrastinated too much and settled in defeat and self-pity. I had truly been my own worst enemy by blocking myself. The answers were to stop allowing the devil inside to tell me lies. Just get up and make something happen! I was thankful that Divinity put The Alchemist in my walk of life to point that out to me.

Even with The Alchemist's intellect his eccentricity went overboard when he actually broke out a ruler to make sure nothing of his goes onto my area of the top part of our lockers, which were side by side. Like it mattered to me. I didn't care if the books he had stacked and other stuff stretched an inch onto my side but he was adamant about having his own space. He would scrub the cell down obsessive-compulsive style. He would neurotically wipe down the walls, floor and even the ceiling. He was a smart guy but lost in his own world of madness.

They drank and smoked weed that night and eventually passed out. I was glad to be free of all that. I couldn't drink even if I wanted to but would have smoked, however, remembering the enhancing effect it had, I was too scared. I was in prison and I didn't want to be there in that kind of mind set.

Something happened to me when I turned 30 after I had moved to Maryland. For some reason beer or any form of alcohol began to make me sick. I often wondered if it was God because no doctor or anyone could give me a straight answer on that phenomenon. Something or some force had put a stop to my reckless drinking by making me feel sick every time I indulged.

Dozer needed a new cellmate because his old cellmate had gotten the crap beat out of him. I had witnessed the whole thing. Some nonsense was going around with Dozer, his cellmate, and these two black dudes. It was 7 in the morning and we were all waiting for the gate of our block to open outside in the concrete yard. The morning was eerie yet beautiful with the sun brightening the dark blue sky. I suddenly heard a scuffle and when I turned around there the two black guys were thumping on Dozer's cellmate! They were swinging on his face and body until he dropped to the floor. They were kicking him as he was down and all the guy could do was cover himself with his arms and just take it. They were relentless and wouldn't stop until the CO's came to put an end to the madness. The prison halted movement as more CO's and a Captain came running. They cuffed all three of them and one by one took them straight to the bucket.

One of the black guys was yelling, "I don't give a fuck! That nigga had it coming! Fuck that nigga!"

I watched as they escorted the guy they jumped. His eye was swollen shut and had blood on his face and head. It was a terrible scene and all I wanted to do was eat. I had begun to recall all the madness I have seen so far in my days of imprisonment. All the craziness, ignorance, and foolishness that went on in that twisted confined society was astonishing. It was then I realized state prison was where you end up when you've fucked up once too often on the streets and you're not wanted in the general public or even in the county jails anymore. I had been to county a couple of times and apparently it didn't seem to work. I felt Divinity had another plan in store for me to get it right and where I was had to be it. I wanted to get out of that block and into the honor block where it was more laid back. I had written a few requests to the honor block unit manager but heard nothing back. I felt in my spirit a good change was coming. I just wasn't sure when.

It was well into October and The Alchemist had moved up with Dozer and I was sent to another cell with a better view. I had the cell all to myself for a couple of days, which felt great! I laid my headphones down and had it echo music through out the lonely cell while gazing out at the changing leaves that fluttered in the midst of the autumn breeze. It was a beautiful escape. I would go to lunch, dinner… come back to my cell and just disappear from the madness of prison.

I felt I could do what I want in having my own cell. I lay on my bunk during the evenings with the light off as the lights from the block shone in. I began to meditate and remember my childhood. The light shining in reminded me of when I would lay on my bed at night with the light out, the hallway light would shine in. The comforting feeling I had in my youth, I brought to my present. With music from the past surrounding me in the cell, it felt like I was reliving part of my early days. With every song, a different distant memory would rush in, giving me a pleasing sensation. I felt free.

My solitude didn't last long as they placed a guy named Joe in with me. He was really cool and easy to get along with. He was transported from another facility on writ. He had to go back to court for his charges of grand theft. He was in his early 30's and was chill with me playing my music. He was soft spoken and wore glasses.

I asked, "what's the prison your from like?"

He started telling me how much better it was. That there were nicer showers, soda machines, could buy ice cream and that it had more programs than the one I was in. I started wishing I had been sent over there. It wasn't much further away from home.

Joe asked, "been to the main yard yet?"

"Here and there. I'm still getting adjusted to actually being in prison."

"Aren't there games and other things to do in the yard?"

"Yeah, but I don't get involved."

He looked surprised. "Why?"

"I guess I'm attached to my comfort zone here and a little afraid to get out there."

He said, "its still early. Let's go to the yard next call."

Not too much later we were called out to the main yard. We both walked out of our block talking as all the other inmates were going to the main yard. I still felt a little intimated but talking with Joe made me feel better. He was easy to talk to and someone I felt I could be opened with. He gave me the confidence I needed in a place like that. I felt more at ease when him and I went out to the main yard. He got me into playing bocce ball and sac toss. Those were things I was too afraid to play with the other inmates. Before I knew it I noticed I was fitting in with the crowd.

There were two other guys from our block that joined in. Square Beard who was in his late 30's was in for kidnapping. A good old country boy from the sticks. He had a good 12 – 24 year term to deal with. He was named after his square shaped beard on his chin. Then there was The Under Bite. He was 28 and had just done a 10 year stint. He was back in… again… for robbery doing a 3 – 6 year stretch. He had a serious under bite and was crazy looking with wild black hair and creepy green eyes, like a villain out of a Batman cartoon. They were cellmates and on a roll in giving each other jailhouse tattoos and they must have had 50 or 60 of them all over their bodies. They were proud in showing Joe and I every one they recently imprinted onto their bodies. The Under Bite said he wanted to have at least 100 tattoos in the next few months. That was actually both their goals. My God I thought. How crazy was that?

There was this older black guy who I called Kool Kev who I talked to sometimes on the block. He was 42 and had a long time to go. He was watching us play the sac toss.

He said as we were tossing the sacs. "I shouldn't be talking to all you short timers."

I asked, "how long do you have?"

"Shit! I have 24 years left to my minimum! I got a 25 to life sentence. I'm 42 and I'll be here probably until I die."

"What'd ya do?"

He gave me a crazy look. "I killed someone."

"Who'd you kill Kev?" The Under Bite asked.

"My step father. The son of a bitch put his hands on my mother. He was abusive and I had to put a stop to that! I had warned him time and time again to leave my mother alone. He didn't listen to me and put his hands on my mother again so I killed him. It was a damn shame he had to learn the hard way."

"Now your mom doesn't have her son anymore." The Under Bite said.

"Yeah, I know," Kev said in sadness. "I love my mother and miss her like hell. She still comes to visit me. But man, she's getting older and I don't know what I would do if she dies. I'm stuck in here for protecting my own mother!"

I remember thinking how terrible that was. He was protecting his own mother. Should they have given him that much time? I remember when I took care of my mother I saw a couple of punks giving her a look like they wanted to rob her. I felt at that time I would have went off on them if they went near her. I was protective of my mother and wouldn't allow some jack off to hurt her! Who knows... I may have killed someone, protecting my mother. Kool Kev wasn't a bad person. He didn't have a criminal record or anything before his murder charge. He worked a good job and had a life. Luckily he wasn't married with children. That would have made it much worse for Kool Kev and his wife and kids.

Our time for evening main yard was getting shorter due to the earlier setting sun. They would announce on a bullhorn atop one of the towers for all of us to take it in. We had to put everything away and follow the crowd back onto the block to wind down another day.

I found a good friend in Joe who was an intellect and easy going like me. Finally there was someone I could relate to and feel comfortable with.

However, it didn't last long and they took Joe to court and moved in a new celli for me. He was a large beastly man in his late 40's. I remember thinking, ah no! This guy is going to be a problem. Like a Big Foot, his looks were inhuman and a little nerve racking, but his spirit was peaceful and kind. I called him Big Boss and to my surprise once he opened up he was a really nice person. He had been in and out of prison for over 20 years of his life. He had made parole and would soon be leaving. He had a television and for the first time in my incarceration, I could watch TV!

The fall leaves were growing in color and the weather was crisp and pleasant as the days went on. I had a choice to go out to the main yard in the autumn air then come back to the cell and relax with some television and sip a cup of coffee. It was one of the best parts of my day being comfortable on my bunk and watching evening shows on the television with no cell light on. The cell door remained closed to keep out the madness that went on in the dayroom.

Big Boss smoked a lot, so him and I smoked in the cell together, which made me feel at home. He told me I was someone who did not belong in prison and the system had made a mistake in sending me there. He also told me I would make parole for sure and I had nothing to worry about. Even with his encouraging words the demon within always seem to peer its vile skull into my enlightened world.

Having the TV was like a present, I felt, as Big Boss said he wanted to give me something nice before he left. I felt like I knew him all my life and I seemed to make him feel better just talking with me. I was finding ways to escape the madness of prison and it felt good. The television was a window to the outside world and I had fleeting moments where I felt I wasn't in prison at all. He was also a drug addict and told me he wanted to make a good change in his life.

He said to me, "you really are a good person and you shouldn't be so down on yourself. I hope you make it when you get out. I would love to get together someday for a barbeque. For what its worth my friend you have brought a smile to my face."

I asked, "how did I do that?"

"Just by being you."

I must have made some sort of impression to him to tell me all those things and to offer me the remote of his television stating it was a gift for me until he leaves. It was a gift from God! Some days, though, I can't understand why I am so blessed. Why me I often wonder. Xanadoo was right in saying I was the light. Big Boss showed me that even someone like him who had been in and out of prison for over 20 years could open up to someone like me. It was a genuine feeling for him to have great respect for me in that place. I was just being myself and it made my confidence grow even more that just being me made a difference to someone else.

Not much later on they had Big Boss pack up and I was going to miss him, even though, I knew him a short while. It was amazing how close people could get in prison when celled up. I was the type to get along with almost anyone and I was grateful that I had decent celli's. I was wondering who my new cellmate was going to be when they had told me to pack it up. I was about to be moved over to the honor block and I was just getting comfortable in my current block. Part of me didn't want to go but it was what I had been wishing for all that time. It was always a pain in the ass to box up all my stuff and move. My possessions were growing the more time I was there. I loaded all my stuff onto a pushcart and before I left out the door I bid farewell to those I got to know. I was happy yet nervous because I would have to start all over again in yet another reformatory community.

A Sequence Of Regrettable Events

I made my way to Maryland in a stupor of opiates in July of 2004. If shooting heroin wasn't enough, I pulled off the interstate a few times and made a hospital pit stop. I wanted to make sure I had enough to get me there. As soon as I showed up on my brother's doorstep, Rich and his wife knew I was on drugs. I must have had that sickly look and they could see it in my eyes. I just lied and said I was tired from the long drive, which technically was true!

I got an apartment immediately and moved all my stuff in. After my mom passed away, my brother's and I had split up all the furniture and I got the couch, tables, TV, entertainment center, dresser draws and my full size bed. I had bought a new computer and finished up my novel. It felt good to be free of the Sunshine State but just my luck it was summer time in Maryland. I wanted to see the change of seasons again so bad! I supposed I had to wait a little longer.

I had stopped cold turkey from the opiates and once again I was ill. I was determined to stay clean in my new surroundings. I drove to every corner of the state to explore and get back in touch with my inner child again. My stomach hurt, I felt weak and ached all over. I was living off of the rest of my inheritance, which took a heavy hit from all the drugs, and recklessness of my past. At least I still had my Mustang and my health.

I got in touch with the courts in Florida and told them I had moved. Luckily I was able to do a plea by mail since my charges were petty. Though I was still angry from that silly arrest at least I could resolve it where I was. All I had to do was pay a fine and court costs then washed my hands clean of that bullshit.

Rich and his family went away to Myrtle Beach and gave me the key to their home. I was to watch the dog and keep the house safe while they were gone. I remember one night I had started drinking a bottle of wine. The fiend within was hammering me and since I didn't have any pills I filled that void with more drinking. I hung out in their basement watching television rocking the bottle hard. I remember accidentally spilling one of bottles making a mess and feeling a little unwell. Fleeting glimpses of my insanity flashed on and off in my mind. I was lost somewhere in the madness of my frame of mind and anger came to pass. Hasty visions of me punching something loomed in thought. I didn't feel real in that moment of time. Leaving the house was barely a recollection.

I woke up in my own bed not remembering how the hell I got home. My hands were bloody and bruised. How did this happen I wondered? I had a bad hangover along with sharp pain when I moved my fingers. Something was wrong and I had no idea what happened last night. I got dressed and went out to my car, which was ok. I drove to the hospital that ironically was around the corner. I walked in the ER and went right up to the desk.

The woman sitting there looked at me and asked, "How can I help you?"

I said as I showed my messed up hands, "I think I broke my hands!"

I waited a short while then was called back. They did an x-ray and found that I had a boxer fracture in both hands.

"How did this happen?" The doctor asked.

"You see doctor. I just moved here and I was organizing my apartment. A table fell on my hands while I was moving," I lied.

"Looks like you punched something." He said in some suspicion. "But I guess anything can happen."

"Yeah and it really hurts." I exaggerated a bit because there was one thing I wanted. "Can I please have something for the pain?"

"Absolutely! I'll have the nurse bring it to you immediately."

I couldn't tell the doctor I got so drunk last night and that I do not remember how this could have come about. I still wasn't sure how it happened. I also know that if I told them I was drunk they may not have given me any narcotics and I had to have that. The nurse came in with a shot for me. That feeling of excitement arose in me. What wonderful opiate was this? I lifted my shirt and she injected it into my shoulder, which burn a bit.

I asked, "What is this?"

"Dilaudid."

"What?"

Hydromorphone. It is 5 times stronger than Morphine and it will ease your pain! I gave you a good dose. Two milligrams, which is what you got, is like 20 milligrams of Morphine. Give it about 15 minutes." She explained.

Hydromorphone. That was a first. No doctor in Florida ever gave me that. From what I had studied in the past about medicine, I learned it's synthesized from Morphine making it more potent. What Hydrocodone is to Codeine, Hydromorphone is to Morphine but on a whole other level of opium derivatives to make people float and feel no pain. As I waited for the medicine to kick in I sat there trying to think of what the hell happened last night when all of sudden I felt a great rush slowly over take me... I was feeling nice and high! At that moment I didn't seem to care any more and wanted more.

I was discharged with a Percocet script and braces on both hands. I got into my car still feeling so very nice from the shot and saw that I had 6 messages on my cell phone. I called my voicemail and that's when I heard it!

My brother was yelling into the phone, "What the hell did you do to my house? Call me back now!"

There was no way of explaining the panic I had. I called him back and he told me I had wrecked up his house. Rich's mother-in-law had stopped by and said the kitchen chairs were punched in and the dog cage kicked in. The mother in law's mailbox across their street was knocked down. Apparently I must have backed up into it in the blackout I was deluded in.

I pulled up to my brother's house and saw the mailbox across the street lying on the ground. I do not remember doing that! I went inside and I saw two of their wooden kitchen chairs broke. The chairs had thick strips of wood in the back and they were freshly busted through. How could I have punched through wood that broad I thought? Why did I go mad like that? Holy shit! I knew I needed help after seeing that! I walked into their living room and saw the dog cage kicked in. Luckily the dog was not in it. I began to have strange flashbacks of last night and felt the rage stirring in my spirit. The alcohol must have enhanced the fury I was still carrying around. The wine combined with my rage seemed to have given me superhuman strength to break through wood that solid. No wonder why my hands were fractured. How the hell did I drive home last night? It was a true miracle that I got home safely. I was grateful I didn't kill anyone or myself. It amazed me that my brain was able to still function on some sort of autopilot. Even though I was unconscious to the real world, my subconscious guided me home. Truly the angels were with me the whole time.

Rich and the family came home and I was so ashamed. I received a good yelling at and all I could do was say how sorry I was. I wasn't welcomed there at the time so I went back to my lonely apartment in deep despair. I was crucifying myself and it made me fearful of my own sanity. I had to reach out and talk to someone. I called the crisis hotline and told them what had happened.

"I got so drunk last night that I punched through my brother's wooden chairs, fracturing my hands and I kicked in their dog cage! I also knocked over his mother-in-law's mailbox by backing up into it and drove home in a blackout!" I come out with to the man.

The man replied, "You have to be kidding me! Come on now... No one does that. Stop wasting my time!"

He hung up on me! I slammed the phone down thinking to myself it was no joke! I needed help and they hung up on me? They must get a lot of prank phone calls and my story must have sounded whacked or made up or something! I felt even angrier that they didn't take the time to hear me out. I was feeling extreme anxiety and fear. I needed something fast! I had my Percocet script filled and popped a few of them and began to relax. My God! What was to happen to me next?

The summer was nearing an end and I had landed myself a good job as a driver. It was a fairly easy job delivering energy drinks. Fate was working for me because I was looking for a different company for a different job. I was lost and walked into an office building to ask for directions and they so happened to be hiring. Irony has a funny way of working. I got to see more of Maryland by delivering all over. It was a peaceful job and we got paid the same no matter how early we got done.

My hands were still healing and I had to see an orthopedic. There I was explaining how much pain I was in to the two doctors that were examining me. As one doctor looked me over, the other began to write a script for Percocets. They gave me the stronger milligram of 7.5 and a 60 count, which worked for me.

I would sit on my couch watching television, drinking beer eating the pills. The beer for some reason wasn't making me feel as good as it used to. After one or two beers, I would not feel well with a dull headache. As I sat there high and reckless in my head, I wanted to venture out.

I went to a local bar and sat down and ordered a strong drink. Maybe hard liquor will make me feel better. I sipped the drink as the opiates circled through my bloodstream, releasing a steady stream of pleasurable chemicals. Feeling great, I ordered another shot. There was this young black woman sitting next to me. I turned and smiled at her.

"Hi," she said sipping her drink.

"Hello," I responded.

She took a sip of her drink and asked. "What are you up to tonight?"

"Just hanging out. I was bored at home so I came out for a drink or two."

We got into a conversation. Nothing special, just small talk. Her name was Peaches and she seemed like a decent person. I wasn't really interested in anything more than to just talk but it seemed like she was trying to tell me something.

She asked, "do you smoke crack?"

"Can't say that I do."

It was in that moment I felt the need in trying something new. The alcohol was still making me feel unwell. I paid my tab and her and I went to an apartment. She went inside and in a moments time came back out with two small sacs of white rock. We went to my place and she took out a crack stem made of glass and put in a filter made out of what looked like a scrubbing pad. She put a small piece of the crack rock onto it and lit the flame. She toaked a bit then took in a large inhale of the smoke. She passed the pipe to me and put a small piece on. She instructed me to hold it up then slowly heat the tip allowing the rock to melt as it sizzled. I followed through and inhaled the smoke and held it. Suddenly I felt an overwhelming sense of pure well being as I exhaled. My body felt lifted and sensual. It was similar to sniffing cocaine but much more intense with a calming effect to follow. I felt like an orgasm had consumed my entire flesh leaving me with a phenomenal sensation. All I knew in that moment was I wanted another hit!

Before I knew it Peaches led me to another girl named Jen who led me to a drug dealer named Pee Wee. Pee Wee was a tall black guy who didn't seem like the drug dealing type. He had a heart and was nice. He dealt heroin and crack cocaine and was often generous in giving heroin to people who were ill. He was curing them with the same medicine he sold them that made them ill in the first place. Irony at its best! His caring ways was great but he was also enabling them with a poison.

Pee Wee had a white girlfriend who was about 30 named Linda. They were together for a while and she was a serious drug addict. Linda was petite with short brown hair and blue eyes. What felt like no time at all Pee Wee and Linda moved in with me. They were both homeless and moved around from place to place selling the drugs. It wasn't much of a choice for me as they just loaded my car with their stuff. I couldn't just tell them no so I let them live at my apartment for a while.

Since I had a car, I had to take Pee Wee down to the inner city part of Baltimore to re-up on the drugs, which made me nervous. In those inner city neighborhoods if a white guy was seen driving a black guy around, it was cause for suspicion. The cops could pull us up for that alone. As if white people don't ride with black people. But given the stereotypical attitudes that's just the way the thinking was for most cops. However, white people, usually addicts ride with black inner city boys. In those cases more than likely there's a crime going on.

I felt relieved once he made his move and we were out of the city. For my services, he would reward me with some heroin and some crack. As we were on the expressway, he would put some heroin onto a dollar bill then hand me another rolled up bill to snort it up as I drove on the way home. Why waste any time we figured? I became wrapped up in the two powerful substances and began to spiral out of control. What was I doing with these people I often wondered?

Drug addicts from all over were showing up at my apartment and Pee Wee was dealing. My place quickly became a crack house and a place to shoot up dope. There were all sorts of characters coming by and smoking crack. Some were over talkative, others became extremely paranoid and some were chill. Well into the night Pee Wee would get so high on heroin he would be standing on his feet completely bent over with his arms hanging down to the floor. How he never fell to the ground was beyond me. That was something I have never seen before!

This twisted nonsense went on night after night.

There were times Pee Wee, Linda and a few other strangers would pass out in my living room. I would walk out of my room with the eerie grayish daylight shining around and see everyone dead to the world and think what have I become! What kind of life have I allowed to have here? It was a form of being dead in our minds and this was our own interconnected personal hell! The pressure was killing me and I felt there was no way out of the madness that had taken me over.

It was affecting my job as I was always late and was making silly mistakes. I was fired and once again was unemployed. The money I had that my mother left me was nearly gone. I was constantly draining my account to buy more and more drugs! In all that time, it came as a huge surprise that the $100,000 was almost gone in no time at all. This addiction I had in me felt like I was being sucked dry!

It was well into November and Pee Wee and Linda had moved on to another place. He said it helped to elude the police in finding out about his business. I was alone on my couch watching television when there was a knock on my door. I opened and to my surprise it was Linda. She rushed inside and needed my help.

She said, "I just stole all of Pee Wee's drugs and I need a place to hide. Please don't tell him I am here. I will share it with you."

My God I thought. Should I really get involved with her I wondered. Once she snorted up a line of heroin and took at hit of crack, I knew I needed some myself. Sure enough I sniffed up a good line of dope and smoked a huge hit of crack. It bubbled and steamed as it melted with a crackling sound. Once I blew out the smoke I was feeling that soothing sensual feeling I could not deny. After that I told Linda that, sure, you could stay here. All I knew was I wanted more and more crack so Linda and I smoked all night. I had smoked so much that I thought there were people outside of my apartment. A strong jittery feeling overtook me. I was becoming delusional! I needed more heroin to calm me down.

The next morning after all the drugs were gone, I was laying in my bed. It was around 8 in the morning and I did not want to get up. Linda, after sleeping on the couch, knocked on my bedroom door and stood there shaking.

She said, "can you take me to the store. I am ill."

"What's at the store?"

"We have to make money. Please?"

I have heard of boosting from stores and pawning it for money. I just never thought I would be exposed to it. I didn't want to get up but Linda begged me.

We had gone to a grocery store and apparently Linda had boosted before. She grabbed a few grocery bags and put them into her purse. I grabbed a shopping cart and went up one of the aisles. She pointed out things that were worth money such as over the counter medicines and other things found in someone's bathroom. She loaded up the shopping cart and we went to an isle where there was no one shopping. She took out the bags and put as much as she could into them. She also filled her rather large purse with the stuff. Alright I thought, this could work. Since there was a pharmacy in the back of the store, the idea was to pretend we checked out there. With a shopping cart full of grocery bags with stolen goods, passing the cashiers, we went out the doors.

My heart was pounding; fear lingered in my spirit as we got to my car. Once we placed everything in my car, I felt at ease.

I said in relief. "We did it! We got it!"

Linda smiled and told me where to go next.

Straight inside the outer edge of Baltimore City to a crooked pawn store was where we ended up. We carried the bags in and took everything out onto the counter. They added everything up and put it all into the back for future sales. We had made $160! The pawn storeowner knew us dope fiends went boosting for those things and he bought them from us at 1/3 the retail cost. Then the silly son of a bitch would raise the prices to re-sale for a profit. What a twisted and bent scheme it was for all of us. It was the devil's playing field I was on and I just blocked out the crimes I was doing just to get high. As Sarah McLachlan said, *"We are companions to our demons. They will dance and we will play."*

We went to a payphone and she made a call. Once all was said and done I drove her to a place where we scored some heroin and crack. She had a cooker with syringes and we wasted no time shooting up the dope. It took away her shaking and withdrawals. I sat there for a moment and thought why I was getting involved in such a disgusting way? This wasn't me I remember thinking then had dreadful remorse. All that was removed once I fired up a good dose of heroin.

It was early spring of 2005 and I was falling in what felt like a bottomless pit. I had no job and no money. Dope fiends came and went, as my place became known as open house for drug users.

My brother had intervened with a friend and had everyone not on the lease to leave because he knew how low and fast I was sinking. In order to pay the rent, I had to sell my Mustang, which I only got $10,000 for. Rich helped me sell the car and got me another. I bought a 1995 silver Integra for $5,000 and used the rest to pay the rent and get food. The rent had been paid up a few months ahead so I had little worry of getting evicted. I had spent a few days in the psych ward of the hospital to recover from the chaos I had endured.

I was back in my apartment all the while trying to get better as the days passed. I was so far down and I was in the hopes of rising above.

With the links between all the yo yo's that been to my apartment, led even more dangerous people there. Linda still came around with heroin and I just had to partake in the fest. She introduced me to a girl named Tammy. Tammy had insisted on doing a few drug runs but in order to do so we needed gas for my car. I remembered I still had my credit card and we went to the gas station. I knew it was over the limit but I tried in high hopes that it might work. I had pumped the gas and filled up my car. I purchased cigarettes and when the attendant swiped my card it was denied. I couldn't very well return the gas I already put in my car and he refused to take the cigarettes back.

When the cops showed up they asked me if I could get the money I owed. I told them I would try my best and they gave me 24 hours to do so otherwise they would issue a warrant for my arrest. Once we left I knew there was no way I would raise the money. I wasn't about to ask my brother or his wife. I was already on bad terms with them. Linda and Tammy didn't have a cent to their name. What else could I do but try to forget it and hope for the best.

What led to more different types of fiends coming by my place, led to a couple of drug dealers who showed up at my door. Since I didn't have any money to give them, they offered me some crack cocaine to use my car to do runs. I foolishly gave them the keys and stayed home and smoked. I smoked and smoked until I was hallucinating. One thing I learned about crack was that it goes fast! I so badly wanted that high I got with the first hit. I never could get it but I tried relentlessly over and over again like an insane person. It was like I was chasing a phantom in the bareness of obscurity. My sexuality was extremely enhanced and I would spend hours watching porn, freeze-framing the women until the drugs wore off.

This shit went on for days and there was no sign of my car being returned. Once the drugs were all gone, I felt tremendous regret and found myself kicking my ass. I would look in the mirror at myself and wonder who that was. I was becoming sickly and losing weight. What happened to the healthy young man I was? I was an A student involved in so many positive activities. I was a writer who had a relationship, a good job, money and a car. I was voted most likely to succeed but was turning out to be most likely to lose my mind. As I felt paralyzed, I stared at myself and saw the madness and insanity that lie in wait, constantly recycling in my mind. While I stayed locked with myself, I saw a corpse before my own eyes. I felt I had crossed the point of no return and I was finished.

A big time drug dealer named Gunz had paid me a visit. He was ruthless, well respected and was in my apartment. He had gotten news that my silver Integra had been totaled. Those two guys who used it worked for Gunz and were reckless when driving and flipped my poor car over. Gunz was yelling at them and threatening them.

He yelled, "you nigga's fucked up this guys car! You owe me money! I give you my word I will find you and fuck you up!"

I overheard the other guy on Gunz speakerphone. "Fuck you nigga! I ain't scared of you."

In that moment, I felt so sick that my car had been wrecked! That car was in my name and I was hoping the police weren't coming for me. What the hell would I tell them? Um, yeah, I let them borrow my car in exchange for some drugs.

In no time at all Gunz and his crew had made their way into my residence, making it a hideout. I had about 10 drug dealers with guns in my place as they blasted their rap music. I wasn't hated the ghetto rap they played because it sounded pure evil.

"Kill that faggot" shouted out often with a gunshot backing it up as the bass thumped.

There was no escaping it! I had made my own hell worse!

Gunz had rented a car and I had to drive the boys around as they sold and picked up crack. They hit me off with the drug and I was foolishly falling into their trap. Some of Gunz boys were on the run and as I was driving around with Flavor, another one of Gunz cronies. I heard police sirens all around me. A helicopter flew so low I could actually see the pilot and hear the police speaking out for the boys to stop and surrender. Flavor was telling me we had to pick them up but there was no way I was getting involved with that!

Luckily we couldn't find them and headed back to the hideout being my apartment. Gunz wasn't that bad of a person because he did help me out with food and drugs. They had a few parties and accepted me as one of their own, even though I was the only white guy. I felt Satan had set a trap and I fell right into it. I could not back out of what I got myself into. My brother had helped me get out of the last mess with the dope heads in my apartment but these guys were not going to leave any time soon or peacefully.

They stored large amounts of cocaine in my heating vents and always had guns on them. I really didn't fear the guns because I sensed an angel was watching over me. I found myself socializing with everyone and noticed they brought over a trick every so often. I had witnessed a pretty young female strip naked and let those guys have their way with her all for some crack! The fact that a female could allow herself to be used as a party favor for a high baffled me. The power of those drugs was unbelievably overwhelming. I realized how deep it brought me down from where I used to be. It was an alluring beautiful impression that made all my problems and pain go away. But when you back up and look at it face to face you could see the ugliness of its essence. Even though I could see the aftermath and destruction of the drug, it still had a way of hypnotizing me and making me believe everything would be ok. It was stimulating insanity mixed with pure deceitfulness, which led to deep denial.

Linda had stopped by and her and I were sitting down as the boys went about their own business.

"Are you ok?" She asked.

"Well, I got myself into a bit of a situation here."

We talked and talked and I felt like I had a friend in the mess I was in. We talked in depth and how grateful she was to me for taking her in and helping her out.

She said sincerely. "Not only did you take me in but you were respectful to me. You never tried to take advantage of me. I feel I can tell you anything. You are my best friend."

The guys had all left and I had the key of the car Gunz had rented. I was trusted to hold on to it safely while they made some moves in the city with another car. He told me I could use it if I needed. Of course I took advantage of that and made a few hospital runs for some pills. Gunz had paid for the pills that kept me afloat mentally.

Linda and I lounged on the couch watching television peacefully while everyone was out. I enjoyed those moments when it was quiet. The only time I didn't feel trapped. I had to take a shower and told Linda.

"Where's the key to the car? You don't want to lose it." She said cunningly.

"Don't worry. It's on the coffee table. I'm going to take a shower."

I went to take a shower and something occurred to me. Was leaving the car key with Linda a good idea? I quickly got out and dried off. I got dressed and went out and saw the empty spot on the couch she was on. The key was missing and I rushed to the window and saw the car had been taken.

"Damn you Linda!" I yelled out.

She was asking earlier if I could take her boosting and that she needed drugs. I had told her tomorrow would be better and I should have known. I wanted to hate her but I knew it was the drugs that took her over. The demon of addiction driving her. Her cravings and need for the remedy of escaping was far worse than mine. That was something I can say I never did. Steal a car, especially from my best friend!

I paced around my empty apartment hoping she would come back.

But she didn't...

Gunz and the gang came back and were not happy about what happened. I was in fear for my life in that moment while I tried to explain what happened. Gunz gave me a mean look and didn't know what to say. Suddenly Flavor punched me in the face and I fell to the couch seeing a white flash! I tried to yell out and tell them it wasn't my fault but it was. I should never have left the key in Linda's reach. I never should have left her alone.

We all went driving around in another car looking for Linda but had no luck. Flavor had apologized for hitting me but said I deserved it at the time. Thank God I was on good terms with those guys. I thought I might have been murdered. I prayed to God to please help me out of that mess!

It was going to be a long night...

We got the car back by some sort of miracle the next day. A very loyal customer of Gunz had given the word she had seen the car. Linda had long since abandoned it in a parking lot a few blocks from my apartment and was not seen since. It was a horrible experience but it had turned out for the best. At least in that situation. I was still stuck with those hardcore guys in my apartment. I would often see the neighbor across the parking lot of my complex staring at us. She was a middle aged black woman who often sits out on her patio to smoke. We had made eye contact a few times and I could tell she knew my situation, what was going on but never said anything. I felt she understood that I was locked in and couldn't get out and was hoping I'd get out.

One peaceful night at home I was relaxing when one of Gunz crew came by my apartment all whacked out.

He told me. "Hey yo son! Gunz got shot! I'm getting my shit and getting the fuck outta here!"

He rushed to gather his things as I stood in shock then Flavor knocked at my door. I opened it and he told me the same story. He went into the vent and pulled out all the drugs and a handgun.

He looked at me and said, "Shit's going down and I need to hide out somewhere else. Hey man! You be good a 'ight?"

They left and I closed the door in fear of what could happen to me. I could not believe Gunz got shot! That could have been me!

Night after night I sat in the dark, hoping no one was coming for me. I was sitting on my couch with only the television shedding light when I heard a loud crash! I peaked out my window and didn't see anything. I went outside and looked to my left. There were a few detectives who had raided the apartment next to mine. I stood there for a moment and wondered if they raided the wrong apartment. I believed it was meant to be my place.

One of them saw me and walked up to me. He questioned me on Gunz and the gang but I had to play dumb. He with another detective came into my apartment and searched around. Since they couldn't find anything they asked me more questions. I told them I was just an addict trying to get myself together. They knew that my place was where they were hiding and they crashed the wrong house. I can't image what those people are feeling! Why was I saved the surprise smash into your house and wreck up the place? My neighbors next door didn't deserve that. It was my darkness that brought it there.

Once they left I was thankful to God for sparing me. Even though someone got shot it was a blessing for me. They were gone! They raided the wrong apartment and I felt bad for those unsuspecting victims that had to go through that. Because of my addiction, my neighbors had to suffer. The detectives must have got a tip and smashed in their windows and rushed in thinking it was mine.

I fell to my knees and with great remorse cried out in shame! I grabbed a knife and held it to my wrists. I slowly cut myself, not having the courage too cut deep. I wanted to kill myself but I couldn't do it for some reason. Why am I breathing Lord? All I do is cause problems! I threw the knife and it stuck into the wall. I needed pills bad! I had gone way to many times to the hospital around the corner. I knew I couldn't go there and I had no car.

I got on my bicycle, the only means of transportation I had left, and rode into the night. I had taken a 20-mile journey to the next hospital. Gliding down and struggling up the hills, I pedaled on. I was deep in the country, hearing the sounds of the night. I felt alone and lost in a realm of peaceful sorrow. The air felt soft and cool on my skin, breathing in the scent of forest and moss reminding me how I felt when I was a child. There weren't many cars on the two-way back road I was on, which made it feel more secluded on my voyage. The streetlights shone an eerie glow on the road as I passed by each one with the fleeting resonance of the crickets and night bugs. During certain moments, I could still feel everything around me as I did as a child. It was near as fleeting as the sounds of the crickets coming and going. I still had great admiration for nature and the night with my inner child still alive somewhere in me.

What kind of person does what I am doing I thought? It was a question I didn't want to know the answer to. I just wanted to be medicated! I didn't care how far it was. Getting to the hospital was all I could think of so I made an adventure out of it.

I checked myself into the ER and stressed a severe pain issue. I lay calmly on the hospital bed as the nurse injected me with a good dose of Dilaudid. It was the relief I desperately needed in that time.

After a short while there, I got back on my bike and rode the 20-mile ride back home. My desire for music was also still alive in me as I had on my headphones for the long journey back. I peddled on distracted in my mind to get back as fast as possible, robbing me of my peaceful adventure. The push of the pedals tired me out quickly and I found myself out of breath and taking off my headphones. Once I got back in town, completely tired out after my insane 40-mile round trip on a bicycle, I got the script for Percocet they gave me filled at an all night pharmacy. I couldn't pay for it, so I had stolen a few things to return so I could get credit at the pharmacy. Including prescriptions.

I hadn't recognized the velocity of time that had passed me by. It was summer already! Where did the time go I wondered? All the psychosis I went through along with the drugs had become mind erasers. Last summer zipped by. I had lost interest in admiring the fall leaves and the season of Halloween with my family. The holidays went by in a blur. A new year had begun, as I was lost in a fog of lunacy. It was 2005, I had turned 31 years old and I was on the verge of eviction. It felt like a bad dream I was slowly waking up from. All my money was gone, I had no car and nowhere to go. I truly missed my mother and wished that I could go home to where she was. There I was on the floor of my isolation with the radio playing. A song called *"Ordinary World"* from Duran Duran was playing.

"What is happening to me? Crazy some say. Where is my friend when I need you most? Gone away..."

I was still lost without my mother. She was my best friend and she was gone away. Perhaps she was there with me the whole time. Many miracles had occurred many times over in that madness. My mother probably told the angels to get rid of those drug dealers. How else could I have been saved from that unharmed?

I didn't have much longer in that residence. I got my eviction notice and began selling my stuff. Little by little people came by and bought the couch, the entertainment center and even my bed. When all was said and done all I had left was a few blankets and my television. I found myself eating pills in an empty apartment lying on the blankets on the floor. Everyone who came and went in that year's time sucked me dry. All the money I spent on those drugs was smoked away leaving me with nothing. I just lay there in ruins watching old reruns of my childhood TV shows all night.

It was 4 in the morning and the rust color streetlight gleamed into the vacant address of my demise, blending with the eerie glow of the television. I seemed to feel safe from 4 am to 5 am. The darkest hours before sunrise. Happy Days and Lavern & Shirley came on. I wasn't sure why that time was like that but it was a comfort zone. I looked forward to that time of night, wrapped in a blanket, head propped against the wall as I lay on the floor watching TV of my past. The ghostly sense of my memories was a vanishing reminder of who I used to be. I just existed in the blank space of what was my extraordinary state of mentality. I could barely define that moment in time.

The next day I was picked up by the police for a warrant I had out for me. The money I owed the gas station a while back when my credit card was denied had caught up to me. I rode my bicycle to the nearest plaza. I was about to go into a store for a boost. I needed money, so I thought if I stole a few things, I could pawn it. A cop drove up on me wondering what I was doing. He asked for ID and called it in. Sure enough, I had a warrant and went to jail. They let me go with no bail only to wait for a court date for a charge of theft under $100. I had to walk a few miles from the county jail to where my bike was and ride home to a lonely dwelling. There was no one who was going to help me where I was. I was truly on my own.

Sure enough a couple of days later, the Sheriff, along with the clean up crew, came to bleed dry my habitation. Luckily Rich had came by earlier to pick up my computer and some memorabilia. My TV was sold that day and all that I had left was my bike, my backpack with some clothes and a radio. I had $75 in cash on me. I left that place behind me and felt something pulling me in the direction of Baltimore City. For some reason there was something influential whispering to me that the city was where I would belong. As I rode my bike with my backpack snug, I saw a husband and wife with their three children standing near the street. All their furniture and stuff was all over the place. They were also evicted with no mercy. They lingered there looking sad and beaten by reality. The man gave me saddened eyes as I cycled on by. How could I feel bad for myself when I created my mess seeing that poor family kicked out with no where to go?

The Look Within

The honor block was different than being in general population. It was more laid back because many of the guys were in the outside work program and or close to going home. Basically, the safest place to be when you want to just go home! There were four 22-man dorms where new inmates go first. Then we sign up on the cell list, which moves us down to an 8-man dorm next. After that, we move into a 2-man cell. So I signed up but the list was long and could take months. I could be out of prison by the time I paired up with someone and get our own cell.

I was sent up a flight of stairs to a tier that led around to the bathrooms and another dorm. I opened the door to my new dorm. As I looked at the rows of bunk beds that were in the dorm, it felt like I was at summer camp. Most inmates had their own televisions and a small amount of space between each set of bunk beds. There were plenty of big windows to look outside that made me more relaxed. I didn't feel so confined being there. It was a much better block than the one I was on. I had a top bunk being a newcomer and had to wait to move down to a bottom bunk, which I liked better. I hated being on the top. I set up my bed and just lay down for a while. There was a lot of talking and the sounds of multiple televisions being played. I just closed my eyes and drifted off in my mind.

I kept mostly to myself as I walked down to the pill line to get my meds. It was a pleasant little walk in the cool fall air. I could see the full moon above, shining down on the entire prison ground. I went onto the pill line, which was always a loony bin. There I saw Square Beard and The Under Bite from the old block. I greeted them and they told me nothing had changed on my old block. They began to roll up their pants and sleeves, showing me the new tattoos they imprinted on one another. There was one that stood out. It was the Latin word, Diablo, meaning Devil. On his same arm spelt the word SLAYER. It stood for Satan Laughing As You Eternally Rot! His other arm had an angel and spelt the Latin word, Angelus, meaning Angel. He was a walking form of good and evil battling one another. I thought it was pretty cool.

"How many does this make?" I asked.

The Under Bite said, "61! A hundred is our goal."

A hundred? Can't say I condoned it but I understood their boredom. As we waited in line for our medication, I overheard two inmates talking.

One guy said, "There is a difference between a thief and a robber."

"Oh yeah? What's that?" The other asked.

"A thief will be in your home and if he went to use the bathroom and saw your drugs and money he would take it without you knowing. He would lie if you were to ask him who took it."

"Yeah?"

"A robber will be in your house, say he went to the bathroom, saw your drugs and money. He would go back and tell you he is taking your shit. A thief is sneaky, a robber don't give a fuck and will take your shit right in front of you."

Interesting discussion. Two other inmates were talking.

One said, "Yo son. I just got out of the hole. I got a stack of write up like you wouldn't believe yo!"

The other said, "That ain't shit. This is my third prison. I got kicked out of two prisons so far."

My God I thought! How does someone get kicked out of a prison? These are the main topics around here? I often used the expression *"UGH"*. The definition clearly defines the word as used to express horror, disgust or repugnance. Ugh! It was a very appropriate word for where I was and the food. So far there wasn't much conversations about becoming a better person anywhere around me.

Suddenly, like a punch in the face, I smelled an awful stink! Everyone who was on the line started covering their noses with their shirts or hand. Someone had farted but would not own up to it. An unsuspecting inmate walked inside and stopped instantly.

He said, "What the fuck?" He stood on line for only a moment. "To hell with this! I don't need my pills that bad!"

He ran himself the hell outta there. The nurses were looking around.

One nurse said, "Oh mercy! What is that?"

A few others got out of there quick and finally I got my meds and left in a hurry! There had to more to prison than passing bad gas, getting jailhouse tattoos and describing the difference between two different types of criminals who do basically the same thing, except one denies it and the other would kill you over it. Also all the other jargon I heard.

I got back to my bed and pulled out some paper. I had to write out my issues and I did it in a form of a letter to Goo.

Friday October 20th 2014

244 days in

Dear Goo,

I have seen some of the madness in this correctional facility and it is time to find peace with myself. I want to find my place and get to know good people. Being stagnant makes my mind attack myself, which makes my anxiety soar! I am a 39-year-old man, soon to be 40, trying to find his way in life. I have diagnosed myself and have to work it out.

Diagnosis: White adult male who is highly intelligent. Has great powers of the imagination and foresight. Has great potential but suffers from generalized anxiety, mild paranoid delusions, obsesses too much and dwells in the past. Possible borderline bipolar disorder. Can do much in a positive state of mind, however, isolates in negative states. Often wallows in self-pity and defeat.

Lows can be overwhelming, including paralyzing low self esteem, distorted views of self image and detachment of society.

Highs can produce incredible artistic activities and intense creative thinking. Able to inspire self as well as others. Has made great differences in many peoples lives being the light. Has a great sense of humor along with unique qualities and persona.

Conclusion: An artistic, eccentric, pure of heart individual battling a very powerful dark side of the mind with great frustration.

My mind, that illuminations my brain, is often the enemy that attacks me. I attack myself putting nothing into life. Like an autoimmune disease where it attacks the body.

Here's a couple of typical silent conversation with my brain when it attacks me...

Driving home from work:

Brain: Pain in lower back. Need pills.

Me: Going home to rest now.

Brain: Hospital run.

Me: I don't really feel like it.

Brain: Hospital run.

Me: Not enough money.

Brain: $35 is all we need. $10 for gas and $25 for the pills.

Me: Let's go home first.

Brain: Okay.

A little while later lying in bed...

Brain: Pain in lower back. Need pills.

Me: I already know that!

Brain: Hospital run.

Me: I'm resting now. I don't feel like it.

Brain: If we leave now we will get back sooner.

Me: Not now.

Brain: Get up! Let's go!

Me: Later.

Brain: whatever.

Later on the couch watching television...

Brain: Bored now. Back still hurts.

Me: I'll take a bath soon.

Brain: Headache forming now.

Me: You're doing that!

Brain: Hospital run.

Me: No!

Brain: Yes!

Me: Leave me alone!

Brain: We're wasting time. Let's go now.

Me: No.

Brain: Pills make me feel good!

Me: Stop it!

Brain: If we leave now we'll have a nice evening. Let's go.

Me: It's too much of a hassle.

Brain: We'll get the good stuff and feel nice.

Me: Ya think?

Brain: Oh yeah! Let's go.

Me: My God! If I go will you shut up?

Brain: Yes.

Me: Okay then. Let's go.

Brain: Coolness! Happy now.

Something stupid I said twenty years ago that my brain would not let me forget...

Brain: That was a stupid thing to say.

Me: I know.

Brain: Why did you say that?

Me: I don't know.

Brain: It was really stupid.

Me: You put it there!

Brain: Embarrassing!

Me: It was twenty years ago. I'm sure no one remembers.

Brain: I remember. You're stupid.

Me: Cut it out! I can't go back and change it!

Brain: You said it.

Me: Can we change the subject please?

Brain: Stomach reporting hunger. Requesting some kind of salt-based food.

Me: Don't really feel like going through all that right now.

Brain: Pizza.

Me: I don't feel like getting up.

Brain: It will be worth it.

Me: Ok.

Later on…

Brain: That was a good pizza! Feeling better now.

Me: I know.

Brain: That was a stupid thing to say.

Me: It was twenty years ago!

Brain: Stupid.

Me: We've just been through this!

Brain: Why'd ya have to say that?

Me: Why won't you shut up?

Brain: Stupid.

Me: I can't believe you don't shut up!

Brain: You should have said something else.

Me: Oh, I can't take much more of this!

Brain: Don't do it again. Getting tire now. Need rest.

Me: Oh, thank God!

I signed and sealed the letter. I have been writing letters to Xanadoo every single day and found it to be therapeutic. It has been showing me myself from a different view. Like stepping out of a picture and gazing back at it. Being inside my head has given me distorted images of my being. What I see in myself someone may see something else. When I feel stupid someone may see me as smart or vice versa. Why does this have to happen? How did I become so discombobulated?

I wanted a better look at things so I went to bible study. I was walking into the chapel when I saw Dale, my old cellmate from the classification prison, sitting there. He gave me a hug and was surprised to see me. He had remained at the classification prison a month after I had left. This was his home prison he will live at for a while… possibly for the rest of his life. He was still fighting his case for his mysterious crime. I still felt it was a terrible sex crime that perhaps he was in denial over. This man had tendencies to judge others. Even Xanadoo and I for not being married. Telling me we are committing the unforgivable sin of Adultery. That this is a sin and that is a sin and I will surely go to hell if I don't change my ways.

Meanwhile, when he was my cellmate, I would get sickening thoughts of him raping a little girl. He had been married to the same woman all his life and the Christian faith keeping him feeling guilty if he doesn't live the strict way he so truly believed. That could have enabled him to fall into that corruption being he was so oppressed all his life going too fanatical with over zealous religious conviction. His belief was the only true belief in the world and if you didn't follow that, you were doomed.

I had a twisted dream one night of him trying to come on to me. He was crawling on my bed as I looked at him in disgust.

I spoke harsh words. "Remove yourself from me."

I heard him whisper, "You know you want to."

Then I woke up! Every time he judged me or someone else, I felt like saying, "Don't judge me! You know what you did!" His repulsive sin I felt reeked off of him! In a strange way I kinda of felt the girls cries. How she felt when that old man made his move on her like in my dream. Him saying the same thing to his little victim. I didn't have all the facts so I really couldn't say anything. I just felt it. Well, whatever it was, it was between the Divine and him.

The pastor started and opened with a prayer. He had us turn to the book of Matthew. Matthew chapter 12 verses 43 – 45 was a very interesting suggestion. It was called "Return of the unclean spirit."

43. *"When the unclean spirit has gone out of a person, it passes through waterless places seeking rest, but finds none.* 44. *Then it says, 'I will return to my house from which I came.' And when it comes, it finds the house empty, swept, and put in order.* 45. *Then it goes and brings with it seven other spirits more evil than itself, and they enter and dwell there, and the last state of the person is worse than the first. So also will it be with this generation."*

That passage had put a daunting revelation of my own soul. In my days of youth, there were always unclean spirits lurking, whispering sins to my essence. Addiction itself is a powerful ill-behaved force. One drug turned into more drugs that were worse than the first. Demons are persistent in consuming human souls and dragging us down into spiritual demise. At first using drugs was fun, exciting and new. Slowly I needed more and I began doing things I thought I would never do. It turned my moral perception evil in ways I have never known. The powerless I had in consuming mind-altering substances were shockingly overshadowing. It was like I could see what I was doing but I couldn't control it.

As I fell deeper into the pits of my own hell, things began to look different. I didn't feel the same feelings I had when I was clear-headed. I felt worthless and unattractive. I isolated on a path of obliteration. I lost the will to live. Addiction and obsession had enslaved me beyond belief and I became a prisoner of my own mind. It was in that passage of the bible that made me realize just how real darkness is. It cluttered the light within my spirit and corrupted me physically, mentally and spiritually. When I looked back on my sickness, it scared the crap out of me that I could have become so confined by the grip of Satan. Messing with my mind and leading me down the wide and broad path to hell.

What was taught in that session was if we remain blind to the wrongdoings that are around us, we become lost and things would always get worse. Jesus Christ showed us the example on how to live, how to be, showing kindheartedness, healing and the ultimate sacrifice. I could see the narrow path of righteousness. With positive thoughts, positive things will occur. Living in a negative state of mind creates problems that could have been avoided. Kindness was always the one key to life I believed in. Being on all those drugs turned me, not only against myself, but also against my family, friends, and Divinity. Anger and resentment grew in ways I never felt. Resentment was like hurting myself expecting the other person to feel the pain. I was only hurting myself.

Nowadays, I see so many ungodly men running around praising sin as if it were a habitual way to be. We see sin in every corner of the world and just accept it. As it states in the bible that in this generation so will be more evil doings. I had no control over anyone around me but I was then in control of myself. I wasn't sure what the answer was in the existence we live. All I knew in that moment was that morality could only begin with me. Perhaps if I were to shed my light of hope and joy, others would follow.

We were let out of bible study and I walked with Dale until we split to our separate blocks. If he was truly innocent, I sincerely hoped his lawyers would get him out. But so far he has been incarcerated for three years now and no luck. Walking back to my block I felt lifted. That message I received in bible study really got to me. I walked into the block and the CO at the desk told me I had mail. He handed me a letter from Goo and I went up to my dorm. I sat down and opened the envelope. The letter was full of love and knowing that she would be there for me when I come home. I could only imagine how hard it must be for her to be all alone. I didn't want to hurt her anymore and I knew I needed to grow into the man I could be. But it would take work on my part.

Ironically she sent me lyrics to a song by Michael Jackson called, "Man in the mirror."

Goo highlighted the words; *"I'm gonna make a change, for once in my life. It's gonna feel real good, gonna make a difference. Gonna make it right...*

I'm starting with the man in the mirror. I'm asking him to change his ways. And no message could have been any clearer. If you wanna make the world a better place take a look at yourself and then make a change."

The synchronicity of the Divine was well balanced. I had that revelation in bible study then I receive a letter from Goo with that song. Words that were truly telling me I could be so much more than what I used to be in my darkness. I felt that since my thoughts were positive, an encouraging message of conviction came to me, reinforcing my sparkle of spirituality. God is Light and Love, which is the most powerful Force in the Universe. I had no doubt that the Deity of Light and Love was real and that if I apply myself I could overcome the darkness. I just needed to be completely opened and ready to hear the messages that come in waves from beyond. And no message could have been any clearer.

I began to socialize more as I slowly opened up. There was this heavyset black man who was in his mid 40's. He noticed me and came up to talk.

"You don't look like someone who is suppose to be in here." He said nicely. "You're not from around this area either I bet. I heard you talk, I bet you're from New York." He said.

I asked, "how could you tell?"

"From the way you present yourself. My name is Andromonous. But you can call me Andro."

"That's a really cool name."

The bell for mainline rang and it was time to eat. Andro and I walked together in the crowd not really looking forward to the crap we were going to eat.

"So what are you in for?" Andro asked.

"I forged some prescriptions. You?"

"I am a parole violator. I had a 12 to 30 year sentence for robbery, made parole, was out for a few years then violated because I smoked a joint." He shook his head. "You seem like an intelligent person, like you have it together."

"Yeah, well, not all together. I'm here aren't I?"

As we were walking to the chow hall, I briefly told him my story and my past and how I kept making the same mistakes.

He said, "have you ever heard of something called 'The law of attraction'?"

"Sounds familiar. What is it?"

As Andro and I got into the chow hall there was a long line and the madness was all around us.

Andro said, "if you were to be in a positive state of mind, positive things become attracted to you. Good things always seem to happen. When you're always in a bad mood or in a negative state of mind there is always some kind of drama in your life. Like certain women who always say they constantly gravitate assholes to them. They are doing something wrong to allow that kind of negative energy to come into their lives. Or when you wake up in the morning and stub your toe and say this is going to be a bad day! You carry that negative emotion with you making the rest of the day a bad one. Just because one has a bad morning doesn't mean one will have a bad rest of the day."

The thought was intriguing because when I look back when I was on all the drugs, I always seem to attract other drug addicts and dealers. My energy was calling out for that kind of company. I had those terrible days when I had a bad morning too because I believed it was simply *"one of those days."* My energy must have been enormously negative when I was writing out those scripts that ended me up in prison! Allowing all those bad choices and negative feelings also attracted warning signs that I didn't want to hear. I was so down that the higher force was calling out to me forewarning me to stop. But I didn't and I ended up paying for the consequences.

"How do you know this?" I asked.

He said, "I may be in prison for something stupid but I love to grow and cling to other uplifting people. I do a lot of reading and avoid pessimistic people."

As we moved up on the line we overheard two inmates talking. They were checking out a short unattractive elderly woman who was a Lieutenant doing rounds.

One said, "Damn she's got the fat ass son! I'd slam old girl in the can! I'd tear that ass up!"

The other laughed and said, "Damn! You've been in prison way too long!"

"Yeah, I'm getting tired of beating off to the hot bitch on the cheese bottle we get on commissary."

"Damn yo! You still beating off to the cheese?"

"Fucking right!"

Andro looked at me. "That's what I am talking about. There are always going to be ignorant people in this world and especially in prison. Grown men who do not want to change or grow and wind up back in prison after they get out. That's why I gravitated to you because you seem to have an inner light about you. You definitely do not belong in a place like this."

We grabbed our trays and sat down to eat. It was some new type of fish that was rubbery. It looked like some sort of pink sea creature stamped into squares! It came across like an ocean cockroach. From what I was told, the fish was actually made up of ground up fish heads, turned into a batter, made into squares then baked. The uncertainty of the origin of the crap before me gave me a real hard time eating it. All around me I saw inmates chattering mindless dribble and stuffing food down their pants to sneak back to the block. Some were yelling across the room with no shame.

Andro continued, "you have a quiet disposition about yourself. Your energy is calming."

"Thank you. I'm a writer and I have done a lot of great things but my addiction overtook me."

"The snowball effect, huh?"

"Snowball effect?"

"I know about addiction and it always comes down to the snowball effect. You start with one then two then four and before you know it your life is spiraling out of control. Before you know it that little snowball rolled and became massive until it was too late. But you look like someone who can make something of yourself. We all screw up. It's what makes us human. Believe me this prison doesn't define me."

Talking with Andro made me see the light that was within me. I noticed that since all the negative energy was out of me and I was replacing it with positive, someone good came to me. I remember learning how holding a good conversation can stimulate the mind. Isolating made me feel like hell and I knew the spirit of Lucifer was lurking. That dark sensation we feel inside that takes us over sometimes leaving us with no hope. I know it all too well. Strength for humans comes with unity. Some things we cannot do alone.

We finished up our shitty meal and started walking back. The weather was cool and the fall leaves were mostly gone leaving them nearly bare.

Andro asked, "you appreciate nature, huh?"

I said, "oh yeah. There are so many guys in here that could care less. Preoccupied with dumb shit."

"That's because they are shallow thinkers. They refuse to step outside of the box like you. Hey you should come to the library when we go. There are a few books I would love for you to check out. You're in prison, may as well make it into a learning experience. Pretend it is a school."

"Believe me I do. I write letters everyday to my girlfriend and tell her about the craziness that goes on here. I believe that with a bad situation we can make something good come from it."

We got back to the block and he had to go to talk to someone else. Andro seemed like a decent well-educated person and the synchronicity was working around me. If I were to keep up my positive energy, I would continue to attract good things.

Andro and I along with a few guys from the block went to the library the next day. There I found a large amount of information. As I looked around, I saw quite a few good men actually studying, making use of their time. It was a better side of the penitentiary community. I walked down one of the isles and saw a book on the universe. I grabbed the book and had a seat at the table. I flipped through the pages seeing captivating photos of our solar system. How all the planets can continuously revolve around the sun was amazing. Hubble had taken so many breath-taking views of the outer reaches of the universe. There were intense images of our galaxy. The sight of the spiraling galaxy, which held billions of stars, began to create a spark in my understanding.

The universe is undeniably vast and expanding at a fantastic speed, so they say… We really do not know for sure. I remember reading in the bible, that God stretched the heavens like a curtain, and spread them like a tent to dwell in. The big bang gave us the scientific theory on how the universe began. What always intrigued me was what was going on before that? What was the spiritual world like before time? Could the universe have existed once before and ended then was reborn like the circle of life?

As I read some of the information from the book I held, I learned that no one could answer that question. Allegedly science claims the universe that holds billions of galaxies, which hold billions of stars and planets, was just an accident. From nothingness it started from a tiny speck of energy that appeared out of nowhere and blew up giving birth to what we see in the sky and beyond. What I felt in my spirit was that God could have been on the outside of what is now our universe and made the explosion giving life all around. I do not rule out either science or religious conviction, I combine them.

The spiritual side of it, as we understand it, was that Divinity shaped existence that took six days. We sense time different and in our limited minds it could have taken billions of years to come together in those six days of Divine creation. Spirituality is the faith in the mystery that a higher power is at work. It gives us meaning to life and that we have a purpose. It keeps us in balance in knowing right from wrong and gives us hope.

Science is the study of the mechanics of how everything works. Science breaks down the technicalities of the universe and analyzes the functions of everything from inner space to the far reaches of the universe. There are so many questions that may never be answered and it boggled my mind to no end! Science cannot explain the force behind the curtain of life. In my mind I have seen so much but it doesn't compare to the greatness that lies outside the material world and even outside the physical plane.

Was the universe infinite or could it be finite? If I were to travel through the cosmos on a straight line would I end up at the same place I started? Go to the end and come back out at the beginning like in a video game making it both infinite and finite. Could the universe be similar to the shape of planets that are simply round and how it goes on forever going round and round? Could the halo of the great universe make it seem endless like being surrounded by an array of mirrors? I often wondered if there were other universes parallel or outside of our own? I wanted to know what existed beyond time and space and who God really was! My energy was lifting, as I felt compelled to learn more. Going to the library was something I needed to open the doors inside my mind.

I have seen beyond this world yet I have a world of my own in my mind. I could pick up on energy in nature, people, and the beauty of existence. I gain energy from intellectual stimulation, music and traveling outside the box of simple thinking. I have noticed I am in sync with people around me and even with the weather and seasons. I can gain information I need when I look for it. Time aligns me with opportunities that come to me at the right time. I have seen many of those chances fly right past me. But there is a circle to life and another chance is given. It was up to me to take hold of that moment and use it to my benefit.

Time has gotten faster the older I got and when I look back at my past its like a transitory blink. The timeline of my life and all the memories inside of it was just as minuscule as grains of sand. Even in the insignificant sequential era of my years, I recall countless moments where I got stuck and time dragged. The seconds that slowly ticked one by one made my misery seem to linger because I desperately wished the moment would end.

Like that moment at the first prison stay where I would stare at the patch of sunlight painfully drag as if it weren't moving at all. I was in pure torture and I felt terrible and wanted out but I could not get out. I was trapped in that cell waiting for the next mealtime that seemed like it would never come. Time is somehow distorted to feel slower than usual in our despair making it a form of personal hell. Great and exciting moments seem to just fly by. Having fun makes us forget the time and forgetting makes time appear, as if it doesn't exist. Before we know it the good times are gone and we wonder where it went. Is all we see and know just a false impression that circles the sands of time? Really now... Where the hell does the time go?

My head began to hurt as I became obsessed with my newfound spark. I looked around the library and felt a strange déjà vu. It was another mind-boggling perception that I never could explain. I never have been in that chair in that library ever in my life. It felt like a fleeting instantaneous shadow of familiarity like a small window through time was passing by. If I could catch it in that instant, I could actually predict what may happen within the few seconds of the mysterious portal of that point in time. Perhaps those passing phenomenons are God's way of correcting the same errors I keep making. Was it the distorted sphere of mirrors of my existence before me going in a loop? I wasn't sure of the answer but I did know one thing. It was time to take out the garbage that was cluttering my mind and recapture what I have lost. There were infinite worlds out there to explore rather than to be forever lost in the circle of my own.

Living Off The Grid

It was late November 2005 and I had lost everything.
When I first arrived in the city, back in the end of August, it was a
new way of living. I rode my bike from hospital to hospital
obtaining pain pills. I was touring the big city and admiring the
Inner Harbor and all the waterfront stores. The harbor glistened
with large boats and some yachts at bay. There were people
everywhere, shopping, walking and eating out on the patios of the
restaurants. I was high and free from the worries of the every day
life. It was like a whole other world with tall buildings and so
many cars coming and going. Fire engines, ambulances and police
cars rang quite often.

I met this woman outside one of the hospitals I was at who
introduced me to a duel diagnosis rehab. I was standing outside
the ER smoking a cigarette and this heavyset woman who was also
smoking walked over to me.

"I'm going to come over here where it's safe where you're smoking."

We started talking and she mentioned having her own personal issues. Struggling with drugs and depression she told me how bad it was for her. She was homeless like how I was in that moment in time but found a safe place.

"Where are you living now?" I asked

"It's a place for people like me who need help. It's a duel diagnosis center for mental problems and addiction," she said. "It's been helping me a lot."

"I need a place like that. Where is it?"

She had gave me all the information I needed to know and hoped to see me there the next day. Fate was working for me by putting that woman in my life at that time but I procrastinated knowing there was a place that could help me.

I continued to get high and sleeping on park benches. My determination for prescription drugs turned dangerous. It was a Sunday and there were no pharmacies opened that day in the city. I didn't give up and rode around with my prescription for Dilaudid, through the worst neighborhoods, on a serious mission, until I found one that was opened outside of the city. All that energy just for a tiny pill that altered my brain for a short time was such a waste. I remember thinking; if I would just use that determination on my writing career, I could be so successful. Clearly my dark side was in charge no matter the cost, putting my priorities way out of whack.

One evening when I was about to lock up my bicycle to crash on the park bench, there were five teenage black guys on bikes circling me and another on foot. The one on foot grabbed my bike.

"Give me your bike!" He said forcefully.

My backpack was on the ground so I put my foot through the strap to make sure that they would not swipe it and held on to my bike.

I stressed. "This is all I have! I am homeless!"

"Mother fucker, you ain't homeless!"

He pulled out a blade and threatened to cut me if I didn't give him my bike but I was still holding on tight. One of the other guys looked at me in concern.

He said in a nice way. "Just give him the bike man. I don't want to see anyone get hurt."

I finally let the bike go and he hopped on it and rode away with his boys. There I was completely alone next to my park bench I usually slept on. I was scared but grateful they didn't take my backpack, which held my clothes and radio.

The next day I went to that safe place that woman had told me about a few days ago and checked in. In my moral fiber I felt it was the Spirit of God who moved in and had my bike taken. Karma had delivered me some bad luck due to my gluttony for more drugs and not wanting the help when it was provided to me. I kept putting off going to the rehab center and went on too many hospital runs.

"I'll go tomorrow," I would tell myself but never went.

A force that was beyond my power came along, allowing those teenagers to take my bike, my only means of getting around, leaving me with no other choice. I had seen the sign. Or perhaps it was inevitable due to my negative ways. Either way it was time to try and get myself together.

The duel diagnosis center provided psychotherapy help along with drug treatment. Basically I was in a mental hospital drug rehab. The first stay was rough as I was withdrawing in observation. They gave us medicine to help with that. We lounged in big chairs that reclined back. It wasn't the greatest but at least I was safe. The night went on slowly as I couldn't sleep. As the nighttime turned into day, I was happy to move on to the next stage of that dreadful place. I was moved into one of the buildings with three floors. The third floor was for the men and there was a huge dayroom with many rooms. They set us up at social services to get us on Medicaid, food stamps and cash assistance. We also were given a monthly bus pass to go wherever we needed to go for free being that we were considered temporarily disabled.

I was summoned to court for my petty theft charge when my credit card was denied and they gave me 18 months probation, which was a bit harsh for my insignificant crime. Luckily I had an address, which was the rehab at the time; otherwise I may have had a bench warrant on me. It was no big deal. I simply had to report to my probation officer once a month. I did really well in the program for a short while until I met a girl named Jessica. I wasn't focusing on recovering. All I wanted was to please the sickly desires that were screaming out to me. Jessica and I engaged in free sex in a dirty abandoned shed. She introduced me to some people who got us heroin and cocaine. Once again I was becoming wrapped up in my addictions.

The counselors knew something wasn't right with her and me so we got drug tested and kicked out of the program. She went her way and I was again all alone. There I was walking the streets of Baltimore City with my backpack during the holiday season. It was nearly December and I had nowhere to go. At first I felt free and adventurous. I had no worries, no responsibly, nothing at all. I had lost everything and I was free to do anything. So I walked the city streets and slept at the local mission. It was another side of the streets I never knew existed. We would all check into the mission, then sit on the chairs in the chapel. We would go to eat dinner then they had us take a shower. They offered me new clothes, fresh socks and underwear.

After, we would sit in the chapel and wait. A pastor would come in and say a few words but I was in no mood to hear it. I just wanted to lie down and fall away. Around 9 PM they cleared the chapel of all the chairs and we lined up to grab a mattress. They gave us sheets and a blanket and we found a spot on the chapel floor. I remember noticing the long thin bright brown wood stripe pattern on the floor. As I looked around I saw everyone setting up their place to sleep. Spreading the sheets they gave us, setting up the pillows, and chit chatting among each other. I looked up at the arched shaped ceiling with the heavy lights beaming down on everything. I just set up my mattress and lay down, covered up and felt safe.

Once the lights went out I would stare at the ceiling asking myself if where I lay was real? I didn't sleep much and heard a symphony of bodily noises from everyone around me. It was a very depressing way to live and I was deep in it. I just wanted to lie there and prayed the time would go slow. I'd stare up at the ceiling with the dim lighting that was all around. I tried to hold on to that moment, feeling safe and warm. I didn't want it to end.

The night moved on and I knew time was getting closer to having to get up. I could hear people talking and saw the lights in the hallway outside the chapel go on shinning in through the window. That dreaded feeling of "Any Minute Now" was all over. I tried to close my eyes and hold on to the comfort for as long as I could. There were a few overnighters that were already up and getting ready to leave. More movement began and I opened my eyes seeing the chapel slowly come to life... Sure enough, those damn bright lights came on and the remaining started to get up. The mission had every one who stayed over night get up at 5:30 in the morning. We got fed breakfast then it was off to do anything.

For me I enjoyed the scenery of the Inner Harbor and downtown Baltimore tooling around the beautiful stores and sparkling waterfronts. People walking around, some alone, some couples in love and families and children. The way I looked and walked, I did not appear as a down-and-out drug addict. I seem to have fit in being disadvantaged, hiding in plain sight as if I were a regular person. There were always people walking around with backpacks. Usually because they were college students or people going to work, which helped me blend in. I was just another person with a backpack and headphones, listening to music walking the Inner Harbor. The water swayed and rippled as there were boats docked. I would smell delicious food as I passed the many restaurants that were part of the walkway off the sea front. I wandered inside the mall like shopping plaza. With no money everything was out of reach and I was so hungry.

I rode the buses and subways to venture the big city. I had neglected to inform my probation officer I was kicked out of the program and homeless. She really didn't ask a lot of questions anyway so I let it be. The rehab I was in was voluntary, not court ordered, so I felt she didn't need to know. I had cash assistance, which wasn't much but it got me by. I was able to get free food with my food stamps and eat at the soup kitchens. I had become strong willed in surviving the streets. I never knew I could handle such a feat. My addiction was on the move and every so often I would go to a motel with the money I had.

A bus ride and a light rail later, I would get off outside of the city and catch another bus or walk the 2-mile journey up the road. I would check into the motel, toss my backpack on the bed. I'd plop on the bed and removed my shoes with my bad foot odor hitting me in the face! Back in my safe zone, I would get undressed and soak in a warm bath. Enjoying the moment, I would try to forget what my life had become. Afterwards, feeling refreshed, I would lay in the king size bed. I loved the feel of after a nice bath, the way the sheets felt. Pulling the covers over me I would quiver in a comforting way. I grabbed the remote and watch television while I popped some pills and smoked cigarettes. I never wanted to leave the comfort of that cozy bed with the television. I became so attached to that room in only one night. I longed so much for the refuge from the storms that were cycling around me and within.

There I was in a lonely hotel room with no lights on and the curtain closed under the warm covers feeling snug and sheltered. The television glowed eerily around me with the shadows dancing on the walls as the heater raddled. I was watching the movie *"It's a Wonderful Life"* completely twisted on drugs and despair. As I got into the movie I felt that no one would have been affected if I were never born. In the movie the main character, George, got a glimpse of how bad things would have been if he never existed. What would have been different if I never existed? At that moment in time I didn't exist in the real world. Life continued to function and I was illusory. Maybe things would have been better if I were never born. I no longer felt the will to live anymore. I just continued to lie in that hotel bed watching the movie wasted and far away from life hoping the night would linger. I felt out of my head and foggy as I tried to focus on the movie. I began to drift with my eyesight stuttering as everything in that darkened room appeared in a strange hazy apparition. The voices on the television became muffled and distorted… I was in nothingness…

The heater by the window would click on snapping me back to reality. I would keep close track of the time trying to stretch that night out as long as I could…

Before I knew it, I saw daylight slip through the cracks of the curtains and my time there ran out. I looked at the clock and it was 10 minutes before checkout time. I hated having to get up, dressed and leave the comfort of that motel room. I had to bundle up with the long black trench coat I had. It was getting cold, and as I would walk up the street to catch the bus, I would stand there with the cold wind blowing in my face. My mind went blank and I felt a strong sense of hopelessness. I was living off the grid with no one but myself. I was lost in a world of confusion and vagueness. The feeling was overwhelming and I didn't know what to feel anymore. I had just given up on life and everyone I had loved had given up on me.

Days went by and Christmas came. I was no one living nowhere. Never before had the holidays felt so grim. It was cold and cloudy and I was walking the streets with nowhere to go. My family was together, warm and happy living a good life. I had sincerely missed my brothers and their family but I was in no position to call them for help. Part of me felt like I was the forgotten brother and was truly on my own in the brutal icy reality I created. As I walked around the practically empty city, I saw all the Christmas decorations and fur trees all decked out. I felt such sorrow and I couldn't take it anymore. What was I to do? I was destitute in a cruel world.

I tried to sneak into hotels and sleep in the bathroom stall just to keep warm. There I was lying next to the toilet using my backpack for a pillow hoping no one would discover my presence. They must have had a security camera because someone came in and called me out. He escorted me out into the frigid night and told me to never come back. I remember thinking of all those warm rooms that were empty and if he had a heart he could have let me stay a night there. All those available rooms and all the down-and-out people with nowhere to go, cold and hungry sounded so immoral. It was 15 degrees out and he was so uncaring. Why did the world have to be so insensitive?

New Years had come and gone and still I was homeless in a bitter city. It was mid January 2006 and I was going on 32 years old. I would see people eating at restaurants, warm with their loved ones. I would often stare into cafes with my black trench coat and backpack snug around me. I saw people laughing and able to buy stuff living out their lives. They didn't know how much emotional pain I was in and how far gone I was. The homeless people and I were cast to the side and considered the forgotten and the parasites of the functioning world. Though I didn't appear homeless to anyone because I took care of myself, I felt useless to humanity.

The snow would fall all around me and I saw so many men and even woman living on the city streets. They had a square space, like a small park, next to a church that allowed the homeless to camp there. There had to be over thirty or forty men and women, many who had tents and basically lived there. Grown men and woman living out their lives in tents scattered around like a little neighborhood in a hopeless way. As I would walk by I noticed there were a few benches where some would sit and talk. Others who didn't have a tent would be sleeping on blankets and sleeping bags. Several big trees stood in the square. They had strings where they hung out their clothes, big metal garbage cans and a few fire pits. It was a good thing that the church allowed them a place to stay even if it was outside in the cold.

There were quite a few men standing on corners, holding up cardboard asking for help. Standing in the median of a divided city street, needing "$". Even disabled veterans, some in wheel chairs, no legs, burnt out, dirty asking for help. Disturbing how those who once fought for this country are now in the pits of reality. Pushed aside, discarded. I can only image what they must have gone through in those wars. Fighting a pointless battle between mankind's divided sides. Mankind fighting each other and for what... really? Geed... Territory... Religion, the cause for most wars. Killing one another over differences in beliefs. Its been going on for centuries and will continue. Too much evil in this world, it will never change!

I was a loner and isolated, not being part of that detached society. Like a ghost in the night I wanted not to be seen or known. I just wanted to drift freely and remain off the radar. Memories were always with me. That one time I was in love for the first time. I remember the video from the song *"I Remember You"* by Skid Row back in the fall of 1989. A very powerful reminder of my first love experience. I remember in the video there was a homeless man walking around the city streets in the winter. He carried around the pictures of his first love. He drops them as he walks the cold streets with the gray sky and the city buildings all around. Being 15 going on 16 as I lay in my bed for some reason I saw myself as that homeless man remembering my first love. I couldn't help but see that as something that drew me in. Every time I watched it, I always thought the same thing about the video. I often wondered would that be me? There were just certain things that stood out almost like a strange premonition. Back then I didn't know what to think about weird stuff like that. It was the time when I was with her and I had a warm home, my innocents, family and friends.

And there I was walking around in the dead of winter with nowhere to go just like the video. Was me watching that back then a vision of my future? In that moment, that was exactly what I became. Part of me also did not want to give up so easily like that and just accept I would forever be on the streets. Deep within me I still felt that shimmer of hope and that there was more to how I was existing in that moment in time.

One night I was walking with nowhere to go and there was an older black man who knew me. He offered me a spot next to him over a manhole, which produced warmth from the stem underground. He gave me a blanket and was kind. All through the night, I couldn't stop shaking, even though I was fully dressed under a warm blanket. I felt horrible and got no sleep with my constant shivering. I had to get up and found myself struggling to walk, feeling sick and weak.

It was 6 in the morning and I staggered to the subway. I went down and waited for the train. It was cold down there and the lights hovered above me in the nearly empty underground terminal. As I stared down at the subway tracks, I often thought about suicide. I would visualize laying on the tracks and have the train run me over, severing my head from my body. Why not I thought? No one would miss a loser like me anyway. I really didn't have the nerve to actually do it and shook off the twisted thought. I felt the air beginning to blow over me, growing stronger, as the oncoming train honked in the distant, deep in the tunnel. I saw the lights in the passageway coming, gleaming in my eyes and the rumble shook around me. There had to be hope for me I thought. The train slowly pulled up and I knew I had to go to the hospital. There was something wrong with me.

Once I check into the ER, I didn't have to wait that long. I went back and onto the bed feeling beaten by the streets. After some tests, the doctor said I had pneumonia and needed fluids and antibiotics. I told him how much pain I was in and he gave me two Percocets to feel better. As I lay there being given IV fluids, I felt I could not go on like that anymore. The streets were beating the crap out of me. I had suffered emotional, mental and physical collapse and couldn't bear it anymore. Once I began to feel better, I got myself together and knew I needed to get help. That was when I decided to go back to the rehab to give it another try.

It was the summer of 2006 and I had successfully completed the duel diagnosis drug program. I made it through the cold winter that led into a warming spring of my recovery. They had diagnosed me with bipolar disorder and put me on medication. Apparently everyone who goes through that program was told they have some sort of mental illness and put of psych meds. I did not believe I had bipolar; instead, I was up and down due to my personality, addiction and the loss of my mother. I was eccentric in many ways along with being creative and artistic. I was unique and did not walk along with others as a follower. I had my own views on life and walked my own path.

I did not pay much attention to what the program had to teach me. A big part of me going there was because I was beat down by the streets and I wanted to better myself as a person. I was still on probation and doing well. I moved into a transitional house that catered to drug addicts. They had rules such as a curfew, to remain drug free and to attend NA meetings. I didn't rebel too much against that. I was grateful I had a roof over my head. I had to pay rent so I landed myself a good job as a valet driver. I was hired and placed at a local hospital downtown. The irony of me working at a hospital I had been too many times over was interesting. It would always be a reminder that I could get pills right then and there if I wanted.

I had to park cars and talked to many people who had pain medicine, which struck a chord within my demons. I tried to fight it off and focus on work. One of my co-workers had a car for sale and I really wanted it. My determination to make as much money as possible to drive again soared! I began taking on extra shifts and working really hard at my job. Each day that I worked, I was fully focused on making the money to get that car. It was all I thought about. My positive energy was streaming and there was no stopping me from reaching my goal. I was working 7 days a week and was dedicated to my work and people skills. I had to be the best worker there because I had a mission.

I had gotten a raise and finally reached my goal of $1,000 to buy the car. It felt great being able to drive a car again and I was lifted. The interesting part of my determination in raising the money was it had impressed my boss. He had called me into his office and commended me on a great job. Not only did I receive the raise for my performance, I also won employee of the month. I gained a credential and won a $50 gift certificate for Best Buy. I remember thinking, I didn't mean to earn employee of the month, and receive a reward for my hard work. I just really wanted that car. My boss had offered me a promotion to become a shift manager if I were to keep up the good work.

I was on a natural high and impressed with myself that I could accomplish such a feat. I remembered going on that mission to find a pharmacy on my bike when I first got to the city. My determination was strong on that Sunday when all the other pharmacies in the city were closed that I did not give up no matter how hard it was. I was successful in getting the script filled, and now, I saw I was successful in my work, even if it was for a car. The point was that I could achieve anything I put my mind to. The mind is a powerful thing and if I were to use it to my highest potential I could do anything.

I was attending an NA meeting when I met an old friend of my brother's. His name was Marty and was serious about recovery through Narcotics Anonymous. I got to know him better and he wanted to become my sponsor. He knew all the ins and outs for the NA program and I figured I could use a few lessons on true recovery. He offered me a room in his attic to rent out for me. I could move in any time I wanted. I thought why not? It could be good for me to live with someone who had over 5 years in recovery. So I packed up my stuff at the transitional house and moved into the upper floor room of his house.

I went with him to a lot of NA meetings and I was slowly getting the idea about the step work. I first had to admit I was powerless over my addiction and that my life had become unmanageable. No argument there I thought. Next I had to believe a power greater than myself could restore me to sanity. I did believe that. Next I had to turn my life and will over to the care of God, as I would understand Him. That I did. I always have believed that, so it came pretty easy for me, even though I had slipped away from God in my darkened days.

Something wasn't right. Marty began to act differently. He showed up at my work one day and handed me a bag with a few pills inside.

"Here," he said. "I know your back hurts and I had a few extra."

To my surprise they were Vicodin pills and I wondered why he would give me those. I didn't question the matter, as I did need em. So I started taking the pills. Marty had two daughters that lived with him. One was 9, Brie and the other was 14 named Paris. Paris was having sex since she was 10, which I couldn't believe. When I was 10, I wasn't even thinking about sex. At least not having it. The girls looked up to me and considered me family since I was living with them. Paris confined in me often about her issues and looked up to me as a big brother. She had told me she smoked weed and she would drink a lot with her friends.

I tried to warn her about the effects of drugs and alcohol but she had her own free will. I could not control what she did. I had my own problems arising. I had obtained a doctor and swore I would not ruin it by over asking for pain meds. My new doctor was the sweetest person I had encountered in my pill popping days. She was a black woman named Dr. Blackman. She always called me Boo and prescribed me anything I wanted. I had abused her kindness in asking for every narcotic, saying one didn't work, and I wanted to try something else. I had terrible guilt by deceiving her but my addiction took over me again. If that wasn't bad enough, Marty began to backslide in his recovery. He started smoking crack and became unstable. I did not understand how someone who was so into recovery could fall back into drugs so easily.

Time flew by and it was late January 2007 and I was turning 33. I had successfully completed my probation and was free. I could wash my hands of that petty arrest. Marty was on a serious downward spiral and I was going down with him. I would make drug runs for him, going to the bad neighborhoods, obtaining crack cocaine. We would split it and he would lock himself in his bedroom. He was so paranoid from the drug that he thought people were coming after him, which was why he locked himself in his room. He had closed all the curtains in his bedroom and swore he saw people watching him from the big-based blue lamp he had. He tried showing me in his messy closed off isolation chamber. He pointed at what looked like long glowy images. It was the other lights he had lit and the design of the lamp base. He really believed he was seeing that people watching him. As if that was even possible! He had lost his mind! The children were a factor, I thought, as I knew he was making a bad example for them. Brie who was turning 10 had told her big sister she was ready for sex. Where was Marty I thought, as I knew that was not a good thing. They were children and on a bad path at such a young age!

My drug use had escalated so much that I wound up being late and screwing up on my job. I wouldn't follow the rules and I was asking some of the customers of the valet company for pain pills. A few had given me some out of the kindness of their hearts. Dr. Blackman got red flagged for over prescribing me pills and could no longer give me any. She was still very nice about it. I understood where she was coming from. I had worked overtime valet parking at a hotel on my day off and smoked a cigarette on their grounds. The hotel manager did not like that and reported me to my boss. I had a sit down with my boss and he told me I was fired. I could not believe I got fired on what was supposed to be my day off!

I went back to my co-worker and told him I was fired. Suddenly my boss came up to me very angry.

He yelled, "you have been asking the customers for pills?"

What could I say but… "Sorry about that."

"What the hell is wrong with you? I want you off the property now and do not step foot here again!"

I left feeling like crap that my addiction had taken away my accomplishments again! I had no job, and my sponsor, who was supposed to help me stay clean, became my enabler. How could it happen I asked myself? Karma was once again catching up to me and my car that I worked hard for broke down on me! The transmission took a giant shit so I was without a car again! I had to make money so I had to walk up to the Labor Ready Program and was sent off doing odd jobs for nonsense pay.

Marty had met a woman named Lisa. Lisa was in her late thirties, not much younger than him. She had moved in and was a part of our madness. Lisa used to work for a doctor but was fired and had stolen a couple of prescription pads. She was too afraid to write them out so I offered to play doctor. I remembered how they did it by studying the many scripts I had gotten in the past. I wrote out the prescription for whatever we wanted. Since I had Medicaid, I could get the pills for free. I knew if I wrote out a Percocet script for 5 mgs, I would eat them up too fast. But if I would write for the 7.5 mgs, I could get them sooner being a new script. Then it was the 10 mgs. I did this over and over again with both of our names writing out for Vicodin and Lortab next.

I was deep into prescription fraud that I didn't realize the consequences. I was in my room in the loft listening to the radio. A talk show was on and I felt the spirit of the Divine trying to reach me.

The radio spoke, *"There are consequences for everything we do. Even if we were to stop what we are doing that is wrong, a price must be paid. We cannot do a bad thing and not expect a punishment. The universe does not work that way. There is no escaping the wrongdoing we carry out. All sins must be paid for. All sins."*

I knew it was a sign that I was Karmicly Fucked!

Marty got arrested for stalking his ex-wife and was put in jail. There was no way to bail him out. How the hell could my sponsor fall so fast and end up in jail? I was seeking recovery but instead I got re-enabled to feed my addictions. It wasn't supposed to be like this I thought. I was becoming scared that something bad was about to happen.

I was on one of the odd jobs and I was called to go on a delivery out of the warehouse I was placed at. It felt great to get the hell out of there and go on the road. The day was beautiful and mild. It was mid April and the trees were beginning to grow little leaves and flowers. I felt connected to the world, as I looked out the window at all the beauty that was around me. Peaceful music played and it was soothing to be in the truck. We delivered to the eastern part of Maryland, which was a 2-hour drive far away from the city. Far away from my madness.

We crossed the bridge over the Chesapeake Bay. Looking down at the sun glistening on the water I felt serenity. I haven't had a wonderful day like that in a long time. I always loved to travel and see all the beauty around me and that's what I was getting. Being on the other side of the bridge looked like I was in another country. The land was flatter and mostly farmlands. I peered into a few of the passing farmhouses I saw. I could actually feel those people's lives and could envision a few good memories. Standing in a clean country home, having a good life. Picturing what all the seasons would be like living on a farm. Admiring the land during the summer. Winter cozy nights by the fireplace, sipping a cup of coffee. Having someone to love next to me. I was feeling what it was like to live in that part of the world even for a short time.

That day felt like a gift from God, as something bad was to come. As if God granted me one last divine day before he brought the hammer down.

Lisa still lived with us and it was up to her and I to tend to Marty's daughters. We had to take care of them while he was in jail. I continued to forge the scripts and was getting in over my head. Lisa and I were getting large amounts of Percocet, Vicodin, Lortab, Valium, Xanex and Soma. I had my computer there and was working on my novel even though I was in a haze of deception and gluttony. I was trying to focus on my career but my dark side was getting the best of me. Signs were all around me that something bad was coming.

It was late April and Lisa and I had a refill left for Hydrocodone. Something felt wrong in my spirit, as I was about to get on Marty's bicycle to pick up the refills for us. I grabbed the disks with my novels on them and put them in my jacket. I never had done that before but something was telling me to take them with me in case something happened. I rode my bike in the cool misty evening to the pharmacy. I walked inside and got the large amount of pills for Lisa and I. I paid for them and walked outside to my bike. As I started to ride away, out of nowhere a sport utility vehicle drove up fast on me. I veered out of the way thinking he was a crazy driver.

The man looked out of his window and said pissed off, "Hey! Come here!"

A pick up truck pulled up next to me so I had stopped the bike, and before I knew it, the man in the sport utility vehicle jumped out and tackled me off the bike! I remember landing on the ground hard and the pills scattered on the pavement. I didn't know what the hell was going as he picked me up and threw me up against the pick up truck. They were undercover detectives and I was done! The jig was up. They detained me immediately and faced me forward.

The one who jumped me was acting like a real jack off treating me like a terrorist. The other was calmer and nice. He asked me some questions.

He said, "We got a report of someone going from pharmacy to pharmacy forging prescriptions." He picked up the pills that had fallen to the ground after I was tackled. He asked, "Are these all for you?"

I said, "Yes. I am a drug addict and needed medicine."

"Who is Lisa?" He asked.

"A friend."

"Well your friend landed you in trouble. We know she used to work for a doctor. We talked to him and he stated she used to work for him and was fired and had stolen two prescription pads."

I asked the asshole detective, "Why did you tackle me?"

He said, "I thought you were going to make a break for it."

"I was dead stopped!"

"I wouldn't worry about that right now."

I knew I was screwed. They searched me and had a police car called for me. Ironically the police station was directly across the street and I should have seen it coming. The signs were all around me warning me of my pending doom. Why didn't I listen to them? Was my addiction that overpowering that it blinded me to the repercussions of my actions?

They read me my rights and placed me into the cop car. I was taken across the street and booked. I tried to plea to the detectives that I was an addict and meant no harm. I was charged with obtaining a controlled substance by fraud, possession, and possession with the intent to distribute. Since I had a high pill count they thought my intentions were to sell them. What they didn't understand was my intention was to eat them. My bail was set for $15,000 and I knew I could not get bailed out. My only hope was to see the judge to see if my bail could be reduced or waived.

I sat in the cell feeling sick with a huge bruise on my hip from the idiot tackling me. There was no need for that, I thought! I wasn't going anywhere. It probably gave him an excuse to use unnecessary force. I had no weapons on me, I wasn't about to make a break for it and I certainly wasn't dangerous. I was just a person caught up with a disease of my mind and spirit. I was called out of the cell. I was a mess. I hadn't taken a shower in a couple of days and my hair was raggedy. I was brought into the courtroom where there were other offenders. Each got their turn to speak and the judge kindly granted a bail reduction. It was my turn to explain to the judge my situation.

I stood up and could not control my shaking. "Your honor I am not a drug dealer." I spoke crazily. "I am an addict and never sold a drug in my life. You can drug test me and you will see I have been taking the pills! Please you're honor waive my bail of $15,000!"

The judged looked down at me and said, "Request denied. I am resetting bail at $35,000."

I sat back down feeling miserable. Why did he up my bail and reduce the other's? I felt like a dumb ass as I thought of how I must have looked. Messy hair, pale, dirty clothes and the look on my face must have screamed help! I was detoxing off the drugs and was anxiously asking to be set free. The judge must have noticed my sickened condition and raised the bail, perhaps for my own safety. There was no more to do or say. It was all over for me.

The Holiday Bridge

The Autumn Bridge had come and gone. Time was moving along so fast that I couldn't believe it. It was mid December and I had became well adjusted to the honor block and living in the dorm. The block was decked out with Christmas decorations, which gave me a sense of the holiday spirit. Some of the inmates would make Christmas decorations out of paper and some would draw their holiday spirit on the wall. There was a small Christmas tree in the corner and it felt good to look at.

Thanksgiving had come and gone and it was sad not being home with Xanadoo, though she did visit me on Thanksgiving Day. I had missed so many holidays and I was in a maximum state correctional facility for that one. The best part of the visit with Goo was the CO was really nice and put on the big screen television for us to watch the Macy's Day Parade. Since there was hardly anyone visiting, she allowed us to have a beautiful

Thanksgiving. It was a shame, I felt, that in the prison I was in, there were over 2,000 inmates and only 3 inmates, including myself, got visits that day. Basically Xanadoo and I had the visiting room mainly to ourselves with the television that was usually meant for children visitors. It was a true blessing for us.

I received my outside clearance and moved on from being a block worker. I was an outside worker who had never seen the outside of the fences. I was placed to work with an electrician that was right outside the prison gates. I was excited to walk out of the razor wire fences to a taste of freedom, but the man in charge of the power plant to where I was placed, worked alone and never took out a crew. I still got paid which was a whopping .24 cents an hour, 6 hours a day for five days. So basically I did not work but still got paid for it. I wasn't about to complain.

I moved down to the lower bunk after my old Bunkie left the block. What a relief it was to have a bottom bunk! My new bunkie was a black guy with shoulder length dreads around 30 who was an intellectual. He and I got along right away and I enjoyed his company. His name was CJ and was doing a 2 – 4 year stint for cashing bad checks and identity theft. I had rented myself a television for $20 worth of my commissary until April. I got it off a wacky skinny black dude named Chicken Stick. Chicken Stick was the type to go around and hustle what he could and gamble since he had no one putting money on his books. I felt it was a pretty good deal and I could have my own television which I allowed CJ to watch with me or when I wasn't there.

My neighboring convict had the bottom bunk next to me. He was known as the Zen Master and had slicked back dark hair with a thin long grayish mustache and a pointed goatee. He was an Asian man in his late forties in for manslaughter. He was a Buddhist; very dedicated to his religion, who was a peaceful person and a blessing to be next to. He received an 8 – 16 year sentence, which I found unfair. He told me he knew marital arts and it was in self-defense. He swore he never meant to kill anyone deliberately. It was against his nature and lived with the regret everyday. He meditated daily and was able to block out the madness in the 22-man dorm. I had talked with the Zen Master often about how to meditate. He instructed me to think of beautiful things and listen to my breathing with my eyes closed. Clear my mind and allow the answers to come to me. He obtained the name Zen Master because he had reached pure Nirvana, which was true enlightenment of the soul.

The Zen Master was someone I wanted to learn from in some ways. I longed for peace of my own mind and wanted to vanquish the demon inside my head. I wanted to reach enlightenment in the lunacy of everything I was around. I was always seeing many of the inmates making hooch, talking about nonsense, blasting their music, watching Jerry Springer every day, and arguing over who is the best football team. It was a place of competition and I wanted no part of it. Why do humans have to believe they are the best or their team is the best? Like the words from the band Boston say.

"People living in competition. All I want is to have my piece of pie."

Grown men arguing over football teams all day long. On the chow line, on the pill line, in the yard, even in church! Apparently sports overruled everything else and that was a damn shame! There was so much more to life that I felt. There is so much beauty in the world to be admired. The Zen Master told me admiring true beauty is conducive to the soul and gives us uplifting energy. That was something I had felt in the past. Growing up in nature, like I did on Long Island, made me feel alive. The Zen Master had appreciated my stories of my youth and my oneness with the natural world.

He said to me, "You are of importance to the world. You just have to believe it."

I had found my own way to meditate and reach calmness. I would lie in bed on my back and close off all disruptive noises. I would close my eyes and listen to some of the more gratifying sounds. I found it pleasing to listen to the rainfall outside brushing against the window. The sounds of someone shuffling and playing cards were relaxing to me. The vibration of the bed when someone walked by soothed me. People whispering and humming a tune calmed me. Some television programs were peaceful to me such as the soft voices on daytime soap operas. The sounds of someone gently ruffling through pages of a book or newspaper gave me a nice sensation.

I found it so amazing that I was able to tap into the sounds around me and block out the annoying ones.... For the most part anyway. It was interesting to know my brain released comforting chemicals throughout my body as my ears absorbed selected reverberations. The Zen Master told me that was key thinking to finding enlightenment and aligning myself with oneness. It would surely release me from the clutter in my mind. To filter out all that was wrong and take in what was right.

The Zen Master's Bunkie above was a young black man about 27 who was in for attempted murder. He told me he got paid to kill someone, like a hit man, and received a 10 – 20 year stretch.

I asked him, "what does killing someone go for now a days?"

He said, "I would have gotten $40,000 but the guy I tried to kill lived after I put a bullet in his chest."

He went by the name the Sand Man because he would put people asleep permanently. The Sand Man was a laid back guy who I got along with.

My thoughts were going a mile a minute knowing I was about to see Parole. I sat on my bunk thinking of all that could go wrong. Creating all sorts of bad outcomes and aggregated situations, worsening the matter.

The Zen Master said, "do not allow yourself to go in there with negative thinking. If you do then you will give off negative energy and others can feel that. Do not try and bend reality with a false spirit and lies. Rather, go in there and be truthful and let them know you are regretful of the crime. Let them know your future plans and the good you wish to do. Illuminate positive energy and you will get positive results. We all have a devil inside of us telling us lies. Know thyself. Know the truth. You are of great value to the world and will be going home in April. Simply believe. Remember the devil is a lie and once we rid ourselves of negative thinking we find enlightenment, our inner light of goodness and love. That is the true essence of God!"

I kept his words alive in my mind. What he spoke of was great wisdom. I went down to the CO's desk to ask for my pass to see Parole. He gave it to me and I had a few minutes to kill. This elderly man named Don, who had life in prison for murder, was walking his dog. The block I was on had a program that allowed inmates to care and train dogs that were strays. The inmates train them and care for them for about 3 months so they can get adopted out. It was a great program the prison had and I was all for it. I tried to join it but my minimum was too short. Don had told me that his last dog bit a CO in the ass and they wrote him and the dog up. They gave Don and his dog 5 days of cell restriction. How does a dog get written up and put on cell restriction? They had to escort them out when the dog needed walking, then right back to the cell for their personal lockdown. I laughed then went outside.

I took in a deep breath as I walked to the education building where Parole was. About a month ago I had seen the Institutional Parole Agent. She was surprised that they put me in prison for my crime. She said they should have given me county time and probation. Even the drug counselor who I talked to a while ago asked me why was I in a maximum state correction facility?

His exact words… "Why are you here?"

I had no answer for him, as the system was a bit off in their judgment of my crime. I walked in and told the CO I was there to see Parole.

I began to grow restless, as I was nervous. I was tired of being locked up and wanted to go home to Goo. Xanadoo was still visiting me faithfully every single week. The blessing of having her could not be denied. She had never let me down once since my incarceration. For that I knew I truly loved her and wanted to go home. My enemy began silently whispering to me that I was not going home in April. Parole was going to give me a year hit streamed through my mind.

"Better get used to being here," The voice told me. "You are not going home in April. Sorry son! Here's how its gonna go down…

Me: I'm a good person and I have everything in order.

Parole Officer: Well, you do have everything in order and you are a model inmate. Institutional support, no write-ups, you were given the early release incentive, first time in prison, good people in your community, an eager to want to change and a regretful attitude. But we are gonna keep you locked up!

Me: But I just heard you gave a repeat offender with write-ups who is a bad example in society?

Parole Officer: Yup! He will go back out to probably commit more crimes, who knows, maybe even kill someone. But someone like you… KEEP LOCKED UP! "

"Oh shut up!" I screamed in my head. "What kind of stupid thinking is that?

I remember the words by my old counselor. *"Why would they give you a hit?"*

Andro in his experience with parole said someone like me does not even belong here, that I would get parole without a doubt.

I was called in and I kept the Zen Masters words with me. I sat down before the man behind the desk and put on a friendly smile. He was a middle-aged man who didn't really smile and seemed unemotional and probably tired of his job. Who knew I thought? I just wanted to do my best.

He went through my charges and it made it seem worse than it was. "Three counts of obtaining a control substance by fraud." He fixed his glasses then looked at me. "Could you tell me what led you to commit that crime?"

"I was in a lot of pain and didn't have my own doctor or health insurance. It was a stupid thing to do, I know, but I was desperate and went about getting the pain meds all wrong. I truly regret the whole thing."

"Were these pills for you or were you selling them?"

"They were for me."

"Do you have a home plan?"

"Yes I do. I am going back to Western New York where I live with my better half."

"What are you going to do when you get out?"

"I am a writer and have a huge idea for a new novel. I already have one novel published and want to write again."

He seemed impressed. "Well ok then. I think that is all I have to ask today. Do you have any questions for me?"

That was quick I thought.

I asked, "are you able to tell me if you think I will make parole or not?"

He smile and said, "I can't tell you that."

"I'm sorry. I just want to go home and start my life over."

He smiled again and told me to have a nice day and good luck. When I walked out of there I started analyzing the interview. Picking at every word I had said. Maybe I shouldn't have mentioned wanting to go home. Did I say the right thing when I told him what led me to the crime? I shouldn't have asked him if I would make parole. That was stupid of me. In the early release program that I have all I would need was one "Yes" to make parole. How hard could that be I asked myself? You better shut up brain because I am going home!

I had gone to bible study and sat next to a man who I found out some creepy news about. Dale, my old cellmate at the classification prison, a Christian minister, received a life sentence for raping a 12-year-old girl many times over. It shook my soul when Goo had looked him up online. It was all over the news with a picture of him that looked pure evil she had told me. I knew it was some sort of violent sex crime! I had felt it in my core when we were celled up together. He had spent over $40,000 in the first two years of his confinement. He told me he had to spend another $15,000 on a new lawyer to continue fighting his case. He was not giving up and it made me wonder if he really was innocent or just in denial?

I wasn't there to judge but Dale had lectured me so many times on reading the bible and not to sin. He made me feel guilty if I decided not to go to bible study. He made me feel guilty if I hung around other's that weren't Christians. In his extreme Christian belief, he swore only his version of "Born Again Christians" go to heaven. So even all the good that people do, they go to hell for not practicing his views. All the good Xanadoo has done for me, saving my life and helping others, she's doomed to hell for not being a Christian? There are no Christians in heaven! No Catholics! No religion! I never did tell him I wasn't a Christian but spiritual. I didn't want to be made to feel guilty for being simply opened spiritually. I stood outside the box of religions. I told Dale I was with Goo who was once married and divorced.

He swore that I was committing the unforgivable sin of adultery and I was going to hell for it. That once two people get married, it is until death do they part. So even if the person married for the wrong reason and married the wrong person they were stuck with them? I did not believe that. I was always able to sense if two people were meant to be married or not. At my brother Rich's wedding, I felt him and his wife were meant to be together. The wedding was the best wedding I have ever been to and I felt joy for them joining as one. The energy there was inspiring and invigorating. I knew they were soul mates and had true love for one another. Their love lit up the whole place! Their marriage was truly blessed. That is the essence of a true marriage.

When my friend Key married his first wife, I knew it was wrong. He was marrying her for all the wrong reasons.

"I don't have anything better to do." He said.

They married because her parents were strict Christians and gave him an ultimatum. Marry our daughter or move out of our home, which was where he was living at the time. He didn't want to be on the streets so he married her even though he did not truly love her. I knew it was not meant to be and felt it in my spirit. It was an outside wedding and I remember staring at the candle in the hopes it would blow out. As I stared steadily at it, the candle sure enough went out. A train horn blew loud in the distance and a bird would not shut up, distracting the pastor who was marrying them.

So my thoughts on marriage was, if I could peer into the hearts of two people and sense whether or not they are meant to be, truly God could. I felt the Divine does not bless and join two people together if it was a slip-up or forced upon. Divinity grants us free will to do as we please but it does not mean that two people who simply made an error should be joined together as one until death. God is Love and only God knows True Love and when two people are connected spiritually, mentally and physically. He only blesses those who are meant for one another and those who share unconditional love, not those He knows are making an oversight and have doubt about Love for one another. He can peer into our souls and know what goes on in our hearts.

Ironically, the pastor was discussing adultery from the Book of Matthew. Matthew chapter 5 verses 27 – 32 discussed the immorality of adultery. Marriage nowadays has been taken so far out of whack and is overly abused!

An inmate asked, "What if the man beats his wife? Does that make a divorce ok?"

The Pastor said firmly. "They are still married in the eyes of God, so no it would not be ok. Remember, its until death do you part!"

"So the woman should stay married to a man who beats her?"

"She should first try to seek counseling with her husband and try and work it out. If not, she can get a certificate of divorce but she may never be with another man because in God's eyes, they are still married. If she were to marry again, she will be committing adultery and so will the other man she marries."

I asked, "so what if two people get married for the wrong reason thinking it was right. Fall out of love and the woman falls in love with someone else that is right for her. Say she finds her Real soul mate after she got married by mistake to the wrong person?"

The Pastor said angrily, "What part of until death do you part do you guys not understand? Love isn't everything when it comes to marriage. It's not about the right fit or soul mates. Marriage is to glorify God. People over use and over play the word love. If you are with a woman who is divorced and you feel you two are soul mates that are in love it does not matter. I don't care if you two were to be happy in love forever! She is still married in the eyes of the church and you are committing adultery and will go to hell if you do not repent."

I had a real problem with that! So if two people are meant to be together but one got married thinking it was the right thing to do in the past and realized it was truly wrong, they were stuck? If they fall out of love or were never truly in love to begin with with their spouse, they were stuck? God does not want us to be unhappy and that goes against the true meaning of love. We all make mistakes even in marriage.

That took me back to when I was living in Baltimore and there was an elderly lady in her 70's who was a Christian. Her husband ran off with his secretary and got remarried. A typical bastard. Yet the Christian woman remained faithful to him and never dated again. How could God want anyone to remain faithful to someone like that? So he went on with his life free and happy and she was left to remain faithful to a man who no longer loved her and never will over a belief system? The Divine wants us to be content and I knew in my heart He forgives those who wrongfully marry.

God does not join two people together who do not love each other or have doubt in their hearts. What form of marriage joins two people? A Catholic priest? A Christian pastor? A Jewish rabbi? A Buddhist guru? With all the religions in the world, which one is the true faith? To me True Love was always the real joining of two souls, not a piece of paper or a religious tradition conducted by man. I guess I felt defensive because I knew I loved Goo and Goo loved me and just because she was once married didn't make her any less my soul mate. Never took away our deep unexplainable connection. In no way did I feel loving each other was an unforgivable sin! Her love saved my life and that's what matters!

The Pastor went on to discuss that if you do not turn your life over to Christ you were also doomed to hell.

He said, "there are so many nice old ladies who are not Christians. If they do not commit to being a Christian and accept Jesus as their Lord and Savior they will go to hell. Now… there will be a lot of nice old ladies in hell now won't there?"

What the hell was this guy talking about I thought? So if a sweet old lady was of a different faith and led a good life doing good deeds they're going to hell? What should it matter what faith we are? To be kind, loving and companionate, the best person we can possibly be is the key to life. The strength of God lives within our own spirit. Unfortunately so does the devil.

There was a man behind me praising Jesus as he stood up. I knew him on my block as Chappy. Not too long ago I overheard that same man talking disgusting to another inmate. He claimed he had sex with this girl then later on kicked her to the curb because he said she smelled bad. He praised himself on how he laughed at the poor girl as she cried, humiliating her. Then there was Dale who shook his finger at me for not always going to bible study or church, meanwhile, he was a rapist. There were many I saw in church on Sunday then went back to cursing and negative behavior right after. We should always remain positive every day of the week as best we can.

Last week I had attended a Pentecostal church service. Another form of Christianity that was very extreme. They believe a person is not truly born again and spirit filled unless they are baptized in the Holy Spirit with the evidence in speaking in other unknown tongues! They live only for Christ and Him crucified, shouting, praising and speaking gibberish. Learned behavior passed down from generation to generation. It comes out of the book of Acts but the true meaning of other tongues meant, people were filled with the Spirit and were able to talk and understand other languages they didn't know. To be able to break the language barrier and communicate. Pentecostals took it to a whole other level and believed in a rather strict way of oppressed thinking. Folk raised and conditioned to think in the way of false doctrine. It made no sense to speak an unknown language that absolutely no one understood, not even the person speaking it. Throughout the centuries, the true word of God got twisted and divided.

I did not believe we had to go to a man made church or confess to a priest to be forgiven. God is everywhere and we take that Blessed Spirit with us wherever we go. I could pray and talk with the Lord anywhere I wanted and ask for forgiveness directly from the Divine. He was always listening. God lives in all of us, therefore he is always present, whether I was talking in a group, with one person or alone. We are all connected to the great Divine. Well, some are connected to Satan, thinking they are connected to God. It's having our own personal relationship with our Higher Power that mattered. I remain spiritual, not religious, because religions have too many rules and they all think they are the only truth. With the thousands of faiths out there who was to say who was right and who was wrong?

Radical Islamism's is evil in a sense. Their Sharia Law states harsh penalties for not obeying like putting people to death. A Muslim man can marry and sleep with a 9 year girl. A woman who gets raped cannot testify in court unless she has 4 male witnesses. Really now… how would that be possible? If the woman doesn't have witnesses she is put to death under Sharia Law for committing adultery but if the man is found guilty his punishment is to marry his rape victim. A Muslim cannot marry a non-Muslim. The punishment is death! Radial Islamic have cut the heads off Christians and set them on fire. I never understood how a religion could be so horrible! Islam means peace and there are many Muslims that practice just that. But like any bad thing, this had been planted into children's heads to truly believe what they are doing is right. Killing in the name of God is not what life is about.

I remember thinking that we are a world of Christians, Jews, Muslims, Hindu's, Buddha's, Native Americans, and so on and so forth. There is truth in every religion out there and they all pointed to one thing. One Higher Power. One Ultimate God. One great source of Love and Light. In some religions there are many gods but the main focus on it was the difference between right and wrong, good and evil, love and hate, hope and fear. I was raised

Catholic but something felt wrong. I was never moved during mass nor did I believe in confessing my sins to a priest who was just a man and a sinner. I didn't believe in some of the rules and rituals they had. I did not feel I had to believe just because someone told me so. Oppressed and made to feel guilty in some ways when there was nothing to feel guilty about.

So I had stepped outside of religion and became spiritually free and connected to nature. In some ways I had joined many faiths together as one including science. Being spiritual was the belief of the Divine and the true meaning of love and faith. Science simply was the understanding of the functioning universe. With all the wars going on over religion, the question of who was right was something I had to find out. Where does the real truth lie? I believed it was in our hearts.

I was lying in my bed during the evening, the near ending of another day, watching Rudolph The Red Nosed Reindeer and it ushered sweet memories in. When I was a child my mother and I would watch this together. I felt the spirit of my mother giving me peace. Thank you mom for being such a caring mother to me I thought to myself. The snow was falling outside of the window. It gave me serenity to see the white flakes falling. There I was all cozy and warm in my prison bed, watching my old childhood cartoons, I thought sarcastically. The Sand Man was looking at me as I was watching the Christmas Cartoon giving me a strange look.

"You're watching Rudolph? Damn son! Your shot out!" He laughed.

I just smiled and continued to watch the end of the show.

The Zen Master looked over at me.

He said, "you are in touch with your inner child. I admire that."

"I always have been," I said.

CJ had gotten a television off another inmate. He had removed the plate off the cable box on the wall. He learned how to connect a short wire to my cable line so he could get free cable. Basically he was piggy backing off my cable, which I didn't have a problem with. It was funny that crimes go on even within the prison walls. He was on his bunk above me watching his TV with his stolen cable. Andro was playing cards with someone and the chatter was all around the dorm.

I overheard someone ask. "What's for breakfast tomorrow?"

The response I heard was... "Probably some bullshit!"

I had to laugh because it was true!

Christmas was right around the corner and I still couldn't believe I was celebrating it in the pen! I got up and walked down the long aisle between the rows of bunks in the dorm. Most of the inmates were watching other programs and it appeared I was the only one watching Rudolph. It didn't bother me much. I was my own person and in touch with my inner child. I stood in the back and lit up a cigarette and took a few drags. We weren't supposed to smoke in the dorm but everyone did anyway. Just keep a look out for any CO's was the number one rule. I saw a few inmates making their late evening meal known as a Chi Chi. They mixed a bunch of soups with chips, sausage, squeeze cheese and sometimes meat they snuck back from the kitchen. A few kitchen workers were running their own business by stealing food and selling it out of their cells. They had a smart way of smuggling food back to the block, which I wasn't sure of. Whatever it was they always got past the pat downs when leaving the kitchen and entering the block.

I sat back on my bunk and began watching the movie "Scrooged" with Bill Murray. It was a comedy spoof of the Charles Dickens's "A Christmas Carol". I knew Goo loved that movie and I thought about her. I missed being with her so much! We had watched Scrooged together every Christmas. Thoughts of my past came to my mind and as I watched more of the movie, I started thinking about my present and my future. I had to write to Xanadoo about my feelings so I got up and grabbed a pen and paper.

Friday December 20ᵗʰ   *305 days in*

Greetings Goo! Here I am at the end of another day sitting on my prison bed watching Scrooged! Yes, I'm watching Scrooged! I think of you when I watch this. This is where I miss you, but you see Goo, watching this, your spirit is with me. I carry you with me always. So here I am comparing the movie to my prison experience. Being here has given me the time to go through

442

my ghosts of the past. To see the mistakes I have made and the people I have hurt. Where I went wrong. I see my wrongs and I want to make it right.

My ghost of the present, I think of you all alone paying the bills, taking care of the house and the animals. Yes Goo, I feel your pain and how on your own you feel at times. Having to come home alone and not having me there to make you dinner, take out the trash, care for the animals and to give you foot rubs. I am so sorry for having you go through all that but its not forever.

I see my future without you. I see myself dead and it scares me when I could have done so much in my life. I do not want to end up dead in an ally frozen solid in some city! That was the vision I had if I lost you and I went back to drugs. The ghost of the future is unrelenting and fierce! Once we die that is it. We can never come back from that and my spirit would probably end up in my own hell reliving the pain and misery not even knowing I was dead! I would feel something is wrong and exist on the plains of the nightmare and darkness I created. I am so much better than that!

I am having my own Prison Christmas Carol! But knowing you are there for me makes me smile! Not many men in here have love or anyone on their side on the outside. I do truly love you! Thank you for showing me the true spirit of Love! I was watching Cops earlier and this man got arrested for drugs. He was crying out to his girlfriend that he was sorry and how much he loved her. He begged her not to leave him and said he needed help. That's how I was when I first got arrested! I was so scared that I was

443

going to lose you. It was touching in the episode of Cops because the girlfriend told the man she was not going to leave him ever. She said she was going to wait for him. Just like the words you told me over and over again. That you would never leave me and you never did! You stood by my side! I dedicate the song "Faithfully" by Journey to you.

"I get the joy of rediscovering you... Oh girl you stand by me. I'm forever yours... Faithfully!"

Love is the essence of God!

Remember that! I love you always!

I signed the letter and sealed it. It always felt good to write her. It was around 10 PM and the lights went out in the dorms but the televisions stayed on. I went downstairs to mail out my letter. I stopped and looked at the Christmas decorations all around the block. I glanced at the Christmas tree all lit up. It was quiet on the block and I felt lifted finding freedom in prison. I may have been incarcerated during the holidays but my spirit was still alive. No matter how long the DOC had me locked up I knew they could not take that away from me.

Rising Above It

I was a serious mess being arrested but I had overcome it. I had spent four grueling months in county jail and tried to make the best of it. I worked in the kitchen and made $1 a day and was placed on the nice side of the jail. I was put on Thorazine and had traded much of my medication with other inmates for a radio and some snacks. I had written a poem and had it published in the monthly newsletter they had. While working in the kitchen there were a lot of shenanigans going on. There was this older heavyset black woman who worked in the kitchen and she had taken a liking to me. When I got involved with some of the tomfoolery such as stealing coffee, sneaking milks and juice from the cooler and sleeping on the job, she stressed a good point.

She said, "you don't need to stoop to some of these guys levels. I can tell you are a good person who does not belong here. You are better than that!"

I did have fun with those guys and we always ate good and found places to sleep since it was a night job we worked. Laying on the benches of the long metal tables in the break room, which was just a short square incased section. The storage closet was another place we had. The guys would move things around on the shelves and try to barricade themselves in. It always enticed me to stand in the storage room, with a light bulb in a metal case lit the room. I often pretend I got locked in there and couldn't get out. Like being trapped in a world of closed isolation. But her words really stuck with me. I am better than that. She was able to sense my inner light and had pointed that out.

It was time to see the judge after four months of waiting because I had that stupid felony of Possession with intent to distribute. I went from a cage to the courtroom and the prosecutor had dropped everything but the only crime that I wasn't guilty for. I was guilty of forging the scripts, and possessing them but I was not guilty of intending to selling them. I was guilty of eating them. Ironically they wanted to charge me with the one thing I didn't do. The DA recommended 3 years probation with 3 years DOC time suspended.

The judge looked down at me and said. "Every time I have someone stand before me, with a serious drug charge, I give them probation and they wind up violating and coming back to jail. I have seen it time and time again."

I began to get really nervous. I think I may be going to prison.

The judge continued, "I will take my chances and grant you 3 years probation with 3 years of DOC time suspended. Please do not come back here ok?"

I was so grateful and thanked the judge for releasing me.

I was released from jail and there was a lit cigarette sitting in an ashtray with no one around. Ironically, I was so craving one in that moment! Strange how that always seems to happen when I'm in need. Synchronicity was at work and I thanked God for having that. I grabbed it, took a hit and went to the bus stop. I inhaled the cigarette and it was a relief after being in that jail for four months! The jail gave me a bus token so I took the bus downtown. It was late August of 2007 and I checked into the Mission for some shelter. It was summertime and I knew I needed something to do to get it right.

The lyrics from Daughtry sang... *"Its Not Over,"* rang in my head. *"Lets start over. Try to do it right this time around. It's not over. Because a part of me is dead and in the ground."*

I had heard that song so many times while I was in jail and it made me realize I could get it right this time around if I try. Part of me was dead and in the ground mentally and spiritually. The kitchen lady telling me that I was better than that. Not going to prison and given another chance on the streets. The signs were all around me to try and get it right for once in my life. I had been given another opportunity at existence. So I joined the drug program the Mission had to offer. It was a spiritual based program but unlike the duel diagnosis rehab, there were no doctors or medication. The Mission took away our benefit card with food stamps and cash assistance. It was a surprising requirement they had to join. Otherwise, they won't take you. Apparently they use all of the benefits of everyone that joins the program and give absolutely nothing to us. That place gets loads of donations on top. I didn't even think that was legal to use someone else's cash assistance and food stamps. I did not agree with that but I didn't have a choice.

There was a 45-day blackout period where I could not leave the grounds. The day consisted of going to morning devotion at 7 am. A preacher would come in and sing the same patronizing religious song every day. We had to go to bible study and learn verses of the bible, which they tested us on. It really wasn't a spiritual based program, it was Christian. I did not agree with the program forcing Christianity on everyone. There were many men of many faiths and the program insisted on becoming a Christian. We had to attend Protestant church services every Sunday and if we didn't go they would put us out. I don't think that quite goes over with what Jesus would really do.

A man of extraordinary kindness, understanding, forgiveness, peace and love would be gentler with us. Kind of contradicts the term "Being a Christian". Even though I didn't concur with the rules, I went anyways with an opened mind. I actually wanted to attend church and hear what the pastor had to say. One thing I liked about Protestants was they were more laid back, not shouting and preaching. There was no shaming like in other parts of Christianity. I actually felt a message or inspiration given to me when they spoke.

The bus ride up to the next county was the most inspiring part. Seeing nature, feeling free as I sat by the window and looked out at everything. It was a church about 45 minutes away that took us in on Sunday services. It was away from the city and when we got there, nature was all around me. I would walk off into the woods alone while the others smoked their cigarettes before the service began. That youthful feeling came over me and I felt like a kid again... free.

I met a very eccentric musician named Funk. His name matched with his persona and musical talents. He had a problem with pain pills and heroin and nearly died at one point in his life because of it. He was nearing 50 years old who had no teeth but could play any instrument and sing. The Mission had a band that played every Friday in the chapel. I didn't feel having religious conviction forced upon me was the right thing. It is said it's not a religion but a relationship with Jesus Christ. Then they pile on all these rules and belief structures and if you're not born again, don't go to church every Sunday, don't read your bible, do this, don't do that, etc... you are doomed to hell. To me, that's what makes it a religion or an organized belief structure. I have my own "personal" relationship with God and I have the heart of Jesus within me.

I talk with God, walk with God everywhere I went. That's a personal relationship. With so many different sect beliefs in Christianity, much of what one does and believes is based on their personality or how they were raised. Like minded people who feel the same way about their beliefs gathering in unity. Worshiping together, feeling lifted. Being born again and devoting ones self to the Christian life has saved many people's lives. However, even in those cases, they still argue over what's right and wrong, how they see the bible and spirituality. Truth is in the heart and I always stood outside the box of religion. But for people who believe that which they believe and it makes them happy, then that's how they see life. It's really not about right or wrong as long as it makes you a good person.

I needed something more and joining the band was it. I went to rehearsal and sat down with the band. There was Fat Chubs, a very heavy black man, with a good spirit. He was the lead singer of the band and easy to get along with. Funk on guitars. Miguel, the drummer, was short with a good character. He was from Puerto Rico, spoke Spanish fluently and really knew how to hit the drums! Then there was a tall Jamaican, named Hawk, who sang back up and played the guitar and keyboard. All were recovering addicts trying to get their lives together. Funk had stated I could play the bass but needed some practice. I really didn't have my playing skills down pat. I dabbled a bit in my younger years when I had my own mini recording studio in my room in Florida. I never performed in front of a live audience.

I got highly involved with the band and enjoyed practicing where I quickly became a natural at rocking the bass guitar. The Mission had provided all the instrument. We were not allowed to play any rock music or anything else but Christian music. I felt like a restricted artistic individual and I knew Funk and I could bring a lot of great stimulating music to the band. The fact that the

Mission put serious restrictions on us made me feel like some sort of puppet on a string. What was wrong with expressing ourselves the way we feel? I did not like being told what I could or could not do and that was why I remained outside the box of religion and organizations.

The playing of the music was still invigorating to me. Funk had so much faith in me, he told the band to let me play live every Friday. He felt I was ready. So we all carried the music equipment to the small stage they had and set up. Every Friday at 1 pm they had graduations of all the phases for us and other things such as motivational speakers and graduates who succeed. Before and after the service, the band would play a few songs. Setting the sound up felt great as we had a mixing board and two huge speakers, one on each side of the stage.

The Mission had over 300 men and I remember standing before everyone. There I was with the strap over my shoulder holding the bass guitar as Chubs spoke to everyone. I had to remember what I learned during rehearsal. The beat started and I laid my finger on the bass string and started hitting notes. Luckily the songs we did were fairly easy songs. I got nervous but once the band began to play, Funk as he played the guitar, gave me a look nodding his head, as I played the bass correctly. Laying my fingers on the strings, changing chords, feeling the sound of the profound music that was coming out of me. I was getting it right! It was such a lifting feeling to be living a dream like that. I never got the chance to do that and there I was.

My confidence soared and I started going to the library to find other songs to play. I found one song by Jars of Clay called *"Flood"*. I related to the lyrics and asked if I could sing that song myself for the next performance. Funk told the band I would do great and they gave me that chance.

A few weeks later, there I was on stage playing the bass and singing the song. Fat Chubs had stepped aside and gave me the chance for that one song. It wasn't as easy as I thought singing and playing the bass at the same time. But I was doing it right again... kind of. It was tricky playing the chords as I sang out the words.

There I was singing words that I was able to express. *"Lift me up! When I'm falling. Lift me up! I'm weak and I'm dying. Lift me up! I need you to hold me. Lift me up! And keep me from drowning again."*

It was truly the way I felt as I sung my heart out. The melody was lifting me up from my darkness as Miguel had a fast wild beat going. Hawk had the keyboard in tune with our rhythm, streaming a peaceful angelic sound in the background. Funk was rocking the electric guitar as I lay down the swift bass line. The miracle of music had raised me from my personal death I had for so many years.

Funk and I rebelled a little and we rocked that song despite what the stupid rules were. We rehearsed the song for the guitar to have great distortion. A harder sound that added a rock edge to the music. We wanted to be free spirits, not held down by the senseless laws of the Mission and their Leave It To Beaver view on things. To some of them, rock music of any kind is a sin! Some how a long the way, the electric guitar and the sound it gave off, became demonized. So, to many Christians, rock music was of the devil. And I get it because a lot of the rock music over the decades did sing of disturbing, sick and twisted things. Growling and screaming evil words for teenagers to listen to and get bad ideas from. It's not the music we play, its what the song is about, the lyrics it speaks.

Funk and I had arranged the song because we had the need to really get the song out there to reach the listeners. We had to deliver the message the song had, which was to be lifted out of darkness. Did we really do something so wrong? So we rocked out a little. It wasn't like we were jamming death metal! We were who we were and no one should tell us different in how to express music. There is a lot of oppression in life and systems.

We got outside gigs with the local university and a couple of churches. We actually got to ride on a tour bus and for the first time in my life, I got just the slightest glimpse of what it was like to be a rock star. Loading the bus with the instruments and sitting comfortably on the huge bus that was very spacious. We had all the legroom in the world and it was a moment of pure bliss. Though it may have seen minuscule in the music world, we were living the dream in a small way for that evening.

Touring the local churches became a regular thing and I loved every minute being on stage. They may have forced creed on us but finding the true meaning of music was what we really needed. God was everywhere and the great Divine was deeply in the spirit of the harmony we played. To me that was what being spiritual was all about. Being free to express our feelings and to share it with others.

Funk and I became best friends and would go on walks in downtown Baltimore. We were allowed to take an acoustic guitar with us. We would stroll on the Inner Harbor, which was beautiful and had many people walking about. The water from the inlets was glistening and a cool breeze blew. Funk knew so many great songs and one song he wanted to sing for the people was The Doobie Brothers, "Listen to the Music". There we were as the populace of the city walked by us as Funk played the guitar. Funk and I both sang the spirited lyrics of the song.

"What the people need is a way to make them smile."

Sure enough those who walked by enjoyed us, giving them a smile and gave us a few dollars.

We sang from the heart. "Whoa oh whoa... Listen to the music!"

It was freedom surrounded by pure enchantment to be alive like that! Divinity had put me in the right place at the right time. Meeting Funk was one of the best things that I really needed to build my musical talent I had buried inside me. I just needed someone to help lift it out. It was just the right thing to make me smile again and really feel the connection to the music.

I landed a Mission job writing for the weekly newsletter they had. I had to come up with stories of inspiration and hope. I found that easy to do and I was having three or more articles published a week. I was given my own flash drive to save the stories on and to turn them in at the deadline. My muse had reached a new high and I remembered the disks of my novel I had saved when I was arrested. That little voice in my head that told me to take those disks just in case like a premonition. I was blessed as I remembered my brother had rescued my computer from Marty's house after I was in jail. It was a miracle I did not lose my gift for writing.

Another blessing came to me when my probation officer told me I no longer had to report to the office twice a month. Since my crime wasn't that severe, I could report every three months to a kiosk machine. I thanked the Lord for that! I hated having to go to the office to report.

Another blessing came to me when I landed a publishing company for new authors. It was an unknown company that was around for a few years so I gave it a shot. I had to go to the library, to use the computers, and go online everyday to go over the publishing steps. All sorts of wonderful feelings were running through me as the dream was coming alive even more. It was then when I discovered that living positive delivers positive results. I remember walking to the library and I thought to myself how much I would love to meet God. Truly know the mind of the Divine.

As I looked up I saw a billboard that said, *"Meeting God is around the corner. Keep your eyes opened."*

I cried out to God in gratefulness and happiness! The great Divine had not given up on me and was all around me. I had realized that I had created my own prison and that I was finally free. I did have purpose.

Months rolled by and so did the holidays and a brand new year. It was mid winter, 2008 and I had published my first novel. It took about 4 months to go through the motions and finally get my story in print. They had sent me a few of my books to me and looking at it was wonderful. I had made peace with Rich and his family and told them the news. I had set up with a couple of bookstores to do a book signing. I talked to the manager of a few small bookstores and landed one. The bookstore had to order 20 copies for me to advertise and sell. The only issue with my publishing company was that they would not take them back if the bookstore wanted to return any extra copies. That was a questionable system they had. I wasn't too sure about my publishing company. At least it was out there.

So there I was sitting at a table outside of the bookstore in the mall as people walked by. I had my books standing up and ready to sign. Only a few people had taken a look at them and since I wasn't a known author, I didn't get that much business. Selling books wasn't that easy. Only 6 people had bought my novel and I singed each of them. It was a great feeling but I still felt insecure because I was hoping to sell more.

I continued on and came across a huge bookstore I use to go inside all the time at the Inner Harbor during my time in the city. I went inside loved the smell of the place. Seeing people walking around the isles looking at all the books the place had to offer. I wrote the escalator up to the manager's office. I asked if I could do a book signing.

"Sure!" He said in a happy tone. "Always like to see new authors take off. Tell me a little about it."

I gave him the cliff notes version and he seemed to like it.

He nodded and said, "Ok, let me see what I can do."

The manager asked my name then went back into his office. As I stood there I saw the wide variety of books that were everywhere. Could my novel be a seller in this very bookstore and all over? I wasn't looking to be rich and famous. I just wanted to live comfortably and help people. I continued to wait as I began to daydream of becoming somebody one day.

Suddenly the manager came out and rushed up to me!

He snapped, "You are not supposed to be in here! You were caught stealing here a few years ago! I want you to get the hell out of here!"

I said, "That was a one time thing and I was sorry for it! I took the wrong in my life and made something right. I am a new man and published my first novel."

"I don't care if you're a new man! Get the hell out of here before I call the cops!"

"I thought I was barred for a year?"

"No! Forever!"

"Well, I'm sorry but they told me one year. I just needed music and did take a CD! I'm not a bad person. I already feel bad enough."

With an unforgiving demeanor, he snapped. "Get out now and if I catch you in here again I will call the cops!"

"Whatever happened to giving a new author a chance?"

"Not in your case, now leave!"

Before I walked away, I said to him. "We all make mistakes you know. People do change!"

He had nothing to say so I walked out of there feeling down on myself. When I first got to the city back in 2005, I had gone into that bookstore and was caught stealing a CD. It was stupid of me but I was desperate. I needed music to listen to. I was caught and they called the cops on me. There I was in the back of the store with two police officers and the storeowner questioning me. I simply told them I was a recovering addict and I needed a CD and that I was truly sorry.

I remember the cop asking. "Do you want to press charges?"

The owner who was a woman in her 40s and as she looked at me, I pleaded with my eyes not to take me to jail.

She said in an understanding tone. "No. But you are banned from my store for one year. If you come back in the time, I will have you arrested."

I thanked God that the owner of the store had a heart and let me go, telling me not to come back for a year. I knew that was what she told me. That was nearly four years ago and my God! Has it been that long since I had been in Baltimore City?

The demons rose up in my mind again. They started telling me that I was not going to make it as a writer. They were telling me to go do a hospital run. Go get some pills! So that's what I did. I told Funk what had happened and he decided to go to the hospital with me. Funk and I started going around to all the hospitals in the area getting back into opiates. We were catching the bus and riding out all over the city. I remember what that heavy set black woman told me when I worked in the kitchen in jail.

"You are better than that!"

She was right and I told Funk I had to move on. Instead of going to hospitals, Funk and I walked around looking for a job. I wanted to work and make a living. It was time to move out of the Mission and get my own place. Funk was easy to get along with and helped me in my search for employment. We toured much of the beautiful parts of the city. It was really nice to have a good friend by my side. There was something I was missing in my life. True Love! I felt my soul mate was out there somewhere.

I told Funk, "I don't know what it is, but there is something about a 40 year old woman."

Even though I was 34 going on 35, I sensed my soul mate was a gorgeous 40-year-old woman. Why I sensed that I wasn't sure. But I kept telling Funk that there was something about a 40-year-old woman! I felt it deep in my soul! I saw her with brown hair and blue eyes. I knew she would be special and have extraordinary artistic talents. It was just a matter of time until I found her. The same woman I have been seeing when I first sensed she was out there when I was 20 after Amanda and I broke up. Even though I loved her, I knew she wasn't the one. That

Eagles song I use to hear when I had my first drivers job in Florida *"One of These Nights"* always came on the radio when I was thinking of my true love? Who is she? Where is she?

As I thought about this woman that song would come on. It always spoke to me knowing someone was out actually out there.

It sang, *"Oh, coming right behind you, swear I'm gonna find you, one of these nights…"* I knew I was coming up right behind her. I knew she was near. Then the radio would sing my favorite part. *"I've been searching for the daughter of the devil himself. I've been searching for an angel in white. I've been waiting for a woman who's a little of both… And I can feel her but she's nowhere in sight."*

That's exactly the kind of woman I knew she was. She had her bad side but she was also an angelic person. I knew it then and then it felt like she is getting closer.

It was getting dark as we walked around and I could not stop thinking about this mystery woman. I thought to myself, I am going to find her and felt her in my heart. It was then when we walked by a streetlight and it went on at that moment. It shone down upon me and I was lifted yet again. I had to take it as a sign because it wasn't the first time that happened. Whenever things were about to go wrong a light would go out as I passed it. Or in that case, a light would go on right above me when I was positive right as I walked under it or for even no reason at all. I did not think it was coincidence but something kept telling me to keep the faith. That kind of synchronicity was so fascinating! The mechanics of how synchronicity works was still something I couldn't figure out. What I did figure out was that it was real and it meant something. And Funk noticed it also so I knew I wasn't crazy!

I landed a job as a host in a restaurant. I started off as part time but I needed the money. I was successful in getting a second job in another restaurant making coffee and doing odd jobs.

Funk and I had an unexpected drug test and we still had those opiates in our system from the hospital run. They tested us and sure enough it was positive for opiates. They wound up taking us to a lab, wasted time and money to see if there was anything else. Funk and I were brought down to the managers office. He told us that his hands were tied and couldn't do anything. We were both kicked out with no resources, advice and anything else. When I went up to my dorm room to get my stuff, they had one of those peacekeepers with a walkie-talkie rushing me to leave.

"Come on man, you gotta go!"

I was like... "Really? Can I get my stuff first please!"

We were 9 months into the program with 3 months to graduation and they just put us out for relapsing once? A mistake every addict makes. What would Jesus really have done? He would show understanding, kindness, forgiveness... Love. Values the mission lacked. We weren't thee average members of the program. I was in the band, I wrote for the newsletter, I just published a novel and landed two jobs. I went further than anyone in the whole mission and they just throw us out? They should have put restrictions on us instead of just putting us out on the street with nowhere to go. Narcotics Anonymous and A.A. even says that relapse is a part of recovery. Not meaning its ok to just keep relapsing over and over as many times as you want. But if you slip and make a mistake, own it, understand it and move on.

Groups like N.A. and A.A. holds much more understanding and forgiveness for fellow addicts who fall into drugs and alcohol then surrender again and come back to the meetings. They took everyone back in with opened arms and love. What got me the most was that it was a Christian program to help people. What they did was NOT Christ like at all! Not even a second chance especially how far I came along in success there. That was what they did often when someone relapses or doesn't follow their belief system. They had once put out a man on the streets for drinking a beer behind a dumpster. He died three days later of an overdose.

I had to sleep in some bushes by the water after work hoping no one would see me. It was an enclosed circle of thick green bushes that had a large propane tank in the middle. There was enough room for me to lie on the ground and rest my head on my backpack. It weighed on me having to do that and work. I also had to go to Social Services and get my food stamps and cash assistance back because the Mission kept my benefit card! They continued to keep using those benefits while I was out on the streets. Really now! Who does that?

I eventually lost touch with Funk after he went to another rehab. He would visit me from time to time at work. Unfortunately the demon of addiction never dies. Funk turned back to drugs and just seemed to have fallen off the face of the earth. Wherever he was I hoped he was safe. I knew I would not forget him and his musical spirit.

I met a server named Mike at the restaurant I worked at who said he had a room for rent. That came at a good time because I was tired of living in a bush by the harbor. The room was furnished with a bed and a dresser. I was able to move in right away after giving him a down payment. It was in a house near the outskirts of the city. All the houses along that block were close together and barley any yard. The room was on the second floor and it felt so good to have a roof over my head again.

It was a bit of a struggle living on my own paying rent for the first time in a long time. Mike was kind and allowed me to be late on the rent. He wanted to help me and I helped him by giving him the best customers that showed up while I was hosting. The ones that tipped! My brother had brought me my computer and I had set it up on a desk that was already in the room with a chair by the window that faced west. I wanted to start a new novel but the one I had published was slipping out of my grip. I was working two jobs and was too tired to promote the book. I got the Internet hooked up and did have my novel online through my lame publishing company. I still talked about it at work to a lot to customers but my boss was a jack off and told me not to talk with the customers. I did not understand why I couldn't simply talk to people at my job. I always made sure I did my job but there was nothing wrong with a little small talk. Was I hurting them? No! I felt I was inspiring them with my words and my spirit. I always had a way of making people smile and I wanted to let them know exactly who I was. I was a published writer and that minimum-paying job did not define me. I was better than some dead end job.

When I came home to the house I rented the room from, I saw a cat sitting outside. She was mostly black with specks of white on her short fur. I said "Hi" and she said "Meow!" She was hungry so I brought her in and gave her some food. Mike came downstairs.

I asked, "whose cat is this?"

Mike said, "you know, the guy who used to rent the room next to you moved out and left her here."

"Would you mind if I took care of her?"

"Go ahead. I wasn't sure what to do with her anyway."

It was a shame that people get a cat then move out leaving it behind. I have heard many stories of people abandoning their pets. I brought her up to my room and began petting her. She would become my very first cat and a new friend. I loved cats and their personalities. What to name her was a thought. I went through many names including Gwen Stafani but nothing fit. It was by chance that I found her and the word Chontix popped in my head. It was a fitting name at the moment. She was a perfect Chontix for some reason!

Chontix became my new best friend and we would lie on the full size bed and we would sleep next to each other. She would always lie on my chest and lick my head and purr. I had to buy cat food and it wasn't easy on the salary that I was on. Even though I worked two jobs, I was just afloat getting by with rent, food, cell phone bill and cigarettes.

My boss wasn't the greatest and knew I was hungry and I would sometimes ask if I could have a left over plate but would always tell me no. If a customer returned a plate of food he told us to toss it in the trash. It killed me to see all that good food go to waste when I was famished. I still snuck in the back and eat some of the food that the customers didn't eat. It was helping me get by.

One day I was in my room eating ketchup packets. Mike walked in my room as I was on the computer and had witnessed me eating the packets.

"Look man. You shouldn't be reduced to eating ketchup packets for dinner. I will go in the back at work and get you some real food on my next shift."

The irony of working at a restaurant and being hungry with no food all the time was astonishing! Thank God Mike was sensitive to my needs and was going to help me. I did not understand the world when there was hunger everywhere and people like my boss was throwing out food to eat!

Time had moved on and it was early 2009 already. I just turned 35 years old and I was alone. My money situation and living situation was fine but I longed for love!

"Where are you?" I often thought to myself? Where was my soul mate? I had a simple routine. I would get up at 6:40 am, pissed off because I hated mornings. I hated when the alarm clock went off, I would punch the bed not wanting to get up! I forced myself up, got dressed and ready. Then I walked 6 blocks to the bus stop, rain, snow, hot or cold… wait… ride the bus downtown to my first job at 8 am. Put on that stupid hat and apron that made me feel like I shrunk down to 2 inches tall, I felt so worthless. Get off at 2 pm and hang around the harbor until 4 pm when I started my evening job at the restaurant. Get off any where between 7 pm to 1 am and ride the bus back home and sleep. Thank God I had days off like my Sundays. I spent a lot of time in my room watching music videos on YouTube on my computer thinking about my soul mate. So there I was listening to a song by Natasha Bedingfield called *"Soulmate"*.

The lyrics belted out. *"Somebody tell me why I'm on my own if there's a soul mate for everyone?"*

Chontix was purring as she sat on my lap. She would look up at me with loving eyes but it wasn't enough. Such a tease I thought for that song to come on when I was desperately searching for my true love! I began to crave drugs really bad again. The loneliness was getting the best of me once more. I had obtained a doctor and he had put me on some heavy shit! I was surprised because usually doctors don't put anyone on strong pain meds so soon. He was giving me the Fentanyl patch, starting me off on 50mcg, which was to be worn on my skin and slowly seep into my blood stream for 72 hours. Fentanyl was a highly potent narcotic painkiller. About 100 times stronger than Morphine! He also gave me 10 mg Percocets with Soma, a strong barbiturate like muscle relaxer.

It was a wonderful cocktail of a mind-altering remedy. The pain medicine gave me that inner glow type high and the Soma was like a modern day Quaalude. Together it was just the right ingredients for a spectacular cozy lightheaded floaty feeling. It wasn't enough to have the narcotic patch on my arm so I started shooting it into my veins. I would cut open the patch and squeeze out the gel into a spoon, add water and cook it up. There I was shooting three days worth of a highly intoxicating drug into my system in one shot! It was grounds for a sure overdose and I wasn't sure how my brain took it.

I had a grim vision of myself suddenly. I saw myself facing my computer and the window that was next to me had glowed an eerily orange as the sun was setting. The room would emerge weird with orange and reddish colors burning around me. I saw myself dead from an overdose as I sat there in my chair with lifeless eyes. There I was sitting in my chair facing the computer with my eyes wide opened and a needle sticking out of my arm as the sun set on my life. Chontix would try to bump me and meow at me but I would not respond. I was dead and forever left in the shady realm of nowhere.

I had shaken my head of the strange vision and looked for more music to listen to. I came across a song I haven't heard in a long time by Richard Marx. The song was called *"Heaven Only Knows"*. I fell under the spell of the beautiful melody.

"Heaven only knows what lies before me. Heaven only knows what all my searching is for. All my life I've waited for a miracle but I can't ask for anything more."

The song spoke to my soul and I was lifted yet again. I was still searching for something and Heaven only knew where it would lie. All those miracles in my life but I was seeking for more.

The words continued to touch me. *"I've always wondered how to know right from wrong. Looking for a reason to replace what is gone but somehow the road just seems to lead back to me."*

With all those windy roads in my life it was up to me to find myself. Still, even with all those encouraging words Divinity was bringing me, I was lost without having someone to love. Love was everything to me. I would rather be poor and have true love than all the money in the world.

"God? Where is she? Please tell me!"

I was in silence and without an answer. I looked up and the song had ended beautifully. It was a heavenly blend of sounds all brought together. I looked onto the comments people post up to see what was said about that awesome song and its inspiring instrumental ending. There was one comment that stood out.

"This song has the most beautiful ending that I have ever heard. The way that Richard sings heaven knows over and over is just so beautiful... So meaningful..."

I didn't think there was anyone else out there who felt the same way as I did. I commented to her and wrote back

I typed, *"I thought I was the only one who loved this song and the end."*

I guess we weren't alone on noticing awe-inspiring music.

She commented back, *"You are not alone."*

I went to another song by Richard Marx called *"Calling You"*.

There she was again! I quickly wrote, *"You again!"*

She commented back, *"It's me!"*

She went by the name Elle and we became YouTube buddies online.

Time continued to move on and it was almost springtime. The weather was getting warmer and I was still shooting up the Fentanyl and popping the pills. Elle and I had been e-mailing one another everyday since we first me on that Sunday evening. I wasn't expecting anything serious, just a friend, so I opened up to her. I told her all about my addiction and the life I had led. She wasn't there to judge me and still accepted me as a friend. It felt good to finally open up to someone. The more darkness I shared with her, the more she seemed to respond in a loving way.

She was going through a divorce and told me she had no children and no other ties. The divorce would go smooth if her husband would sign the papers. They were splitting up because they had a difference in opinion… many differences, but feared the town she lived in would talk. She lived in a small city in Western New York State and almost everyone knew her. She sang and taught dancing at her own dance studio, which was well known. Her husband has been her dance partner for years, before they ever got married. It had been a 15-year relationship and partnership with 7 of those years married. She also feared losing him as her dance partner because they did shows around the area for special events. She was really driven to be a celebrity and a light to people. She really stood out being artistic and eccentric and was active in the city.

I noticed she was a lot like me in worrying too much. Making things bigger than they are. She seemed very OCD like me. I had inspired her that if she wasn't happy, she should do what she must do and not to worry what anyone may think. People talk when they have nothing better to do. Then they forget and move on with their lives, meanwhile, the person who was afraid would stay trapped in their unhappy life just so others won't talk. I found that to be highly unfair. The tabloids completely attack super stars, showing the worse picture of them and making shit up! What killed me about that was a lot of people believe that crap because they want to. They aren't happy in their lives, so they need to see other people go down. She seemed to be more at ease when I wrote her.

I was working at the host stand at the restaurant when I received a call. To my surprise it was Elle. I was flabbergasted she called me.

She said my name in a cute voice.

"Elle! Hi! How did you find where I was?" I asked.

Elle said, "you told me in one of your e-mails where you worked and I looked the number up. I had to hear what your voice sounded like!"

My heart fluttered in the notion that someone would go through the trouble just to call me. I was deeply touched and moved. The synchronicity was there again, as I noticed the date was 3/21, the first day of spring. To me the date numbers of 321 appeared like a countdown to my future. The first day of spring represented my new beginning when everything is re-born. It was all in sync to my new found meaning to life.

There were both good things and bad things about my life at that time. I would talk to Elle on the phone, as I would stick my arm with the syringe and fire up a blast of Fentanyl. I would get that soothing rush of the painkilling treatment as we spoke. If only she knew what I was doing at that moment. I was sure she would have nothing more to do with me. On the good side she began to open up to me more and started giving me hints of her attraction to me.

She had sent me pictures of her and she was dramatically extraordinary. Her pictures captured her uniquely big pretty eyes and stunning full lips. She had long wavy brown hair and blue eyes. She loved being a dancer and singer and had sent me a few of her dance videos. She was very affectionate as a person. Elle was very much in touch with the rhythm of music and life like I was. She had an up-beat personality and spoke encouraging with a dash of sexiness and charm. The more pictures she sent me the more beautiful she appeared.

I had begun losing myself in her untamed beauty and sex appeal. I had sent her pictures of myself and she was bowled over by my looks. She had told me many times over I was incredibly handsome and it was a shame I did not have a girlfriend. What was going on I wondered? Could a woman of her caliber even be remotely interested in me? She was 40 years old and it took me back to when I told Funk there was something about a 40-year-old woman just a few months ago. Did I have a premonition that love was on the way back then? It seemed my senses were still alive. She sent me a song by Barry Manilow online called *"Ready to Take a Chance Again"*.

The song spoke to my heart, *"You remind me, I live in a shell, safe from the past and doing ok but not very well. No jolts no surprises, no crisis arises my life goes along as it should. Its all very nice but not very good...*

And I'm ready to take a chance again. Ready to put my love on the line with you. Been living with nothing to show for it. You get what you get when you go for it. And I'm ready to take a chance again with you."

The mystical forces were sending me messages through music again. I was living in a shell doing ok but not very well because I was without love and I was back on drugs. It was all very nice but not very good getting high like that I thought. I looked around my room and realized I didn't have much to show for myself. I have been living with nothing to show for it. It was true that you get what you get when you go for it. I felt in that moment I was ready to take a chance again for love. It had been too long and Elle was the first person to accept me for my grim past. She didn't judge me for being homeless.

She even told me, "I would have been homeless with you."

No matter what awful thing I told her she seemed to love me more. Was this real I thought? Was Divinity granting the one thing I have been praying for? I wondered is this Love? The question remained, would I give up the drugs, settle down for a change, and for once in my life be happy?

The Winter Bridge

I was in the visiting room with Xanadoo holding hands. She always came with money to buy us real food they had from the vending machines. I knew if I got too use to the shitty prison food I would become immune. Someone once told me they were in prison for a long time and when he got out he ate real food and vomited. He wasn't used to outside food, which made me wonder about the crap I was eating behind the walls there. The moments I spent with Goo were so nice and I was grateful I had a break away from the madness of prison.

Xanadoo and I got to know some of the people who visited regularly. There was an elderly man in his late 60's named Barney who was convicted of murder. With the gentleness that came off that man, I couldn't image him killing someone. His wife Jane who lived on the other side of the state came to see him faithfully.

They had met in prison. I didn't understand how that was even possible as Barney explained it.

He said, "I was on a visit with a friend and this stunning lady named Jane was there and it was an instant attraction. We started writing each other and fell in love."

I thought it was an amazing story of true love! I would never imagine two people could meet like that while the other was behind bars. I had asked Jane what was it about Barney she fell for?

Jane said, "when I came with his friend I wasn't expecting anything. It was Barney's light and energy I felt. It was love at first site."

So they got married while Barney was in prison and Jane has been visiting him for the past 8 years. Love knows no bounds, I believed, as I sensed the loving energy coming off the two of them. Barney was a Christian as well as Jane and they always held hands lovingly and read the bible together. I felt it was really good for a man who had life in prison to have that. He had been locked up for over 25 years so far and will never know freedom again. But the love he had with Jane would give him freedom beyond the razor wire that incased him. Barney did not belong in prison I felt. He was a God fearing man, very faithful to his faith and seemed so kind. With the crime he committed was 25 years enough time? Should they give a good man like him another chance at living free?

There was a young man named Jake who had a wife named Jenny that came to see him every week as well. They had a baby girl together and she always brought the infant to see Jake. Jake and Jenny were in their mid twenties and were always friendly towards Xanadoo and I. I had talked with Jake and he told me he was doing 2 ½ to 5 years in prison for possession a large amount of marijuana. He wasn't a drug dealer; as far as I knew, he just liked to smoke his weed. Since the amount of weed they caught him with was well over an ounce they charged him with a felony and added Intent to deliver a controlled substance. The man was a good father and loving husband, which really showed in the visiting room. The question remained, should he have gotten a prison term for a plant? Should he have been taken away from his wife and baby? He said he had a great job and Jenny had to struggle on her own to take care of their baby.

It really pissed me off to no end to see that going on! So what if he smoked some weed or even sold it. Many states have already legalized medical marijuana, two states that even legalized recreational cannabis. I had learned that cannabis was used as a medicine for centuries until government became misinformed and banned it. Considering what Refer Madness taught everyone back then, it was no wonder they banned it. But what they didn't know was, prohibition doesn't work. They didn't learn from alcohol prohibition, that all they did was create a black market. Criminalizing it also ruined billions of people's lives since 1937 and set us back decades on research on the plant. They have been discovering so many more benefits of marijuana. A plant some religious people call "The Devils Lettuce", was actually the opposite of what they believed. Its actually saving lives!

Also, it was our free will to smoke if we wanted to. He wasn't hurting anyone. It made no sense that alcohol is legal, a substance in which kills more people than any other drug and causes more violence and accidents. In my opinion who was the government to take away our God given free will? To spend all that money on law enforcement and overcrowded prison systems over drugs is ridiculous. The billions of dollars, time and resources wasted on law enforcement over marijuana alone. I felt they should make natural drugs such as opium, marijuana, peyote, mushrooms and the coca plant legal. I believe God put these natural medications here for body, mind and soul. They are naturally growing plants and because it gave people a buzz the government made it illegal. They will never win the war on drugs and they should just make them legal and provide the rehabilitations for those who want it. Save the billions of dollars wasted on law enforcement, jail and prisons. Take in billions from tax revenue and put that into treatment and education. Whether someone uses it for fun or has an addiction, jail is not the answer when there are real crimes going on out there. Take the focus off the drugs and redirect it into addiction, the unseen demon of the mind and spirit. A real disease and obsession of the mind.

With all the killings that go on with the drug cartels, in the black market and down to low-income neighborhoods, it would be a more peaceful world to decriminalize all drugs. I was watching a show on the television and the police were entrapping people with undercover cops who were selling small sacs of weed. The unsuspecting victims were arrested and the police seized their car.

The people would have to buy their own cars back to them after they get bailed out. I could not believe they were doing that. I thought entrapment was illegal? I felt that the police seizing the people's car and selling it back to them was robbing them but created a law to protect them. One of the persons who had their car seized and arrested told the police he just bought the damn thing! The question remained, was what the police were doing wrong? I felt it was! To me it was just a way for the law enforcement to legally cheat people and make money, especially over nature.

I asked Goo what she thought about all that?

She said, "it sucks! But it is what it is. You can't change the way the world is."

Perhaps she was right but it still pissed me off. All I could do was change the man I was.

There was a true blessing going on as I told Xanadoo I made parole! I was so scared wondering whether I would make it but I did! I kept beating myself up thinking I would never get out. One of the guys on the block worked in the drug and alcohol program and saw my name on the computer. Once an approval is made they send it to all the counselors.

He said, "Congratulations."

I asked, "for what?"

"Making parole!"

It was like God knew I was worrying and sent him to tell me ahead of time. All that wasted energy for nothing.

The letter I received a few days later stated:

478

You are granted parole. The reasons for the board's decision include the following:

Your reasonable efforts to comply with prescribed institutional programs.

Your positive institutional behavior.

The positive recommendation made by the Department Of Corrections.

Your acceptance of responsibility for the offense committed.

Your development of a parole release plan.

All that was left was for New York State to be contacted and go to inspect my home for approval. It was another worry that arose. What if they do not approve it? Where would I go? Xanadoo was so happy and relieved that I was coming home in April and I needed to be there, not a halfway house. It was mid February already one year ago that I got arrested. I had been incarcerated for one entire earth orbit around the sun. The world still spun and life continued while I had been removed from society. I could not believe how fast the time was going. I really thought my life was over when they first cuffed me. I saw the domino effect go down bit by bit but I had made it. I had turned 40 years old and it was a new dawn in my life. I felt so good to be holding Goo's hand in the chair next to her. It was frustrating not being able to make love to her. It was torture to not being able to touch her the way I really wanted to. Xanadoo always said prison was so ridiculous to take a man out of his life over something stupid and stick him behind the walls. What was it all for? So many man made laws, so much madness.

Xanadoo and I always sat in the same place in the long row of chairs. The wall that Goo and I saw was all painted up for the children visitors. It had all different cartoon characters such as Bugs Bunny and Mickey Mouse. Behind that same wall was the hole loaded with inmates who were locked up 23 hours of the day. Sometimes we would hear the men trapped in there screaming and yelling. I heard stories of the guys in the bucket who would throw shit and piss on the CO's. It seemed that when a human becomes locked up and in solitary like that they become reduced to animal like behavior. Humans weren't meant to be caged but the world was so screwed up and man went crazy with incarceration. I learned that in some states they were taking away funding from education, closing down more schools and building more prisons. There was the answer I thought sarcastically!

The time had come and our visit was over already. Goo would get to the prison around 9 in the morning. I would be called down to visit and strip naked for a search which I become use to. Then we would hug and kiss and eat something. It felt so good to drink soda and eat real food and be with her. But the time went fast and it was 3 pm and she had to go. We walked up to the CO and told her our visit was over. The CO behind that desk always enjoyed our visits and told us our love for one another really showed. She also had mentioned that I did not belong in prison but I was.

We would see Jake and Jenny getting sad knowing their time was also up. Barney and Jane did not want to separate but it was the rules of the DOC. I embraced Xanadoo and held her tight. As I ran my hands down her soft hair I thought there had to be another way than to simply throw us in prison. So many lives were ruined and it affected more than just the inmate. All the lives around that inmate were impinged on as well as the children. Prison was no place to bring a child to see his or her daddy.

I moved back from her and gave her a long kiss.

"I love you!" I said. "Remember, I will be coming home in a couple of months."

"I can't wait! I love you too!" She said with a smile.

I walked over to the door and waited to be buzzed in. She went over to the door to freedom and always waited until I went in before leaving. There she stood as the door I was waiting at buzzed me in. I opened it and peaked out at her as she waved goodbye, blowing me kisses and sending her love. As I slowly let the door close I waved bye to her until the door closed and I could no longer see her. I turned to the CO at the desk and knew it was time to strip one more time and go back to the pits. I may be confined in a silly system but I had Goo's love and no one could take that from me.

Wednesday   February 21ˢᵗ
368 Days In

Good morning Goo! I thought I'd take you on a ride along today. A day in prison. A day in Ugh!

5:30 AM – Dorm lights go on. Ugh! I'm going back to bed.

6:13 AM – Woke up to the CO yelling, "Count Time! It's a standing count!" Ugh! 5 minutes later here they are with their clipboards as we all stand for the dumb count!

6:55 AM – The bell rings for breakfast. The CO yells, "Mainline out!" Ugh and stuff!

7:11 AM – Just got back from chow. Cream beef and rice crispies. What a meal! It's so cold! I'm going back to bed.

10:45 AM – Rolled out of bed. My Bunkie CJ just told me the governor wants to close down a bunch of schools in Philadelphia and build more prisons. That's worse than ugh! That's a down right shame! What does that say about our country's future?

11:30 AM – The bell rings and the CO yells, "Mainline out!" Lunchtime.

11:51 AM – Just got back from lunch. Shitty Italian Sausage and Pea Soup! The Italian Sausage looked like a giant dog's dick or something you'd find in a toilet! Next time you do the litters and you scoop out a perfectly formed piece of cat shit, that's what that thing we ate looked like! Major Ugh! I'm now making coffee with lots of cream and sugar to drown out that awful lunch!

12:10 PM – The bell rings and the CO yells, "Everyone take it in! Block workers!" So now as the block workers are cleaning up the rest of us go into our dorms and cells. I'm going to enjoy my coffee and watch the news.

12:18 PM – My God! In the news: Terror threats in the Olympics, chemical spills, robberies, murders and devil babies! Ugh X's 10!

12:22 PM – I Miss You!

12:23 PM – I Love You!

12:24 PM – I Want You!

12:54 PM – The bell finally rings and the CO yells, "Count time! It's a standing count!" Like we don't know that! 5 minutes later they come in with their clipboards again. Ugh and stuff!

1:09 PM – Just went to the back of the dorm to smoke. This is what's going on. Some are playing cards, watching TV, sleeping, talking and reading. I just found out the prison removed all the oranges because of the unbelievable amount of hooch being made! Ugh!

1:21 PM – I'm watching Sex and the City and they are eating N.Y. Style Pizza! Between craving real food and the sexual frustration is a BIG UGH!

1:30 PM – The bell rings. We're free again yay! Well, kinda. I am going to work out now.

2:16 PM – Ahhh! That was a good work out! I am so glad they have weight machines inside this block! They didn't have that on the other blocks. I'm going to make a protein shake I get off commissary. This is a non-ugh moment!

2:30 PM – I went outside and it is so cold out! There I was in our block yard admiring the glistening snow from the sun and the painted blue sky with the bare trees in the background. Truly not an ugh moment!

3:15 PM – The bell rings. Take it in again!

4:00 PM – Bell rings again. Count time again! We all have to stand... AGAIN! Ugh! Everyone is watching that stupid Jerry Springer! Today's topic is Lesboliscious! It boggles my mind how that is one of the most watched shows. Double Ugh!

4:25 PM – They are handing out mail. Nothing for me today. ☹

5:00 PM – I'm getting my sneakers on, dressing warm to go wait for the feed bell to ring. Seriously Ugh!

5:26 PM – Just got back from dinner. Ground up fish heads made into a patty with rice and apple crisp. The walk to the chow hall was beautiful. The sun was setting with high clouds that stretched across the sky. An Ahhh Moment! I'm going to get naked now and take a shower.

5:50 PM – Ahhh! That shower was most enjoyable! I still miss taking a bath. I am going to wind down now with a cup of coffee and the news.

6:45 PM – The bell rings and the CO yells, "Medication!" Pill line.

7:02 PM – I'm back from the pill line. This is the time I roll myself some cigarettes and watch Inside Edition with a cup of Green Tea. Some of the guys are using their stingers to boil water to heat up the food they brought back from dinner. They add some yummies from their commissary to make their own meal.

7:23 PM – Done rolling cigarettes. Gonna kick back now and watch TV.

7:30 PM – I Love You!

8:03 PM – I just got back from a smoke, sipping my Green Tea. I was watching the doggies playing together out in the yard. One dog had the other by the lower jaw! This is the time I see what's coming on the television while I write you my daily letter. I could either watch Cops or Nightmare Nanny. I'll put on Nightmare Nanny playing on Lifetime. They say its TV for women but some of us men here watch it too!

8:45 PM – The bell rings. Everyone is told to take it in again for the night. Ugh!

9:01 PM – The bell rings again. Count time! We all have to stand one more time. Ugh and junk!

9:55 PM – Well Goo, the lights are about to go out for the night. This is when I settle in on my prison bed and watch TV or listen to music and wait for a new day just to do it all over again! I think about my life a lot! I think of you a lot too Goo! I cannot wait to come home! I miss you every moment I am away! Remember how much I love you. You are ALWAYS with me! ☺ This concludes our day...UGH!!

They finally moved me out of the big dorm down to the little dorm. The little dorm had eight of us and I felt good being out of that loony bin! There was always chaos going on up there from loud televisions, thunderous talking, and having a barbeque. The guys sometimes took a whole roll of toilet paper, put Vaseline on it and set it on fire on their round metal stool. The Vaseline would prolong the flames and they would cook some kind of meat over an opened bonfire. There was always something illegal going

485

on there from stealing cable to giving jailhouse tattoos. They actually made a tattoo gun from a fan they get off commissary. They take it apart and somehow fix it to use an ink pen. There were so many smart men locked up!

It was so much quieter in that small dorm and I loved it. My new Bunkie's name was Baltizar. He was a laid back white man in his early fifties. He was in for a parole violation for smoking crack. His original charges were multiple burglaries. He had told me he had burglarized the Mayor and the Chief of Police but didn't know it. So they hammered him with a 12 – 24 year stint! He did his 12 years and made parole. But he was a serious crack head and that's all he talked about. He was very proud of his bowling ball sized hits of crack and when he gets out he wanted to continue his crack fest and invited me down to show me how it is done. He said he could show me how to get a real bell ringer of a hit. I told him those days for me are over.

I was lying on my new prison bed watching television. They were crucifying Justin Beiber on national TV due to his arrest. I suppose I should be thankful I didn't make it in Hollywood because look what they do. They took a talented young male and blow him up into a superstar. They robbed him of his youth and placed enormous pressure on him to keep up appearances in a means to make money. Then when he makes mistakes for being only human, they put him under the microscope and even make stuff up. The media, the press, critics, even comedians all attack him and tear him down. It was no wonder why so many artists become addicted to drugs, some even overdose and die.

I did not blame Justin Beiber for his behavior. He was a 19 year old stripped of his growing years and those who judge him dare to make him look bad. Hollywood created him and was destroying him. Being a super star was a means to lose your soul, having to keep up by re-inventing yourself, causing stress just to keep fans happy only to have them forget you when you are washed up. Hollywood to me was a hideous bitch goddess. When I look back at all the big stars of my time they were mostly forgotten already. All their past efforts and success meant little to nothing in the present day and future days to come. It was inevitable that anyone who worked hard to become a star always falls and becomes forgotten for the most part. There were only a few that may still have a small impact on the world in the later years to come. I used to beat myself up for not making it in the business but I felt it was for the best. I would have had a hard time dealing with all that Mickey Mouse bull shit.

I got up and went outside into the bitter cold for a smoke. I placed my cup of tea on the counter and looked outside the yard fence into the prison grounds. I saw a few CO's along with a Captain running towards my old block. Looked like another fight had broken out. I inhaled my smoke and thanked God I was no longer there. Sure enough, moments later, they were escorting someone in cuffs to the hole. Whenever they brought someone to the bucket, they would halt all movement in the prison. They didn't want anyone getting involved while they were bringing the unruly inmate to RHU. There were a couple of blocks that they had to lock down do to a stabbing. The insanity that went on in prison was astonishing.

I grabbed my cup of tea and walked back inside. As I walked around I saw some inmates working out and others playing cards as the televisions were on. As I freely strolled around I saw a small group of men in a circle praying. Whenever I saw men praying like that I would always bow my head out of respect and to wish the blessings they seek unto them. It was my way of remaining connected to the spirituality by secretly being a part of their circle on the outside. It made me feel good to see grown men who were incarcerated gather in unity and pray together. It was like that when I went to church on occasion. So many inmates changing their lives and finding God to become a better person. That was the part of Christianity I admired. I sometimes wondered what the world would be like if Jesus never died on the cross for us or if there were no bible.

I had lost my lighter a few weeks ago and had asked around. There was this one big guy named Wil who had found it. I was told a couple of inmates had lied and said it was theirs but he would not give it to them. When I approached Wil I told him what the lighter looked like and where I had lost it. He gave it back to me with a smile.

I asked, "how come you didn't give it to those other guys or keep it for yourself?"

He said, "because I felt that was wrong. I knew those guys were lying and I wanted to make sure it got back to the right person. I know if it were me I would want someone to do the same thing."

Wil showed me that there were honest men locked up. Not everyone in prison was a bad person. It was then I came to the conclusion that prison was a place of madness and miracles. It was madness by those who remained in that criminal mindset. Those who just didn't care about anything including themselves. It was madness to see all the fights, the gambling, and the negative thinking, just remaining in the sickly prison mentality. It was a miracle for those who allow the prison experience to make a good change in them and grow from it. I had made the experience a good one. I had checked out quite a few books and read like I have never read before. I could feel myself growing and learning. I even checked out books that had pictures all around the globe. They were stunning pictures of how beautiful the earth could be. I was able to travel around the world while I was locked away. It was a extraordinary escape in my mind.

I went into the bathroom to relieve myself. When I went to wash my hands I took a look at myself in the mirror. I was 40 years old but didn't look it. I wanted to stay forever young but I knew that no one does. I noticed my hair was thinning but no grays were present. I saw on my chin a few gray stubbles. There it was, the signs of my aging. I looked my whole face over and didn't see any wrinkles yet. My eyes showed that I had been through a lot. They seemed weary of my old life and that it was time to move on. I had some small bags under my eyes but felt grateful that I was able to see. When I looked down at the back of my hands I moved it back a little and noticed there were some small wrinkles. I put my hand on my stomach and felt I was slightly overweight. I had always been thin but I was feeling heavier. I was working out again and had built muscle but had a bit of a tummy. I didn't like it. How does it happen I thought? We are born only to age then eventually die. What was the point of that? Some say it is a testing ground for us humans and when we die, we evolve on to a higher form of continuation. Others believe there is no point to life and that we were just a bunch of fumbling dopes bumping around aimlessly. That when we die our consciousness becomes extinguished like the flame of a candle being blown out.

I knew there had to be more to life than that. I felt deep inside that my heaven I will be a god of my own imagination. I'd be able to do anything I could think of. I do not believe those who go to heaven will be praising and singing for all of eternity unless that is what their passion in heaven is. It is beyond our mortal's minds to know what heaven is really like but I do know I was looking forward to it. I had made my peace with God and held the Spirit within. Everyone's reward in heaven is different, its just a matter how wee see it. Our greatest passions and desires come to life. I felt I knew my place in heaven.

Just knowing I had no liver damage from all the drugs and alcohol I had consumed over the years was a wonder. How was that even possible? I had a strange way of keeping positive, which I believe was healing myself over and over again unconsciously. The Zen Master once told me that keeping our energy lifted keeps us in harmony with existence. It's a healthy way to keep the mind, body and soul in good shape. It was a true miracle I survived all I had been through not having any organ damage or brain damage. I really had nothing wrong with me but the bad karma the drugs and my negative mindset brought. I really should have been dead many times over. There really wasn't anyone who could answer that mystery.

It was the Divine on my side keeping me alive for a reason. Even though, I was in prison, I couldn't help but feel blessed. I was able to move my fingers and my arms. I was able to wiggle my toes and walk. All of my senses were unbroken and in great shape. I had my health, my intelligence and my talents. There was no reason for me to feel sorry for myself anymore. It could have been so much worse. I was 40 years old and it felt like my life was getting started. I could have a great future ahead of me as long as I hold my head up and stay positive. I didn't have much time left and I knew I had to live the way I deserve and to be rid of the darkness for good. By overthrowing my dark side and allow in the light. To end the pointless war that battled in my mind and to rearrange the clutter. It was up to me to simply believe.

A Different Corner

I was at the Baltimore Grey Hound bus terminal close to 2 in the morning waiting for my bus. I had bought a round trip ticket to Erie Pennsylvania to meet her physically. I was on my way to meet Elle for the first time. How could it happen I wondered? There I was on the computer listening to a song and found love. We were at the same place at the same time. Elle had sent me a song by George Michael called *"A Different Corner"*.

"Turn a different corner and we never would have met."

It was an amazing phenomenon how two people from two different parts of the country could meet like Elle and I. What if I wasn't on the Internet listening to that song at that moment? Would we still have met? What if my brother never rescued my computer when I was in jail? Would we still have met? Was it fate that brought us together? All these ifs boggled my mind because if things were somehow different we wouldn't have found each other. I simply believed it was that Divine force that was beyond our comprehension combined with synchronicity. We are all connected and are joined together when the time is right. Elle was perfectly placed in my life at the right time and everything fell into place. I was still struggling and Elle started doing something no one has ever done. She actually mailed me food and other wonderful gifts. She sent me candleholders, curtains for my room and new sheets and comforter for my bed. She had told me she wanted to make my lonely room a home for me.

It was summertime of 2009 and my room got really warm and it was uncomfortable. She sent me my own fan! So I returned the favor by sending her cookies from my work and a signed copy of my published novel. She had told me I had saved her from having a break down. My words had encouraged her to smile again since she had been through her divorce. For the first time in a long time she was happy and it was because of me. I was just being myself. She had lost her mother to breast cancer at the age of 62. That was the same age my mother had passed away from complications of MS. We had our mothers who were our best friends both die at the same age. We also had absentee father figures so there was bonding between us.

So there I was in the bus station at 2 in the morning sitting in one of the rows of chairs in the brightly lit huge waiting room. There were some people lining up on lanes of the cities they were going to. There was something I liked about being at a bus station at night. There were a lot less people traveling. The place was mostly quiet as I waited. Erie was the closest the bus took me to Western New York.

They had called for us to board the bus and it wasn't crowded at all. I was able to sit comfortable next to the window. Elle and I had fallen deep in love over the past six months we have gotten to know each other.

One of my coworkers asked me. "How do you fall in love with someone you never met?"

Our spirits simply connected through the telephone and Internet and we shared in a lot of things we both loved. We were both artistic and eccentric.

The bus had begun the journey and I sat back as I saw the high-rises of Baltimore City slowly fade in the distance and into the beautiful darkness of the country. Our love was no ordinary love. We were always on the phone together enjoying every minute of our conversations. I took her everywhere on my cell phone with me on the city streets. I laid down a memory of our love on every step I took on the streets. Every night when we got ready for bed we would lay our phones down next to each other and fall asleep. We may not have been sleeping next to each other physically but we were together in our hearts with a little help by modern day technology.

The drugs were playing a serious issue onto my spirit. Elle and I began making love over the phone and I was distant at first. I had a hard time getting involved since it had been a long time and the fact that my brain was cluttered with mind numbing chemicals. I was walking on the city streets and made a decision. I would either choose love or the drugs. If I wanted to love Elle with all my being, I would have to stop the pills. Since I had that sickly vision of me dead with my eyes opened in front of my computer with a needle sticking out of my arm and the room glowing orange from the setting sun I chose wisely. I would have to give up the drugs.

In those moments of time I kept hearing Kenny Loggins *"This Is It"*

The lyrics shouted out to me like a sign from Divinity. *"Are you gonna wait for a sign, your miracle? Stand up and fight... This is it!"*

So I simply stopped going to see that doctor and detoxed terribly from the medicine all on my own. I was so sick I had to miss work but Elle was with me the whole time. It wasn't an easy thing to do but I did it. Elle's love had saved my life and I was so grateful for her because I would have ended up dead. Elle always made sure I was up by calling me in the morning when the phone sometimes disconnected us in the night. It was cute when our overnight phone sleep together would not disconnect and last through the night. As the daylight began to shine in my eyes I would hear the sweetest voice.

Her soft spoken words first thing in the morning. "Good morning. I love you!"

It was so much easier to wake up to a day where I would have to walk six blocks to the bus stop and wait rain or shine warm or cold. Then it was a twenty-five minute ride downtown to be at work at 8 AM. I was not a morning person but Elle made it great to wake up even for a grueling day of working two jobs.

Elle wasn't always the easiest to get along with. She had a way of taking things out on me when she was upset about something. Quite often she would break up with me over the phone but it never stuck. She always called back to say sorry. I had become her personal punching bag. Perhaps she was just a little scared of our new found love. One time I was in the bank and had her on speakerphone waiting to cash my paycheck. The bank had tall ceilings and was large and she was on one of her vocal rampages. She began yelling at me and it echoed through the entire bank. It was so loud that everyone in the bank got quiet and looked at me. I had to hang up on her and try to smile.

I told the teller. "My girlfriend is having a bad day."

Elle was rather childish and over zealous in her ways and some days it was nerve racking. She was not the average woman. I certainly was not the average man and Elle loved that about me.

I was growing tired and had to put my head back to try and sleep. I still had a long way to go on that bus ride.

The bus had pulled into the Erie terminal and Elle was right there waiting for me. I had not seen her just yet but I had just gotten off the phone with her and she was inside. I began to grow a bit nervous and wondered what it was going to be like meeting her for the first time. In the past six months we had become close and in love, we had our own relationship before we actually met. I grabbed my bag and walked off the bus. I stepped into the terminal and looked to my right and there she was. She was even more beautiful than the pictures she had sent me. Her eyes lit up when she saw me.

She said in happiness my name and ran to me. We hugged for the first time and it felt immensely soothing. Finally we were able to embrace and feel and smell one another. There were a few others getting off the bus looking at us.

Elle said, "this is our first time meeting!"

No one really shared in our personal joy. We walked outside into the warm summer day and she was all over me wrapping her hands around my arm. The first thing we did was go to see Lake Erie. I had never been to that part of the country and it was incredible. It looked just like an ocean that went on forever. We walked on the sand and saw a lot of seagulls. Elle and I were sharing a moment together in that corner of the world. It was truly a different corner of our lives. It still touched me to think if we turned to a different corner we may not have met but we did!

Elle and I got back into her car and I drove for the first time in a long time. I was still on probation and wasn't really allowed to leave the state but I felt it was worth it to meet her. I often worried what if they wanted me to come in. A little bit of fear ran through me thinking I could go to jail for that. I was hard to explain but my senses told me I would be ok. That calming feel that came upon me like God resting his hand on my shoulder whispering "Do not worry." Whenever I worried and got that feeling, it always did turn out ok. I didn't think I was meant to meet her just to go to jail and lose her.

We had pulled over and I wanted to kiss her for the first time. I was nervous but she seemed up beat and secure in our love.

I said, "I really want to kiss you now."

She said in a sexy tone. "You think we should?"

She was giving me all the signs by touching my arm and leaning forward showing me her cleavage. She had quite a body on her and her eyes were so bright and alive. We kissed for the first time and it felt like I was kissing for the first time ever. I haven't felt that way in years. She sparked that old flame within my spirit. Something I lost over the years was now on fire again.

We drove in New York holding hands and happy being together. I heard on the radio a song by Rita Coolidge called *"Your Love is Lifting Me"*.

"Your love is lifting me higher than I've ever been lifted before."

I was so lifted I couldn't help but smile! There it was again. Synchronicity of life singing to me again.

As soon as we got to her house we wasted no time making love! It was intense and I couldn't believe it was so long for us both. I had no regrets making that 12-hour trip to meet her. I felt the way I did when I was a teenager. Like it was the first time. Elle had another house where she actually lived, which she would soon be selling. The house we went to first was the house she had grown up in and she would soon be moving back into. She had rescued a few dogs and cats. I wanted to go to the other house to meet them but she had told me one of her dogs was temperamental and was nervous about it. The dog had been beaten as a puppy and was not friendly with outsiders, especially men. I told her to give me twenty minutes and I would have the dog licking me.

I told Elle about my encounter in Florida with that guard dog who ran at me but stopped when I showed no fear and I began petting him. The woman who owned the dog couldn't believe it and didn't understand why he didn't attack me. I also told Elle about Key's Rotweiler who was chemically insane whom I play fought with. Elle felt comfortable with me and brought me to her other house where she lived. As soon as I walked in there the dog began barking and growling at me. I sat down in the kitchen and just ignored the dog's aggression. Sure enough, after some sniffing around and curiosity, twenty minutes later the dog was licking me! Her name was Haddy and she was a 30 lbs Whippet Terrier mix. Elle could not believe it! She also had two black Labradors who I called the Dopey Brothers. They were calm dogs that were twin brothers and stuck on stupid but they couldn't help it. I went around the house and met all the cats. I always loved animals and Elle was impressed that I had that kind of connection with them.

She took me across the street to her neighbor's house. They were going to toss the dog they had out into the woods but Elle wasn't going to let that happen. The dog, that was a Pit Bull Labrador mix, had come running down and ran right to me. He was a white loving animal and I wondered why anyone would want to get rid of him. So Elle and I adopted him right away. I named him Barisnikov and brought him to his new home. I knew

499

then and there I wanted to spend the rest of my life with Elle and decided to move up. We spent every minute together in the four days I had away from the city. We made love 16 times, which was a new record for us both. There really wasn't much holding me back from leaving the city.

Like all good things it had come to an end fast. There we were back at the bus terminal saying our goodbyes after our four-day love excursion. I didn't want to leave but I knew I had to go back and take care of a few things. We kissed and hugged and we had to be detached again. It was heartbreaking having to go back to that city but I knew I'd return to Elle. I got on the bus and sat there for a few minutes. I knew the bus wasn't leaving just yet and I saw Elle by the door crying. I got up and ran off, grabbed her face and kissed her passionately. I looked into her big bright eyes and told her we will see each other again. I had to find a way of getting off probation and leave the two jobs I was working and the life I had lived in the city.

Time moved quickly. It was February of 2010 and I had written to the judge in Maryland. I told him I was working two jobs, writing a novel and I had not violated nor tested dirty for a urine test. I also added that I had a better opportunity in New York, which I did! I needed to move and have the fees waived.

I got the letter in the mail back with *"Granted"* written on it. The judge had dismissed my probation 8 months early and waved the $1400 probation fees. It was then I knew I was making the right choice. Elle had driven down from New York and helped me pack up my stuff and moved Chontix and me to our new home in mid March. She had sold her other house and we moved into the house she grew up in.

Time continued to move into summer then into the fall and I had gone a while without looking for a job. I was becoming attached to the comfort Elle was giving me. In many ways Elle became my new enabler. She had told me many times that I was her little New York boy and wanted to take care of me. So I began seeing a doctor and got on Tramadol. It was a non-narcotic painkiller that worked like one. I didn't feel being on that was wrong in any way.

I began to feel things I haven't felt in years. I was able to feel Elle's memories in the house she grew up in. As I would walk around the house while she was at work I could see her as a little girl. It was a fascinating sensation to be able to feel those memories I never lived. How was that even possible? Were we that connected?

Another strange thing occurred when we made love. For some reason after I had an orgasm I would feel a powerful feeling of that overwhelming thirst and naked feeling come over me. It was as if I was exposed before some higher spirit and it was watching me knowing my thoughts and feelings. I haven't felt that way since I was a child. There I would be lying beside her out of breath sensing that entity watching us. I wasn't sure if the being was good or evil, I just knew it was there. Did the release of chemicals in my brain after the orgasm spark some sort of higher sense? How I knew that entity was around as a child I may never explain but it was so real I became fraught!

Living with all the cats and dogs was a new found sense of joy. I loved all the pets we had and I felt like I had my own family again. We still had Barisnikov, Haddy and the Dopey Brothers. Elle and I took them on walks around the neighborhood and it was special to be walking our dogs. I could actually say "Our Dog!" Something I never was able to say before. We had a few cats that she had rescued including Chontix who rode calmly in the back seat as we moved to New York from Maryland. She quickly dominated the house and became Queen Bitch. She even put the dogs in their place! There were two orange cats that were brothers that Elle saved from someone who moved to another state. They were reckless and very playful. I had named them the Shenanigan Brothers due to their constant tomfoolery!

There was a new cat we saved who always jumped the other cats. He was overly playful and the other cats hated him. So I named him Lil Bastard because that's what he was. At least to the other cats. We loved him no matter what. We had an older cat with a bobble head due to a brain tumor. I had named him Bobby Bushea Bobble Head. He didn't know whether he was coming or going and was often jumped by Lil Bastard. Then there was Magoo and his big goofy brother The Doppelganger. They were big, calm and not very bright tomcats. There was a small skinny cat that would eat like a fiend. If another cat would vomit, he would rush and eat it! I named him Alexander A. Fiend, better known as A Fiend! Lastly there was a rust and brown color calico cat that looked like an alien. I immediately named her the Space Cat.

Doing the litters was a new thing for me. It was something that had to be done everyday and feeding them was always interesting. It would start out as a meow fest as we brought the cat food around. Then it turned into a swat and hiss fest as we would fill the bowls, fighting over it like there wasn't enough for everyone, but there was. Then it became a crunch fest as they ate.

I had begun to call Elle, Boo Boo's, because it fit her. Over time my Boo Boo became my Goo Goo. I couldn't quite understand how my Boo Boo became my Goo Goo but she did. More time had past and she became Goo. Elle = Goo and she thought it was cute. Then I started calling her Doo and Xanadoo. My unique creativity had always been with me.

Xanadoo and I had judged a karaoke contest and it felt like we were on American Idol. To watch and judge those singers was the lift I needed. It reminded me when I was in plays, being all connected. We enjoyed seeing all the talent that was in that town. We got to give our thoughts and comments as we spoke into the microphone. Goo was overly giving perfect scores but I saw their gifts well. It sparked a new idea for a story to write. So I went home to the room I had to myself and began a new story.

With all that I was experiencing I never took the time to realize how fast time moves. It was well into 2011 and I was still unemployed and I had brought Goo with me to my doctor. I selfishly felt that if Xanadoo was with me, the doctor would give me stronger pills and he did. Goo had no idea what addiction was about and wanted to see me happy. She would always be happy for me when I got the pills I wanted. I was given Percocets, Soma and Tramadol. I also had seen a different doctor and he gave me Valium. What I didn't realize was that I still was me on the inside. Moving to another state didn't mean I would leave my addiction behind. It followed me wherever I went so did my dark side. I was falling off the grid of life once more and Goo's love couldn't help me. Addiction was so powerful, cunning and it would always find a way to lure me into the shadows of spirituality.

I tried to justify my drug use but it all boiled down to one thing. I was back on my mind-altering substances again. Goo was not happy and was often giving me messages but never directly. I remembered one day she pointed to my bag next to me with my pill bottles and cigarettes.

She said, "that's all your life is about! Pills and cigarettes!"

I didn't want to hear it. I was comfortable in my wallowing pity and dim lit lifestyle. She continued to grow angry at my lack of employment and drugged out ways. We began to fight a lot. I knew what I was doing was wrong but I was being foolish. Being on all those pills, I felt nothing could harm me.

The moment I found out Xanadoo was becoming attracted to another man it woke me up. The pain within me of her being with someone else scared me. So much anger filled my spirit, as I knew all she wanted was a better life. I was not the man I should have been. She deserved so much more and I was failing and being really stupid. I remember taking my pill bag and throwing it across the room and Goo grabbed me, holding me, showing her love and support. Luckily the other man lived far away and never came around again.

Enough was enough I thought. I went to see my doctor and told him I had to stop taking the pills. I told him I had an awakening and wanted to be free. It wasn't easy but I had stopped the pills once again.

Time moved on and I was more focused on finding a job. It wasn't easy where I was living finding a good job. The Holidays passed quickly and it was 2012. Another year had passed me by. I keep searching and searching as the seasons continued to change into spring then into summer as the earth kept turning. Time had no mercy on me but I knew I couldn't give up.

I landed myself a job as a salesman for a car dealership during the summer of 2012. It was fun at first but the weight of having to manipulate people into buying a car was not for me. I remembered making calls and getting into a conversation with some of the customers. The boss didn't like that. I was just too friendly to be a salesman. I had told one of the other salesmen, who was a young punk around 20, about my friendly conversation with a lonely elderly woman and he laughed.

He said, "I don't give a fuck who I'm talking to or what their situation is. All I want is the sale and the money!"

I could no longer be in that sort of business. I had to quit and kept looking for another job. After some searching I found the job I was looking for. It was a driver's job, which I always loved.

I felt free on the road and I wasn't held down in an office somewhere. It was a stable job and I made pretty good money. I was finally being the man Goo deserved.

That dark force was still there and was telling me since I was making good money I deserved a reward. Hospital runs became a part of my world once more. I would often think how sick it was to drive far to get pills. Who does this I thought? But that inner force always took me over and I continued on. I tried to get the pills from my old doctor but he would not prescribe them to me anymore. I had to handle a lot of heavy deliveries and my back really began to bother me again. I had terrible pain in my elbows and needed relief but could not find any.

It was late 2012 and I went to see another doctor but he also would not give me any pills. There I was in his office waiting for the doctor to come in when I noticed a prescription pad lying there.

My inner voice said, "there ya go! You can write out your own if you want."

I told the voice in my head to shut it but it kept convincing me that there was nothing wrong with writing out my own scripts.

"Just do it, "the voice said. "No one is going to help you."

I leaned over and grabbed a few sheets and put them in my pocket. I began to grow nervous knowing that what I was doing was illegal.

When I got home I took a hot bath not wanting to forge those scripts.

The voice said. "If you write them and go into Pennsylvania no one will know it."

I got out of the tub and wrote out the scripts for some Hydrocodone and Soma. I drove into Pennsylvania and I was shaking. I was so scared and did not want to be doing that but that voice would not shut up! I felt like I was being torn all different ways. The voice convincing me that what I was doing was ok and the angels above sending me signs that it was wrong. I felt guilty and wondered about getting caught.

After picking them up I was thinking about getting caught as I listened to Pink Floyd *"Yet Another Movie"* waiting for the pills to kick in. The road was dark with only a few passing streetlights. I started thinking about all sorts of different possibilities that scared me. Images of going to jail and losing everything. I remember thinking will I get caught?

Then as the Pink Floyd song was ending in a peaceful instrumental way, I heard a man speaking low...

"Maybe not today, maybe not tomorrow but soon and for the rest of your life."

That was clearly a message from the powers above warning me that if I do not stop I will get caught. The evil force had a way of begging to differ. Just do a few more and be done with it.

My guilt was getting the best of me. Xanadoo and I had gotten into a fight and I was going to go on an all night hospital run. I wanted to hit as many hospitals as possible and get as much drugs as I could. There I was telling the doctor my exaggerated pain. She told me she would get a shot for me. I felt good about that. I got up to use the bathroom and I limped to pretend I was still in pain. I saw an inmate from the local jail in an orange jumpsuit. The two police officers that were watching him seemed to be giving me a look of suspicion. Did they know what I was doing was illegal or was it another sign telling me to stop?

On the way to do another hospital run Xanadoo had called me. She was sad and missing me telling me to come home. I could not continue on my hospital runs so I turned around and went home. I believed Goo might have saved my life that night. If I would have kept going I may have been over drugged and killed someone or myself.

Things became weirder as I was down to my last refill. That silly voice once again spoke, as I wanted to stop. I was taking a bath trying to relax.

The voice said, "you know, if you use a fake accent with your acting ability you could get another refill for the pain pills over the phone."

I said out loud. "No!"

"Just do it! One time is all I ask."

I screamed. "No! Leave me the fuck alone!"

The voice would not quiet down so I gave in and made the call. I was actually talking like a foreign doctor and it seemed to work.

The pharmacist said, "ok we will refill this."

I said in my fake accent, "thank you."

He replied with, "thank you doctor."

The power I felt for being able to do that was astonishing!

I was making a delivery from Buffalo to Erie and I was detoxing off the pills again. I had tried calling in my last refill but the pharmacist told me it was too soon. I had to wait and I hated it. I was having a day of pure bliss even though I was unwell. The music was playing on the radio and every song seemed like a message. It was in sync telling me my time was short and a change was coming. The day was clear blue and cool out. It was February 2013 and I felt bizarre in my own spirit. As I was driving I looked to my left and saw a prison. I was meant to make a delivery there but it kept being delayed. In that moment I felt outside of my strange world like nothing else existed. The space between my own existences was parted from the real world as that prison stood out. I felt like I was in slow motion with the music telling me it was too late. I had crossed a line I could not rearrange.

I made the delivery the next day to that same prison and did not like the looks of it. I knew what I was doing was wrong. Through the fence the vision made me sick. Before I left the prison parking lot I pulled over.

I said, "God? I only have one refill left for my phony prescriptions. Please allow me to get that last refill out and I will be done. You know that if I know that refill is there I will not stop thinking about it."

I began driving back to the warehouse and the music was still talking to me.

Super Tramp sang the *Logical Song.*

"When I was young it seemed that life was so wonderful. Oh it was beautiful, magical. And all the birds in the trees they'd be singing so happily, oh joyfully. Oh playfully watching me...

But then they sent me away to teach me to be sensible, logical, oh responsible, practical."

Life for me in my youth was wonderful and bright. Then I grew older into the brutal realities of the world. Were the angelic powers going to send me away to prison to save me from the person I became?

It was these words of the song that really hit me. *"The questions run so deep for such a simple man. Please tell me who I am?"*

Did I really know who I was? I was a 39-year-old man who was breaking the law and could be so much more. However, the devil within me felt what I was doing was just fine.

A few days later I was on my way to another prison and I called in for my last refill. The pharmacy told me no problem and I would pick them up after my prison delivery. I rolled into the prison and backed up the truck to the prison docks. The inmates unloaded my truck and it was then I was grateful that I wasn't locked up. The irony of committing a felony on company time while at a prison rang in my mind. God wasn't going to put me in prison I felt. I would be ok.

I made my way down some windy hilly roads and I wanted to pick up that Soma script and do a hospital run. I had lied to my boss telling him I had to leave early because of a made up issue at home so I can get high. I remember last time when I did a hospital run on that route seeing all the hilly roads seeing the Amish riding in their horse pulled wagons. I was rushing home one night and saw them, almost driving into them. Thank God I was alert. But what if I were to kill someone with a bunch of pills in a different name on me? The thought scared me but I would still do it.

I walked into the pharmacy and told the woman behind the counter the fake name I used for that refill for Soma. It would be the last time I do that and I couldn't wait to be done with it. I hated doing it but I knew I had to get the last refill out. I was waiting and waiting wondering what was taking so long.

I looked to my right and saw a police officer walking my way. I looked to my left and saw two more cops coming in from the back. In that moment I knew they were there for me. I felt frozen and helpless. I knew I could not make a break for it. One officer approached me and asked if I were the person using the fake name for the medicine. I lied and told him I was picking it up for my cousin.

They brought me outside and asked me all sorts of questions. I finally gave in and told them it was for me. I gave him my ID and he wrote down my information. They had told me that my calling in for the script too soon sparked suspicion and the pharmacist called the doctor. So when I called back for the refill they lied to me and told me they would fill it. The moment I arrived there they hit the panic button and the cops were on their way. In my sick mind I was hoping they would cut me loose but that didn't happen. He told me to turn around but I tried to reason with him.

I said nervously, "please don't arrest me! I needed medicine! I will lose everything!"

They grabbed me and turned me around as I cried out. They forced me into cuffs and leaned me on the hood of the patrol car. There were people around looking at the fool I was. It was all over for me!

I said, "I just needed medicine! Please! I will lose everything!"

One officer said, "do you expect us to feel bad for you? There are other ways to get medicine!"

It was that time I felt everything fall away from me like a domino effect. How stupid I was for doing that crime. What was I thinking? If only I had turned a different corner I may not have been in that situation. It was that moment I felt the reality of just how sneaky the disease of addiction really was. I was duped yet again and would lose everything I worked for. What will Goo think of me I thought frantically? My work truck was parked in the front of the pharmacy and I was going to jail. What would my boss think? I waited for that driver's job and it was being taken away from me. All was going to be lost but I did it to myself! Was it the end or had it just begun?

New Beginnings

It was officially spring 2014 and the weather was getting warmer. My Bunkie Baltizar and I were walking the ¼ mile track in the main yard. The sky was clear blue and felt mild and refreshing. Baltizar and I started walking 8 laps making it two miles. Yesterday we walked 10 laps making it 2 ½ miles. Our mission was to do a total of 12 laps that day giving us 3 full miles. I felt so alive and free as I walked with my head held high! I looked at all the other inmates working out, walking, playing handball, and there were some tossing the football around. On the flip side of the seasons, last summer into early fall, I felt so scared and stumbled when I walked thinking everyone was watching me. I didn't have the energy to walk 1 lap and did not feel well at all. It was a new place of hell for me and I didn't know what to expect. I remember sitting at the table staring out past the fences to freedom feeling alone. I was never really alone. My angels were always there.

I came to believe that entity I have been sensing all my life was my guardian. I told Dale, my old celli, and he swore it was a demon. The entity never made me fearful nor did I sense an evil presence. I knew the spirit knew my thoughts and stood there in the imperceptibly of the spiritual shadows. Another person had told me it was a

guardian. Why I always felt naked and thirsty when I felt it near I still couldn't explain. Why that feeling arose during heightened sensations like having an orgasm after making love or when I was in my youth still confused me. If I focus intently I could sense the entity was right there beside me. What did it want I often wondered? Why did I know the being was there as a child, even as a baby? Where did it go as I entered my older years?

I did not know what the mysterious immortal face looked like. It was invisible to my eyes but in my mind I saw shadowy robes with a binding hood over the guardians head. The entity would stand there with no words and no movement as the eyes I could not see watched over me. I felt my soul was naked before many heavenly beings. When I focused harder I could feel the vast amount of immortal souls in the uncertain cloudy distance. I would become overwhelmed and found it hard to breathe as I felt the presence all around me as I was exposed in the illumination that was beyond time and space. Along with the intense thirsty naked feeling, I would experience a strange sentiment like a tickle embedded in my spirit. Whatever that occurrence was, it was beyond my comprehension. I can see back to my birth but I started to see towards my death. I knew it wasn't my time... yet, but I was somehow able to start feeling my timeline before me. There was time left to correct myself and become what I can be.

I was protected all throughout my prison time as I sensed. My home plan was approved and all I had to do was wait for the day to go home. I had a few days to go and I couldn't believe how fast it went! The ride the drugs took me on felt a little like Alice in Wonderland. I followed those mind-bending substances down the rabbit hole and was in for one hell of expedition. It took me to places I would never think I would ever have gone to. I met all sorts of colorful characters along the way and gained so much knowledge of the dark side of existence. I felt like I had passed through death and hell for so long but survived. Being dead to the world like I was in my mind gave me a newfound appreciation for life. Seeing my own personal hell gave me joy in finding heaven again.

I felt the breeze blow and the smell of the fresh spring air. It felt so enticing and gave me a lift. Once again I was in sync with the seasons. My release from prison happened to come on a spring day. Spring is when everything is renewed and new beginnings arise. Flowers grow; baby leaves form on the trees and the weather brightens and warms nicely. As the seasons changed I was able to finally let go of much of my demons. Before I was arrested I used to have weird dreams of having fights with my mother. Her and I used to get along so well and really didn't argue much. She was my best friend and I could not understand the dreams or why we were always fighting.

Guilt played a big roll, as I felt bad for not being a better son to her. I always felt I could have done so much more especially if I weren't on all those pills! What I came to realize was those dreams were not my mother haunting me but me fighting myself. I was battling myself with guilt using my mother's face in my subconscious. I had sat down and wrote my mother a heartfelt letter and sent it to Xanadoo to read. I had to confess to God, to myself and to someone else the immorality of my ways. It was a way of forgiving myself for the wrong I had done and sharing it. I was not a bad son I was just mentally unwell. Even though that doctor from my youth had told my mother she would lose me emotionally, it offended us then but it turned out to come true.

I wondered about all those I met along my journey. Last I remember Wayne from the county finally got a break and was offered the help he needed. Xanadoo had looked him up and turned out he was sent to state prison for 2 ½ to 5 years. I was sure Lil Bastard had to still be in the hole and would be maxing out his entire sentence. I didn't see much hope for him. I did miss Andy and thought about him a lot. Andy wasn't a bad person just a little lost. I was grateful we got sentenced together and had each other's support to face the hells of first going to prison. Dale I visualized raping that 12 year old girl. I felt her pain and that sick sexual touch as he forced himself on to her. He was supposed to be a father figure and a pastor to her. He took advantage with his

sexual desires that he could not contain. I just knew he wasn't truly innocent but deep down inside I knew he always was guilty. I felt bad for his wife having to be alone after being married to him for 40 years. That had to be so hard especially living states away.
.

I heard Dozer was put in the hole again and the Alchemist moved to a different block. Rumors were floating around that the Alchemist turned gay but I had a hard time believing that. Andro was just released on parole again and I wished him well. The Zen Master was soon to be up for parole himself and was confident he was going home. Just simply believe was the words he taught me.

As I walked along side Baltizar I felt I had a good experience all in all. It was hard at first but I made it. I never thought I would have come as far as I did. With the guiding Light of God, having my Goo's Love and my positive mindset, I can honestly say I made it and I am a better person for it. I simply had to believe.

Baltizar and I made our last lap just in time because yard time was over. We had to line up at the gate and wait to be turned loose back to the pits. We were all called back to the block and I sat down on my prison bed to write one last letter to Goo.

Tuesday April 1st
407 days in
Welcome Goo to New Beginnings. All the bridges have been crossed. It is finally over. This will be my last letter to my Goo. I can only say it has been quite a wild ride. As I look back I

517

saw I was in a loop of a never-ending cycle. Then God stepped in. Now it is the time for my new beginnings. I had been my own prisoner for so long and didn't know who I was. I am a beacon of light and all the dirty layers have been pealed away showing my inner light again. How do we start off innocent as children then slowly become consumed with sin? How did I become cluttered with personal sickness and twisted thoughts? Darkness flowed through my veins at one point. How could I be my best friend and my worst enemy at the same time?

As I walked the track in the main yard I saw so many inmates with their own stories. I always asked myself who are these people? Who were these faces? What brought them to prison? Did they know when they were a child they would end up in prison? I can now look back on my life and see the turning point in my life when I fell into darkness. Did having an absentee father and a sheltering mother add to my fate? Where did I get all these amazing gifts and talents? What lies ahead of me once I get out? So many questions still remain unanswered. But with my new beginning I will find them. With you my Goo I will be the man I know I can be. Thank you for believing in me!

The day had finally arrived! I had to pack up everything and brought it down to where they would soon be releasing me. All I had to do was wait for them to call me down. I said my goodbyes to everyone I came to know. It was a little after 8 in the morning and I was sitting at one of the block tables. As I looked around I saw all the inmates doing their everyday routine. A few were working out, some playing cards and others reading or talking. The chatter echoed around the entire block and I knew I wasn't going to miss that. It was interesting to know that after I am gone prison life would continue to go on. Other will leave and new faces will appear as time rolls on like it always does. Everyone around me, other than the few I came close to, had no idea I was on my way out the gates.

My predictions came true when I had mapped out my prison experience. I felt when I was in county I would go down state in May of 2013 and I did. Then I wrote Xanadoo that letter telling her we would have to cross the summer bridge, the autumn bridge, the holiday bridge and the winter bridge into new beginnings. I sensed I would be in the classification prison in June and into my home prison by August and I was. I had predicted I would be settled into a routine by October and released in April 2014. Everything I had laid out in my mind came true even though I doubted myself and let fear over take me. How I knew that I wasn't sure. I always had that gift.

My name was called and I took in a deep breath. I took one last look around the block and slipped out unnoticed. I passed through the yard and out the first gate onto the grounds. I had to sign out a couple of days ago for the library, medical and the barbershop. I had to walk around the entire prison and in a way it felt like I was getting one last view of everything. The walk felt great knowing I was going home. I passed the kitchen and I knew I was not going to miss the food they served. I passed the medical building and remembered how nervous I was about that Hep C test. Thank God I did not have Hep C or any liver damage. That was a true miracle!

Another interesting thing happened when I had one last test for my hyper thyroid. It mysteriously went away! I thought I was going to have to take medicine for the rest of my life. I never did worry about that and I sensed I would be fine. The doctor was baffled because that wasn't something that went away on its own. Perhaps the stress and fear I was having then made my thyroid overact. Perhaps my positive thoughts and activities cured me.

I walked into the place where they first brought me from the classification prison. A sergeant was there with one other inmate who was also going home. I looked at the holding cells and couldn't believe I was in there when I first got there. My body tingled and I felt joyous that I would never have to sit in one of those cells again! I had to sign for my property and the sergeant gave us some new clothes to wear. It would be the last time I would have to wear those prison browns forever! I went into a small cell and took off my incarceration and slipped into freedom. Once I stepped back out I grabbed my boxes and followed the sergeant back out to the grounds.

We followed him through the first set of doors where no inmates were allowed. I was no longer an inmate of the system. We continued to follow the sergeant down a very long hallway with a green carpet. They called it the green mile and I could see why. Xanadoo had told me that was the walk she took every time she came to see me. Once we finally made it down the long hallway I instantly saw Goo. She began to cry as she saw I was again a free man. She ran up to me and hugged me. It was a moment of bliss in which we were back into each other's arms no longer separated by the state.

We walked out into the parking lot and for the first time in a long time I was on the outside of the fences looking in. The sky seemed bluer and the air smelt fresher than usual. We got to the car and placed my boxes in the trunk.

Xanadoo said, "this was where I parked every time I came to see you. I never missed a visit. I couldn't leave you in there all by yourself."

I said, "I know. Thank you so much for not giving up on me." I smiled as I looked into her eyes. "Let's go home now."

We got into the car and it felt so nice to sit in a car again! Xanadoo started the car and that was it. I would leave that prison behind forever. As we drove I saw all the beauty of nature I missed so much. I leaned over and put my hand down Goo's shirt and it felt so good to feel her again. I really did miss touching her the way I waned to. She sighed and put her hand over mine in comfort. In some ways I couldn't believe I was free again. I only had a short prison term but at times it felt like a lifetime. There were those moments I thought I would be there forever! I did a total of 13 ½ months or 412 days. Thank God I was granted that early release, otherwise, I would still be locked up and not riding home with my Goo. I would have had to wait until August and I was grateful that I didn't. August would have felt so far away being in that place.

We continued to drive and by the time we got to the pharmacy where I got arrested we stopped.

I said, "that's it. That's where I thought my life was over. I will never forget that moment when I got caught."

Xanadoo said, "please don't ever do that again! I don't think I could handle going through that again."

"Believe me, after what I went through, I will never do that again!"

We then drove up the street and parked in front of the county jail that I was held at. We took a good look at it. I saw the window from the block I was locked up in. So much madness went on in there and I felt so thankful I wasn't there anymore. It was interesting to see it from the outside since I was on the inside at one point in time. I felt that I had my freedom again and I was well on my way to a new life.

Back on the road we headed north. In no time at all we crossed over into New York and before I knew it we were home. For a moment it felt like I never left. We walked to the door and as soon as I walked inside the dogs were so happy to see me. I wasn't sure after being away for that long they would have remembered me but they did! They probably thought I was dead! They continued to lick me and wag their tails in excitement and I never realized I was so loved. I went around the house and saw all of our cats, especially Chontix, and greeted them though they weren't as excited as the dogs were. They were cats and had their own personality but I knew they were happy to see me. Chontix could not stop meowing at me welcoming me home.

Xanadoo showed me the box of all my letters I had written while I was away. She had kept every single one of them and for over a year they piled up. There had to be well over three hundred and I couldn't believe I had written that many letters. Xanadoo told me those letters got her through being alone. She had a basket full of small teddy bears. She called it my bears of hope and they were there to welcome me back home with a new sense of hope for the future. I started thinking was there hope for me? Strange feelings began to arise. As I looked at Xanadoo smiling that I was home, I thought, was she really my woman? Was that house I stood in really where I lived? All these animals, were they really mine?

I began to grow fearful and saddened of what had happened to me and I saw the timeline of my life and all the bad things I had done. I left Xanadoo and the animals all alone for my own selfish stupid needs! I was 40 years old and starting over yet again sensing the time was moving on into my older years. I felt in my spirit that my time was getting short. We all inevitably die and I was beginning to see my life slowly flash before me with old thoughts, dreams and memories I forgotten about. I came to realize the sickness of the disease of addiction. How could addiction have ruined so much of my life and hurt the ones around me? I started to feel less than deserving of what I had and having Goo by my side. I should have felt happy being home but instead I felt scared and guilty of my past.

Xanadoo asked, "what's wrong?"

I said, "I'm having that feeling again of worthlessness."

She grabbed the camera and we sat down on the couch.

"Maybe this will make you feel better," she said.

She started showing me videos she took while I was in prison. All the holidays I had missed she captured on video. She went to a concert and recorded some of it for me. Then she had spoken on the camera stating how much she loved me.

"I recorded all this for you because I didn't want you to miss anything." She said with a smile.

I still didn't feel worthy but touched that she thought of me the whole time. She showed me a very disturbing video of myself when I was all drugged up before I went away. There I was sitting on the couch, my eyes half opened and I was just mumbling senseless dribble. As I continued to watch myself I felt appalled. I looked like a real loser as I was trying to stand up not knowing where I was. I was watching myself as I was fumbling to put on my shoes.

Xanadoo said in the video. "Where are you going?"

I had said. "I... I... want..."

"You want what?"

I slurred the words. "I want to smoke."

I stood there not moving looking lost and wasted. I was so wasted that when I turned to the camera I thought she was taking a picture and I struggled to smile looking like a fool.

Xanadoo had said. "I'm not taking your picture ya goon! I'm video taping you to show you how bad you look on all those pills!"

I looked so sloppy, unattractive and sickly. I had not shaved in days and looked like a bum. It had taken me a long time to get myself to go smoke and I couldn't understand what the hell I was saying. I did not even remember that night.

She stopped the video and I felt even worse.

She said, "I wanted to show you how you were on those drugs. They made you into someone else and I didn't like it."

I said, "I am so sorry for all that. I am not the same person as I was then."

"I hope not. I can't go through that again. It wouldn't be fair to me."

"How did you do it while I was away?"

"I had my friends, my work, and the television. The animals kept me company but it wasn't the same without you. I slept on the couch the whole time because it was too sad to sleep in the bed without you. I missed holding you at night and falling asleep in your arms. I missed talking to you when I had a problem. You were always the first one I opened up to because I like your words of comfort and support. I had to eat microwave meals because you always did the cooking. I missed that so much. I'm still not sure how I was able to pay all the bills on one income. By the good grace of God I made it through. It was a miracle. I'm letting you know now that if you go to jail again I will have to leave you. I can't ever go through that again."

I hung my head for a moment then said. "I am so sorry for leaving you. I didn't want to go. They took me from you but it was my fault. I love you so much and thank you for not leaving me!"

I felt anger towards my addiction! All the demons in my head and all the mistakes I had made. What was it all for? I may have been released from prison but I was still in the grips of my dark side. It would take a lot of strength everyday to have to deal with it. I began to grow cravings for pills. I felt anxiety and restlessness. I was missing the drugs in my system. The question remained of how the hell I could miss something that ruined my life and nearly killed me?

Xanadoo put her hand on mine and smiled. I felt lifted knowing I had love on my side. She had done so much for me while I was away. She never gave up or left me there alone. She managed to pay the bills and take care of the animals. Guilt rose up within me and still the anger remained of how I was missing those stupid drugs? That was as bad as someone being in an abusive relationship and missing the person who beat the crap out of you. My inner demon whispered that I like the abuse. From my younger years until I was an adult I always beat myself up. I was free from prison but I had a void. The drugs filled that void and they were gone. In some ways it was like a death I was going through. It was the death of altering my mind and living in a shell of false serenity. They gave me comfort and shelter from the madness of the world. I knew it was going to be a struggle but I had Goo. All I wanted to do in that moment was hold her in loving comfort and forget everything else.

I had to report to parole and the ironic part of it was the parole office was next to that same prison I made the delivery to. The first one I saw off the interstate when I was having a day of pure bliss. The same prison I had gone to the day after and stared out into the fences and knew what I was doing was wrong. After checking in with my new parole agent, I got all the paperwork and finger prints done. I sat in the parking lot for a moment. I stared out at the place where I spoke to God. When I told Him to allow me to pull the last of my refills and I would be done. Was having to report to my parole officer at that same prison a Devine reminder of my past? To remind me never to do what I did again each time I would report? The interesting part is that not many from my area go to this parole office. It was further out of where I lived so I would say it was a reminder every time I go see the parole officer.

I began to drive on leaving that memory behind me. I could tell the angelic forces were going to be around me guiding me on the right path. There was really no way of escaping that. I was driving and thinking about my parents. They were both dead and it felt strange that they were once alive. Walking, talking, heart beating, blood flowing through their veins, living life and going through the moments of their years. We are all born only to age and enviably die. So in the end would my prison experience even matter? Does anything we do while on this earth really matter? It was a haunting question that I may never know. All I did know was life, as we know it, mattered then and there in that corner of time. There was a time when I couldn't even look at myself in the mirror. I hated the way I looked. Then I realized I was wasting my life and it wasn't that I didn't like the way I looked. I hated who I was.

I just wanted to die but I knew if I would have died during that miserable time in my life I might have taken the sadness with me. My soul may never have gotten to rest and move on to the great divide beyond the physical realm. I may not have even known I was dead and been stuck in limbo. How many chances do we get in life anyway? I had screwed up so many times and I should have been dead many times over. But there was always that force beyond my comprehension that saved me again and again. There was a purpose to my life and I still had to find out what that could be.

Feelings of worthlessness consumed me again when I had gotten back in touch with some of my old friends and my brothers. Both of my brothers had steady jobs and were married with children that were growing up. As I thought about my nieces and nephews I came to the conclusion that part of me turned into my father. My father was an absentee father and I saw I had become an absentee uncle. In my sickness of addiction I never sent them birthday cards or called them for the holidays. I had been a selfish, insensitive jackass!

My uncle Cory was known in the family as the burnt out loser. He had been to jails, was homeless and a waste of life according to my mother. He was the baby of my father's side of the family. I was the baby of my family and my life was similar to my uncle Cory's! Was it a pattern in the way the family lines ran?

My mother had broken that chain of dysfunction and made me aware of the wrongs I had done and the will to change it. I knew I deserved so much more than what I had given myself.

The friends I had in Florida also had good jobs and their own homes. My ex-girlfriend Alyssa had three children and two steady jobs paying her bills responsibly. My friend Key was married with two children and owned his own business. He had just bought a house in Georgia and was doing well. When I went online to my Facebook account I had seen more of my old friends. Facebook was a great thing to have because I loved keeping in touch with everyone I knew. All the kids I grew up on Long Island with had great lives and lived like normal people should. If only they knew the shit I had been through. All in all I had felt like the biggest loser of all the people I knew.

I got home but Xanadoo was at work for the evening. I walked inside the house and looked around. I still couldn't believe in all the lives and places I had been that where I stood was my home. I was born in the Bronx, raised on Long Island, moved to Florida when I was 16. I traveled across the country to California and back to Florida. I lived in the suburbs of Maryland, Baltimore City and moved on to Western New York. What the hell was I doing there on the other side of the state I was born in? I felt I was born in the east of New York and will die on the west side. This was the last stop in my life and I always knew that after I met Xanadoo. Felt like the sun rising in the east of my childhood and setting in the west of my older years and I saw the sun getting low. How much more time did I have? I began to feel I was in the beginning of the endgame of my life. The last chapter has begun in my existence. It was a feeling I could not escape.

What would I have been if I never moved out of Florida? A thought that always made me wonder. Would I have still been homeless and bad on drugs? What if I never met Goo and remained in Baltimore? I really believed I would have been dead. Goo's love really did save me! She was all the support I needed. She had printed up a few posters for the novel idea's I wanted to work on to get me going.

It was a beautiful day so I took a walk around my yard. I noticed our yard had so many trees and bushes surrounding the entire yard that gave it the "away from the world" like feel. The same way the house I grew up did and now being on the other side of my life, I have it all over again like a blessing. It felt like I was given my own mini park like the one I volunteered at back in my childhood. I had an idea to build my own pond in the yard like the one at that park in my hometown. To fully bring the feel and peace of my youth and hold on to the moments even in my own backyard.

We had about a half-acre on top of a hill where I could see downtown and the hills beyond. It reminded me of my youth and how I always admired nature. I took in a breath and looked at all the trees and the buds that were starting to bloom on that warm sunny spring day. I gazed down and looked at all the blades of grass and the sun shinning. I heard the birds chirping and a mild breeze moved me. I was starting to feel childlike again. I was able to blend the feel of my childhood into my older years where I stood and looked around. The feeling was amazing as so many memories ran through me. Many memories I had forgotten about or haven't thought about in years were popping up more and more in my mind. I couldn't have asked for a better woman in my life and a better place to live the rest of my days. It was ironic that the beginning of my life seems to be similar to the endgame of my life especially that I am seeing it like I did as a kid. God has blessed me with more than I deserved. It was time to get going with who I could really be.

I went inside the house and I walked upstairs to my writing room and put on some music. She decorated my computer room with all sorts of inspiring sayings...

"If you're handed it you can handle it."

"Don't think too much. You will create a problem that wasn't even there in the first place."

"It is not who you are that holds you back. It is who you think you are not."

"In a world where you can be anything... Be Yourself."

"Dream – and the future takes form. Believe – and you're halfway there. Work – and climb to fulfillment!"

All were the perfect words to remind me that I can be successful. I began to feel hopeful again. I may be 40 years old and starting over again but at least I was not dead. I had passed through death when I was dead within myself from the drugs. Those days I would sit before the television staring at the color bar completely twisted on drugs and alcohol. Why did I fall into the spell of that pattern? As I can see myself staring at the color bar I

531

came to the conclusion that all the colors that were there represented the many parts and shades of my life. So many colors, chapters and so many lives I had lived. The piercing noise off the television, as I stared at the color bar, represented the blank void I was stuck in. It was like riding the wave between life and personal spiritual death.

Like turning off the television of the same old reruns, it was time to turn off that part of my life and move on to my new beginnings. The blank pages ahead...

I could not go back and change anything; all I could do was move forward. Just like that song by Phil Collins that I had playing *"Long Long Way to Go"*.

"So it would seem we've still got a long long way to go, I know."

I continued to let the music off my computer play randomly as it inspired me. It was a new beginning for me and I knew that I still had a long long way to go. I had been given yet another chance to make it right. As I closed my eyes I realized those color bar days were over. I was beginning to really feel my entire timeline from when I was born all the way through, able to stop at any point in my life and feel, relive and cherish that I had a lot of good moments. Even the bad times held a place in my heart because its part of who I am. It was like being able to flip through a book and go to any part of the story. My connection to music was stronger and I could really feel the memories like a taste of heaven more than I ever had. I was able to close my eyes with music and relive any memory as if I was almost there in my mind.

Every precious moment when I was growing up on Long Island soared within my spirit. There were so many songs that brought me back when I lived in Florida. My time in Maryland and the big city all held a piece of me. I was able to hold that extraordinary feeling the entire time the song would play. Music really marks the moments of our lives. It's like a heightened sense of my youth and the things I have been through. I had realized the speed of time just seeing how 40 years has come and gone. I could only imagine what my future could hold and where I was going.

At that moment Dianna Ross came on next with the song. *"Do You Know Where You're Going To"*

She sang as I loved that song. *"Do you know where you're going to... Do you like the things that life is showing you... Where are you going to... Do you know?*

Music slipping in at the right moment was fascinating. I couldn't believe, still, after all this time how it works. How I am thinking something and that happens. I did like the things life was showing me. All the wonders of my youth and years I got older til now rushed in my mind. Life has given me a lot of madness and miracles, many that I still couldn't explain. Where I was going to I was afraid of … succeeding at something great. I still wasn't sure if I could do it.

I sensed there wasn't much time until I pass on. I felt a strange feeling of inevitability. Feeling my past more in depth, little by little, I have been remembering old dreams, thoughts and memories. Out of nowhere an old dream I haven't thought about in years and decades will suddenly pop in my head. Strange meaningful dreams almost as if I lived them started to accumulate and recycle through my mind over the last few months. Those dreams I had felt attached to and I wasn't sure why.

Just then *"These Dreams"* by Heart began to rock out. I looked up and around my room knowing something was with me again. The perfect timing moments were happening more and more. I fell into the rhythm of the song and many thoughts started popping up. An old thought or memory that I forgot will arise then lead to another. It felt like my life was slowly flashing before my eyes, which confirmed my suspicion that I am getting closer to the end. Just knowing that one day I will inevitably die really hits me. I began to sense a closeness to the conclusion of my life. Time just keeps moving faster and though there was still time for me, I felt it on the distant horizon. Always noticing the sun getting lower in the sky every time I think about my death was telling me where I was at in the timeline of my life. I always felt I will pass when I'm half a century. That was something I always felt in my heart through the years.

Like a premonition and all these signs around me telling me when my time will be. It felt like my childhood was mirroring my present adulthood. Where I began in life and now where I'm ending. Humans age the moment their born, slowly grow up into adults and go through their life cycle and inevitably die. My Goo will inevitably pass away. All of my friends and family will one day pass away. The sweet release of death is something no one can escape! It was something I was not afraid of. In fact I was looking forward to evolve into the heavens, beyond time and space. To be free of the material world and everything in it.

What was next after we die? How will heaven really be? I began to dwell it was all in the power of the imagination. Heaven can be anything we wanted that makes us truly happy along with our greatest desires and passions. To be free of pain, hunger, violence, war and death. We will forever feel joy, happiness, ecstasy, and orgasmic feelings flowing through us with peace and love. We will see God in all his brilliance who in heaven is the source of light and love. The great Divine would shine like the sun as an inspiration of all that is pure into our souls. He is a light so powerful there is not one speck of darkness. We are all gods in our minds and carry that same divine inner light within us. God, Light and Love are always in our spirits.

I somehow knew my place in heaven and was looking forward to the sweet release of my death. I've never been of this world though I live in it. I wanted to be free of this existence, of the material world and soar beyond time and space and be a god, create my own world, have powers as an immortal and unleash my imagination! I wanted to see those I have lost in the material world and teleport at the speed of thought to worlds of their creation and be reunited. Heaven is infinite and I believe there are worlds among worlds that go on forever.

With the crazy way time moves I knew it would be happening before I knew it! I was beginning to see and feel in the future what life will be like in the house Goo and I were living in. We will grow older then carry on with the others who we have lost in the past. That one day there will be new people moving in the house Xanadoo I shared so many beautiful moments in during our time there and begin their lives after ours is gone. Then the new people that live there will create memories throughout their lives and generations. Life always carries on. And it was time for me to carry on the remaining years of my life the best way I can with everything I have been given and learned.

I began thinking how I would ever become what I'm destined to be… what I can be. I looked over at the picture I had on the wall. It was Jesus knocking on the door framed in gold with a light on top that shown down making it look brilliant. Exactly how I felt. He's been knocking all my life, I just never answered or told him to come back later. Just then a song by Olivia Newton – John called "*Magic*" began to play.

The lyrics spoke out to me, as I got lost in the melody feeling my inner child. *"Come take my hand… You should know me… I've always been in your mind… You know I'll be kind… I'll be guiding you… Building your dream… Has to start now… There's no other road to take… You won't make a mistake… I'll be guiding you… You have to believe we are magic… Nothing can stand in our way…"*

Wow I thought. I got a tear in my eye for knowing that God was still with me. Love was still with me. Divinity has always been in my heart and mind. That song has spoken to me before and now that I was looking at Jesus and thinking about my future, those lyrics play. It also brought back feelings and beautiful memories of my childhood. Combining my childhood with my adulthood was amazing. I felt the way I did when I was young and I'm moving on in my life with the dream. I see the way daylight makes our house look just like it did when I was growing up. It seemed brighter and my senses felt greater. Even after all I have been through, my guiding light was always with me. I knew it was time to start writing again. It would be the last thing in my life I had to do. Recapture what I lost and just believe.

God has blessed me with many gifts though sometimes it feels like a curse. I just had to know how to use the gifts I have been given. It was time for me to finally trust within myself, within my mind and within my spirit. Listen to the spiritual messages, feel love, and be young again. My moment will come when I am set free of this world before I know it but there was still time. Time to cherish every day, what I have and to be the best version of myself. To live, be grateful and spiritually free. In the end it won't matter what faith we are. Its having faith. In the end all that matters is forgiveness, kindness, understanding, peace and love.

When you believe... Great things will happen.

Made in United States
North Haven, CT
14 October 2021

10336379R00295